FROM AW ~~AI~~ **OF HORROR FICTION COME 30 HAIR-RAISING TALES TO SHATTER THE IMAGINATION. . . .**

In "Soul of the Beast Surrendered" by Wayne Edwards, a tortured adolescent finds good reason to fear his own imagination. . . .

A haunted young girl traces her ancestry to the dark, underground sewers of Manhattan in Caitlín R. Kiernan's "Tears Seven Times Salt." . . .

Adam-Troy Castro's "Family Album" gives us a chilling account of the victims of a serial killer's rage. . . .

Enter a world of madness and African witchcraft in the lush and horrifying "Scars" by Lucy Taylor. . . .

. . . and 26 more stories to tantalize and terrify you!

DARKSIDE

TERRIFYING TALES

DARKSIDE

Horror for the Next Millennium

Editor: John Pelan

A ROC BOOK

ROC
Published by the Penguin Group
Penguin Putnam Inc., 375 Hudson Street,
New York, New York 10014, U.S.A.
Penguin Books Ltd, 27 Wrights Lane,
London W8 5TZ, England
Penguin Books Australia Ltd, Ringwood,
Victoria, Australia
Penguin Books Canada Ltd, 10 Alcorn Avenue,
Toronto, Ontario, Canada M4V 3B2
Penguin Books (N.Z.) Ltd, 182–190 Wairau Road,
Auckland 10, New Zealand

Penguin Books Ltd, Registered Offices:
Harmondsworth, Middlesex, England

Published by Roc, an imprint of Dutton Signet,
a member of Penguin Putnam Inc.
Previously published in a limited editon by the Darkside Press.

First Roc Printing, January, 1998
10 9 8 7 6 5 4 3 2 1

(The following page constitutes an extension of this copyright page.)

REGISTERED TRADEMARK—MARCA REGISTRADA

Printed in the United States of America

BOOKS ARE AVAILABLE AT QUANTITY DISCOUNTS WHEN USED TO PROMOTE
PRODUCTS OR SERVICES. FOR INFORMATION PLEASE WRITE TO PREMIUM
MARKETING DIVISION, PENGUIN PUTNAM INC., 375 HUDSON STREET, NEW
YORK, NEW YORK 10014.

This book (as they all are) is for my wife, Kathy,
and for absent friends who helped
so much in the beginning:
Karl Edward Wagner & Roy Squires.

The editor would also like to thank
the following people who've made ten years
in this crazy business possible:
Tim Powers, Matt Hargreaves,
James P. Blaylock, Charles de Lint,
Bill Trojan, Bob & Phyllis Weinberg,
Mark & Cindy Ziesing, Edward Bryant,
Michael Shea, Robert L. Brown,
Paul Dobish, Don Jerome, Mary Pelan,
Alan M. Clark, Lucy Taylor,
Wayne Allen Sallee, Adam-Troy Castro,
Nancy Springer, Kim Antieau,
Thomas Ligotti, Jessica Amanda Salmonson,
Mike McLaughlin, & Alan Newcomer.

CONTENTS

CONTENTS

Skinwriters

Robert J. Levy

She was the palest human being Kurt had ever seen. For that reason alone he decided to talk to her. She looked "unusual," and unusual women, he had found, were often an inspiration for his work. That was, after all, what really mattered.

He first spotted her through the blue-smoke haze of a party, one of those downtown affairs populated by the black-denimed art school crowd of which he was marginally a member. Her name was Rye ("spelled like the bread, not like a witty remark," she explained). She was pretty enough, intelligent, possessor of a liquid voice and charmingly reticent smile.

It was her skin, however, which first intrigued him—marmoreal, immaculate, whiter than white. Yet she was not albino for her hair was black as jet and her eyes an unearthly jade-green.

He explained that he was a published poet. She seemed politely unimpressed, and he found himself titillated by her indifference. She casually mentioned that she was a "performance photographer." He quizzed her further, but she remained vague about her work. His interest piqued, they sidled off to a darker, quieter corner of the room. They had talked for about a half hour when she began to allude to her past.

"It doesn't sound like the happiest childhood," Kurt said, giving her the option of elaborating, though the hoped she'd refrain.

"It wasn't," she began tentatively. "My earliest memories are of my dad beating up on my mother. Then, later, on me." She smiled ruefully. "It took many years and too much expensive therapy to even recall that last part."

"I'm sorry," Kurt said, realizing that he wasn't, that all

the while he was watching her and listening to her heart-breaking tale he could think only one thought, feel only one desire: to touch that amazing skin. Not her, but her skin.

"Well, it was a long time ago," she continued. "Besides, they're both dead, and I've managed to deal with it—in my life and in my photography."

"In your photography?"

She looked at him from her bright eyes, green gems set into alabaster skin. "Maybe sometime I'll show you."

Mark smiled what he knew to be his most winning smile, the one that bespoke strength and fragility. "You're a very serious woman, aren't you?"

"Sorry. I know I can be too intense about my work at times. But I'm better now. People have even told me I'm developing a sense of humor. You see, I've learned that obsessiveness has its place, but too much can destroy you."

Kurt did know, at least from other writers of his acquaintance. He'd been to arts colonies and conferences, and he'd heard the tales of suicidal depression, writer's block, the agonies of art. He would listen uncomprehendingly—and, perhaps, less than sympathetically—because, for him, writing poetry was a joy. He'd had fair success at it, too—a few chapbooks, a volume from a respectable university press, some part-time teaching coupled with his recently won fellowship. It allowed him to exist, albeit meagerly, in a tiny sublet studio apartment uptown. He wrote his verses, sent them to journals, shrugged off rejections, took solace in acceptances from increasingly elite publications, and always tried to stretch himself further with each new poem.

Kurt and Rye agreed to meet in a few days for coffee. Suddenly, it all seemed too easy. As she left the party he turned to her.

"You might as well tell me now. Is there anything important—wonderful, horrible or otherwise—that I should know about you before we meet again?"

She stared at him, smelling of vanilla, her skin gleaming.

"Yes," she said. "Like a fruit, I bruise easily." She pulled on her knit cap and strode out into the chilly swirl of autumn leaves.

Kurt lay in bed that night replaying her parting words. They were strangely enigmatic. Was she warning him that she was easily hurt in love, that he should be gentle with

her? Or, more unsettling still, was she hinting—as her vaguely flirtatious tone had conceivably suggested—that she liked a little "roughness" in her romantic life, perhaps a perverse need resulting from the beatings of her childhood? The latter possibility did not intrigue Kurt at all. The more he debated the ambiguity of her parting words, the more he resolved to call her the next day and cancel their meeting.

In the morning he sat at his ramshackle desk, his hands occasionally roving toward the phone, but he was at last unable to make the call. The reason: her creamy, ungodly pale skin. He wanted to see her; no, he wanted to touch her. Something about her singular appearance had inspired him. He had even woken with some lines from a new poem caroming in his head, lines connected to his image of Rye as he watched her disappear into the cab the other night amid the churning of dry leaves, the promise of colder weather and snow. He began writing as he sipped yesterday's reheated coffee from a chipped mug. The lines flowed effortlessly: *Unlike snow in any other place, city snow withholds itself. Days now we've been waiting, the air itself petulant with cold, our noses etching clear question marks along glazed window panes. Still, nothing happens.*

Then he stopped, stretched his arms and legs, and began to think about Rye. He would see her Thursday evening for coffee, maybe a movie if things went OK.

Did he like her? He wasn't sure.

From somewhere in the back of his mind, the idea that he was using her crept into his consciousness. That her image had triggered a new poem only gave credence to the idea. He turned back to his poem—which he knew, at least in some metaphorical way, was about Rye—picked up his pen, and found that he could not write. He put the pen down, stood up, walked about the room, sat back down and picked up the pen again. Nothing.

Damn, he thought to himself. He should never have taken a break after writing a phrase like Still, nothing happens. It was practically inviting writer's block. He lit a cigarette, the first of many that long, unproductive day during which, for the first time in his memory, he did not—no, could not—write a single other word.

Later in the week he hunkered at a corner table in a coffee bar, angry with himself, tense, frustrated. Four

straight days he had stalked his tiny apartment like a tiger, unable to find a single word or image he could commit to paper. His throat was sore from too many cigarettes, his temper frayed, his mood bilious. The crippling words echoed in his head: Still, nothing happens.

He'd been fraying a paper napkin into tiny pieces when he realized that Rye had sat down next to him. He found himself newly mesmerized by her eerie, waxen appearance.

They talked about movies, books, the usual mix of banalities intended to slowly tease out, through misdirection, another person's essence. At one point Kurt admitted he had begun a poem, partly (completely, he knew) inspired by her.

"Oh," she said, not exactly flattered, but not quite disappointed either. "You mean about my skin?"

Kurt, momentarily stunned by her bluntness, mumbled something about how he found her interesting and intelligent and attractive, but she waved her hand.

"No, it's all right, really. Maybe all that other stuff is true, too. I don't know you well enough yet to accuse you of being a liar. You're not the first person to notice my skin color, or lack of it."

"Look," she continued, laughing momentarily at his obvious discomfort, "I like you, and you're being honest. How about coming back to my place for a drink. No strings, seriously. The fact is, I'll just explode if I have any more coffee."

They split the price of a cheap Bordeaux at a liquor store on her corner, then sat on the floor in her meagerly furnished loft. Her apartment was barren of color. The walls held a few black and white prints, photos of the "street grunge" school—grainy shots of garbage, cigarette butts, often at jarring angles. Kurt had tried several times to broach the subject of her work, but she still seemed reticent to discuss it. He was unsure if she was merely being shy or condescending. He felt exposed, however, for he had given her a copy of his poetry volume, and she had asked him to read one or two aloud.

"Your poems . . . they're intellectual without being chilly. Funny, too. Their brevity works to their benefit. They seem to linger in your mind and expand after you've read them."

"Wow," Kurt said, laughing. "I'll pay you to write my next jacket blurb!"

The Bordeaux was long gone, and they had nearly finished another half-bottle of wine Rye found in the fridge. She leaned against him, and rested her head on his shoulder. He took her hand in his. His blood raced: He was touching that incredible white skin. Through her hand he could see the tracery of blue veins, a road map leading into some mysterious, dark part of himself that he had never known existed, the nature of which he could not guess.

Kurt woke with a tangle of black hair before his eyes and the feel of Rye's warm, still-drowsing bulk pressed against him. She shifted in her sleep, and her buttocks pressed his flank, arousing a pleasant, erotically tinged torpor.

Their love-making the night before had been unexpected, gentle and exciting by turns. The only awkward moment had been her out-of-character request, as she undressed, that they turn off the lights. Stray moonlight through a skylight illuminated their tryst.

For Kurt it was like falling into a melting snowbank of supernatural whiteness. Her kisses had been white, her caresses white, her smell one of utter whiteness. And yet now, as he grew more wakeful, the tense, irritable feeling returned—he was still bereft of words, of images, of language. He was "poemless," and a sickening unease welled up inside of him.

Rye shifted again, and the covers started to slide down from her upper body. Kurt noted this with satisfaction, anticipating another glimpse of her creamy breasts and stomach. Still asleep, she turned towards him.

His breath caught in his throat, and he stared in horror.

Where her skin had been a flawless white expanse the previous night, now her entire body was covered with bruises, but unlike any such marks Kurt had ever seen. They were not livid purple, but ink-black, as though someone had daubed Rye's breasts, neck, arms and stomach with kohl. Kurt stared in disbelief. More disturbing still, on some of the bruises he believed he saw his own handprints emblazoned on her flesh.

Kurt had never been a violent man. His first reaction was self-loathing; he must have gone insane last night, and, to

make matters worse, with a woman with her sad past of physical abuse. He tried to think back, to recall some primal, feral rage during which he might have wreaked such havoc upon her body. Maybe he'd had some sort of blackout, or was schizophrenic. Maybe he had become violently drunk, though he could only recall having consumed four or five glass of wine.

Then he saw that Rye's eyes were open.

"It's OK," she said, sitting up against the backboard, pulling the covers up around her.

"OK? My god, look what . . . I did to you. I don't understand what happened . . ."

She put her hand over his mouth. "Calm down," she said. "It wasn't you. I tried to explain at the party. It's me. I have very . . . sensitive skin. The technical term is purpura simplex, though my case is apparently more, well, complex. It's defied all the specialists. It started when I was very young. Anyway, the fact is, you were lovely last night, sweet and gentle. But it doesn't matter how gentle you are. Anything, even the merest touch, a tight watchband, belts or shoes . . . even applying makeup bruises my skin."

"I see," said Kurt, vaguely relieved, though still disquieted. "I've never heard of anything like it."

"My case is unique. I've turned it to my advantage, though."

"I don't understand."

She looked at him seriously. "Well, you've handled this well so far. I guess it's time to show you my portfolio." She threw on a bathrobe and padded out of the room. Kurt's first thought was to put on his coat and flee, but he couldn't, not with the memory of her formerly unmarred skin still in his mind.

When Rye returned, she carried a large leather case and a tall glass of grapefruit juice for Kurt. She sat down on the bed next to him. It was Kurt's impression that the black marks covering her body had already begun to fade.

"This is a series I exhibited last year at a gallery." she said, "I did the photography using a time-released shutter."

Kurt watched in amazement as she turned the plastic-encased pages. Each contained an 8×10 black and white photograph of Rye, usually naked, sometimes in various forms of partial dress, displaying either her front or back,

sometimes lying in various positions on her side. In each photograph her basic skin color showed up as a pure, marble white. However, her body was covered, head to toe, in carefully orchestrated patterns of black and gray bruises. Body painting, thought Kurt, and then he suddenly realized it was no such thing. Rye had merely applied pressure to her own skin. She explained that when she had finished her "painting," she would set up her camera, lights and a time-release shutter, and take a series of pictures of herself in various positions. Later, she'd whittle the developed shots down to the best one, which became the final work.

The photos—the whole idea of them—disturbed Kurt greatly, examining as they did the idea of a woman's body as a canvas for physical abuse. Oddly, though, as upsetting as they were, he could not turn away, for they were not in any sense "ugly." Some could even be thought beautiful, though by no means erotic. Kurt understood intellectually that by photographing herself as objet, metaphorically bruised, she was attempting to transcend her personal history of abuse through the medium of her art. Emotionally, though, he recoiled, but whether it was from the photos themselves or from his own dawning fascination with Rye's work he could not say.

Clumsily, he tried to say kind things about her photographs. She was obviously timid about showing them to Kurt, but she seemed elated at his words, and her excitement showed at being able to speak freely.

"I usually used a blunt plastic stylus to make lines," she explained, "and a stiff-bristled brush to fill in larger areas. I've even used an air-brush, turned up full, for some of the stippling effects. All the work, of course, is temporary. As you can see, the bruises from last night are already fading. So when I take the photograph, it becomes the only record of the actual work. I print small limited editions, then destroy the negatives. They have sold fairly well. An exhibition I had a year ago got good reviews."

"I'm not surprised," Kurt said. "It must have been hard to even conceive of this project given your past."

"It took a long time. When I was a kid people used to make fun of me. One time a bunch of girls held me down and wrote FREAK on my forehead with their fingernails.

I hid indoors all the next day, looking at a mirror, reading it backwards over and over to myself. The fact is, I used to think I was some kind of monster. I mean, I'd even come indoors from a windy day with my face completely bruised. Can you imagine what that must be like?"

"I doubt anyone could."

"Funny, it did have one benefit. After it started happening, my father was terribly afraid of hitting me. I guess because the evidence of what he'd do to me was there for all the world to see. Anyway, these photos were an important series for me, but ultimately a dead end. I've kind of been searching around for another angle ever since. Maybe collage or a collaboration."

"So what sort of work have you been doing?"

"For money? I work part-time at a gallery. As far as my photography? I've been taking other sorts of photos—you know, street work—but nothing's really grabbed me."

"Except me," Kurt said, reaching out towards her.

"Very funny," she said, playfully batting his hands away. "The fact is, if I were actually in the middle of a project like my 'self-battered' series I wouldn't allow you to touch me while we made love. It would . . . ruin the 'canvas,' so to speak. So how about that poem you said you were working on, the one that I gave you the idea for?"

"Oh, that. I'm blocked. Totally. It's never happened to me before. Usually I just sit down, grab a pen, and words just flow, like there's this river rushing inside me."

"But it's dammed up at the moment?"

"I guess," Kurt said, staring at her skin again, noticing that the bruises had almost faded away, and realizing that the first glimmer of a strange notion had crept into his consciousness.

"What are you looking at?"

"Nothing," Kurt said, embarrassed, turning his glance away from her.

"Do you think I might see the first part of that poem you're working on. Maybe I can be of help."

"I never show uncompleted work . . ."

He realized she had seen his gaze linger on her arms a moment too long, and she looked at him oddly. "Maybe you need some sort of change to spur you on."

"I need something, that's for sure."

"Look," she said, "please write out that first verse for me."

"OK, I'll make an exception. Have you any paper?"

"You won't need paper," she said, opening her bathrobe and letting it fall to her waist.

At first he was shocked. Gradually, though, he admitted to himself his true desire. Her skin had now cleared of the previous night's dark scrawlings, and was again approaching its former pristinity. She was offering her body to him as a blank page onto which he was expected to write his poetry, and the idea of it tantalized him in a way that even sex with Rye had not. The peculiar thing, thought Kurt, was that his need was entirely writerly, completely unerotic.

He was tentative at first, but she suggested that he just use gentle finger pressure, starting below her left breast. His index finger trembled, moving in light, cautious strokes. She urged him to press a bit harder, and slowly the bruise calligraphy began to show up.

He learned as he proceeded how to anticipate the amount of space remaining on that particular line on her torso so that he might fit all his words. She breathed softly, occasionally making a suggestion ("apply less pressure over a rib bone, more over unsupported skin") so that his lettering was even and sure. It took all of a half-hour, even though he was merely rewriting what he had already committed to paper from memory. Then, as he approached that final phrase, Still, nothing happens, something tensed inside of him.

He froze for a moment, running up against the wall of his writer's block. Yet the feel of her warm skin against his hand—its life, its receptivity—seemed to give him courage. So he pushed onward, and as he wrote that immobilizing phrase, he suddenly found himself changing the period at the end of happens to a comma, and he kept going, going, writing new words, new poetry, for the first time in days:

Still, nothing happens, and the belly of the sky grows fat with northern promises, and we, made weary by the weather man and all his inklings, disbelieve in any but real presence's . . .

At last he stopped, not because the poem was done, but because he suddenly knew he had so much more within him to write. In fact, he had begun to see "Waiting for

Snow" not as a poem, but as a series of poems about inextinguishable desire, winter, whiteness—and about the blackness that always lurks at the center of what is most white. He reached out to grab Rye and hug her gratefully for being the key that unlocked his writer's block, but she stopped him.

Kurt watched as she threw her thin robe about her again and brought out lights, reflectors, lenses, filters. She unrolled a large, seamless scrim, which she attached to hooks built into one wall. Then she set up her Nikon on a tripod, inserted a lens and began to take photographs of herself and Kurt's words. She posed on her knees, facing forward, her robe unfolded down to the top of her pubic thatch, her black hair obscuring most of her face, which was turned in profile. Kurt watched, fascinated by the care and craft and slow decision-making involved.

When she was done, she dressed.

"That was wonderful," said Kurt finally.

"Which? Sex? Your writing? My photography?"

Kurt simply smiled.

"Yes," she said, "they were."

A few days later—days without Rye, days during which Kurt's writer's block returned with renewed force, leaving him pounding his desk in frustration—a manila envelope lined with stiff cardboard arrived in the mail. He opened it, suspecting what it would be.

Rye's printmaking abilities were formidable. She had turned a simple black and white shot of herself into a superbly textured surface of subtly contrasting whites, light and dark grays, and rich ebonies. In the middle of it all, on Rye's body, was his poem, perfectly legible.

"Your photo is wonderful," he told her that evening over pasta puttanesca he'd prepared at her apartment.

"Our photo," she corrected him, slurping up a linguine strand. Later they sat sipping brandy, listening to the wind outside. As they talked, Kurt found his mind drifting. Holding her hand, he began to focus increasingly on her skin, its receptivity to his words the other day.

"I . . . I want to continue our project," he said at last.

She looked at him, and for a moment he thought she might be insulted. "I was hoping you would."

This time he wrote on her back the long way, as she lay

on her side, using a blunt plastic stylus she provided for him: We go on waiting for the snow though when, at last, it comes, we will not see the drifts collect from this fifteenth floor apartment without a view. Snow will not change a thing for us, any more than strange tales of other snows from ages past . . .

He wrote and wrote, the long, horizontal line of her back dictating the length of his lines, which flowed with an oceanic, wavelike motion unusual in his work. At last, he stopped, and she photographed herself.

"Perhaps this is the beginning of a new collaborative effort," she said when done.

"I'm beginning to hope so. I don't see this as a single poem, but as a longer, multipartite work. I think it might be book length. Maybe a hundred short poems."

"I'd love to work on it with you."

Kurt looked at her, at her skin. "You already are."

And she came towards him, wanting, he could tell, to make love. Suddenly, he did not wish to. Something new had surfaced within him, holding him back, as though he were afraid of despoiling his blank page, his working surface, his inspiration.

"If you are going to work on this project, we must do things a bit differently from now on," she said, kissing his neck gently.

And they did do things differently. They made love almost without touching, to keep her skin as white and unmarred as possible. He kissed her face gently, supporting himself above her on his arms so his body weight did not press against her. At other times she sat atop him, but barely so, so that they touched only as much as needed to complete the slow, rhythmic movements of sex. It was not that he didn't enjoy it, but rather that he was literally going through the motions. True, he wanted her, but now in a manner so different from the ways he had ever wanted any woman that he felt he must keep the intensity of his need a secret.

In the weeks that followed, Kurt and Rye practically lived together. Their combined daily rhythm became the ongoing momentum of the composition of their mutual poem/photographic series, "Waiting for Snow."

During that time they made love less and less frequently.

This was Kurt's doing. He tried to be subtle about it, feigning exhaustion or headaches, but the truth was that as his poetic inspiration took hold, he increasingly demanded an unblemished surface upon which to write, and he came up with ever more intricate excuses for avoiding lovemaking to assure that his writing medium was pristine.

Meanwhile, Rye had taken the liberty of showing several photos to a gallery owner who was eager to do an exhibit when the work was finished, and an agent Kurt knew had expressed early interest about showing it to several publishers.

Their life together soon took on its own cadences. Rye left early each morning for her gallery job; Kurt traveled uptown to his own apartment to write. However, he did not tell Rye that he was now completely unable to write at all except on her skin. Once home, he'd finish up a couple of free-lance journalistic assignments; edit the introduction of an art book for a friend; mark some student papers for a writing class he taught one day a week. But of his own work he did nothing. It was as if her shining skin had become the only light by which his poetry could see its way into the world. Without Rye's body, he was in the dark, a black hole of imageless, parched spaces, trackless and frightening. Those days alone in his apartment soon grew nightmarish for him, hours upon hours in which he had to face squarely the new, terrifying emptiness of his own imagination without Rye's body. And during those hours some dark part of himself began to wake from slumber, and slowly it began to engulf Kurt, warping him gradually but inexorably.

He began to feel that Rye was more than a lover, more than a collaborator. If, indeed, he could never write again except on her magical skin, then he must make sure no harm came to her, that nothing except his own words blemished her flesh. As the lonely, fruitless days at his desk went on, he sat for hours sometimes, going over the ramifications of this strange dynamic between him and this relative stranger, and he came to realize that if she—her actual physical person, her body—were the magic by which his creativity lived, then she had tremendous potential power over him, which she might wield as she chose, kindly or

cruelly. Above all, he knew, no harm must come to his work surface.

It was morning some days later, and Kurt still lay in Rye's bed watching her dress for work at the gallery. They had finished another section of "Waiting for Snow" the previous night, and he felt energized and excited, yet at the same time he was filled with a sense of foreboding: Large canvases were being freighted to Rye's gallery that day.

"What are you going to be doing with them?"

"What do you mean," she said curtly, buttoning her blouse. Her increasing annoyance with him had become palpable during the last few days. His constant refusals of her sexual overtures had clearly begun to offend her. "The canvases. They're pretty big aren't they?"

"Enormous. Wall-sized in some cases."

"You . . . you're not going to carry them or anything?"

"What?"

Well, I mean, if you hit yourself, or if one of them lands too hard on you . . ."

"I'm not lugging them around, if that's what you're asking. I'm supervising workmen on the installation."

"Good."

"Why? What's your worry?"

"Well, look now. I mean we're doing this collaborative project, and I'm in the midst of the best thing I've written. A magazine has already committed to publishing part as a self-contained chapbook. You know I've had some trouble writing on my own lately. I mean, if you came home one night from work all bruised, I wouldn't have a usable writing surface."

She stared at him. "I'm so glad to see it's my welfare that concerns you. Anyway, what's the big deal? If I did get bruised, you could just write that day's installment on paper and rewrite it the next day."

"I don't think so."

"Why? What are you talking about? You leave here every morning and go to your place to do your own writing."

"No. I . . . well, I haven't exactly been honest about that. The fact is, I haven't been able to write a word of poetry without you."

Rye looked down at her feet. "I had no idea. I'm sorry

about that. I really am." Then, putting on her knit cap, she said, "But I can't accept responsibility for it. Kurt, listen, I care about your work, our work. But you don't own my body. It's . . . on loan to you, understand. If I want to get a goddamn tattoo, I'll damn well do it!"

"Of course," said Kurt, momentarily cowed by her anger. "You're right. I don't know what I was thinking."

Rye softened. "I know how you feel. This project's important to me, too, you know. I won't do anything to jeopardize our work. I swear." She kissed him and left for the gallery.

Kurt dressed after she left, and let himself out, but as he headed for the subway that would take him back uptown, he became frightened that she was taking unnecessary risks with the canvases, risks that might bruise the waiting page of her flesh, and he began walking crosstown instead, through the maze of crazily angled streets that was the old city. Twenty minutes later he turned the corner he had sought and grew more cautious.

A truck was parked in front of the gallery. Rye was on the street, talking to two workmen who carried a huge, flat crate through the doorway. Kurt inched further down the street and peered in through the window. Rye was showing the workers where to prop the enormous canvases. At that moment she turned, and Kurt fled, ducking into a nearby coffee shop.

No, he assured himself over a steaming cup, she hadn't seen him. She couldn't have seen him. Everything would be fine.

What am I doing? he asked himself, a new sense of desperation creeping into his mind. I have to make sure she doesn't break up with me. I must do whatever she says or I won't be able to write ever again.

Taking the subway back uptown, he determined to try and maintain a necessary composure regarding Rye, so that he might complete the great work in which he was involved. He was a writer first and foremost, and if he needed this woman to complete his magnum opus, so be it. After that, perhaps, if he could write again on his own, he might break things off with her. But for now nothing must interfere with "Waiting for Snow."

On the way home, he stopped to take in a film; feeling

relaxed afterwards, he wandered home by way of the park. The first thing he noticed when he entered his apartment was that his answering machine was blinking. The message was the last thing he expected. It was Rye, furious. She had seen him outside the gallery, and she was screaming: ". . . how dare you stalk me like some psycho! I never, ever want to see you again you lunatic bastard!" The sound of her slamming the phone down was a gunshot; the bullet seemed to pierce Kurt's heart.

His first reaction was sheer panic, his only thought the completion of his poem. He had to do something.

The rest of that day was a blur in which all other concerns faded into a gray background. He was consumed by his own terror at the loss of Rye, the loss of his poem. He tried reading, going for walks, turning the television on and off. Nothing took his mind off his fear. Slowly, inexorably, the dark, misshapen part of himself tightened its grasp, as though it were pressing blunt fingers against his very soul, bruising him black.

Late in the afternoon, he found himself downtown again. He turned a corner, hunching against the now-frigid wind and squinting into the steely glare of the sky.

He headed up a flight of stairs and let himself into Rye's apartment with the key she'd loaned him; he wanted to be there when she came home from work—to apologize. He'd even beg her forgiveness, anything, any form of self-abasement that would enable him to complete "Waiting for Snow."

As soon as he entered he knew something was wrong. Lights were on. Rye's jacket lay on the floor along with her boots and scarf, as though she had hastily thrown them off upon entering. He took a few steps into the room and heard sounds. Then he smelled the acrid stench.

He ran into the kitchen. There was Rye, on her hands and knees, dropping the last of the negatives into a metal wastepaper basket. From the basket poured black smoke, and tiny flames licked its blackened edge.

"What are you doing?" he screamed wildly.

"Who gave you permission to come in?" she blurted out. "Get out! Get out." She turned her back on him, grabbed a large sheet of negatives and readied them for the flames.

Kurt ran towards her and grabbed her viciously around

her waist, pulling her away from the flames, but as he did so, she dropped the last leaf of negatives into the fire. They curled and melted in upon themselves, a sickening chemical stench filling the air.

Rye and Kurt fell heavily to the floor. She kicked and screamed furiously. Kurt, still clutching her hard around her middle, tried to keep her pinned so her flailing hands could not find his face. Finally, they fell motionless in a heap. They separated and stared at each other.

"What the hell is wrong with you?" she finally yelled at him. "Are you insane? You break into my home and then you attack me?"

"You destroyed them!" he screamed at her. "They weren't yours to destroy! They were mine, too."

"You . . . you thought I was burning 'Waiting for Snow'?"

Kurt stared at her blankly. "You weren't?"

"That was just some random rolls of film I took a few weeks ago. I hated everything about them so I just trashed them."

"By burning them?"

"I find burning bad work exorcizes it from my mind."

"Rye . . . oh, God. I have no words. I am incredibly sorry for everything, for all of this. I have just been in a state these last few weeks . . . I'm sorry about following you, for not trusting you . . . for what just happened now."

Rye glared at him. "I promised myself long ago that I would never again let anyone, man or woman, touch me in anger. I should just tell you to get the hell out." She wanted to do just that, Kurt could tell, but somehow she managed to control herself and continue. "I guess even a bastard deserves a second chance. Besides, we have work to do."

Kurt was stunned. For the first time he understood what should have occurred to him long before—that just as he was using her, she, too, was using him, and when "Waiting for Snow" was finished, she might discard him lightly.

Her coolness sent a chill through him: Here was a woman who had been physically abused as a child, and Kurt, by his actions, had probably brought all that horror back to her in full force. Yet she was going to put that aside, ignore the fact that she must utterly loathe him at this point, in order to complete her work.

It angered him, and yet, on second thought, it relieved him of some of his own misgivings. Weren't they both, Kurt wondered, in some sense monstrous?

Kurt had every intention of leaving, but she seemed reconciled to his presence, so he remained and helped clean up the mess made by the burned film. They tried to make small talk, but all their efforts ended up in mutual discomfort and protracted silences. Finally, she suggested they try doing another page of "Waiting for Snow."

Rye disrobed, and then they both knew it would be impossible. Kurt, in grabbing her, had horribly bruised her entire torso—his own hand marks were evident in several places.

"Oh, well," she said, suddenly sounding drained and apathetic. "Tomorrow morning, first thing then, when it fades."

So they went to sleep—she in her bed, he on the couch. They were no longer angry, it seemed to Kurt, but resigned to the truth that both only had use for each other in so far as their mutual project must be completed. It was cold and bloodless to give one's own artistic ends such terrifying primacy—something, Kurt realized, he had never had trouble with before. Just before nodding off, he started momentarily at the sound of the wind rattling the loose windowpanes, as though winter were screaming to get in.

Kurt woke to an empty bed and the sounds of water running in the bathroom. Rye walked in wearing her bathrobe and a curiously sour expression. "What?" he said, knowing something was wrong.

She hesitated, then removed her robe.

The bruises were still there, still as black as the day before when Kurt had inflicted them upon her. Kurt still saw his own incriminating handprints on her torso.

"I don't understand," he said.

"Neither do I," she said.

"Maybe I should wait awhile. Maybe they'll fade."

"Sure," she said. She made coffee, and they sat in silence together, she leafing through a magazine, he staring anxiously out the window, trying not to look at her to see if the marks were fading.

"They are always gone after this many hours," he said finally.

She glared. "I don't know what to tell you."

Morning dragged on toward noon. Every hour or so Rye would examine herself to see if the bruises had faded, but each time they were still there, black and unforgiving. As Kurt made lunch for both of them, he admitted to himself that the bruises might not fade that day. Perhaps she felt the same. "Look, maybe I'll just go, and we can get together when they fade and finish 'Snow.' "

"Fine," she said, emotionless.

Suddenly there was nothing more to say to each other, so he left. No words could rectify what had transpired between them—his violence towards her, his own admission to himself that Rye was never more than an agent that triggered his creativity. It was as though their ongoing story, the narrative of "Waiting for Snow," had somehow come to a brusque conclusion—or non-conclusion.

Over the next few days he called her several times; she was never in. He was panicked: Without any copies of Rye's photos he could not remember the lines of "Waiting for Snow." Unable to write, unable even to copy his own work from memory, he grew frantic. In all his phone messages, he tried to express some human concern for her, ask the appropriate questions, but he never managed to refrain from asking about her bruises. He heard himself, and it made him vaguely ill—the tone in his voice that clearly said he cared only about his writing, his need to use her skin. Yet he could not stop himself.

This, he realized now, was who he really was. Strangely, it was a revelation that, while painful, also felt oddly liberating; at least he no longer had to hide from his own true self.

One day, a week later, he came in from the icy air to find a message on his phone machine: "Kurt, I hope you're well. The bruises still have not faded. At this point I do not expect they will. I've started taking other sorts of photos. See you soon."

That last sounded about as hollow to him as his own concerns for Rye had sounded. Kurt knew they would not see each other soon, nor did he understand if the bruises had truly not faded. It sounded like a story Rye had invented to explain their break-up. Was she saying that marks upon her body made in violence would never fade in some greater emotional sense? Or was she simply noting the bizarre fact that she, whose skin had always been a renewable

white surface, had suddenly, for some inexplicable reason, decided never to return to its pristine state, as though it had been sullied forever by Kurt's hands.

Then one morning, a few days later, a large envelope came in the mail: It contained all the photographs of "Waiting for Snow" up until the point they had ceased work. Kurt was elated, until he saw that the envelope also contained one other photo, not part of their series.

It was a picture of Rye, naked to the waist, horribly bruised, his own hand marks evident on her skin, dated one week after his assault on her. It was a photo of what he had done to her, of the bruises that would not fade.

He tried calling her, but there was no answer, and what could he have said anyway if she answered? Finally, one day, a computer message announced that the number had been disconnected. She had obviously moved, and though Kurt felt he ought to try to find her, he could not come up with any decent reason why he actually should do so.

He sat at his desk the next morning. The photos of "Waiting for Snow," which had seemed so important a short while ago, were packed back in their envelope in his desk drawer. On his desk was the other photo Rye had sent; he'd been staring at it obsessively ever since he received the package. It, too, was a collaborative work of sorts, Kurt thought grimly.

He still had not written a word in his notebook since he began his project with Rye. He stared at the photo, then out the window, at the steel-gray sky. It seemed fraught with some sort of dark promise. Thick clouds obscured the sun, a harbinger of something grim, but a promise of change nonetheless.

As he looked out over the bleak cityscape, he saw the scene quickly obscured in silent, drifting whiteness, like soft static blurring the picture on a television screen. It was a windless snow, a thick, obscuring, magnificent snow that threatened to cover up everything—cold, relentless, uncaring. He felt as though he were looking deep into himself, perhaps for the first time in his life—honestly, unflinchingly. And he suddenly knew that he need wait no longer. Kurt picked up an old ballpoint pen, turned to a blank, white page in his notebook, and he began to write.

Ice Dreams

Elizabeth Massie
&
Robert Petitt

He remembered . . .

It snowed. Blew in from the north and blanketed the piney woods of East Texas. Came in on black clouds, near dark, falling fast and furious. Came down at the wrong time, when he wanted to sit and watch it but could not. Came when she called him in. The first snow he had ever seen and she called him in.

He shivered, glanced at the filthy curtains, and wished he could open them just a crack to take a look outside and see what real snow looked like covering the yard and the rows of collards. If he were in his own room he would have done just that.

But he wasn't in his room, with the ragged quilt tucked between himself and the chill of the sheet, creating a warm and tangled cocoon. He was in her room. And her worn quilt hung on the foot of the wrought iron bed, a forbidden comfort. This night, as had been many others since he had grown the body of a strong young man, was a night of cold secrets. He lay on top of the spread, naked and shivering, cold being only part of the reason for his tremors.

On a small table by the window was a lantern which tossed tiny flickers of light but offered no real heat to the room. The small brass insets in the frame of the bed caught the light and they winked at the boy in blood-red anticipation. On a straight-backed chair, coiled like a huge, mindless snake, was her cattle whip. He had never felt its bite, but had seen the animals disciplined by it, and he prayed he would never offend her and stir her wrath.

A floorboard creaked in the adjoining bathroom and the boy's gaze jerked upward to where the rubber hot-water bag was hanging. It wasn't filled with hot water, he knew. It was for other things.

The door opened. The boy flinched but did not move to cover himself. A woman came to the bed, her face in silhouette because of the pale lantern light. The long braid of her gray ponytail, frighteningly similar to the whip, hissed audibly across the flannel of her nightgown, reaching all the way to the baggy bulk of her ancient buttocks.

She sniffed and ran a hand beneath her nose. She had a cold, but it would not stop her. This was her pleasure. She would have it. She climbed onto the bed beside the boy, grunting with exertion. She hiked her gown up with one hand. The boy felt his penis twitch with fear and excitement.

When the woman was still, he rolled over, knowing what was expected of him, positioning himself between her legs. He kept his face as far from hers as possible; she smelled of stale sweat and old onions. She made a clucking sound, took the bag down, and inserted the tip into the boy's anus. She tilted it, and the icy river invaded the boy's bowels. He cried out. His penis immediately became erect.

She pulled him into herself.

The area was cordoned off, and Harry Jessup stopped his jeep as close to the line as he could without knocking deputies on their asses into the snow. He pulled his gloves on and stared out through the windshield. People were everywhere, milling just outside the line, trying to see. Harry licked his lips, wishing he were somewhere else. He didn't have the time nor desire to be doing this. It wasn't as if he wasn't busy enough with his full time job as the only gynecologist in the area. But he had been coerced into temporary service by a friend on the police force until they could get a full time man.

"Just now and then," Harley had promised. But then the murders had begun, and now and then had closed the distance between themselves. Harry Jessup had been called in for his medical knowledge and his two cents worth, which had escalated into a couple dollars worth. Working with the dead wasn't the problem. Harry just didn't like playing

detective. He hated the Quincy jokes and the questions his regular patients asked him during office visits.

"But, Doctor Jessup, isn't it really disturbing, dealing with all those dead people?" The old ladies would try to look horrified as they dropped their wrinkled panty hose.

Harry knew the bent little women were just fishing for gory details. It drove him nuts.

At times he wished he'd never felt the urge to be Mr. Nice-Help-The-County Doctor.

Like now. A little boy out for a skate on the semi-frozen pond had tripped on the ice and slammed into a snow bank on the pond's edge. The boy had righted himself and then screamed. There, protruding from the snow bank was a hand, a hand he had recognized by the high school ring and the little dangling monogrammed bracelet.

Curtis, the young forensics specialist who had come in from Dallas to help Harry Jessup with Danville's increasingly notorious situation was still back at the lab, still studying the latest bloody installment. Curtis was a young shit who never would come to the murder sites with Harry but preferred to sit in the comfort of the morgue and poke at the bodies. Curtis would have some live company while he worked; Harry's retarded cousin Brian had a custodial job at the hospital, and he liked to watch autopsies and eat M&Ms.

Harry sighed heavily, grabbed his bag from the seat, and stepped from the uneven heat of the Jeep into the cold. A stone-faced deputy lifted the yellow tape and Jessup stepped under. He moved directly to where Sheriff Harley Billings was in animated discussion with two other deputies. Judging from the look on Harley's face, it was obvious the man was in a mood. And not a good one at that.

Harley scowled when Jessup came into his line of sight, nodded slightly, indicated with a hook of his thumb and a savage jerk of his head where the snow bank with the body was, then returned his attention to the deputies. Harley was a quiet man, but his voice carried in the frozen air.

"You ain't gonna sit on your fucking thumbs on this one, neither," he said. "This is piss in the bottom of the outhouse. This is so goddam low and sick I want to kick the ass of the whole county for letting it happen. You boys understand what I'm saying?"

Walking over to the sight, Jessup thought he could almost feel those deputies nodding vigorously. The investigators had uncovered enough of the woman for positive identification, Jessup noted as he stood over her. She was—had been, he corrected himself—the waitress at the Longhorn Diner. Donna Sue Giles was her name, and she had been sweet on sheriff Harley, but Harley had repeatedly talked himself out of asking her out because he felt she was too young for him.

Jessup bent down, looked at the high school ring, checked the date. Donna was young, all right, but not too young. She had been out of school for a few years. Jessup figured she was at least twenty-two. No longer jail-bait, but just fresh enough to make men of all ages want to take a sample. Sweet and tender, what some men considered to be prime meat.

That had been the Longhorn Diner's claim to fame, the serving of prime meat. This young girl had brought the steaks out, hot and steaming, served up on big, heavy platters. That was the way most of the rough and rugged men in the area liked their meat served, hot and steamy, on a hot metal platter.

Yeah, most men. But not one, for sure.

No, there was one who liked his meat served cold, in a bed of snow, or atop a sheet of ice. Prime meat, like this waitress. Or like the first one, that pretty little librarian from over in Hanley. Or the court steno, Tammie Shelton, from right here in Danville. Or the one found just two days earlier, the candy-striper out at the Sunshine Acres Retirement Center. The candy-striped was at this minute under Curtis's knife, dead, cold and alone. But she wouldn't be alone for long. Donna Sue would be with her shortly.

The sound of approaching sirens brought Jessup out of his thoughts and back to the moment. He straightened and turned back toward his Jeep. Let the paramedics handle this end. It was time for him to go back to the hospital and take the elevator down to the basement.

And the morgue.

"Well?"

Jessup peeled off the rubber gloves and tossed them into an already bloody pan. He turned to Harley. "Like the rest. What did you expect?"

Harley angrily passed his gray Stetson from one hamhock hand to the other. "I expect to catch this son-of-a-bitch. I expect you and that specialist. . . ," he spat out the word as if it had a nasty taste, giving young Curtis a look that would have killed if given substance, ". . . to give me something more than what I've been getting. I don't want the fucking NATIONAL INQUIRER down here, making us look like down-home dumb asses. Can you see it? 'Serial Killer Runs Amok in Texas, Law Enforcement Unable to Contend.' "

Jessup scratched his nose. Donna Sue's blood was under his fingernail, and it smelled like copper. He put his finger down.

"I want some fuckin' answers," Harley went on. "Not this gobbly-gook you've been giving me."

"I know what you want," said Jessup. "But we can't give it to you yet. All we know is what we've told you. The victims are all roughly the same age, same build, same color eyes and dark hair. They all worked in public places; they were accessible to everyone and anyone."

Harley shifted his two hundred forty pounds from one size twelve to the other. He was not happy.

"They died the same way; they were strangled with an object or objects unknown. And they were sexually assaulted, before or after they died. But no traces of sperm was found, and no pubic or other body hair was found. No skin or blood of the killer for us to study. In short, nothing."

"Except for the water," Harley added impatiently.

"Yeah," Jessup agreed. "The traces of water in all the victim's vaginas. Plain county tap water. The same amount of chlorine and additives our sewage treatment plant uses, so obviously it comes from any house or business in Danville. It wasn't melted snow or ice as we first thought. It could be anyone who lives around here."

"But, goddammit! Who?" Harley was livid. It looked as if he might cry or explode. Harry wondered if Harley had cared much more for Donna Sue than he'd let on. Harley stormed back and forth. He rammed into the trash can beside the morgue's door and it crashed to its side. "Fuck it," Harley said. He scooped up the trash and crammed it back into the uprighted can; papers, rags, paper clips, an

empty yellow box of Kodak film. Then Harley pulled himself upright, shut his eyes for a moment, and spoke again. His voice was softer. "Just what the hell are we in for here, Harry?"

Harry Jessup felt a sudden, unexpected sympathy for the big man. "I don't know," he said. "I really don't."

He remembered and dreamed . . .

It was cold in the bathroom, but he was used to it now. She was in the tub; the icy water had hardened her nipples and they jut erect, like purple mountain peaks above the white clouds of her breasts. Her long braid floated in waves, like an eel surfacing the water. She smiled up at him wistfully; she told him she was getting old.

He denied it, shaking his head vigorously. He knew that ice preserves, cheats age, for she has told him often. He believed; to him, she was beautiful. She smiled at his denial, drew herself up so that her head leaned against the cold porcelain. She spread her legs beneath the rippling water. In invitation. He could not move for a moment, but just stared.

"Take a picture, it'll last longer," she joked impatiently.

He climbed in, his testicles shriveling, but his member hard. He tasted the purple peaks, penetrating her at the same time. She slipped a finger into his rectum.

. . . and he awoke with a start, his penis hot and ready. He tried to recall all of the dream, but could not. He knew what he would like to do, but she was gone. Long years gone.

He thought of them, then, the young girls. The frozen night wind blew through the open window, caressing his skin. And in the dark, atop the sheets, he brought his organ to release and planned his next encounter.

The next girl was as easy as all the rest. And he stood for a very long time after it was over, shivering in the cold and wet and glorifying in it. He left her in the cellar of the deserted bank where they had fucked, the newest of the ice bunnies.

Harley didn't know why he went back to the morgue. He knew Jessup was at his office, doing his put-the-feet-

into-the-stirrups and spread-the-knees routine for all the who's who in Danville County, and raking in the long green. He got a sour chuckle from that thought, just imagining getting paid for inspecting pussy.

As he reached the morgue door, he damn near got his head smashed in as it swung outward. Harley ducked back, grateful that his reflexes hadn't gone with age.

The man who came out looked startled to see Harley, his green eyes widening, then narrowing as he recognized the sheriff. He nodded as greeting, shifted the old-fashioned hot water bottle from left hand to right, and moved off down the hallway. Keys rattled on his belt, the black wrist strap of a small camera dangled from his pocket. His clodhopper shoes squeaked on the tiled floor.

"Hey, Brian," Harley said, but the orderly did not turn back. Harley shoved thumbs into his waistband and watched as Brian Jessup rounded the corner and disappeared. Brian was Harry's simple-minded cousin. Harry had pulled some weight to get Brian on at the hospital after the state had given the boy all the help they would, and then turned him loose.

The way Harry explained it, the boy had been raised by their grandmother Ruth since an infant. Brian had been sixteen when she had died, and he had gone berserk. He had succeeded in digging the grandmother up out of her grave no sooner than the soil had been worked over the hole. After replanting the grandmother, the state snatched Brian away and performed their wonders. This consisted of training Brian as a janitor, giving him group therapy sessions, then releasing him. Harry did not have room for Brian in his small house, not that he really wanted to be a babysitter. And Brian, who had been conceived out of wedlock by a father unknown, and whose mother hadn't been seen since the birth, had no other relatives he could claim. Harry made arrangements for Brian to go back and live alone at Grandmother Ruth's farm. For several months now, Brian had been employed by the hospital, and for several months, Harley has thought he was one weird fucker.

"Weird fucker," Harley muttered, then opened the morgue door and stepped into the frigid air. He flicked the switch inside the door and waited for the harsh fluorescents

to kick on. They flickered, brightened, then bathed the room in glare. He blinked, momentarily blinded, but not before his eye caught the edge of something caught in one of the sliding vault doors.

He walked over, saw it was the corner of a sheet. And he knew who was under that sheet. It was all he could do to make himself open the drawer, but she had been kind to him, sweet on him it was said. So it was the least he could do, return her kindness with a small consideration of his own. He pulled out the drawer, saw the tag attached to the big toe, shuddered, and quickly tucked the sheet back over the exposed foot. He moved to close the drawer, but noted a wet stain in the middle of the sheet, right where it curved. Over the pubic mount of the late Longhorn Diner waitress.

He froze. Something painful flared beneath his ribs, then rocketed upward to his brain. When it hit, it hit hard, and rage took Harley Billings as nothing he had ever experienced.

Brian Jessup had been carrying a hot water bottle.

Harley's fingers caught the sheet and lifted it from Donna Sue's body. The hair of her triangle was fringed with water. There was water, also, on the slab between her thighs.

The phone on the wall rang. Harley threw the sheet back into place and grabbed the receiver. His ears were roaring.

"Billings," he hissed.

"Harley?" It was a deputy. "Another one's dead. Down at the old condemned bank building. I guess you . . ."

But he didn't get to finish. Harley had looked into the trash can, and seen an empty box of Kodak film. Cameras and hot water bottles.

Hot water bottles were used for more than just heat compresses. They could also be used for enemas. And douching.

The receiver hit the wall with a thud. Harley was out of the morgue and running before he knew he was doing so.

"You don't have to go in if you don't want," Harley told Harry Jessup. "It's family, and it could be an ugly scene."

The men stood outside the cruiser at the end of the farmhouse's long dirt driveway. There was little snow on the

ground now, but crusted ice puddles littered the drive and the rough yard surrounding the house.

"No," said Harry. "I'll go with you. Certainly Brian is not who you want. He's harmless. Believe me. This is a mistake. Let me do the talking, will you?"

The front door was closed but not locked. The men entered the foyer, straining to see in the near dark. There was a cluttered living room to the left. Down the hallway was the kitchen. The air hung heavy with the smells of fried food. On the right was a set of steps.

"Think he's gone up?" asked Harley.

Harry shrugged.

Harley led the way to the second floor.

There were only two rooms upstairs. One an attic storage. The other Brian Jessup's bedroom. Harley lifted his foot to kick the door in, but the door was not secured, and he stumbled into the room.

"Shit," he swore.

Brian was not in the room.

"Shit!" Harley stormed about the floor, pacing between the twin-sized bed, the wooden rocker, and the trunk beneath the single window. Harry stood back and watched. "There has to be something here," Harley said. "That little bastard is too dumb to hide evidence!"

He turned over the mattress, glanced under the bed, opened the trunk.

Then stopped. Harry came closer to look as well.

There were packs upon packs of developed pictures. Yellow packs crammed into the trunk along with old clothes and junk. Harley opened one pack and flipped through the contents. His eyebrows drew together in confusion, then straightened out in horror.

"Christ, this is it."

Harry looked at the photos. At first he saw nothing but blurs. Colors running together and forms without meaning. And then he saw what Harley had seen.

"He took pictures of the act," Harry said. He fought to control his breathing. "All these pictures are close-ups of his goddamned penis. Of girls' pussies. He held the camera as he was fucking them and took pictures!"

Harry dumped more packs of photos. The pictures were all blurred, all barely distinguishable. Lighting was different

in many, some were nothing but smears of flesh tones. But they were without a doubt a penis. And spread thighs and wet cunt.

In another packet, there were pictures of a penis penetrating bare, white pelvic bones.

"Christ have mercy on us!" shouted Harley.

Then Harley lifted something else out of the trunk. His hand spasmed and he dropped it to the floor where it lay like so much dead and grayed grass. A long, thick braid of hair.

"What the hell is this?" Harley said.

"It looks like grandmother's hair," said Harry. "She always had a long braid of hair, even until she died."

"Cut if off after he dug her up, I'll bet," said Harley. He went to the window and slammed his fists against the glass. He stared out at the backyard. "And I'll bet hair can choke a woman as easy as one-two-three. Goddamn it, Harry, didn't you know? Didn't you even suspect?"

"No," said Harry.

"Why, then?" asked Harley. "How could someone be so perverted?"

Before Harry could answer, Harley yelled, "Look! He's out of the shed! Headed for the woods!"

Pictures fluttered in the wake of air as the men ran from the room.

The cave was not far from the farmhouse. Drink cans and M&M wrappers alerted Harley to the presence of the chink in the earth. The deputies, who had come along, were commanded to stay outside. Harley and Harry went in.

It was dark, and the men felt along the sides as they moved. Icicles dripped from the ceiling of the cave. The floor was slick with water.

"What the hell am I tripping over?" Harley swore softly.

"I don't know," said Harry.

And then Harley cried out and went down. Something rushed past the men in the blackness. Harley shouted, "He's going out!"

A deputy, from somewhere outside the cave called, "We've got him, sheriff!"

Another one said, "You ain't going to believe this."

Harley and Harry worked their way out of the cave.

Brian Jessup stood, his forearms secured by the deputies. He wore a coat and pair of moth-eaten gloves. His pants were unzipped and his penis stuck out. In one hand he held a human skull. On his erect penis hung a human pelvic bone. His green eyes stared, huge and wild, at his captors.

Harry ran one hand along his face. Harley said, "Fucking skeletons. Raping girls with hot water bottles. Killing girls. I think justice here calls for an old and swift judge. Let me find a rope."

One deputy laughed abruptly and uncertainly, staring at the bewildered man with the bone hanging on his dick. Another glanced around as if actually looking for a rope. And in that moment, their grips loosened a bit on Brian's arms. The retarded man jerked free, pulled an icicle from the edge of the cave's mouth, and lifted his head to the sky.

"Cold and beautiful!" he cried, and crammed the frozen dagger through his eye and into his brain.

"That should about do it, don't you think? I mean, except for waiting on the report of who the girl in the cave might have been."

Harry Jessup didn't respond to Harley's statement. He just sat staring into his drink. On the jukebox some guy was singing about drinking himself to death because his woman done left him for another man.

Harley nudged Harry with an elbow, and Jessup finally looked up. The sheriff had a sour expression on his face.

"What Harley?" Harry asked. "I've been listening to my drink, not to you."

"I said we got him dead to rights. He shit in his own back yard and stepped in it. Left sperm in the girl in the morgue. And there's the photos. Can you imagine he was smart enough to send them to different developers, though? And we got that braid of hair. One sick fucker, Harry. I know he was your cousin but I can't help but want to celebrate his passing. Our girls are safe now."

Harry nodded. "Brian's funeral's tomorrow. Guess nobody'll be there except for me."

"That doesn't dredge up any sympathy. Sorry."

"At least it's solved."

"Yep. Convicted, sealed, and dead-on-arrival."

Harry Jessup stared at Harley, grunted, slowly shook his

head from side to side. He pushed his chair back, stood, and bade Harley a brusque good-bye.

He caught the waitress on the way over, explained that he would finish his drinking at home, in better company.

She laughed understandingly, accepted his money, then flashed a white smile and an even whiter ripple of thigh as she strolled to Harley's table.

The drive to Jessup's home was a short one. Once the car was parked in the garage he went inside and straight to his study, and the well-stocked bar. He poured three fingers of scotch and added two cubes of ice, stripped, and fell naked into the soft and comfortable old leather of the couch.

He rattled the ice against the side of the glass, the sound reminding him of Vegas and rolling dice.

"Gonna roll them bones." He said it aloud, even as he thought it. And that prompted another thought. "Bones," he repeated.

He remembered . . .

The bones in the cave. The bones Harley would try to put a name to, but never would. Because those bones were old and the teeth had fallen out of the skull long ago. Because those bones belonged to Harry's mother's younger sister, Julie. Harry's sexy Aunt Julie. Brian's mother.

Grandmother Ruth didn't like babies being born out of wedlock. And especially when she found out who the father was. Brian was not only Harry's cousin; he was Harry's son. Harry and Julie Jessup's son. As a doctor, Harry knew that children born retarded because of incest was not as common as laymen would believe, but as the dice of egg and sperm had rolled, they had come up snake-eyes.

Harry sighed, took a drink, and found his eyes drawn to the old whip hanging above the mantle. Grandmother Ruth's whip, used for ornery animals who wouldn't pull or plow. Cut the hide right off their backs. Killed one once with the blows.

And once upon a time, as the saying goes, she took it to a fifteen year old girl and a thirteen year old boy, in a cave. She'd balanced the tiny baby Brian on her bony grandmother's hip and let the lash take its skillful vengeance. She carried what was left of the boy back to the farm house where she nursed him to health.

The girl never came back.

Behind the couch, someone entered the unlocked door to the house.

"I'll be right up," Harry directed.

The whip. The hair. Almost identical to each other, and such a personal part of her. Like father, like son, he thought. Both Brian and Harry had been initiated into the world of erotica by Grandmother's skilled ministrations of water and ice.

Only Brian could never have seduced women. After Grandmother Ruth had died, he fucked who he could. The dead ones. Cold ones, alone in the morgue. And then photograph it to prove to himself it was real.

On the other hand, Harry never had trouble attracting live women.

Harry took the whip and his drink upstairs to his bedroom. He opened the drawer of the nightstand, removed a condom, puts it on slowly, savoring the elastic-like feel on his skin. The charge was much like the sensation he got when he donned his gloves to perform an autopsy, especially on unblemished young females. The waitress was smiling on the bed, her eyes closed. After all, why not trust? He was her doctor, as well.

He turned off the lamp, his fingers found the glass on the nightstand and removed two cubes of ice. Deftly, he slid them into the woman's vagina. She moaned in surprise and passion as the cubes began to melt.

Like his son, Harry liked his sex cold. Grandmother had seen to that. But Harry liked it with real, breathing women.

But afterwards, yes, he could really get off then. Slip the whip around their throats, feel the power Grandmother Ruth must have felt over her farm animals and the boys she had trained so well.

And later, he could put on the elastic gloves, feel the tingle begin anew. Spread parts of the bitches all over the cold metal of the autopsy table, and get paid for it by the county.

The woman on the bed moaned, more urgently. Harry smiled.

And lowered himself into the cold.

Wasting

Lauren Fitzgerald

It was one of those dismal tract homes, with a brick front and square windows that look out over a sea of rooftops and perfectly manicured lawns. I pulled into the driveway, double-checked the name on the mailbox, and killed the engine.

It had been four months since my last assignment. Four months since the Kimner boy. I sighed—briefly, sadly—at the memory. The only thing worse than watching a child die of cancer is to witness a child's gradual wasting as the disease devours his hopes along with his aspiring body. It's enough to destroy a person's sanity, not to mention their faith in God.

I worked my way up the driveway and along the steep walk to the house, admiring the immaculate lawn and the neatly trimmed hedges. So green for early Spring.

I tucked my briefcase under my arm and rapped twice on the door. Momentarily, the door inched inward and a tall, shapely woman appeared beyond the threshold. Her hair was perfectly groomed and her skin flawlessly madeup. She wore an attractive silk suit with exquisite gold and sapphire jewelry, and smelled of freshly applied Channel no. 5; a markedly polished look for nine-thirty in the morning.

"Mrs. Cook," I said. "I'm Ms. Ackerman from the school system. Elizabeth's Home Instruction teacher in American History. You were expecting me?"

She surveyed me from head to toe, her steel colored eyes settling briefly upon my hips. Child-bearing hips, my mother benignly labeled the broad rear end that afflicted all of the Ackerman women. Big fat ass would have been more accurate.

I must have passed her inspection, for her face lightened and she offered a brief smile.

"I've set up two chairs and a card table on the back porch," she said, stepping back to provide me entrance into the house.

"I'm sure I can see myself," I said, "if you're in a hurry to get someplace."

She closed the door, gazed at me curiously. "What makes you think I'm going somewhere?"

I shrugged and shook my head stupidly.

The house resonated with the steady drone of the heat pump, which must have been running at full force, judging from the hot, dry air. Yet the heat did nothing to warm the interior's cool, pristine personality. Every room we passed was sparsely furnished and immaculately kept. There was neither a blemish on the walls, nor a spot on the carpets. The furnishings, what few of them there were, seemed virtually unused. Even the window treatments appeared newly ironed and perfectly draped.

When we came to a small porch behind the kitchen, Mrs. Cook stopped, glanced uneasily around the room, and wrung her hands nervously. Her lips parted and trembled as if about to utter something unspeakable. "I'll get Ellie," she said, and disappeared into the spotless sanctuary behind her, leaving me alone in the screened room with its three pieces of furniture. Ellie. Her school papers had said Elizabeth.

I opened my bag and unloaded the books and papers I had brought for the lesson. I loathed the fact that the school system provided me with out-of-date copies of *"America: A Narrative History"* and *"The Challenge of Democracy"*, when their peers were using the latest editions. It was almost as if they didn't expect these kids to recover, that they would either die or become so mentally destroyed that they'd never be of any use to society, so why bother spending the money.

"Good morning."

I let the stack of papers fall from my hand and turned toward the airy voice behind me. I had not known what to expect. All I knew was that she was fourteen. The Home Study system only reveals the nature of a student's absence from school if it is infectious or potentially hazardous to

the teacher's well-being. In this case, the file was simply classified, "Personal Difficulties."

The face belonged in a Dickens novel, so thin and wide-eyed she seemed to be looking at me through a magnifying glass. Her skin was sallow and resembled flour paste. Upon her small body hung a short dress that draped her skeleton like a burlap sack, the deep neckline providing disturbing glimpses of her sunken neck and chest. Her forearms were as slender as shower curtain rods, making her skin seem so tightly wrapped around her bones it pained me to look at her. Her entire being, what little of it there was, was dwarfed by a flowing crown of golden hair which fell in thick curls around her shoulders.

Anorexia. I had seen it many times before, but not to such a degree. I recognized immediately that this one was in a whole different category altogether. I swallowed and managed a smile.

"Elizabeth," I said, moving toward her. "I'm Ms. Ackerman." I offered her my hand, troubled by her initial reluctance to accept it. She wrapped her thin fingers tentatively around mine, then quickly let her hand drop to her side.

"They call me Ellie," she uttered weakly.

"We only have two hours, Ellie, so shall we begin?"

The girl nodded and drifted toward the card table, her legs shuffling slowly beneath her dress. She settled carefully into her chair and folded her hands in front of her.

How much could she weigh, I wondered. Seventy pounds? Sixty? I struggled to keep my eyes on the text, fearing I would gaze upon her and discover some new, horrible feature. She was nothing like the Kimner boy. Even near the end, when he was fed by machines and weighed no more than a dog, he still had presence. He still appeared human despite his ghostly pallor and loss of hair. Ellie was different. She looked more like a caricature of a human girl than the real thing. She was pitiful to behold. Silently I pledged not to allow this one to affect me. No matter what happened with this new pupil, I would remain detached and cold and uninvolved. God knows I couldn't survive another one like the Kimner boy.

That night in bed, I thought about Ellie and my own battle with weight loss. About the pills and fad diets and

memberships at health clubs where I was too embarrassed to go. As a child, I had promised myself that I would never become like my mother. I would be thin and beautiful and perfect, and never, ever grow larger than a size eight. Twenty years and two-thousand root beer floats later, I had become my mother's twin. How did it happen? I wondered sadly.

I rolled onto my side and wrapped my knees around my pillow. Knees that had never known the feel of a man's body between them. Knees so big and fat they had grown weak and painful from the burden of obesity.

I tried to cry, to squeeze the pain from my body in clear, hot tears. But the tears never came. Only memories. And dreams.

The next time I saw her she had shaved her head. She looked like a toothpick with an olive stuck through the end. She must have seen the shock in my eyes because she smoothed a bony hand over her bald head and uttered, "Hair. Three pounds, six ounces."

I nodded, remembering her beautiful, thick mane. Funny, but I'd never considered hair as part of my total body weight.

Ellie's first assignment, a paper on John F. Kennedy, was brilliant. I already knew that she was a straight-A student from her school records, but the manifestation of her intelligence went beyond grades. Not only was her work virtually flawless, the presentation itself was something to admire. She had written the entire report in long hand, making certain that every letter of every word possessed a uniform look. Then she bound it in a white plastic cover and presented it to me a week before it was due. The paper was impeccable except for a few technical problems. I gave her a ninety-eight.

Ellie took the masterpiece in her tiny fingers and held it to her eyes, scanning the cover page for a moment before planting her gaze upon me.

"I'm not perfect." Her voice was flat and bitter.

"Ninety-eight is an excellent score," I said. "You have an impressive command of the material and your writing skills are quite advanced for your age. Your only errors were in spelling and word usage. You should be pleased."

Her lips soured and she delicately returned the paper to the table. A soft spring breeze filtered through the screen, carrying in the scent of rose blooms from the garden. Ellie turned and gazed outside. She seemed to be looking beyond the yard, past the brick and vinyl houses that lined the street behind hers. Her eyes glazed over with a dark, blank stare, as if she had slipped from her body completely, leaving behind the cold, empty husk of her skin.

She suddenly snapped back when the aroma of tomato sauce and garlic drifted in from the kitchen. Ellie held her stomach and grimaced at the smell. I imagined the wars that ensued after I left for the day; the mealtime battles between she and her mother: Ellie sitting tight mouthed at the table, her mother struggling to wedge a spoonful of soup between her lips. Laxatives, enemas, two hundred sit-ups before bedtime . . . the sickness that undoubtedly consumed every moment of the day . . .

Stop it! I told myself. *You're doing it already.* I bit down hard on my pencil and turned to the next chapter.

"Any questions about last week's assignment?" I wedged my thighs under the card table and scooted in my chair.

"No."

She was even thinner now, the map of her veins pressing against her flesh so that they bulged in narrow tributaries along her arms and forehead. Her head was smooth, her scalp sinking into the imperfections of her skull.

"Let's discuss Watergate," I said coolly. I opened to page 302 of *"Democracy"* and handed her the lesson outline I had prepared the night before.

"Do you know much about physics?" she asked. A small, brown ant traveled the inside of her arm toward her armpit.

"A little," I said, pretending not to see the bug navigating her flesh. "Sometimes I substitute teach science."

She fingered the fabric on her skirt, a sheer silk print that showed through to her cadaverous thighs. "How small can an object become before it disappears?"

I could see where she was headed. "Well, some organisms are so small they can't be seen with the naked eye."

She shook her head, frustrated. The insect had disappeared into the meatless hollow of her armpit. "Yes, but if something is very, very small, does it take up space?" Her

knees tapped together nervously, sounding like two bowling pins butting heads. She gazed up at me with eyes dull as bricks. Just how thin *could* she become, I wondered? How long before her organs collapse beneath the weight of her heavy skin? How many pounds before her flesh decays and her limbs drop away from her body? How long before she fades away?

I could feel the ache of sympathy creeping into my heart, could taste the sour knot of compassion tightening in my gut. I willed it away.

"Ellie, do you have a . . . therapist? You know, someone to talk to?"

"You mean a shrink?" Her choice of words was priceless.

"Yes. A shrink."

"I used to. But he couldn't answer the question either."

"You're fat."

"I've always been a big girl," I admitted. "It's hereditary on my mother's side. Did you do your assigned reading?"

Ellie nodded delicately and rested her head upon her hands. The semester was winding down. Ellie's eyes had turned yellow from a lack of iron, and her skin had soured into something green and blotchy, like turned fruit. She had lost two fingers on her left hand when she burned them on the kerosene heater she kept constantly at her side. When I asked her about it, she merely groaned and uttered, "Three pounds, two ounces." The crimson scabs on her knuckles were thick and fresh; I was surprised she hadn't peeled them off for the sake of a few grams.

"You take up a lot of space," she said, matter-of-fact.

"Does that bother you?"

Ellie shrugged and gazed past my shoulder at the garden. It was early May and the yard was a rolling bed of colors and fragrance.

"It's a lovely garden. Are you the one with the green thumb?" I asked.

"I collect insects," she said. "When I work in the garden, I find lots of bugs. I want to be an entomologist someday."

"Good for you," I said. "It's important to have goals."

"What do you know!"

Nothing, I thought. Absolutely nothing.

*　　　*　　　*

Mid-June. Ellie's mother wheeled her onto the porch next to me, a blanket thrown across her lap. I could see her heart beating slowly in her chest. Her breaths were quick and unsteady. I couldn't believe how thin she had become. I didn't see how it was possible.

"This is our last session," I said, trying not to stare. "I'm certain you won't have any trouble passing the final exam, Ellie. You're a very smart girl. I'm sure you'll get an "A" for the course." I placed the test in front of her and helped her grip the pencil between her brittle fingers. She stank of antiseptic and bile.

"Eeee." Her voice was unintelligible. No teeth. They had fallen out some time ago. Four pounds, two ounces.

"You may have the entire two hours, Ellie. I'll wait outside."

As I left Ellie to her exam, my body grew ill with pain. It was the same pain I had felt with the Kimner boy. The same despair that had grabbed my soul, held it in its fist, and squeezed. Perhaps somewhere within my sick, bloated body, pain felt good. Maybe that was the reason I had allowed myself to become so fat and so alone.

I wandered down the hall and found Mrs. Cook sitting in the living room.

"Mrs. Cook?" I said.

She stood and gazed at me expectantly. She was wearing a beautiful red satin dress and her hair was wrapped neatly around an ivory comb.

"I try to stay uninvolved . . . I usually don't butt in . . ." My voice trembled. "I think she needs help."

"Help?" she said.

"For her problem."

"Problem?" Her eyes were distant. *Denial,* I reasoned silently.

"*Anorexia Nervosa.* Maybe some psychotic tendencies. It's a very common disease, Mrs. Cook. You shouldn't feel ashamed." She suddenly found me with her eyes. I went on. "Maybe if you let up a little. Perhaps if you didn't insist on having things so perfect and spotless, she'd put less pressure on herself."

Her mouth dropped, her eyes narrowed. "If it were up to me, Ms. Ackerman, I'd live in a pig sty. She's the one who insists that I dress like this! She's the one who keeps

me up half the night cleaning and scrubbing and feeding those God damned bugs! She's the one who carves away at her body and keeps the heat blasting so that she'll sweat herself smaller! Five pounds here. Two pounds there. Let up on things? I should be so lucky!" Her pale, smooth hands clenched at her sides.

"She needs to be in a hospital!" I screamed.

"She'd die in a hospital. They'd kill her. Ellie has a brilliant mind. She knows enough to keep herself alive, don't you see? She knows just how far she can go. In a hospital, she'd be treated like a freak! She'd let herself die before she allowed anyone to study her like a God damned laboratory rat!"

Though I hated to admit it, she was right. I had worked with children in hospitals before, had witnessed the guinea pig effect first hand. No doctor, no matter how legitimate, would see Ellie as anything more than a case study.

Poor, tortured woman, I thought. I wanted to embrace her; to hold her and absorb her pain with my own flesh until it consumed me. I wanted to, but didn't. Instead I turned on my heels, hurried out to my car, and waited there for the rest of the session.

It was raining the night I brought Ellie her graded final exam. It was a perfect "A".

I stood on the stoop in the front of her house, dripping wet. Mrs. Cook did not invite me in.

"I'd like to say goodbye to Ellie," I said, speaking through the half-opened door, hair dripping wet. It was dusk, and I could barely make out her face in the gritty shadows of the house.

"Ellie isn't taking visitors now, Ms. Ackerman. I'll tell her you came by." She slammed the door.

After a moment, I crept around the side of the house, through the muddy garden toward the back porch. I waited until I saw Mrs. Cook in the upstairs window before tiptoeing up to the porch. The porch was lit by the glow of a small, black and white television set. There was a distinct clicking sound, then a hiss and a snap.

"Ellie?" I whispered.

Click. Hiss.

Snap!

I moved to the other side of the porch, closer to where the television was, "Ellie?"

I put my face to the screen, the cool metal pressing into my nose. From my new vantage point, this is what I saw: ticks, hundreds of them, big and plump, gathered around her sallow, deflated flesh, dark and pregnant with the juice of her veins. They drove their teeth into her skin. Click. Vibrated their crisp bodies against one another in voracious ecstasy. Hiss. Fed until they burst. Snap!

Blood.

Forty pounds, five ounces.

I vomited into my hand, studied the half-digested meal on my fingers, then wiped it across the damp ground and went home.

I have returned to teaching in the classroom. In the schools, the worst problems we get are drugs and pregnancy and an occasional suicide. Pretty mild, when you think about it. Of course every now and again I'll get a student who appears painfully thin. Sometimes they stay the whole year, managing to hang on with the help of enemas and liquid nutriment. Other times they leave in mid-semester, never to be heard from again. It is during these times that I think of Ellie. I wonder if she is still alive, and how much of her is left. Then I force myself to think of other things.

This is not to say that the experience had no effect on my life. The impact was monumental. And for this I am grateful. Because of Ellie I have come to accept myself for who and what I am: a large woman taking up lots and lots of space. Even more, I am a woman who feels for others, even if those feelings singe my soul. And whenever I start to feel sorry for myself—wishing I could shave a few pounds and become something closer to perfect—I sit in front of the television set, throw back a few root beer floats, and remind myself that I am only human. God bless my big fat ass.

Backseat Dreams and Nightmares

K. K. Ormond

On the corner . . . standing. . . .
Face made-up, although not overdone. Just a touch to
give that right
   amount of painted seduction . . .
   Just a bit sullen . . .
   Just a bit nervous . . .
Cruising past, foot a surrogate erection, he egged the gas
pedal harder and harder. He rounded the corner, and
parked. He sat and thought for a while. He sat and
dreamed.
On the avenue the man sauntered casually, common
frame blending nicely as eyes were kept busy and hands
twiddled aimlessly at his sides. Spotting the treat again, he
smiled. She was still standing there, as she had been five
minutes earlier, clad in tight jeans and a bright pink halter,
with just that slight hint of nipple peeking through. As the
material near his fly bulged, the man stepped up the pace,
strides echoing off the pavement and rebounding between
the crumbling tenements that lined the avenue.
Minutes ticked by almost audibly as the girl stood in a
wary stance, shifting from foot to foot every so often, glancing about. A bus stop sign loomed high above her head,
and the man silently commended such a nice choice of
cover; one could stand beneath its ordinary shroud of safety
for quite a while before hassles arose. Judging from the
look of the treat's nervous demeanor, the police had already been cruising. The blue and whites were also the
reason for his acquiring pedestrian status. A plush vehicle
would be more suited for comfort, but his late model auto
meandering through the neighborhood would surely bring
unwelcome attentions. He was less conspicuous on foot,
and with a bounty of coal black gangways and passages

leading from the street to the rancid darkness of slum alleys, he stood a better chance of losing cops who caught on to his game.

Sidling closer, the crunch of broken glass and gravel providing a fitting herald to his arrival, the man stared as she turned and looked. Nice, she was, with a mouth designed solely for sucking. Pouty little lips—no, not pouty—they were sarcastic, substitute labium, well schooled in organs no proper mouth should know. Tipping his head, the man smiled like an old friend, producing a likewise gesture at this stranger out for a stroll. Quickly though, she looked away, and he dropped his own eyes also, savoring the last few steps before actual contact.

As he placed his hand on her left arm, a fragile face jerking in confusion, he suddenly knew she'd been beaten, stripped of innocent play in years past. The brutalization of the weaker sex was not something he could get used to and the sight gave him pause. He felt sorry for her and for his own participation in blatant exploitation. And, he was aroused. Despite the premature aging of youthful features, her body contained enough pure sex to pique his cravings. Cravings that would not be denied. He wanted what was his.

Spotting the bulge on his otherwise lean stomach, the girl gaped, and tried to bolt, but was brought to her knees by a sudden grab. A quick, violent pull served to snap her up.

"Get the fuck up." He said it with a snarl, in no mood for emotional outbursts. Her fear was not his concern, and the object would not be used on such a love anyway. A quick smack connected with the side of her cheek, and the girl was in shock.

Frenzied steps thudded across concrete. The weapon nestled in a leather belt slapped against the man's belly, bringing a downward glance and sly grin; no one would be scooping this prize from under his nose. Large fingers fondled the necessary pistol, with the streets deserted and not too many receptacles out on the warm, quiet street corners, competition could be fierce.

Next to him, half-trotting, half-dragged along, the treat stared vacantly, and again, the man felt a twinge of pity for such a jaded creature.

"What do you think you're doing? Get your filthy hands

off her! We don't need the likes of you on these streets, dammit! This town is cleaning itself up! Get your hands off her, you filthy bastard, I'll call the cops!''

The obese woman attacked from a doorway, scratching with purple lacquered hooks that left pink trails on the man's biceps. With a punch to the jaw, he sent his attacker to the pavement, her sweaty body rolling about and collecting bits of glass and old gum. Surveying the jellied mass, the man swore rudely under his breath. There would be no cleaning up this neighborhood—murder, robbery, exploitation, sex crimes, and all the other symptoms of a diseased metropolis inherent in its very molecules. One look at the face of his soon-to-be intimate partner sealed that theory. She was hopeless, and a slut.

"Do you want something to drink?" he asked, pulling a flask from the pocket of his trousers. Whiskey droplets stained the front of his fly, remnants of earlier dribblings. The girl stared and said nothing, cringing slightly as fingers ate deeper into the flesh of her arm.

"Your choice, but it will numb the pain of your life some." He tipped the flask with his left hand, the right still clutching brutally. He could imagine already the games to be played in a backseat brothel. The girl continued to gawk with a comatose vacancy, and he wondered if the gun was really that much of a big deal. "Oh well, too bad if it is," he muttered. Their time together would last just long enough to get his rocks off and then home he would head. He was sure the little 'street executive' had been used by many much more dangerous-looking than he, was all part of the life. He finished his swig as the car came into view.

Inside the vehicle the man paused for inspection, hand exploring the length of his penis as he savored the look of the meat. It sat rigidly on the passenger seat, staring about nervously and glancing continually into the back of the car. Thin fingers toyed unconsciously with a small silver ring, and again a sudden wave of empathy grabbed him. The man could truly feel for her. Poor thing had probably been busted one too many times, forced to either exchange favors or spend sleepless nights behind bars. He knew how the cops around here were, couldn't let a working girl earn her wages.

"Do you want a drink? Offer still stands from before.

I'm not a cop, you know. Not even a narc." He smiled harshly, front tooth the color of a razor blade.

She remained silent, eyes darting, practically ignoring his presence. It pissed him off.

"Here." With a brutal motion the flask was shoved against pert lips and she yelped, taken by surprise.

"Drink it. Now."

The girl hesitated, growing moist around the eyes, but the pain of metal against her teeth brought quick obedience. He forced her to drink half the contents before allowing her to cease the suckling. Taking the flask, he replaced it with his own liquored orifice. A shallow gag fought his tongue as it probed and darted, seeking pleasure in a long, wet kiss. His finger traced her lipsticked mouth, imagining what other kinds of suckling it could do. He groped her pubic mound roughly, and put his penis away before inserting a key into the car's ignition and shifting into drive.

A large arm pulled the treat closer, sliding ninety-eight pounds of sex across smooth vinyl. The treat stared at the dashboard, a slender crease around her mouth. It was erased with a single slap. She smiled rigidly then, trying to appease and avoid the inevitable. A silver tooth exposed itself again, the man knowing that deep down she enjoyed, received pleasure in punishment, hating herself to no end. More than likely the girl had been molested since puberty and now found herself earning a living in the only way such a ruined young flower could ever know, fulfilling the prophesy of an older brother, stepfather, cousin, or perhaps, even a mother. Callused fingers pinched a shy nipple, she'd been broken in right.

"How many times has this happened before?" he asked, guiding the car down a narrow sidestreet. Glancing thoughtfully at burned out shells, former homes now grim from the kiss of arsonists' fingers, he wondered if she'd ever known the inside of one of these tenements. Probably.

"Never." She said it softly, with just a hint of babyish recalcitrance.

He smiled and slapped her again. Little vixen. Little dog in heat. Nice ploy, attempting to make him believe the merchandise really wasn't all that trodden upon. But then they all did, either claiming he was the first one of their

lives, or of the week, or if he really pushed, of the night. Not that it mattered, he just liked to start a little something on occasion.

"Okay, I believe you." The words came out sarcastically, and his tongue licked the edge of a lower lip. The girl stared at her raving suitor and then dropped her head. He cocked his own quizzically. Perhaps she thought him diseased.

"Listen, girly. I took a bath this evening and I don't have crabs. No reason to stare at me like I'm repulsive or some grimy old man. That kind of behavior just doesn't cut it. I work out three times a week, and let me tell you, plenty of women would love to put their hands on this body. They could too, if I wasn't so . . . averse to long term relationships. So don't get uppity, pretending you're being soiled or something. That don't work with me, sister."

Another smack and she curled up by his side, loving and hating every erotic tingle of pain, that he was sure of. He jabbed at her crotch with hands roughened by work, and she curled even tighter. He knew then she would give him everything, and even more. He'd brought out the masochist in her.

The rumble of cylinders echoed off pylons. Reining in the powerful motor, the man parked his car under a viaduct, left hand already removing his penis from his pants. Grasping the treat by her wrists and then ankles, he heaved the girl into the backseat, savoring pale, undernourished features, and moist, pleading eyes. Excitement grew harder, he rounded his fist and began.

Punching and twisting, jerking and shaking, he used the treat like a little rag doll. Head lashing from side to side, the treat thudded hard against the armrest, and smooshed softly against the stuffy surface of the backseat cushion. Hands clenched and little feet arched, instep curling as tendons climaxed in painful—and what the man was sure were sexual—spasms. The treat sobbed hysterically, and then cried out for help.

"Dammit!" The fist smashed her nose and the man paused, chest heaving as he tried to catch his breath. He stared silently at the treat, watching as her little lips dripped spittle, little eyes leaked tears.

Little eyes that riveted, no matter what the violation, onto the gaze of his own baby blues.

Pulling back from her pulpy face, the man howled in fury at the accusing stare. He kicked at her thighs in a fit of pique, and clawed her cheeks as visions attacked. Years of incest, of hate, of the girl's quest for that certain hero who never arrived. Former beatings and occasional rapes—all adding up to birth her sunken existence, eked out day by desperate day.

Appalled at his own weakness, the man shrieked loudly, she was supposed to be, needed to be—

Dammit! It always turned out like this.

A heavy tear wound its way down her nose, and he wondered whose eye exactly, it was from.

"Mother Fucker!" Fighting back his emotions, the man worked a size 6 pair of jeans down bony hips and ripped away bright pink panties. He regretted not having been more gentle, but what the hell? More than likely .99 cent jobbers from K-Mart. She wouldn't be missing them. He forced a smirk at the thought, and hit her again as a fading erection swelled anew at the sight of her anonymous, tempting sex. He cracked her soft legs apart like a wishbone. His penis lined itself up to enter.

"No? Please?" The plea brushed across smeared lipstick, bubble gum and booze, and he plunged in rapidly, wanting to get this over with as fast as possible. It was all wrong now, everything had changed. This girl didn't deserve such a hard life, could not be held responsible for decisions made before she knew what she was doing, and it was right that he stop her self-imposed degradation in as quick a fashion as possible. For if he didn't, if no one ever did, some day she would snap, would scream and scream and never stop, wanting to die, needing to die, slicing a pair of thin wrists, or downing an entire bottle of Tylenol #3's, or stepping in front of some speeding trucker, laughing as her ending came, and then wailing as the scenes of a life of horror passed before her eyes, clenching small fists in solid resolution as the swift scythe of death came swinging down, without pause, or remorse, without—

"Stop it, stop it! I don't want any more—NO!" He pulled out as she screamed, and as the man understood completely, so too did the object which had materialized in his

hand. Dark splatters hit the seats, his face, flew into his mouth and eyes and nostrils. Private regions spurted as he burrowed into the cause of her exploitation, jabbing soft, moist folds and crevices. Bowels evacuated as he continued to thrust, the knife both savior and cruel, exaggerated penis, raping and caressing at the same time, making his mind squirm. He should have never picked her up, should have stayed at home, degrading only himself and his hand. For to have subjected this poor child to the stench of filth from his own dirty adult regions was unforgivable.

He lay there panting.

Trying to catch a breath which could not be slowed.

Trying to steady a trembling beyond conscious control.

As the still child reclined on the backseat, the man reached out, pushing a frozen smile onto blood-sticky lips. The wall was threatening to crack now, sudden truths (rapist) and revelations (killer) oozing through the crevices like some toxic, gelatinous obscenity. He slammed his mind shut and continued with the posing, determined the girl would smile in death, she would, she would, she would! As his hands continued to work, the broader the expression on the corpse, the more pinched became the appearance of his own sallow face.

"Thirteen year-old girl snatched from bus stop at gun point as local woman attempts to help. Thirteen year-old girl found raped, mutilated, and murdered."

Black and white, it sat there on the kitchen table, screaming from the page in a little girl's voice. Screaming out his—

As the scenes from a backseat abattoir flashed briefly, the man fought to blank his mind and carefully turned the page. Fingers explored the depths of his trousers, even as tears flowed ever freely.

The Stick Woman

Edward Lee

"I certainly didn't become a millionaire by wasting my money, so why waste good money on toilet paper, hmm?" he'd told her that first night six years ago. "*You,* my dear, are my toilet paper now, and that's what you will continue to be unless you want me to kill your son."

Would he really do that? "No," Priscilla said. She didn't believe him. Even a sociopath like Fenton wouldn't kill their only *child.* And of the request he'd made? What kind of a deranged person would want such a thing?

The answer came that same night, however, when her loving husband had piped down some video tapes onto the television, one of hundreds she would have no choice but to catch glimpses of over the next half a decade. Snuff films, she guessed they were called. Homemade. Men in masks beating children, then raping them, then killing them. Priscilla felt certain one of the masked men was Fenton. *Anyone that . . . sick,* she supposed, *must be capable of. . . .*

Well. Of anything, right?

"Okay." The word scratched out her throat, like a nail against stone. What could she do? Call his bluff? Ricky was all she had left in the world, even *this* world, even this world Fenton had consigned her to, this chamber of dementia that would make the Marquis de Sade hurl his lunch. "I'll do anything you say," Priscilla Brentworth had agreed the next day. "Just don't . . . hurt . . . our son."

Moments later, Fenton was bent over, his Italian slacks at his ankles. Priscilla's face wilted, but she did it, and she knew now she would always do it. *He'll kill your son. He'll kill Ricky. So do it! Do it!*

"Good, good, that's a good dutiful wife," Fenton chortled. "Nice and clean. . . ."

A psychopath, but a rich one. Priscilla had discovered

Fenton Collins Brenthworth's pathological quirks only *after* her own greed allowed her to marry him. *Too late,* she thought.

For fifteen years, she'd been his pretty piece of country club furniture, the ex-model socialite wife who'd given him a beautiful child. She could not account for Fenton's sickness, only snippets of an abnormal psych course she'd taken at Maryland. *Emblematic rectal fixations. Stage sociopathy. Transitive oral-analism with conative misogynistic-obsession-syndrome.* Fenton's perversion lay deeply rooted in a multifaceted hatred of women, and by making her do this, the symbol was made flesh. Hence, her imprisonment in general, and the anal thing in specificity. One night she'd merely awakened in the basement with a bump on her head. "I told everyone that you left me for another man, went back to your hometown." It was so flawlessly simple. With no living relatives, no friends to speak of? Who would inquire? Why would anyone suspect something so utterly depraved of a multi-millionaire loved by all?

The basement had a toilet, a Trinitron 35" television, and a chair. After the first year, the chair had been replaced with a *wheel*chair, to accommodate her sudden lack of feet. She'd tried to kick him one night. Big mistake. "Next time, I'll cut your hands off, darling. If you ever try to hurt me, ever again. And if you ever even so much as hesitate to tend to my need, I'll kill Richard. He's a freshman in college now, Princeton. Marvelous grades, just like his dear old dad." Over the years, Fenton would pipe down other videotapes onto the tv: Richard's first car, Richard in a tux before the senior prom, Richard's high school graduation, etc. Priscilla wept.

"So," he'd clarified for her, "you will lick the feces off of my rectum whenever I desire you to."

"Why? Why?" she'd sobbed, convulsing. "Why are you doing this to me?"

"Why?" He'd chuckled. "Because I can."

So here was Priscilla Brentworth's plight, in order to keep her son alive. Two, three, even four times a day, Fenton would unlock the basement door, come down, and have a bowel movement in the toilet. Then he'd lean over, standing in front of the wheelchair, whereupon Priscilla would bury her face in his bulbous buttocks, licking him clean.

And he had a knack for amusing little comments during her ministrations. "Kung Pao Shrimp last night. Can you taste the peppers?" or "Pardon the diarrhea, dear. I've been a little queasy of late." On feisty nights he'd haul her out of the chair and sodomize her, coming into her bowel and then instructing her to fellate him. "It's only proper you have a taste of your own on occasion." And sometimes he'd urinate into her bowel too, filling her up till she bloated. "Don't worry, darling. That was nearly an entire bottle of Montrachet '57. I only piss the very *best* up *my* wife's ass." Afterward, of course, she'd struggle to the commode and void it all in a, forceful, still-warm stream.

After so many years, her clothes had rotted, leaving her to sit naked in the wheelchair, mindlessly watching soap operas and talk shows. Once Donahue had hosted a coterie of adults who belonged to a "Diaper-Wearing" Organization. Yes, seemingly normal adults who would come home from their respectable jobs and then don diapers and sit in playpens with their spouses. "It's perfectly healthy," the club's chairman insisted. "It reattunes us to our childhoods, reformulates infant ideals to relieve the stress factors of adult life." "You're *sick*!" an audience member bellowed in reply. But all Priscilla could do was shake her head. *Buddy, if you think he's sick, you ought to meet my husband.*

The worst part, of course, was the taste of his excrement in her mouth. Semi-sweet, with a creamy sheen that lingered for hours. All she had to wash her mouth out with was toilet water since Fenton had deliberately neglected to supply her with a toothbrush, a sink, Listerine, etc. Priscilla's teeth had corroded to black, furry pebbles by the fourth year, each of which she'd spat out like malformed pills.

He fed her when he remembered, an opened can of spaghetti and a tumbler of water, generally twice a day. Every so often, however, he'd forget, sometimes for days such that, by now, her physicality had reverted to something akin to a living skeleton, less than ninety pounds, her head a skin-covered skull. The once ample breasts had shrunk to empty flaps of flesh. The lines between her ribs reminded her of death-camp footage, and her hair, long-since gray now, had grown to the floor. Clumps of hair under her arms, a clump of hair between her legs like a rat's nest,

hair tracing her legs all the way to the bulbed stumps where her feet used to be. And not being able to bathe for six years only provided the finishing touches onto the horror show that was now her life. Her own smells appalled her. Every night she dreamed of herself in Bosch's Hell: a stick-figure cretin with jutting hipbones and fleshless buttocks, being eaten by beaked demons.

The television couldn't be turned off, nor could its volume be turned down, and anytime Fenton desired to sicken her further, he'd pipe down still more underground pornography. Images that beggared description and only increased her conviction that she had married quite possibly the most depraved person to ever live. One minute she'd be numbly watching *The Simpsons,* and the next it was some new excursion of disgust. *Where does he get these movies? And who makes them?* It was hard to imagine even the worst sort of human scum purveying such tapes, but then there was always Fenton himself proving the validity of the market. Bestiality seemed a Fenton Brentworth favorite, some even complete with coy titles like *"Makin' Bacon", "Horsin' Around",* and *"Dog Day Afternoon".* Here was another one called *"Natal Attraction",* in which several men fornicated with a drug-gazed woman clearly late in her third trimester. Their intercourse grew so frenetic that eventually she broke her water. Men urinating on women, vomiting on them, inserting any conceivable object, including dead snakes, eels, and fish, into their rectums and vaginal barrels. More women, obviously drug addicts, chugging down goblets of urine, eating excrement with a spoon, shitting on each other as they twitched for their next fix. In one film, a woman extracted yeast and chlamyidiotic effusions from another woman's vagina, with a spoon, then ate the dollop of paste without a flinch, while yet another woman sucked pus from herpetic rectums and gonococcal penises with equal disregard. More films proved even worse: gang rapes, beatings, torture. Restrained woman screamed bulge-eyed as long needles were calmly inserted into breasts, nipples, clitori, and even their open eyes. And of course, the aforementioned snuff movies. In one film a woman was skinned alive, in another rectal retractors were utilized to distend a woman's anus to a wide open whole; she screamed and vomited as hooks were inserted, her lower g.i. tract slowly

but surely dragged out in pink loops. Women strangled, knifed, shot in the head, women forced to eat parts of themselves and eventually bleed to death via the wounds. In one film, a woman's head was cut off with a coping saw, whereupon some demented soul inserted his penis into the open esophagus, to copulate.

No, there was no end to the movies, and obviously no end to the absolute evil of men.

And, just as seemingly, there was no end to Priscilla Brentworth's travail as a living host to that same evil.

It was not until late in the fourth year that he cut off her hands. She'd been watching some cop show, where a tactical officer had cited the dangers of human hands. "Only twenty-six pounds of pressure is required to break a human neck," he'd gone on in this supreme expertise. "I once saw a dealer take out a trooper's eye with a single swipe of the thumb. I once saw a crazed girl in an ER kill a doctor merely by slamming the heel of her hand upward into his nose. We're talking a one-hundred-pound junkie taking out a healthy man twice her size. The blow pushed the sinitic filament straight into the brain . . ."

This dissertation enthralled Priscilla—the hope of the damned, and she'd followed the good officer's advise to the letter, with all her might. But, alas, the faltering blow had only bloodied Fenton's nose. He'd said nothing, leaving the basement only to return a few moments later with some string and a hacksaw. Then he'd choked her unconscious. She awoke to find stumps at the ends of her arms, the bloodflow staid by tourniquets. Her hands, tossed into the corner next to her feet, decomposed to a state of mummification. Over time, she noted that the fingernails continued to grow minutely.

Eating came with much more difficulty now, but eventually she learned to utilize her stumps with at least enough dexterity to keep from starving. She now had chopsticks instead of hands. Like an insect wielding its appendages, she would upend the spaghetti can with the nubs and shake out the contents, then eat it off the floor. Grasping the tumbler of water proved harder but she learned that too. A resilient woman, in other words, sheerly adaptable. The nodelike carpel bone on right wrist enabled her to change TV channels, and getting onto the toilet soon became noth-

ing more than a little inconvenience. Now she was a true stick woman: sticks for legs, sticks for arms, a death-camp scarecrow with skin white as a trout's belly.

And at least she noted a consolation. What else could he cut off without killing her?

"Ricky graduated from Princeton today," Fenton proudly announced as Priscilla rose from a starvation-induced unconsciousness. "I flew up for the ceremony—that's why I wasn't able to feed you for several days."

Like an animal, then, Priscilla jacked the spaghetti out of the can and sucked it off the floor. Fenton, next, had his expected bowel movement and turned his buttocks to her attentions. "God, I missed this," he informed her as she licked up the residue. Then he raped her, pissed volumi-nously up her vagina, and ejaculated in her hair. "And I have more good news, darling. Our son is officially engaged!"

Priscilla nearly passed out again as her husband hoisted up his suit pants and further enthused. "The DePiester girl, you know, from Potomac? You used to go to bridge club with her mother. They'll make a lovely couple, won't they? Soon we'll have grandchildren, honey! Isn't it marvelous?"

Tears burned Priscilla's eyes as she looked up at the grin-ning monster. Then she passed out again.

Every so often, Fenton would bring her what he referred to as "treats." Bums, vagabonds, homeless persons. He'd bring them down blind-folded, then show her to them. "A thousand dollars, just as I promised," Fenton would an-nounce and give the money to the bum. They never said a word as they raped her right there on the floor, their bodies reeking, their skin pocked with all manner of sores, rashes, eczema, etc. All the while, Fenton stood aside, glee in his eyes as he watched the degradation. Performing fellatio proved the worst part, a stench like she could not imagine: sagging scrotums unwashed for years, foreskins heavy with smegma which dissolved on her tongue as she gagged. "Oh, don't be such a whiner, darling. A little dickcheese never hurt anyone. If you're good, maybe next time I'll bring some crackers to go with it." Her stumps askew, she'd lain paralyzed on the floor as they left, covered with atrocious glue-like sweat, flecks of crust, scabs, and dandruff, and drying semen. Once he'd brought in a vagabond whose

penis was so large she felt gored. "I found him just for you, darling. Women always want the big dick. Well, honey, here it is!"

Her rectum had bled for days.

Suicide was beyond her means. With what could she kill herself? Breaking the television screen was impossible; it was mounted in the wall and covered with Lexan. Drowning herself in the toilet, bashing her head on the floor in hopes of a hematoma? No, even in her hell, she couldn't bring herself to attempt it, for if he caught her, and she survived, her tortures would be worse. Besides if she succeeded what might he do to her *son* . . . But deep down, even though she may not have been consciously aware, there was indeed some potential happenstance she was living for.

Fenton's death.

Another day with no food or water. Priscilla knelt at the toilet to drink, as the TV blared. In the water's reflection, she glimpsed her face, and her heart missed a beat when she realized that *she* was the creature looking back.

"—by U.N. estimates, at least another 10,000 Rwandan Tutsis reported murdered by militia members as they attempted to flee," a wooden-faced newscaster dryly recounted. Then, more news:

"—charged with forty-four counts of child abuse over the three years he served as pastor. Authorities claimed that Father Winherst would regularly molest the children in the confessional."

"—eventually found the one-week-old infant in the bag of the family's trash compactor."

There's evil everywhere, came Priscilla's harried thought. And what kind of god can there be to allow all of this?

"An angel came to me," a woman boasted tearfully when Priscilla changed channels. "I saw her, standing right in front of me. She was all glowing in light and smiling, and she told me that Sue Ann's cancer would disappear overnight. And it did! The next day the doctors MRI'd her, and it was all gone, as if it had never been there at all! There really are angels! There really are miracles!"

Angels? Miracles? *Not here,* Priscilla thought.

But when she changed the channel again, her gaze locked on the scene. An ambulance parked before a great posh

outdoor display. A huge white cake, long tables draped in pink linen. Grim-faced men in tuxedos and over-dressed blueblood wives looking on. Two more looked on as well. A pretty girl in a white bridal dress. A tall, handsome young man whose worried face looked all-too-familiar. It was her son. It was Ricky.

EMTs rushed the stretcher to the ambulance.

On the stretcher lay Fenton.

"—an untimely tragedy as multi-millionaire Fenton Collins Brentworth, respected businessman and philanthropist, collapsed of a heart attack during his son's wedding ceremony."

Priscilla stared dumbstruck. She thought of angels. She thought of miracle. *If there really is a god,* she thought, *if there really are miracles . . .*

"—entworth's estranged wife, a beauty pageant queen and former model with the renowned Kinion Agency, could not be found for comment."

Please die. . . . Please say that he died. . . .

"Mr. Brentworth died while in transit to South County General Hospital. Services will be held—"

She didn't need to hear any more; her prayer had been answered, her miracle had arrived.

Priscilla's heart raged. Someone will come to the house soon—Ricky, lawyers, auditors—someone. If I can get to the top of the stairs and pound on the door . . . they'll hear me . . .

I'm . . . I'm . . . I'm . . .

Priscilla's skin prickled in something akin to new life.

I'm free.

It seemed like a week that she waited there, though it was only a day and a half in actuality. Time dripped like tallow. Her wristnubs had bled pushing the infernal chair's rubber wheels to the end of the malodorous room. On her forearms, then, she'd struggled up the stairs in the fashion of an inchworm, dragging hair-veiled, tinderlike legs behind her. Three times she'd had to repeat the trek, in order to drink from the toilet.

And she waited and waited, until. . . .

Clicking sounds and a metallic *snap!* woke her from a throbbing sleep. The door was opening.

"Help! Help me!" she wailed as best she could, pounding her scuffed and bloodied nubs on the door. "Let me out!"

In her zeal, though, in the rigors of this exciting and even angelic revitalization, she lost her balance, canted up on a hip, and—

"Oh, shit!"

She wobbled back and tumbled down the stairs.

Some god. Nevertheless, Priscilla could hack it, couldn't she? After being raped by vagabonds, pissed in, starved, and divorced of her extremities? Disallowed to bathe, forced to watch underground pornography, threatened with the murder of her only child, and coerced to lick fecal residue off her husband's rectum—for *six years?* Certainly, a spill down the stairs amounted to nothing compared to that.

She thumped down head over proverbial heels to the bottom, groggily rearranged herself, and focused her sunken Dachau eyes up the flight of stairs. A timid, hesitant figure lingered—

"Help me!"

The figure then began to come down.

Then this person, this angel more resplendent than the Archangel Gabriel Himself, stepped into the fetid light. It was Ricky.

"Are . . . are you . . . are you all right?"

Priscilla crawled forward on wristnubs and knees, her matted hair shaking white flakes, her gut sucking. "Ricky!" came her parched scream. "I saw the wedding on the news, the heart attack! I know what I must look like but don't be afraid! It's me! It's your mother! Fenton cut off my hands and feet and has kept me down here naked for six years!"

The figure above her stood poised. "Ah, well . . . I know."

"You . . ." Priscilla swallowed her perplexity as surely as she swallowed so much feces, semen, smegma, urine, and—of course—spaghetti, in the past.

"Dad told me all about it," her son affirmed, "while we were upstairs watching the videos. Great stuff, huh? Especially the snuff. But I just want you to know that everything's fine."

Fine, she thought, staring as the dead might stare up out of a corpse-pit.

"Fine?"

"I even came down here some nights, when you were asleep in your chair, to look at you. You really are very beautiful, Mother." Ricky, then, set down two opened cans of spaghetti. "Sorry you weren't fed for so long, complications, you know, with the wedding and Dad dying and all. Wendy's wonderful. Wendy DePiester? You remember her. You used to go to bridge club with her mother. She's so beautiful, Mother, and—well, I didn't tell Dad this but—she's already pregnant. You'll have a grandchild in eight months!"

The word burped from her soul. "Fine." Then two more words. "My. God."

"You'll do it, right?" Ricky politely inquired of his mother. "I mean, you know, if you don't, I'll have no choice but to kill the kid. You don't want me to do that, do you?"

Priscilla simultaneously vomited and shit bile when she saw what her beloved son was doing next.

He'd dropped his trousers, sat on the toilet, and was quite loudly moving his bowels.

Then he stood up and turned, leaned over, and spread his buttocks with his hands.

"You'll do it, right, Mother? Like you did for Dad?"

Priscilla, then, with no other recourse, by instinct, began to crawl forward on her nubs and knees. After all, she had the baby to think of, didn't she? And, to tell the truth, you got used to the taste.

"Just promise me two things, Ricky. Don't bring any bums down here, and please don't make me watch those awful videos."

"Sure, Mom," Ricky promised and leaned over a little more intently.

Soul of the Beast Surrendered

Wayne Edwards

Since he was very small, the basement of Brad's family's small house was his refuge. There was a special place he could crawl into, behind where the furnace and water heater lined a damp basement wall, to remain unobserved. Not missed, but absent. Here he could wait out the verbal barrages his mother and father regularly hailed each other with. He could still hear the words bleeding through the floor above him, but in his sacred special place he was able to distract himself with his own imaginings.

There were pictures on the wall, ones he'd drawn by digging into the aging concrete with his soft fingernails (and later a screwdriver, then a knife) and others only imagined. The pictures were of many things: son and mother, father and son; pets he'd not ever had, dogs and cats and birds; unborn sisters and brothers, allies against the fear of cruelly brandished hands and feet and tongues. Even if they had been real, Brad realized a sister or brother couldn't stop actual punishment, but the beatings were the least of it. Oh sure, when he was being whipped, he thought nothing could be worse *at the time*. But when the anger wasn't directed at him, when his mother threatened his father or vice versa, he was completely out of the loop, had no influence or control. That was the worst, and that is what siblings *could* help him through. And he could help them.

Sometimes the pictures would move, sometimes they spoke. "I love you, Brad," they might say, or, "I'll always be your friend and no one else's." These were their words in the young boy's ear, the words he had wanted to know someone, even an imaginary someone, would speak. Brad made no mistake—he knew the pictures were not real. He started at the top, of course, by wishing some actual person would befriend him. When that failed, he looked to animals

lower on the food chain. Then, finally, there were the imaginates—never "fakes," but *imaginates.*

When he got older, Brad went to the basement less, but not very much less. At least once each week he would squeeze behind the furnace and in the dark retrace the trenches of his designs, trying to forget the latest foray in the upper-world. The place was still special, still a comfort, but its messages had become more serious and thought-provoking, more disturbing. At times, it was a toss-up which was better: to listen to his parents scream about money and infidelity and "that fucking kid," or to hear the cartoon-Brad's confessions of its dreams.

All of the drawings had the face of Brad. Most of them old, loose gougings in the crumbling foundation. Some were newer; he added, on average, one a year now. The newer figures took a more active role in the concrete tapestry, usually reprimanding or throttling or otherwise pounding an earlier version of themselves. Brad saw this as nothing more significant than symbolic growth, casting out of the old, so to speak. It was symbolic because the pictures never told an entirely true story. Always there was an air of flamboyance in their performances, an abstraction. But their intent was never difficult to ascertain.

Yes there was conflict, sort of a multiple personality clash between old and new. Even so, perhaps in spite of this, there was a camaraderie between the imaginates. Whatever horrors they played out for Brad's benefit were just that: play-acting. There was never terminal damage, and no true grudges were held. They seemed to think he would understand their message better in pictures. Or was it that Brad could speak to *himself* better this way? He was never really sure. When he was younger, when he had still thought of himself as a boy, he knew the drawings were a fantasy. He had much the same view now, only he wondered whose fantasy it was.

"Brad?" the Imaginate asked—capital "I" imaginates were the ones that skittered about without the aid of physical creation, whereas the lower case variety were the ones hand-picked in the wall by Brad. This particular Imaginate sported a mohawk haircut, in cruel contrast to his true personality, which was weasel-like. "Brad? Brad? Brad? Which way today, old buddy? Which way today?"

Brad ignored the little fucker—he was borderline M.R. and an all-around pain in the ass besides. Brad called this one Brando, for no good reason.

Brando stood beside Brad's left ear, shouting. "Brad! Buddy! C'mon, dickweed, lay some teeth on me! Let's see 'em, bay-bee!"

"Piss off."

"A reaction!" Brando jumped up, spun in circles of undefined imagination. "Parents got ya down, feller? Fuck 'em, says I, fuck 'em 'til they fuckin' rot. Know what I'm sayin', brown-pounder?"

Brad looked at the Imaginate. Brando was about four inches tall, made of non-existent chalk sticks, grinned like a lunatic banshee. All right, maybe he wasn't borderline, but he certainly was obnoxious. Brad spat a mucus wad.

Brando jumped like there was some need to get out of the way. He wagged an accusing finger at Brad. "That's not the way people who care about each other are supposed to act, you know."

"I don't care about you, Brando, and you're not a person. But I guess you're right, I shouldn't waste my spit on you. Shithead."

Brando sprang. Since he never actually left the wall, he descended rather than arced. He was gone.

For a while, Brad thought.

Brad regarded the other i(I)maginates. Kuhn[I], a provocative little sprite with a taste for dissent, napped. Ruby[i], an occasionally treacherous little rube, attempted to engage Sartre[I] in a truce between nations ([I]v[i]). Sartre would have none of this, of course. Frege[I] was absent, as was Erskinne[I]. There were maybe one hundred altogether, more [I]s than [i]s, a symptom of Brad's laziness, he supposed. He never concluded there was a necessity for balance. He couldn't control the number of Imaginates, the ones that created themselves. He could have, had he wanted to, tried to even up the armies by scratching more imaginates into the walls. But what was the point?

They are all so different, so individual, and they all look just like me, Brad thought. That should probably mean something, too, but Brad never fully appreciated the discontinuity.

Why did he keep coming down here? he often asked himself. He didn't exactly enjoy it. A form of avoidance, he concluded finally, a way to put off, well, doing anything else.

Like being around his parents.

He looked at Humphrey[i]. Humphrey was not Brad's first creation, but he was the favorite. Presently, he was being gang-raped by a bunch of [I]s. Brad took note of this, but did nothing. He never interfered.

Humphrey wept, embittered and degraded. He was an easy target; all [i]s were, since they had a limited field of motion compared to the marauding [I]s; they seemed to be anchored to a small parade ground within inches of their birthing spot. Humphrey took it like the brave little stick figure he was. He didn't fight back, because he knew the futility of such an act. Why waste energy in an action that returned nothing? Brad was proud of him.

Each abuse left the imaginates more decrepit, but they weren't about to give the bullies any satisfaction by participating in the usurped society, by acting the part of plebeians. How had it happened? It didn't matter; it simply was. When did the Imaginates first appear? That was known, but it too did not matter. They obviously were not going away. They could not be fought. It was the way of things.

Brad closed his eyes, suddenly weary. He laid his head against the cool concrete blocks, crossed his arms, and immediately began to fall asleep.

Dante[I] watched him, mimicked his position and expression, then stood and smiled.

"Brad? Wake up, Brad, please," *came the desperate whisper.*

"Quiet, Ruby, I'm tired."

"You, shssh, be quiet," Ruby said emphatically. "This is important. *Listen* to me. They've taken Humphrey."

Brad opened his eyes. Ruby stood in her usual place, her narrow arms forming a petulant posture. "Where would *they* take him? Where could they go, Ruby? C'mon, leave me alone."

"It's true. We saw them. We don't know where they've taken him, but we know he's hurt. Look for yourself!"

Jesus, it was just like having kids. That thought put him

in mind of his parents and their attitude toward him. Now he was awake.

Brad straightened himself, rolled his shoulders trying to work the stiffness out of them. He looked at Humphrey's spot.

Yep, he was gone all right. Most of him, anyway.

His leg (left?) was still in place, as were some other unrecognizable pieces. For the most part, though, Humphrey was gone.

"I *told* you. What are we gonna do?" Ruby was pacing, shaking her round head in dismay.

On hands and knees, Brad looked at the spot more closely. There was the leg—yes, definitely the left. A couple short lines indicative of stubs were there as well, ragged on the edges. The rest of Humphrey's arena was smooth. Not smoothed out, as in rubbed over; smooth like nothing had been there before. Ever.

"You know what they'll do with him, don't you?" Ruby was saying. "They'll *eat* him, that's what. They've already pulled off his leg and fingers. Oh, *do* something, Brad. You have to help us."

"Get serious, Ruby. You guys don't eat."

"There'll be nothing left but the bones soon. And when they get done with Humphrey, you know what they'll do? *I'll* tell you. They'll eat the *rest* of us. One . . . at . . . a . . . time."

Brad could see her dusty tears.

This is ridiculous, he told himself. They don't eat, they don't have bones, they aren't *real*.

But they talk to you, don't they.

"The [I]s have never liked us. Please, Brad, do something. They're going to kill us all! *Kill* us and *eat* us!"

Brad noticed all the [i]s were looking at him now, all expecting something. He heard the floorboards above him creak, heard the shouting of his parents. It must be evening; they were both home.

He looked to the moist floor and saw it: scrawny delicate white lines. The imaginates followed his gaze and gasped in a horrified chorus. He pulverized the ridges with a gentle touch and thought of how easily sardine bones could be crushed by his tongue.

Humphrey's skeleton.

Brad stood, looked at the powder on his finger. *Humphrey.* This was beyond the realms of jest. He did have an affinity for the [i]s, no matter how indifferent he could act. He *did* feel sorrow for their plight. After all, he had put them in this position. His doctrine of non-interference seemed suddenly archaic. Maybe some action was called for. "But what can *I* do?"

"Take us away from here," Ruby said. Dozens of tiny voices echoed her words.

"Before it's too late," Brad agreed.

Brad had become philosophical in his teenage years—philosophy and cynicism were compatible bedfellows if the proper system was adopted. Nietzsche was right.

He thought at first it would be best to kill them all. All the [i]s, that is. That way, they would not fall victim to whatever horrors the [I]s had in mind. Death before dishonor? No. Death before pain.

Then he thought he could do better. He would simply move the imaginates across the room, carve them into the far wall. He had never seen an [I] leave the original wall, so he was relatively certain the [i]s would be safe in their new home. It would take some time, but what, if not time, did he have?

He set about scratching definitions in the new homeland. Ruby first. He ignored the commotion across the room. Brad couldn't help it if a few citizens were lost while he moved them. The best he could do was work fast. He knew his parents would never notice that the basement lights were on, but they would eventually bellow for him. Not for dinner, of course, but at eleven o'clock they would make certain he was in bed. They would want to clear the deck, so to speak, for what was shaping up to be a major confrontation. Thin sheets of dust encouraged by their stamping feet enveloped Brad almost continuously.

He knew something was wrong the minute he finished with Ruby. She didn't look right—a little plumper, a little, ahh, sexier, perhaps a symptom of his changing priorities. He went to the first wall to compare features. The Ruby there was hysterical.

"You can't do it like that! You'll never get it right! You are just making more of us. You have to be *exact.* You

have to copy us exactly as we are, *then* put us on the other wall. It's the only way!''

He knew she was right; it was obvious. Ruby Two wasn't even a good likeness, when examined closely. She still had Brad's face, of course, but the resemblance ended there.

"Hurry." Ruby One's voice trembled.

Brad looked to his right. The Imaginates were gathering in force, obviously positioning themselves for a full-scale assault. Brando was running around relaying orders, slapping the lesser [I]s when they complained. He was Dante's messenger, clearly, and Dante had a plan of his own.

Brad thought frantically, becoming increasingly concerned about the fate of the [i]s. He couldn't let this happen. The imaginates were part of him, a *good* part of him. Sure, they were a pain in the ass sometimes. They were also the only thing that had kept him from killing himself for almost ten years. They were his confidantes, his explainers, advice-givers. The Imaginates were something else, something Brad didn't really understand. Sinister and mean-spirited, most of them quiet (excusing, of course, Brando and a few other instigators of conflict), seeming always to plot. He didn't like any of them. He most definitely did not trust them.

He had to work fast. He needed something to copy the [i]s onto, like paper. He could then scratch them out of the original wall and embed them precisely in the new one. But there was no paper in the basement, and no pencils or pens, either. He couldn't go upstairs. If his parents saw him, he would be ordered to his room straightaway so they could get on with their doings unencumbered. He needed something else. What did he have on him?

One useful item: his penknife.

And what for paper? There was only one answer, and it did not please Brad. Maybe he could do it if he didn't cut too deep. He pressed the blade against the biceps of his left arm.

When nothing happened he pressed harder. He was rewarded with a white line that faded too quickly to be useful. This was going to be more difficult than he had imagined. He leaned into it.

Blood spurted from the wound, and a yelp escaped from Brad before he could halt it. He'd chosen his biceps be-

cause he saw no veins, thought he could scratch the skin without major incident. Obviously, you didn't need a visible vein to create a fountain of blood. You just needed torn tissue, deeply severed skin. The blood was under there waiting. He would have to be more careful. And quicker.

He wiped the blood away and started again.

By angling the blade to his skin rather than approaching perpendicularly, he found he could just scratch the surface, leaving a red line bubbled with small beads of blood. He was no artist. Anyone looking at the imaginates would know that. Flesh wasn't a cooperative medium, either, not like cement blocks. It had the unfortunate characteristic of squirming away from the blade. It took Brad almost half an hour to copy Ruby. When he'd finished, the flesh Ruby had no life, no animation. He knew it was because of the temporary nature of her construction. When recomposed on the opposite wall she would be fine. Still, her face—*his* face—staring up at him, smiling blood, allowed him to think only of death.

He started to discredit Ruby One's figure from the wall with his knife. Her voice stopped him mid-torso. It was a good thing he'd started with her feet.

"Brad, you've got to work faster. Dante has begun his attack."

It was true. Frightened wails surrounded Brad as imaginates on the fringe were assaulted by the [I]s. Fine dust poured down the wall as if from a flour sifter.

"You'll have to do as many of us as you can all at once, *then* put us on the other wall. If you copy us one at a time, only two or three will survive." Ruby One's expression was all misery. "You're our only hope."

Brad's arm hurt, was swelling around the puncture wound. This operation had changed from an absurd diversion to an urgent responsibility. He didn't want this onus, but he had put it on himself by even beginning the rescue. He was therefore committed to the effort. Again Ruby One was right. All at once was the only way. He started taking off his clothes.

From the corner of his eye he saw Dante. He had accessorized since Brad had last seen him; he now sported an imaginary sword and eye patch. *How tacky can you get?* Brad wondered. The other Imaginates he could see were

also armed. The basement wall had become a tapestry depicting a slaughter.

Entirely naked now, Brad began to cut. He couldn't be cautious to the point of merely scratching, for that would surely lead to the virtual annihilation of the imaginates. He worked furiously, erasing each [i] from the wall as soon as it was copied. In all, he was able to duplicate fifteen of them. Fifteen of his subjects, his children, his creations. His friends. It wasn't enough, but it was the best he could do. There was no space left unbloodied and available on his body. None he could reach, anyway.

Brad made it to the new wall—barely. Every inch of him was a rage of pain. He sweated, was dizzy and near vomiting. But he had won. All he need do now was etch the imaginates into the concrete. If he was too weak to finish tonight, he could pick it up tomorrow. He guessed it would take weeks for the wounds to heal.

He would do what he could before he was summoned from above. He wasn't worried about having to explain the scars. His parents never really looked at him, so they wouldn't notice.

He sat next to the new world, holding his tool of creation before him. It was covered with blood and dirt and small lumps of flesh. He pressed it to the wall.

And heard a smooching sound, like an exaggerated kiss. He looked at Ruby Two, knowing before he saw her she would not be alone.

There stood Dante, now adorned only by a crude loincloth. He held the head of Ruby Two in his hands, kissing its eyes. Her body lay prone, still, about a foot away.

Brad didn't pause to wonder how Dante had gotten to the new wall. He was too busy working out his next move. He couldn't put the [i]s on the wall now, not any of the walls. He thought about taking them to another room, some other wall upstairs, but he realized that if Dante could get across the room then he could probably get upstairs, too. Besides, no matter how out-to-lunch his parents were, there was no hiding place as good as the basement. Eventually they would happen upon the [i]s, and Brad didn't like to think about what they would do then. It was enough to surmise that his parents would be even worse for the imaginates than the [I]s.

Dante bit off a generous chunk of Ruby Two's chin. Chewed.

And then the answer came to him, so simple. The work was already done. He would leave the [i]s where they were. They would come around eventually. Once they realized that his body was their new home, they would take to it. He might have to trace over the outlines, make sure the scars were permanent. Maybe move one or two to places on his body that would routinely be covered by clothing. He could do that. Anything to keep them away from Dante.

"Hah!" he spat. "Gotcha, you dim-witted twig-dick. Whattaya think of that?"

It really annoyed Brad that Dante smiled, but he figured the little bastard just couldn't admit defeat. It didn't matter; Brad knew who had won. That was enough.

He turned and saw them. Not dozens, but hundreds of Imaginates standing in the middle of the floor.

Standing?

For the first time ever, the [I]s were three dimensional. They had color and texture. They had intent. Their tiny metal weapons glinted in the forty-watt light. They advanced slowly on Brad. He divided his attention between staring at the legion in disbelief and listening to Dante chuckle.

Then they swarmed.

October Gethsemane

Sean Doolittle

-1-

That's why he keeps on working, trying again; he believes each time that he will do it, bring it off. . . .
— William Faulkner

By not showing until almost half-past eight, Soames ended
up merely fashionable. Truth was: he hadn't planned on
coming at all. Everything about it stifled him, clenched his
throat, simmered him into a mood. It was four days since
he'd sliced open the top of his forearm, and the cut hadn't
yet begun to heal. Inside, the Fire Gallery was fittingly
abuzz; thousand-dollar yip-yups stood in clusters, sipping
from crystal flutes. They positioned themselves before canvases and sounded intelligent, punctuating what passed for
thought with toothpicks from the rumaki.

He was scanning. Looking for cover.

Track lighting had been implemented sparingly above,
soft and well-placed; there was ambiance piped in, unobtru-
sive—Tangerine Dream giving way to Enya as he finally
made his way to the perimeter of the room. Dark, melodic,
ethereal—Soames marveled at how efficiently the music
had been gutted, pasteurized and canned. Upstaged by this
trendy gathering of status jockeys and their boilerplate New
Age drone.

He found a corner and lurked in it. This was pointless,
an opening for some Upper East Side painter he didn't
care to know. Sullen, wishing for something along the lines
of codeine to pass the time, Soames settled for the cheap
champagne. Swilled quickly, it managed—a creeping tingle
that took the sharp crimson edge off the pain. Ten minutes
and Soames was draining his sixth glass, exchanging it for

the last one on the passing server's tray before the hapless bow-tied lad could make his getaway.

Soames was in the process of flagging another server when he was finally made from across the room.

"Aaron."

The voice belonged to Randall Gerard, his beet-faced agent. Randall's eyes illuminated and he hurried over, dabbing great droplets from his balding head with the handkerchief he clutched in one hand.

Slightly breathless, now: "You're here."

Soames waggled his fingers. "Hello."

Randall was looking into his eyes, then at the champagne flute tilting vaguely in his hand; the momentary relief appeared to be nudged out now by something that turned his complexion slightly pale.

"Please, God. Tell me you aren't drunk."

"I'm not drunk."

"Jesus, Aaron," he whispered, stepping in close, clutching him around the shoulders. "Stay together here, will you? This could be a thing for you."

"A thing?"

"Be nice."

Randall was leading him into the murmuring throng, toward a small group gazing at a narrow mural, which was lit portside by a medium-stark halogen bar. The tall one Soames recognized: Phillip James, proprietor of The Fire. He was standing with a willowy blond and an Italian-suited man that sported an immaculate mahogany beard and expensive-looking tortoiseshell frames.

Randall transformed magically as he moved, kick-shifted into high shmooze. Open went the grin, and he said: "Everyone. I'd like you to meet Aaron Soames."

Conversation in progress hitched and broke; James looked up, as if there had been a gnat, before grinning coolly with a reach to shake Soames' hand.

"Glad you could come, Aaron." Crisp, turning to the man beside him. "Mr. Soames will be opening with us in October. Thirty-first, I believe?" He raised an eyebrow to Gerard, who was nodding enthusiastically.

"Aaron, this is Nathan Brenner. Mr. Brenner handles almost all of the opening reviews for the *Times,* these days."

Soames took a sip from the glass and nodded politely, wishing immediately that he'd saved the energy. Brenner's glance was perfunctory, disinterested. Short. "Lovely," said the critic, and returned to the mural.

"Mr. Soames," he went on after a moment. His voice seemed wistful, vaguely distracted. "What do you think of the piece?"

Soames felt Gerard stiffen beside him. Horror: spotlights turned unexpectedly on the Incredible Human Sponge. Says he's an artist. Does he talk? Do any nifty tricks? Randall's poor sphincter must have clenched like a desperate fist. Silence around the horn.

Soames did the civil thing. He looked at the painting.

Woeful. Derivative at best, corporate at worst, an obvious attempt at alien whimsy *a la* Hieronymus Bosch, lacking the technical brilliance, bastardized by chummy pastels. There was a leaf, a piece of twine, and what looked like cottage cheese embedded in a mound of paint at the lower corner. Soames pretended to give it pause as his arm gave a vicious twang. After a few measured beats he straightened and drew a thoughtful breath.

And said, "Guess it pretty much blows." He caught Brenner twitch as Randall deflated beside him with a hiss.

Phillip James was positively glaring. "*Mister* Soames," he said, locking his spine, presenting his willowy blond. "May I introduce you to the creator?"

Soames turned, but the woman had already jerked her arm free, collected herself and stalked away. James scampered off quickly in pursuit. Randall was clutching his head in both hands. It looked as though he might cry.

Soames looked at Randall apologetically. Shrugged.

Then he noticed that Nathan Brenner had turned. He was grinning. Very widely.

"Mister Soames," he said, and extended his hand. Aaron drained his glass and took it, what the hell.

"I'm looking forward to Halloween already."

Randall Gerard peeked carefully out of his cringe *(he said what*?) as Brenner moved off. His grip had been firm, double-handed, left clasping high above Aaron's wrist.

Soames managed to wait until the man was gone before dissolving, drifting along the top of the pain.

*   *   *

"Jesus."

Soames doesn't notice that his shirt sleeve has matted to the gauze.

"Oh. This."

Shot glasses upturned, a field of dead soldiers between them. Small platoon of reinforcements at hand.

"Aaron." Eyes wide.

Concern.

"Hey. Drink up. It's a party."

The city was riding out one final heat wave; even in the dead part of night the air remained humid and thick, heavy with exhaust fumes and decay. Manhattan clung to the skin like oil; it coated the sinuses, turned clothing wilted and damp. The sidewalks and streets perspired it, smelling like iron, like rust. Like pennies in a warm sweaty hand.

Soames needed the walk, metabolism to dissipate the booze. After The Fire, Randall had been so goofy with delight he'd paid for the cab to Garboni's in the Village, and by the time Soames left him there it was almost two. He needed to clear his mind for work; he needed the walk, the motion.

The street lamps threw reaching shadows. In the alleyways, the shadows moved. Soames passed them, among them, and none pounced; he syncopated his stride with the dull aching throb in his arm.

"Somebody should see that."

"I'm sorry?"

"You're arm. You should have somebody look at your arm."

"Pardon?"

"Goddammit, Aaron."

"Mother. Please."

There was a guy on the corner of Nassau and Ann, leaning against the grimy brick directly beneath the inset plaque that claimed Edgar Allen Poe wrote "The Raven" on this very selfsame spot. He was small and rat-like, hands shoved deep into the pockets of his chinos, staring toward his shoes. He spoke as if by radar, muttering "Smoke, smoke," to his feet as Soames reached him and passed on by, three minutes away from . . .

*   *   *

Home.

The loft topped a defunct warehouse; he'd combed the lower reaches of Soho and Tribeca for months before stumbling across it, tucked away in an unlikely upper section of Nassau. The place was perfect, sheer studio; rough concrete floor, echoing cinderblock walls, steel beams crossing twenty feet overhead. He'd cordoned off a small space on one end with drywall for mundane necessity: there was a circa 1972 naugahyde sofa group and an aluminum utility locker *cum* wardrobe crowded into one corner, in the other a chain-pull shower above an open drain in the floor. By the outlet on that side he put up a folding card table with a coffee pot, microwave, and hot plate, dorm-sized refrigerator beneath. He had a toilet. One small mirror, spidered with cracks.

The sinks were cavernous stainless-steel industrial jobs spanning the wall on the other side. Soames peeled out of his shirt and went to them, where he finally unwrapped the gauze.

Infection had set in. The wound was feverish and swollen, red-rimmed, pushing itself apart. A raw wide mouth from the top of his wrist to elbow, already suppurating; the edges of the bandage had crusted, the center glistening with yellow goo.

Soames left the dressing in the sink and returned to the canvas that remained on its easel in the middle of the room.

Sit. Focus. Breathe.

He was cross-legged in front of it for nearly an hour before feeling centered, merged with the hot infected throb, ready to proceed. There was a stiff wire brush in his tool box. Soames found it, brought it back with him and sat down again. Inspiration: he plunged it into the open can of pain thinner first.

Inhaled, released. Began.

The pain was spectacular, blinding. Soames squeezed his eyes shut, biting a scream, riding it up and over. He scraped the brush down the length of the cut again. Bearing down. Again.

He did it until he found the window, until the vision blossomed inside his skull; he worked the brush down and back, scrubbing in circles until the pain was a keening wail, opening like a fissure across the surface of his mind.

When the groove appeared, Soames dropped the brush and leaped for it.

Starting desperately, with both hands, to paint.

-2-

Before subterranean forces will feed the creator back, they must be fed, passionately fed. . . .
—Tillie Olsen

I mean: The pain teaches you and you teach the pain.

—Wayne Allen Sallee

It was one of those accidents artists talk about, the way Soames discovered the groove.

This was ten years. A decade of emotional spelunking, exploring the twisted caverns of his gray matter and trying to make it back with at least some piece of what he found. His soul, such as it was; his *serious work*. Which he could have Xeroxed and passed out on the streets, for all anybody cared.

The only reason Randall Gerard had stayed with him for so long was out of respect for a quiet friendship that had developed between one-time brothers in law. When Soames had been beyond young, a different kind of human; when he'd still introduced himself to people by his first name, still had illusion enough of hope to buy an old manual typewriter for things like grant proposals and applications to prestigious fellowships. Sharla was no kidder; she'd gotten out early on, while the getting was prime, never stopping long enough to look back. Her wayward elder sibling Randall, in fact, hadn't even been an agent until he met Soames.

Nice, that in the time since at least somebody had been able to piece together a career. While eventually whoring himself to dentists in midtown, doing seascapes for their lobbies to support a frivolous, nagging jones he'd developed for food, Soames amused himself with the irony. Sometimes he'd think of it and cackle as he prowled the streets at night.

By morning, the canvas was finished.

When dawn leaked in through the gray-filmed windows near the floor, Soames unfolded himself and stood. He stepped back and allowed himself to look at the thing at last; the vortex of apocalyptic color, the aggressive slashes and whorls. It was empathy, rage, despair. It was incineration. The concertina wire was a ghost note—a transparent suggestion, snaking from deep inside like an umbilical cord, an entrail, connected somewhere beyond the edge of the canvas.

Whatever it was, he'd almost pinned it. So very, very close.

It was finished.

Throb, gentle as a whisper. Soames looked.

The arm had healed, but badly, sealed itself into a gnarled and fibrous scar.

He maneuvered himself across the floor, past the drywall partition, making the sofa group just as the sun gained window level and sliced the room into arcs of light. He thought, Inventory: before function was squelched by a greedy, fitful sleep.

Inventory:

Five six-by-nines. Randall had gotten them the gig at The Fire Gallery on the basis of these alone. Last night was the first full canvas; Soames estimated he'd need ten more pieces, minimum, to bother even showing up. After as many years of waiting for a serious exhibition, something credible, he wasn't about to skimp on incidentals. Say, artwork.

Chest deep in seascapes, cute fuzzy animals and bowls of fruit, Soames discovers the groove.

Random collision; a bottle cap slits the tip of his tongue while opening a beer with his teeth. The pain is a surprise, an infuriating instant. Reflex, Soames closes his eyes . . .

And it's there. Something, a momentary flash. He's painting before he realizes it, catching the thing and pinning it down. Furious. Quick. He's riding a shallow channel, racing for the end before it bottoms, disappears.

Honest. Visceral. No bigger than a magazine, the purest thing he's ever done.

While he looks at it, Soames swallows a warm mouthful of blood.

Notices that he is running the point of his tongue, which has knitted itself pink and smooth again, back and forth along the edges of his teeth.

Soames counted days in his head. October the thirty-first wasn't quite two months away. For the first time since he began working again, he considered process.

The scar was wide as a pencil; it's the first time the healing has gone this way, cosmetically incomplete. Soames traced the new scar absently with his fingers, thinking about the wonderful resilience of the human body—its ability to raise thresholds, build up tolerances against the world. It was a holistically interactive machine; it elevated itself, absorbed.

A vacationing gringo in floral print trots off with salmonella to *el hospidal* just by looking at tap water the wrong way.

A smack draws the plunger further back each time, palsied and sweating, struggling to reclaim the high.

Soames stroked this first scar slowly, reading it like Braille, like evidence left behind. Five pieces before last night. Not easy, not a jog, but so far never more than one sitting on any of them. He'd chosen a title for this newest; it had been in progress just over four and a half days.

Thinking now of process, and of October, he was satisfied with what he'd eventually come up with.

Earth Inferno had a certain ring.

-3-

> From the first rhythmical urge of the inward creative force . . . what a struggle, what Gethsemane.
> —Thomas Mann

Process:

Someone became deliriously rich off a bumper sticker for simply recognizing that the single most vital step in an omelet was the breaking of the eggs.

Destruction first.

Process:

Experiments in pain. More difficult, each time out, coaxing the Phoenix Inspiration to spread its wings from the steaming rubble. More difficult, each time, to capture it.

Soames works until the studio reeks with fumes, head pounding with them. He learns quickly how to wear a filter mask to increase his stamina, give him more time to work before he's forced into the night, the deserted streets. Ventilation becomes critical; the fumes inevitably find their way beneath the mask. They slip in and drug him to dullness, cloud the vision, screen it in a chemical haze. He roams into bad parts of morning and breathes.

Returns to begin from scratch again.

More difficult each time. When it does happen, Soames must be very good. Very, very fast.

Process: Creator, re-create thyself.

September, in and gone like a breeze.

"Aaron?"

He smears the receiver with paint and blood, fumbling it to his ear. Randall's voice is soft, almost surprised.

"Aaron? Hey, are you there?"

"No." He slams down the phone as hard as he possibly can, bells clanging as if wounded from somewhere down inside. He turns back, stops; wraps the cord twice around his fist and jerks it from the wall.

Soames is so furious that it takes him almost twenty minutes before he's able to start over from the beginning.

Outside, the leaves are dying, whisked into the gutters by a saw-toothed wind. It howls in the ventilation shafts of the building as October moves on around him.

Process:

Needle-nosed pliers are the most efficient for peeling back fingernails. The rip-off, heh heh so to speak, after the first couple it doesn't really hurt all that goddamn bad.

Whoever came up with that saying about salt must have been a pansy of the highest order. Rubbing alcohol is better. Bleach actually works the best.

Stay away from the hands, what the hell are you thinking?

The guy beneath the Poe memorial is wearing three flannel shirts and fingerless leather gloves. "Smoke," he is saying. "Smoke."

"Not interested." This is a moment of weakness. Painkillers? Anyone out there from Poughkeepsie? Soames stands in the cold until the rat-man looks up.

"Pills. What've you got for a toothache?"

The rat-man's eyes are pasted wide. "Hey, man." Awe. He shifts his feet. "You all fucked up."

The air is metallic, cold; breath puffs between them like smoke. Soames puts him against the wall with an arm across his throat. "Heey. *Man.* You a doctor or a fucking salesman?"

Too late anyway; the chill has cleared his head, sobered him like a backhanded slap. Soames has come to his senses, changed his mind. He leaves the guy staring, limps back the way he came, moving between shadow and light. From an upper window of a condemned building, two cats scream, killing each other over turf.

If you've got a very sharp paring knife, you can slip it beneath the front edge of a scar, and using your thumb, peel the whole thing back like de-veining a cocktail shrimp.

Process:

Jesus fuck.

Randall won't stop pounding on the door. It's hollow steel, and the echo inside is deafening.

Soames finally opens it the length of the chain and thrusts his face in front of the crack.

"If you interrupt me one more time, Randall. Just one."

"Oh. Christ."

His mouth drops. He can't stop looking at Soames's face.

Few more scars there, since Garboni's. We have traveled beyond the point of getting away clean.

"What are you doing to yourself?" He shoves against the door. "Let me in, Aaron."

"No. Go away. I'm working."

"I'm calling off the show!"

"Fine."

"I mean it!"

"One of us isn't listening." Soames steps back, narrowing the crack an inch. "Call off the show, don't call off the show. I'm working anyway."

Randall is closing his mouth. Opening it. "This is insane."

"Hey. I yam an arteest."

Slam the door.

* * *

Inventory:

Five six-by-nines, still untitled. *Earth Inferno*. Earth Inferno Jr., and three retarded cousins before the canvases get bigger.

How big are they going to go? Soames thinks of the willowy blonde's mural and giggles around his swollen tongue.

Nothing hurts anymore.

Flesh has become mundane; the scars have begun to overlap, mapping the surface of him. Thoroughfares and inroads, cul-de-sacs. There's almost no fresh ground left.

Soames is becoming something of an artwork himself.

Discovery. Skill only takes you so far.

The Phoenix is getting to be one bitch of a big bird. Too big to see all at once, too exquisite to render with anything like accuracy. Soames goes for likeness. A resemblance, at least. Canvases finished and shoved aside, leaning like hoodlums against the walls.

Who heals?

He is a work in progress. Always a good thing to add color: the artist, one notices immediately, favors intricate shades of red.

Outside the city burns. Inspired by recent cinema, participants approach Devil's Night with a new sense of rejoice, remembering what it was about fire they loved. Along the river, the buildings churn thick black smoke into the sky, an illusion of production, industry. The water reflects the flames, shimmering, allowed for a short time to be beautiful. Garbage blazes in the streets.

Randall finds it easy, if expensive, to rent a fireman and two paramedics on his way. They're everywhere, tired and massively pissed. It only takes them three running tries with the battering ram to finally punch in the door.

The man on his knees in front of the wall is shirtless; slick, raw, bleeding. He is holding his arms out wide beside him, head back and lolling slightly to one side. His skin litters the floor around him in wetly glistening piles.

The wall before him is covered in fresh canvases, framed in heavy silver tape. Randall has arrived just in time. One of the paramedics is leaning over and puking on his shoes.

For a moment, arms outstretched, Soames looks vaguely like someone they once read about. Until he breaks position, plunging his hands into the can of thick adhesive by his knee.

Then into the broken glass.

-4-

For the eyeing of my scars, there is a charge.
　　　　　　　—Sylvia Plath

The State Of The Art: Openings in Review
by Nathan Brenner.

After a disappointing All Hallows' Eve postponement, The Fire Gallery displayed the work of Manhattan painter Aaron Soames to enthusiastic survey Wednesday night. The artist himself remained conspicuously absent for the duration. His presence was sorely missed by the gallery patrons, and altogether irrelevant to the show.

A pity it couldn't have been Halloween.

Dark, brutal, relentless: all of these apply to an exhibition that cannot be precisely described. The work of Aaron Soames is a psychological blitzkrieg, an experience only to be had.

Where has this man been hiding?

Mister Soames, a rare plea: More.

—for Henry Desmond,
　　with gratitude and affection.

Scars

Lucy Taylor

"Give me his blood," hissed the Tokoloshe.

Bucket crouched on his bed. His penis was stiff, and he was afraid the demon would see. A man's soul could be won that way, by the stealing of his seed.

"Tuttle's blood," said the Tokoloshe. "His or yours."

The circular, mud-and-thatch room that was Bucket's home reeked of evil, of rut-smell and semen and sweat, odors that enveloped his cock like a warm throat and filled his pious heart with aching dread.

"Leave me alone," he pleaded, staring down at the baked earthen floor. He found the demon unbearable to look at: both hideous and alluring. Raised stains the color of raw liver disfigured half its head and mottled parts of its serpent-smooth body. To look upon it made his blood heat like he was falling sick with malaria. In desperation, he grabbed the whiskey bottle beside his bed and sucked from it. Another sin, but at least the alcohol enabled him to bear the demon's visits.

He heard the creature shuffle up from the floor and move behind him. A cool, clawed hand rested briefly on his back, then traced the damp ridge of his spine, caught and plucked between his legs. Bucket shut his eyes and prayed:

Yea, though I walk through the valley of the shadow of Death, . . .

as the tongue of the unholy thing teased, seduced, befouled him—

. . . I will fear no evil, for Thou art with me.

"His blood or yours," murmured the painted demon, withdrawing its moist mouth at just the critical moment. With a soft moan, Bucket toppled forward, wrenching at his sinful flesh that brought him so much shame and pleasure.

* * *

In the daylight, sober, it was easy for Bucket to imagine he had dreamed it all. Vivid, terrifying dreams had often plagued him. In the bad place in Harare, where he'd spent eleven of his thirty-two years, he'd been given drugs that enabled him to fly, that floated him to a placid, cottony sky where sounds were big and slow and soft, like a hippo rolling and rooting in river mud, and other drugs that produced a half-sleep in which his dreams were as crimson as the African sunset, where his mind leaped and skittered like a troop of baboons.

When the demon had first begun to menace him, Bucket had thought those dreams had returned, especially since, upon awaking, his mouth often felt like he'd gorged on river clay, and his hands trembled violently before he took a drink.

But then he commenced to finding marks upon himself, places where the flesh was torn and blood had seeped into the sleeping mat.

Then he knew the Tokoloshe had come for him, indeed, and that all the years imprisoned in the terrible place in Harare had been for nothing. The spirit of the boy he'd murdered long ago had sent the demon to hound him, tempt him, drive him mad. Bucket had nowhere to flee.

As a youth, the seizures Bucket suffered, the trances he sometimes slipped into when he neither moved nor spoke for hours at a time, had aroused the interest of Zihute, a powerful *nganga* or spirit medium. Bucket had studied with Zihute, learning how to cast spells that would ensure abundant crops or cause a man to sicken and die or make a woman give herself sexually. He learned spells to conjure up the demon Tokoloshe and tricks to recognize one, for the creature could seduce its prey by shape-changing into a person or an animal. Recently, Bucket had put his sleeping mat up on a pile of bricks, for the Tokoloshe was blind and snake-like in its true form, and the bed on bricks was designed to fool it. A futile effort—the creature had transformed itself and attacked him anyway, leaving shallow, bloody teeth marks along his penis shaft and scrotum.

Proof that the demon was no dream and that he was—again—a sinner.

In Harare, a priest had converted Bucket to Christianity with promises that his new faith would save his soul from

hell. Bucket had vowed to give up witchcraft, to abstain from what the priest called "self-abuse" and to forego alcohol.

But the Tokoloshe was here and now, commanding him to shed the blood of an innocent old man, and no shining white Christ had appeared to challenge its malevolent authority.

If Bucket had had reason to fear or hate Sol Tuttle, obeying the demon might have been easier. Years ago, he had killed his cousin, because the boy had mocked him in front of all the village, calling him Zihute's dog, a dullard whose trances were a sign of an enfeebled mind, not supernatural powers.

Enraged, Bucket had lured the young man out into the bush and bludgeoned him unconscious with a stone. Then he summoned up the Tokoloshe, a slick and squat abomination, with breath that reeked of feces and blind, white eyes, and watched it flay the skin from the boy's body while he was still alive.

But Sol Tuttle, unlike the boy that Bucket killed, seemed no threat to anyone. He was a rich and generous Texan— a Christian, no less—whose handsome, educated daughter, Celeste, had lived among the Tongan people for several months. He was going to build a hospital for the village, where the very old could go to die and the woman could give birth and those with birth defects and disfiguring scars could be treated.

Surely such a decent man was completely undeserving of misfortune.

Bucket reached for the bottle beside his pallet. Although he hated whiskey, he loved where it transported him, a place where sounds caressed and touch enthralled and the spurting of his own flesh was like death and resurrection.

He finished off the bottle slowly and thought about the man the Tokoloshe would have him kill.

Late November, the start of summer in Zimbabwe, was the suffering time for humans and animals alike. The stony soil reflected back heat in white, shimmering waves. Choking dust rose from the fields. Occasionally Bucket guided tourists on camera safaris into the bush, but more often he

joined the rest of his people in eking out a mean existence from the parched soil bordering Matusadona National Park.

Visitors during the heat of summer were infrequent, so when a landrover, chalky with dust, pulled up, most of the villagers, including Bucket, assembled to stare.

Four men, dressed incongruously in suits and ties, got out of the vehicle. Bucket had seen them before. They were governmental functionaries from Harare, here to make the final arrangements for Mr. Tuttle's hospital.

The men unfolded charts and diagrams and walked over to the field across from the provisions store, with its hand-lettered signs for beer and beans and cigarettes.

Presently, the two Americans, the old man and his daughter, came tramping across the field. Bucket watched, not moving, but his guts churned as though demons sucked themselves and copulated in his bowels. The old man, Sol Tuttle, was short and burly with an over-large head that reminded Bucket of a warthog. The woman, Celeste, was tall and straight and seemed to suffer from perpetual sunburn, her skin brightly flushed. Each carried a pair of binoculars, a camera with zoom attachment, and a canteen. Although it was still early morning, Bucket guessed they'd already been hiking in the bush for several hours.

As they passed, the old man paused to stare openly at Bucket. His daughter tried to hurry him along. "Daddy, let's go."

Tuttle ignored her. He was looking at Bucket's arms, which were ridged and crisscrossed with scars.

"What happened?" Tuttle said, taking one of Bucket's mutilated arms.

"It was my initiation into manhood," said Bucket automatically, "a custom of our tribe, to see if young boys can stand the pain." He tried to pull his arm back, but Sol Tuttle held him fast.

The white, raised scars resembled a collection of overlapping grids. Celeste shuddered and looked away. Bucket could see the gooseflesh pucker along her arms so that her flesh appeared to roll like the surface of a lake disturbed by wind.

Tuttle seemed fascinated by the scarification. He ran a fingertip along one ridge of scar tissue with the wonderment of a child.

"Daddy, the men are waiting," said Celeste.

"Let 'em wait. It's my four point two million dollars. It's my hospital. Right now I want to look at this man's mutilation."

Celeste shivered in the merciless heat. Bucket wondered if she was ill. An anthropology professor from an American university, she was writing a book about African mythology and folklore and had lived in Bucket's village for several months. It was after her father had flown over to visit her that the poverty of the Tongan people had moved him to put up money for a hospital.

"Are you another African that carves them little gew-gaws for the tourists?" said Tuttle, still unwilling to relinquish Bucket's arm. "Or you farm the dust in this godfor-saken place?"

"I farm," said Bucket. "When tourists come, sometimes I help them find animals to photograph."

"Daddy, you can talk to Bucket later."

Tuttle released Bucket's arm with visible reluctance.

"Before I fly back to Dallas, I want to get some photos of black rhinos. I'd go by myself, but Celeste won't hear of it, says I'll just get myself killed. Think you can find me a rhino?"

Bucket nodded—were it not for his skills as a tracker, he might never have been accepted back into the village after his release from the asylum—but his heart felt leached and calcified, like the white, bone-rich turds of the hyena.

As Celeste linked an arm through her father's and hurried him away, the old man called back, "I want to hear the whole story behind those initiation scars."

Bucket watched Mr. Tuttle and Celeste conferring with the officials from the Capital, while the village elders and the *nganga,* smoking her pipe of pungent-smelling tobacco, gathered round. He crossed his mutilated arms and thought, "How can I kill a God-fearing man who's done nothing to harm me?"

And he remembered the hiss of blood pumped from open arteries and the rip and rending of flayed flesh and something mucusy and mottled red, like a length of intes-tine lined with teeth working over his screaming cousin, and he prayed that the Tokoloshe wouldn't come for him again, that he wouldn't have to carry out its demand.

Presently, when the sun climbed high and blistering in the scalding bowl of the sky, Bucket made his way up the road to the provisions store. A few children shouted names at him—"Imbecile! Crazy!"—but Bucket was used to such abuse and barely heard them. He bought cigarettes and a sack of cornmeal and a bottle of the rough, locally-brewed whiskey.

That night he drank and dozed and awoke to drink some more.

The second time he woke, something breathed there in the dark next to his pallet. For a moment, Bucket thought he was a boy again and his mother was tending him through the malaria that had almost killed him, when his fever had risen so high that his thoughts and feelings muddied like bright dyes that turn an ugly brown when spilled together, and the line between reality and dreams became a confusing, easily-lost thread that was never again mended.

Then he felt the Tokoloshe's tongue flick over him like the winging of an insect, caressing him in places where he both loathed and longed for touch.

"Kill him."

"But why?" gasped Bucket, although, even drunk as he was and mortified by his erectness, he knew it was absurd to try to reason with a demon. Perhaps the Tokoloshe had chosen Mr. Tuttle to die precisely because he was a good man, a generous man, because the village needed a hospital so desperately.

But then the Tokoloshe slid down and murmured soft, vile words that slithered over Bucket's pillow and slimed into his ear, and the words jetted out of the demon's mouth like feces, hard little black turd-sounds that soiled Bucket's soul, until, in the end he understood why Sol Tuttle had to die.

For the Tokoloshe explained to Bucket what the word hospital really meant. Bucket had imagined a white, gleaming building full of kindly doctors, where skinny children with their bellies full of worms would be made well, where people bitten by tsetse flies, people dying of AIDS, and those driven mad by spells would be healed. Never had it occurred to Bucket that the hospital Mr. Tuttle planned to build would be like the place for the insane, where he was sent after his cousin's murder.

That was not a hospital, but a place of torture and squalor, where those whose relatives didn't bring them food went hungry, where the biggest, strongest men took the younger, weaker ones for wives, where those who fought back were tied down and had by all or had their heads pushed into the toilet buckets.

It was from that last experience, oft-repeated, that Bucket had acquired his name. He'd had another name one time, a Tongan one, but he no longer knew it.

"The hospital's being built for you," the demon whispered, words that echoed in Bucket's head long after he was alone. "When it's finished, they'll put you there and never let you out."

At the end of the week, the village elders held a ceremony to bless the land on which the hospital was going to be built. For the occasion, a goat had been selected to be sacrificed, and several neighboring villages assembled. People drank beer, played radios. Many of the women smoked long, colorful pipes. To facilitate this, most had had their six front teeth hammered out by the tribal dentist while they were still little girls, a custom favored among the women of Bucket's tribe for both its beauty and utility. Children scampered about, playing with the few ribby dogs. The older ones were beautified with nostril piercings— mimosa thorns for the girls, a porcupine quill for the boys. Watching them, Bucket felt enraged that Tuttle should come here and construct a place of torture.

Presently, the goat's throat was slit, its blood caught in a basin. The *nganga* produced a pouch of dung-flavored tobacco and two bolts of cloth, white and black. She wrapped the befouled tobacco in the cloth and dropped it into a hole that had been dug where the cornerstone of the hospital would be laid. Then the entire group set out to walk the perimeters of the hospital grounds, with the *nganga* sprinkling the goat's blood along the way.

Bucket followed the procession led by the witchwoman and Sol Tuttle. He prayed that God might strike Mr. Tuttle dead, but the old man strode on, vigorous in spite of his age and the punishing heat, while the *nganga's* ritual ululations rose up like the screech of a leopard caught in a snare.

When the procession had completed the periphery, the

nganga crouched, reptilian eyes shut to mummified slits, and released a keening wail. In the trees behind the village, the baboons began to shriek, adding to the unearthly cacophony.

The witchwoman pushed her way through the crowd toward Bucket. Her body convulsed in a kind of spastic caper, like the k,ad monkeys that Bucket had seen children affix to a set of crude sticks and strings and make dance.

"Tokoloshe!" she shouted in Bucket's face and spat on the earth at his feet, muttering incantations.

He dreamed that night of the bad place in Harare, of being the "wife" of an ape-faced thug and being shared, his insides cored like an impala being gutted by a lion. He woke up gasping, sure the Tokoloshe had seized him, but he was alone, trembling on his bed of bricks, thinking about the hospital.

The next day, Bucket took his rifle and followed Sol Tuttle on his afternoon trek into the bush. The old man was easy to track. A child blind in one eye could have done it. He meandered and wandered, pausing to look at birds through his binoculars: a carmine bee-eater, a nightjar, an oxpecker. It was obvious that he was headed for the waterhole, a dried-up pond of mud this time of year, but the only place for many miles for the animals to drink. Even the most timid would come to the waterhole under such conditions and risk the lurking predators, the lions and leopards.

Bucket knew the thrill of the predator. It was an ugly feeling, one he'd tried to forget, but it sang in his blood like strong whiskey. Only a dozen yards or so behind Tuttle, he could see the old man's khaki safari hat, hear him mutter to himself as he scribbled in the margin of his bird book.

"Yea, though I walk through the valley," Bucket began and then fell silent, for he knew he had no right to pray his Christian prayer, that the Christian God had abandoned him long ago.

Then the wind shifted and Bucket heard the elephants.

Squinting through the glare, he saw three cows, two with newborns. They stood motionless among a cluster of flame acacias, trunks lifted high to pick up the human scent.

Tuttle, who was closer, was unaware of them.

Under most circumstances, Bucket knew elephants weren't dangerous. But a cow with a calf—that was the most dangerous elephant of all, and these cows were stressed from thirst. Tuttle was blundering directly toward them, scanning the treetops with his binoculars.

If there had been more time, if Bucket had been capable of thinking more by reason than acting from instinct, it might have ended differently. For the cow with a notch in her ear, a notch which might well have been put there by a poacher's gun, teaching her forever the connection between human scent and mortal danger, trumpeted and charged.

Reflexively, with an instinct borne of dozens of safaris, Bucket slung the weapon to his shoulder and fired just over the cow's head. She screamed and wheeled. Bucket fired once more into the air.

Only when Tuttle staggered up to him, flushed and gasping, and gripped Bucket's hand did he realize the enormity of his misjudgment.

He had come out here to kill the old man, and the charging elephant had been an answered prayer. For a second, he thought how easy it would be to simply bludgeon Tuttle on the spot. By the time the hyenas and vultures finished with the body, it would be impossible to tell whether a blow to the head had felled him or a heart attack or heat stroke.

But Tuttle's gratitude filled Bucket with guilty dread.

He found it impossible to use the gun as the two men headed back to the village.

In its fury, the demon pleasured Bucket that night and then tormented him. Its red talons prodded him cruelly in that place where he'd been split so many times that there were raised painful welts that never healed, as though he was in the slow process of shitting out parts of himself.

Bucket began to tremble.

"*Your* blood," the demon whispered, and Bucket, moving as if in a trance, reached for his skinning knife. Holding out his left arm, he cut into the already corrugated flesh. Bucket always told those who asked that the mutilation was from ritual scarification administered during rites of puberty. His own people, of course, knew that for nonsense. They knew Bucket punished himself to make amends for the hideous death he had inflicted upon his cousin, but the tourists were fascinated with the initiation story and

sometimes—like Mr. Tuttle—wanted to touch and photograph the scars.

He snicked the knife tip underneath the skin just inside the elbow and drew downward, opening a long, straight seam. Again, another cut parallel to this one. The blood poured down Bucket's arm.

"Again," whispered the Tokoloshe.

Bucket switched the knife to his left hand and went to work on the other arm.

"Tuttle's life or yours," the Tokoloshe said and Bucket, weeping, nodded.

"I saw rhino tracks this morning," Bucket told Mr. Tuttle.

"We'll go out this afternoon."

"Great," said Tuttle, then added in a softer voice, "You'll have your gun, right—just in case we run into trouble?"

Bucket nodded. "And we'll go slow. It's very hot."

"That sun is treacherous," said Celeste, who sat on a camp chair with a laptop computer on her knees. A light sweat sheened her face, and her skin glowed ruddy with what might have been painful sun exposure. "Before the elephant charged him, Papa thought Africa was like Disney World, only bigger. Now he's learned the animals can kill you."

The word "kill" made Bucket shudder as if a snake had crawled between his shoulder blades.

In the bush, Mr. Tuttle ambled slowly and still tired fast. It took him and Bucket over an hour to cover four miles, and then the old man wanted to rest and eat an orange before they continued.

Bucket agreed. They reached the crest of a ridge and sat beneath a huge baobab tree whose brown, bloated trunk resembled the swollen body of an obese drowned woman. Mr. Tuttle took two oranges from his daypack and offered one to Bucket, who declined.

His stomach was already roiling like the inside of a termite mound, and the orange peel reminded him of the Tokoloshe's red and rubbery, discolored skin. He got up and walked a few yards away to vomit.

Doubled over, he saw something glinting whitely in the

dirt. He wiped his mouth and kicked at the thing with his toe, picked it up. A rhino's skull. The horn was missing, of course, meaning poachers. Lions or hyenas had probably devoured the carcass elsewhere; ants had cleaned out the skull.

How quickly the ants did their work.

"You know," said Tuttle, who was gazing through his binoculars at a flock of Egyptian geese when Bucket returned, "you still haven't told me about the initiation ceremony. I'd like to know how—"

Bucket brought the skull down just above the red fold of sunburnt neck. Tuttle cried out and toppled, spitting out orange. Bucket brought the heavy bone down again and again, crushed Tuttle's skull to the consistency of macerated cornmeal.

When he was finished, the old man's brain lay exposed to the ubiquitous ants. Bucket crouched to watch the procession of tiny pinchered bodies across the crevassed terrain of the man's smashed skull. His vision blurred and it was as if he could see two scenes at once, superimposed: his cousin writhing on the ground next to an ever-growing mound of his own skin, and the ants that tore off tiny chinks of fat and muscle from the exposed, raw flesh, an endless procession of tiny black bodies, each with a red dot of flesh in its pincers.

And he remembered the slimy, slug-like thing that ate its way across the boy's flayed body, the wet sound of the creature's teeth between his cousin's legs, and the bloody clutch of genitals, like some obscene grey tuber bleeding from the root, that it waggled from its mouth before devouring the abominable prize.

The memory of that horror merged with the reality of this one.

Thinking to perform the mutilation before the demon did so, Bucket pulled out his skinning knife and reached down to Tuttle's groin.

"Don't touch him."

Bucket looked up in fear and confusion and saw the mottled visage of the demon. It was wearing Celeste Tuttle's khaki safari clothes. Celeste's dark hair, pulled back in a braid, swung down its back. In its hand, the demon gripped a revolver.

Before Bucket could speak, an explosion lifted him up and slammed him onto the dirt with the force of a lightning strike, as blood the color of the demon's marks spewed from his neck.

Smiling, the Celeste-demon crouched down and squinted into Bucket's eyes. She pulled a compact out of her trouser pocket and a tube from which she squirted a pale glob of paste into her hand.

"You don't find my birthmarks sexy, do you?" she said to Bucket, dabbing the clay-like substance onto the dark, discolored patches on her face and neck. Bucket moaned and the Celeste-demon laughed. "If that was a 'yes,' I didn't hear you clearly.

"No, Bucket, don't lie now. You found my naked face so repulsive, you imagined I was a demon come to pay you back for a murder you committed twenty years ago."

She reached forward to touch Bucket's neck where the air stuttered out of the hole in his throat. Bucket lunged at her and tried to bite, but she escaped his feeble effort easily and went on smoothing the paste into her skin.

"Yes, I'll bet you like me better with my theatrical makeup on, you poor retarded sot. Too bad my father didn't feel the same way. He always told me the marks made me beautiful and special. He'd rub the stains and get a hard-on like when he touched your scars. Since I was a little girl, he told me I must never go to a hospital and have the marks removed."

At the word hospital, Bucket tried to get up, but a great weight collapsed his chest, and he seemed to be breathing flame.

The Celeste-demon gazed into her mirror.

"Now my father will never build a hospital . . . here or anywhere else. Can you imagine, Bucket, the thrill he would have gotten, visiting that special wing he planned for the deformed and the disfigured, admiring their afflictions, their dwarfed limbs and scars, perhaps caressing a child's cleft palate and inserting his fingers in the flesh and becoming aroused? Playing god in the presence of the maimed and the grotesque.

"Now his hospital will be as much a fantasy as your Tokoloshe."

An ant was crawling across Bucket's open eye. He tried

to blink it away, but his eyelids were immovable, like stone. The Celeste-demon had finished smoothing the paste over her blotched and mottled skin. She snapped the compact shut and gazed down at him with loathing.

"So now you know the truth about me, Bucket. Now go ahead and die."

Bucket watched her while the light glimmered out of his eyes and the weight on his chest and the hate in his heart became unbearable.

"No," he murmured, and the words that came to him were not the prayers of the Christian God, but the curses taught him by the old *nganga,* Zihute, the summoning spell he'd used once, long ago, to kill his cousin.

When he was finished, the light in Bucket's eyes was almost gone, and the ants feasted avidly at his wound.

Celeste, satisfied that he would soon be dead, turned and made her way back through the tall grass.

Something wet and mottled with stains the color of dried blood ate its way free of Bucket's wound and hobbled after her.

ystery orm

Brian McNaughton

In his junior year Redfield arranged a schedule that suited his habits. None of his lectures started before eleven, leaving him free to study through the night. Hoping for a dreamless sleep before dawn, he would begin to drink beer after midnight, however. After his third or fourth can, he would forget the text in his lap or the paper in his typewriter and fall into the grip of imaginary dialogues with his parents or his professors, with Mary, whom he had lost, or with the literary world he hoped to win.

Furious pounding on his walls or floor would often shock him out of these conversations. He would realize that he had been stamping back and forth, shouting and gesticulating at people who had seemed far more real than the strangers behind the stained plaster. He was spared the shame of having revealed his secrets, for few of his neighbors spoke English.

Tiptoeing laboriously, he would return to his book, but meaningless symbols would dance on the page. He would return to the typewriter he had mounted on a cushion to muffle its noise, but the type would bunch together in a skeletal fist when he tried to build up speed. Mumbling resolutions to pull himself together, he would fall across his unmade bed as his window grew gray.

Despite his schedule, he rarely got to his first lecture on time. He usually had to wait for the mailman.

"When are you going to fix my mailbox?" he asked the janitor, who had woken him to take measurements and drill holes.

"*Si,*" the man said, flashing a gapped grin.

"Mailbox. *Postale* . . . oh, shit . . . *boxo.*"

"*Si, si!*" A dialect or speech impediment forced Red-

field's imagination to supply the vowel in these brusque affirmatives.

Looking beyond green work-clothes and brown skin for the first time, he saw that it wasn't his janitor, an older man who knew enough English to say, "No *poss-ee-blay* now, later, maybe." Except for the grin, this one might have posed for an Aztec idol of the nastier sort: his bald skull narrowed toward the forehead in a obscurely disturbing way. He was a specialist, an electrician perhaps, who couldn't care less about mailboxes.

He envied Shelley and Swinburne all the Latin they had learned in childhood. If he'd had a proper education, picking up Spanish or Italian now would be easy. He felt like a decadent Roman in the twilight of the Empire, able to understand neither his glorious ancestors nor the barbarians swarming around him.

The man went back to work when Redfield turned from his aggressive smile. Gray ashes sifted past the window, as if someone were burning papers in one of the tenement's unsafe fireplaces, but the volume and persistence of the fall convinced him it was snow. Below, the mailman left a glistening black trail in the pale street as he crossed to the opposite side.

"Lock up?" Redfield said as he stepped through a tangle of thick cables to the door. "When you finish—the door—*porta—fermez?*"

"*Si.*"

One of his neighbors lurked in the foyer, but perhaps he was no neighbor at all, a Latin androgyne in oily and strangely patterned black leather. He had hastily withdrawn his hand from the row of mailboxes, but Redfield saw no key in his hand, nor any mail. As always, his own box hung open.

"Do you live here?" Redfield asked.

The boy's eyes sparked with black venom, his lip curled in a sneer. He said something, or made a noise, that suggested spitting. Then he spun on his heel and vanished into a blast of snow, slamming the outer door behind him. Even if he was someone Redfield saw but failed to notice every day, his anger seemed disproportionate.

Perhaps he was one of the neighbors who believed he was a religious maniac. More than once he had been jolted

out of imaginary arguments with Mary. He would grumble *sotto voce* through these monologues, but it was his unhappy habit to shout her name for emphasis. A fat, beige woman who lived down the hall shared his rumored devotion to Our Lady, for she would jabber at him and hold up a fist intertwined with greasy black beads whenever they squeezed past each other on the stairs.

He unstuck his carelessly wadded mail from the box. He found no check from his mother; perhaps the leather-boy had stolen it. The only thing of importance was a letter from one of the university's computers. It told him that he was failing a course in anthropology.

This was nonsense. He was taking no courses in that department. The number of the course, 312, meant nothing to him. He checked the addresses on the flimsy envelope. It was not impossible that two Thomas Redfields were enrolled in the university, but it was strange that he hadn't heard of the other one before.

He supposed he should have been angry, if not worried, but he felt almost grateful. Raising a fuss at the administration offices would be a pleasant change from sitting passively through another lecture on Gerard Manley Hopkins. Overcoming a petty obstacle where success was guaranteed by the justice of his case was preferable to racking his brains for quibbles to raise without contradicting a professor's prejudices, the secret of success in the English department. He envied people like the electrician, whose straightforward puzzles were answered in some book as valid here as it was in Guatemala.

About to leave, he noticed a letter that lay on the floor where he had dropped it; unless the mailman had, or the angry stranger. Large and square, it looked like an invitation. Consistent with that was its elegant calligraphy, now bleeding under a wet footprint. He knew of no one who would invite him anywhere. But—he felt a thrill that was not unmixed with dismay—it was from *Ed Tourmalign,* who didn't know him, who had surely never heard of him.

He believed that Edward F. Tourmalign was the greatest living writer of—well, there was no way around it, of *horror stories,* although that grouped him with the morons who scribbled tripe about gluttonous zombies and libidinous vampires. But it grouped him with Poe and Kafka, too.

Tourmalign dove into the abyss of his subconscious and broke the surface holding up objects of questionable nature that were both foul and beautiful: objects that Redfield, to his frequent discomfort, found familiar.

He had tried to write horror stories. He often wondered why his dreams were frightening while his stories—most anyone's, really—weren't. No words on a printed page ever forced him to check the locks on his doors or windows, turn on every light he had, and sit up through the dark hours jumping at noises and shadows. No story had ever bathed him in cold sweat or wrenched screams from the depths of his lungs. But his dreams had.

Conversely he wondered why such dreams were merely boring if he tried to retell them the next day. "I dreamt a snake swallowed my hand." He could have described the oily blackness of the snake, he could have described his pain and terror and despair, he could have told how he clutched the hand to his breast when he woke, sobbing and crooning over it, half afraid that the snake might get it again. Such a thorough account might convince his listeners that he was crazy, but it would never *scare* them.

The fault, he believed, lay with the language, which was not that of dreams. Shakespeare had known the language of nightmares, for Macbeth had spoke it fluently. But Redfield wasn't trying to write Elizabethan poetry. More to the point, he wasn't Shakespeare. To translate dreams into plain prose, into the bald speech of post-literate America, seemed impossible until he read the tales of Edward F. Tourmalign.

In Tourmalign's stories, wind-blown leaflets, clinking light-stanchions in empty streets, neon signs with missing letters—such banal images assumed, in waking life and in cold print, the horrific significance they so often radiated in nightmares. It had been said of many pathetic hacks that they should never be read at night, but it made no difference when one read Tourmalign, for his work was a poison that infiltrated the bloodstream and altered the structure of the brain. It had taken root and grown inside Redfield like a cancer whose existence he could never forget, one that seemed, when he could inspect it with critical disinterest, complex and gorgeous.

Why should Tourmalign write to him? Redfield had

never published his own feeble efforts. He had never so much as written a letter to the ephemeral magazines that printed the master's stories or to the unheard-of publisher who had collected them in a pair of slim volumes. He sometimes regretted never having written to the man himself. It was inevitable that Tourmalign should be neglected by the herds who trooped to worship the fatuous, and he surely must know that, but the knowledge might bring no consolation. He might be glad to learn that he wasn't merely talking to himself, that his words had been heard and understood by a receptive spirit.

What had stopped him from writing a fan letter was his suspicion that the man who could create such tales was probably insane and possibly dangerous. He knew that this attitude was downright illiterate, that he was no better than the yahoos who ascribed Poe's vision to drink and dope. The fact remained that Tourmalign scared him.

He opened the envelope carefully, conscious that this was not just a letter but a document. It was no invitation: the oversized envelope held only a piece of notepaper with the author's letterhead. Water from the footprint had seeped through, and already the black ink bled. At least he learned that Tourmalign used a fountain-pen, which seemed appropriately stylish and old-fashioned, but which left him defenseless in a world designed for infinitely replaceable computer-flimsies, where venal landlords, wouldn't fix mailboxes, where mailmen trod on their sacred trust with wet boots.

He held the note up to the subaqueous snow-glow seeping through grimy windows. Some of the words had dissolved, but it seemed that Redfield was being thanked for an "amusing" letter of his own, one that had expressed—what?—"dismay." As far as he could make out the sentence, Tourmalign wrote: "Such genuine dismay always evokes empathy. But you—" illegible—"most important that you—" illegible—"dreams—" illegible—"need help, do not hesitate—".

The note became even harder to decipher as Redfield's hand began shaking. What was this? The letter seemed urgent, its contents ominous. He was being *warned,* and the warning concerned those very dreams that frightened him

so much, that the author knew more about than anyone on earth.

He had to examine the letter in a strong light. He should dry it immediately, blot it dry, but he was reluctant to return to his room while the electrician worked. He wasn't afraid of him, not exactly, but he was afraid of the impression he would give to a plain man with real work to do: a gormless booby of a student who typically didn't know if he was coming or going.

And he was going. He hadn't fallen into the clutch of a Tourmalign story. He hadn't written a fan-letter while drunk or invoked the magus while dreaming, he had merely misread the first sentence. Like everybody else, the mad genius was out to make a buck. He had found Redfield's name on a sucker-list of pollutant fantasists and was probably offering help in the form of an expensive critique. That hypothesis matched the invitational envelope. Everything would fit once he had deciphered the message under a decent light.

He folded the note into the envelope and managed to slip it into an inside pocket of his jacket only by bowing it slightly. It annoyed him that he still treated it with such reverence.

He prided himself on wearing only a tweed jacket with a scarf and cap, just like his notion of an Oxford student, in the northern winters. Today he would gladly have abandoned that image if he hadn't pawned his overcoat. His ears began to ache the minute he stepped into the storm, so he wrapped the trailing end of the scarf around them and around the lower half of his face. By the time he was finished his hands had numbed under gale-driven nails of snow. He jammed them into his pockets and curled his shoulders into his chest as he lurched through a white-out of Polar intensity, not unaware of his likeness to a revenant from meretricious films. The few shamblers he glimpsed at distant intersections when the snow caught its breath were a match for him.

Because it was lunchtime, or because of the snow, the administration offices had been all but abandoned. He wandered through fluorescent halls, poked into empty offices, scrutinized confusing directories, questioned students who

knew less than he did. At last he found what he hoped was the right office. An African-American woman sat and stared bemused at the vaporous giants attacking her tall widow, swirling up like all white hell broke loose, only to fall away, twirling and dividing and reforming to return as new giants for a fresh assault. Redfield grew bemused, too. It seemed to him that one cowled monster had brandished its coils at the window more than once, and he waited for its next materialization, but that never came.

The woman started and stared with such aggrieved incomprehension that Redfield felt obliged to say, "I'm a student." When she only glared more suspiciously, he unwound the muffling scarf from his face and repeated the words. He tried to shake the crusted snow out of it, but enough had melted to soak the wool deeply.

She composed her features into official belligerence and swayed toward him, a huge woman, the silhouette of a galleon under full sail. "I got this letter," he said, digging it out. He let her examine it while he fussed with his scarf.

"What you trying to tell me?"

"No, not that." He snatched back Tourmalign's letter. She seemed to be debating whether to call a security guard while he rummaged through his other pockets. The flimsy was now a wet wad, and she blamed him for this, if not for the weather itself. She smoothed it out.

"So?"

"I'm not. . . ." A feature of Tourmalign's envelope, unnoticed before, so gripped him that he forgot her completely.

"Am I s'pose to take your courses for you? So you're failing, so?"

"I'm sorry." He had to force his mind back to the matter at hand, which had seemed so urgent only a moment ago. "I'm not taking that course. I never enrolled. It's some kind of mixup."

"Sure," she said, or something like it, as she sat herself heavily at a computer by the counter and jabbed at seemingly random keys.

He ignored her to examine a printed sticker, or half of one, that was affixed to a lower corner of the invitational envelope. It read, "ystery orm." He thought at first it must be some scrap from his pocket that had mated with the envelope, for his pockets were full of odd, forgotten bits of

paper, but it had clearly been stuck on with intentional firmness. His thumbnail failed to raise an edge.

"Professor Winfield?"

"What?" Redfield said.

"Professor Winfield, Anthro 312, *Serpent-Worship in Pre-Columbian Meso-America,* is that the course you be flunking?"

"I'm not flunking anything. Is that the course I'm supposed to be enrolled in?"

"It say here."

"Well, I'm not in it. I'm not taking any courses in that department. Would you take my name off, please?"

She laughed richly. Her face lit up when she smiled, but not with kindness. "You got to tell Professor Winfield all about it, and then you come back here with the form he fill out."

"And where do I find him?"

Her smile blackened to a scowl. She poked more keys, swearing under her breath, while Redfield examined the sticker. Unlike something that might belong on an envelope, giving additional information to the Post Office or the addressee, it had been placed vertically.

"Carter Hall, number 215. He have office hours now—" she swiveled to check on the snow—"if he there."

"What do you make of this?"

She turned the envelope this way and that until he stretched a finger beyond the counter and put it trembling on the sticker. She said, "Nothing much. 'History dorm'?"

"No, I don't think so. Thanks very much."

"You bring that form back from Professor Winfield, you hear?" She seemed suddenly friendly. "Then we fix you up."

Unwilling to brave the snow again, he loitered in the main entrance and puzzled over the sticker. *Mystery Worm,* or *Mystery of the Worm,* perhaps? The *orm* could be anything, but *Worm* seemed to fit *Mystery,* if that was indeed the other world. In the curious tongue of the English, a worm was not just an earthworm or a tapeworm, it could be a serpent, a dragon, Satan himself.

The university and the city's slum were krakens that had hopelessly intertangled their tentacles. Carter Hall lay on

Market Street, whose shops proclaimed *ropas* and *zapatas,* suggesting to Redfield that bandits might here be hanged. These shops were closed, along with the Cuban-Chinese restaurants where joints of pork would normally sizzle temptingly—but never quite enough to tempt him into assault on a double language barrier—in the windows on spits. He had passed through before, but he had never noticed Carter Hall.

He might have missed it entirely if he hadn't been arrested by the window of a *botanica* that displayed a statue of the Blessed Mother, standing on a wreath of hooded serpents. The garish figure was identified as *Caridad del Cobre,* and he wondered at the path by which a Nazarene virgin and an African snake could achieve religious symbiosis in the Caribbean.

The unexplained events of this day had a common thread of plausibility that especially disturbed him. Writing a fan-letter to Tourmalign and taking a course on Central American serpent-cults were things he might have done, might very well have done. He admired the one and was curious about the other. But he hadn't done either. He knew he hadn't.

The rear of the shop-window held dim objects that might have been balls, gourds or skulls. He had wondered where he might buy a skull to give his dingy room its decorational *coup de grace*. The entry to the adjoining building gave him a view into the side of the shop-window. Backing into it, he glanced over his shoulder and saw that the fanlight was lettered "Carter Hall."

Eager to escape the cold, he abandoned the quest for skulls to lurch into the foyer and puff gently on his reddened hands. The directory he examined had been usurped as a bulletin-board of flyers for weirdly named bands, curled and discolored index-cards soliciting roommates or offering questionable services. He saw nothing suggesting the office of a Professor Winfield, and the foyer looked like that of an ordinary tenement, its floor tiled with scaly, black-and-white octagons. He wrenched his eyes from their hypnotic spell and ascended the stairs, keeping his hand off the cold metal rail after the first painful trial.

The next floor ballooned into a wooden cavern, as if the university had gnawed out the insides of the *bodegas* and

ristorantes to create a vast hollow wherein to hoard its atmosphere of dust and disinfectant and ancient wood-polish. Only a bluish glow could penetrate the fog and soot on tall Gothic windows at the end, though it shone enough to make the floor look waterish. He ventured into it like an inept skater.

The hall was so large that it concealed the doors of the offices it was meant to service, all of them half-glazed with frosted panels. He veered toward the distant side and studied one after another, but none bore the name "Winfield." None seemed to be lighted within. After he had tried a few and found them locked, it struck him that the numbers on these doors were wrong: *four*-twelve, *four*-fifteen.

He screwed up his courage and called, "Hello? Hello!", but got no response.

Near the windows at the end he found an unglazed door with the faded legend, *Gentlemen,* and he entered gratefully. It contained a single toilet whose black seat was askew. The bowl was crazed with a thousand tiny cracks, and its monumental stain had leaked into all of them, but it served his purpose. Raising his eyes, he saw something he had only been told about by old people, a coffin-like box with a chain at the side. Pipes ran down to the bowl, which had no usual tank or handle. An image of Mary as a Swinburnian *demimondaine,* constricted by stiff corsets, stirred him. He zipped up hastily, remembering why he was here. His imaginary enrollment in Professor Winfield's course was a real threat. He was unprepared for the roar of the toilet, the violent scouring of the bowl, when he pulled the chain beside the box.

He thought he heard voices outside the door. He was sure he heard voices.

"By swallowing its tail," a voice seemed to say, "the worm ouroboros swallows all."

". . . Tourmalign," a second seemed to say.

Redfield tried to pull the door open. He wanted to burst upon them and demand answers. The door refused to budge. The toilet continued to roar, then gurgle, obscuring the conversation. He hammered the door, kicked it, and at last it burst wide. The huge hall was empty, but the persons he had heard would have had more than enough time to disappear by unremarkable means.

*   *   *

If he was on the fourth floor of Carter Hall, the second would be in the basement. This was not impossible. Market Street followed the crest of a hill. The main entrance to the building might be on the downward slope of that hill. If he had entered there, he would have entered on the ground floor. That he had come in by a back entrance to the third floor would explain, too, the absence of a valid directory.

He approached the windows and tried to rub them clear with his forearm, but that had only dirtied his sleeve. The snow spattered hungrily against the glass shielding his arm, and he jerked it back.

He saw a downward stair to his left, dark and unpromising, but he took it. He reached a narrow landing lit by a caged, naked bulb. Three doors led from it, but none was marked and all were locked. This would be the floor by which he had entered: the third? He must be descending a disused fire-exit, not a main stairway. Serpentine graffiti tangled on walls of bare brick. "SNAKE 312" one of them read, which struck him as a very strange coincidence, but it must have been the work of an anthropology student playing at street-hooligan.

The next flight was brighter, and he took heart from this until he saw why: it ended at a glass door to the outside. It was obviously at ground level, but by his reckoning this should be the second floor.

No interior door led from this cramped entrance, but the stairway continued down. The hill might be irregular in shape, and the true main entrance could be somewhere to his right and another floor farther down. He pushed on the pressure-bar and managed to force the door open a few inches against drifted snow, but he was unable to see much of the building through billowing white clouds when he squeezed his head outside. He retreated and let the wind slam the door, regretting the horrendous clang that echoed and re-echoed through the stairwell.

The downward stairway was very dark, it smelled dank and musty, but the alternative was to go outdoors and slog his way across the drifted hillside in the teeth of a gale, looking for another entrance that might not exist. At very

least, he might find a janitor below who could set him on the right track.

The steps under his feet were utilitarian metal now, but the rail didn't freeze his hand. It seemed to have been coated with a thick, rubbery material that gave in unexpected ways, as if with a life of its own.

He reached the bottom and stepped into a puddle on the concrete floor. That and his blindness should have oppressed him, he knew, but for the first time in a long while he was truly warm, and that counted for a lot. The atmosphere of the basement was muggy. He might not have been surprised to hear the cry of an exotic bird or monkey in the humid blackness.

"Hello?" he called. "Is anyone here?"

Listening intently in the silence that followed, he thought he heard a hiss of steam, and a rustling that suggested stiff garments brushing the floor. Swinburne's street-walkers strutted luminously before him, but he tried hard to replace them with a man erratically plying a broom in the distance. Whatever the sounds meant, someone was down here with him, who might not have heard him over the noise of his own work.

He advanced by tiny steps with hands outstretched, jumping and nearly losing his balance when drops of tepid water dribbled on them. This could be nothing but the basement, the ultimate, subterranean floor of the queer building. He had overlooked some obvious feature of the structure, or he had simply miscalculated. When he found the janitor, he wouldn't be embarrassed to admit that he badly needed guidance.

The musty smell became distressingly sour. He was about to retreat and call this day a total loss when his path grew lighter. Blue, but more intense than snowy daylight, the luminance ahead suggested electricity. A fizzing sound rose as he advanced. He could easily picture a welder repairing a boiler. He saw that he walked in a corridor roofed and walled with a tangle of greasy black cables and sagging ducts that seemed to convulse in the uncertain light as it brightened. Shadows that made no sense jerked and writhed.

He rounded a curve and nearly blundered into the back of a kneeling man whose hunched shoulders cherished the source of the brilliance.

"I beg your pardon. . . ."

The workman sprang to his feet and whirled in one motion. Against the undiminished glare of the welding torch, or whatever it was, his silhouette radiated not just shock but outrage. His alert crouch and outstretched arms threatened immediate attack. Redfield stumbled backward.

"I'm sorry, I've lost my way, I was wondering—"

The man shrieked with fury and spattered a volley of sibilants. His bald skull gleamed in the light behind him. Oddly wedge-shaped, it recalled the electrician, and Redfield was willing to accept the improbability that his wayward course had led him to the selfsame man.

"My name is Redfield, I'm a student, I—"

Whether or not the man understood, this only enraged him more. He advanced, spitting and hissing in a language that bore no real resemblance to Spanish or any other tongue on earth. Redfield felt in danger of immediate and violent attack. Screaming, he turned and ran. He fell, scraping his knees and hands, but he could spare no time to rise as he hurled himself forward on all fours over rough concrete, through tepid puddles. Banging his head sickeningly into a wall, he only changed his course without interrupting his abject flight. He sensed that his pursuer hovered behind him, but his own hoarse screams drowned any noise of pursuit.

He clanged into the metal stair and flung himself upward, somehow regaining his feet and clinging to the handrail. It must have been a different stairway, for the rail was plain, cold metal, uncovered by any rubbery substance. He hesitated when he saw a bluish light ahead, but then he realized it was only daylight and sprang toward it. He battered his way through a door with a pressure-bar and fell full-length into deep snow.

The shock restored him. Again he must have misinterpreted. He had crept up on a workman and scared the poor fellow out of his wits. He had been angry, yes, but even more frightened than Redfield himself. No one was treading on his heels with the intention of killing him. But he scoured the snow from his eyes and peered back at the door to make absolutely sure this was true as he tried to catch his breath in agonizing whoops.

"Go back and give him *a piece of my mind*," he muttered, mocking a favorite phrase of his mother's to cover

his shame. He feared had already given him a piece of his skull. He touched his forehead, but the blood he saw on his fingers might have come from his scraped hands.

He wrapped his scarf around his head. By now it was completely soaked, but the honest wool could still hold warmth. He burst to his feet and lurched down the slope.

He might have persisted in looking for Professor Winfield, but the wind promised to be at his back all the way home. Even so it pierced his jacket, seemed to pierce his skin and meat and bones. It might have been the cosmic wind of atoms that eternally replaces flesh with dust and dust with flesh, that replaces Redfield with snow and snow with the equestrian statue across the way. That was the meaning of the worm ouroboros, the serpent eternally swallowing its tail.

He found this thought more distressing than any of his real problems.

Soaked, he hauled himself up the banister with numb hands on numb feet and with legs pierced by knives. The last thing he needed, the fat woman with the rosary, blocked his way. He shrank to the side as she said something and exhibited her fist. Her ample thighs billowed against him. He couldn't believe it, she aroused him.

"Si, si, Santa Maria," he muttered, smiling and nodding, wanting only to slither past. *"Mucho*—Christ!—*bona."*

"Santa Maria!" she repeated, but with—loathing? And then she dealt him a profounder shock than any he had got today by spitting in his face.

"You cunt!" he shouted after her, scouring the spit from his face with his sleeve, as she tramped heavily downward. "You and your Virgin both!"

God, he was losing his mind! The house was probably crawling with her relatives, one of whom had to speak English. They would tear him in chunks and eat him. He continued on his way at a fast hobble, slammed his door behind him and locked it. His clothes hit the floor in soggy wads. He pulled a blanket from the bed, the first thing that came to hand, and scrubbed his bare body furiously. He wrapped the second blanket around him and coiled into his one upholstered chair with his blue feet jammed under his quaking buttocks.

He breathed deeply, sighed, surveyed his home. No one pounded at the door. He was safe. He got up and pulled a can of beer from the little refrigerator. It was far too early to drink. He would fall asleep in the early evening and wake up in a darkness that would last for hours, but he needed a restorative now. He sipped and stared at the snow against his window, hoping the storm would last a week and cover the earth to a depth of fifty feet.

He forced himself to get up again and retrieve Tourmalign's letter from his sodden jacket. The envelope bore only illegible smears, the letter was the same. Only the author's letterhead—without his address—and the sticker could be read: *ystery orm.* He could call and ask the author what the hell this was all about, but he had no phone. Dressing and going to the pay-phone on the first floor would be a daunting task, especially since he remembered only that Tourmalign lived in Michigan, or was it Illinois? The phone would be unlisted, he would run out of coins, the beige woman would return to spit on him.

He still had the erection she had improbably provoked. He toyed with it listlessly. Swinburne would have begged her to spit on him—*Our Lady of Pain!*—and her ample figure might have appealed to his taste. She wasn't all that bad, merely older than Redfield by ten years or so and unfashionably buxom. Black eyes, rose-beige skin. *The heavy white limbs and the cruel red mouth like a venomous flower.*

He pictured her fist, so tiny against her huge breasts, her thick lips. He saw it with the rosary entangled—but was it a rosary? When he tried to see her, he saw a smooth, black, shiny thing entwined in her fingers, a greasy black rope. Before he knew it, his seed was spurting into the blanket.

He woke up wet and shivering. He blamed what he once would have called his sin, and it seemed sinful, or at least shameful, to masturbate and sit dully while the slime cooled enough to rouse him. But it was dark now. Hours must have passed since then.

He had spilled his can of beer in his lap. He swore and stilted up on cramped legs, flinging the blanket aside. He tripped over something, shouting in fear as he fell forward. The sensation in the arm he had tried to fling out in defense

was more like a white bolt of clear light than a pain, but it very soon became a pain. He could recall none worse.

His fall seemed to have shaken the building, and he lay waiting for the neighbors to hammer, but they didn't. The distinctive zones of human and electronic gibberish that defined his space were silent. He heard only a pervasive rustling that he ascribed to a grittier sort of snow against the dim window. It must be later than he was willing to accept.

He rose to his knees. His right arm wouldn't bend. He tried to gather it against him with his left, but the pain made him cry out again. He found a table-lamp and pushed the switch, but nothing happened. He had probably tripped over the cord and unplugged it, although his best recollection suggested a more substantial obstacle that had no business cluttering his floor.

"I have a serious problem to deal with," he muttered, and the words almost pleased him, they were so true, so unlike the usual drift of his life in their precision. The only people within shouting distance disliked him or—as that woman's behavior suggested—detested him. He had earned a name as a late-night howler and midnight stamper. If he caught their notice, would they do more than hammer for peace? If they came to his door, would they help him, or would they break his other arm and go back to bed?

And it was broken. The elbow no longer conformed to his deeply-ingrained image of his own elbow, and that rupture with accepted reality was almost worse than the pain itself. The pain, though, was bad enough. When he fondled the break, bones ground audibly, and he fell to his knees with a scream.

When his sobs subsided, he listened hard. He heard nothing but the rustle of incipient sleet, even though he had hit the floor with all his weight. He had screamed very loudly.

He needed light. He got to his feet, noticing how unexpectedly important it was to have two sound arms in order to stand. He went to the door and fumbled beside it for the light switch. His hand rocketed away from something that should not have been there.

The electrician, of course, the electrician: he had been drilling beside the door, and he had . . . what had he done? The light-switch was missing. Through the hole he had

drilled, a thick cable, thick as Redfield's arm, had been inserted. Something about its texture made him jerk his hand away.

But there would be a light in the hall. When he tried to verify this by peering through the crack, he saw nothing. He fumbled with the doorknob, turned the catch of the lock, but the door was immovable. He pounded on the door, kicked it, but when he paused, out of breath and strength, he heard nothing but his own wheezing gasps.

He tried to organize his thoughts. The hall was dark, and the electric clock by his bed did not shine. The power in the building must be out. Brilliant! He couldn't read his cheap watch in the dark. He took it to the window, hoping that a streetlight down the way might help him, but that streetlight was out, too. He saw no light, just a pinkish pallor in the gap where the sky should have been. Unseen snowflakes pattered against the window.

The power-failure was general. His neighbors had abandoned the building. Why? The heat wasn't electric, it was steam, but he noticed now that he was cold. The boiler must be controlled by electricity. He had been abandoned to freeze in darkness with a broken arm because they hated Anglo-Saxons; or more likely, because they had knocked on his door, hadn't been answered, and assumed he was out, or occupied with those concerns he had never condescended to tell them about. He should have been nicer to them; but they had always scared him, he had to admit.

Turning inward, he found that he could very nearly see in the pervasive pallor, but not quite. He could discern shadowy shapes he knew and some he didn't know. The floor seemed especially thick with long shadows that he avoided. He heard a thin hissing that suggested the heat would soon return.

He would have liked to have a beer, but the effort to reach his chair, only a few steps away, was the most he could manage. The refrigerator lay in far deeper darkness. He found his blanket, not all wet, and gathered it around his nakedness. He stared at the dim window and tried to tell himself that he was reasonably comfortable, that he could last until morning.

The pain in his arm now throbbed to the rhythm of his heart. It was hard to shake the delusion that he had an

enormous, red-glowing arm that was twice the size of his body. Leaning to the right and letting his knuckles rest on the floor seemed to minimize the pain. Capt. Scott—". . . these rough notes and our dead bodies . . ."—would never have whined about the mere *inconvenience* of a broken arm.

But Capt. Scott in his antiseptic Antarctic had had no snakes to deal with, and now the thick shadows on Redfield's floor were on the move. He gathered his feet into the chair, screaming, but he could not gather in his right arm. He heard the hissing he had thought was snow, the rustling he had dismissed as steam, but the writhing and interwreathing shadows now told him what those sounds meant.

He tried to rise—he would have leaped naked through the window into the snowstorm, if he could have—but his hand was held. A numb constriction spread upward toward the splintered elbow by slow degrees. He was being swallowed.

He plunged his left hand down into the darkness and seized the thick, rubbery sleeve that muffled his right hand and forearm. It was ponderous. He heard a rustling of monstrous coils as the creature that held him set itself to resist. The abomination slipped from his grasp in its sliminess until he dug his fingernails in, and the pain of wrenching his elbow upward was all but fatal: yet these things had to be done. He dragged it within reach of the only weapons he had, his teeth.

Those teeth were strong and sharp. He gouged great chunks from the worm, the Mystery Worm, that his neighbors had sent and that Tourmalign had tried to warn him of. He pulled out tubular things and sinewy things, he cracked long bones that seemed anomalous to the anatomy of a snake, but he knew that this was no common snake.

No wonder, it seemed, as he gouged and chewed and spat, that the blood pumping into his lap was warm.

Dedicated to Thomas Ligotti.

Tears Seven Times Salt

Caitlin R. Kiernan

Jenny Haniver sits with herself on the always damp mattress in the center of her concrete floor, damp cotton ticking mildewed dark, and no light comes through the matte back-painted windows of the basement apartment. Her books are scattered around her like paper bricks, warped covers and swollen pages. And the candlelight flicker and fluorescence steady from the dozens of aquariums bubbling contentedly, rheumy, omnipresent whisper of air through charcoal and peat and lavalit. She knows the words by heart, sacred interplay of Latin and English, holy pictures of scales and skin flayed back, ink glistening muscles and organs open across her lap.

If this knowledge was enough, she'd have gone down to them a long, long time ago.

Jenny's fingers follow the familiar, comforting lines, and her lips move, pronouncing soundlessly, bead counting each razor thin flare of cartilage and needle stab of bone, hyomandibular, interoperculum, supraoccipital crest.

Necessary but utterly insufficient, dead end to salvation or evolution, transcendence, and when she finishes, Jenny closes the big book and sets it aside.

The apartment is too small, and her tanks line every inch of shelved wall; her long and cluttered tables, stolen doors laid across crumbling cinder blocks take whatever space is left, uneven surfaces crowded with formalin cloudy jars and wax-bottomed dissection trays, rusted pins and scalpels. The dumpster scrounged mattress at the center, and her at its soggy heart. She opens her eyes, irises the color of kelp, slick hazel-brown and dead star pupils eating the tiny pool of yellow candlelight and the greenwhite flood wrapped around. The air stinks like everything wet, fish and fish shit,

mold and algae and the fleshy gray mushrooms that grow unmolested everywhere.

When Jenny Haniver stands, rises up air bubble slow from her careless lotus, some of the layered bandages on her long legs tear, gauze crust clinging to the jealous old mattress fabric, tearing at the useless scabs underneath. She ignores the pain, not even an inconvenience anymore, just a distant murmuring taunt of failure.

Rumors of rumors reach even into her basement, and tonight Jenny Haniver has come out to see if there's any truth between the lines. She comes here less and less often now, this cavern of steel and cement, warehouse once, and the tainted Hudson sighing past outside so the air tastes safe enough. She wears a dingy black and silver body suit to hide the marks, the bandages, sips at salty tequila and watches the dancers, bodies writhing seagrass and eel tangled in the invisible current of sound, alternating mix of industrial clatter and goth's sultry slur. Grease paint vampires and boys with bee stung lips the color of live gillflesh, ravestench reek of sweat and smoke and the fainter, briny tang of spilled beer and come.

"Jenny," the girl says, shouts softly over the music, and sits down in the booth across from her. Jenny looks up from her drink and waits until she remembers the face, puts a name with the hair bleached white and eyebrows shaved and penciled back in place.

"Hello," she says, "Hello, Maria."

"No one ever sees you anymore," the girl says, leans in closer to be heard and the black light strobes catch on the silver stud in her tongue, the single tiny ring in her lower lip. "Someone said they saw you up in Chelsea last month. Pedro, yeah, he said that."

Jenny nods, neither yes nor no, faintest smile showing her teeth, sharp and plaque-yellowed triangles, incisors and canines filed piranha perfect. She lets her eyes drift back down to her glass and the girl keeps talking.

"Jamie and Glitch got a new band together," she says. "And Jamie's singing mostly, but, Christ, Jenny, you know she can't sing like you."

"I heard that Ariadne came back," Jenny says, and the girl says nothing for a long time, a stretched, uneasy space filled

up with the grind and wail from the speakers, calculated pandemonium, and the background rumble of human voices.

"Jesus, Jenny, where the hell'd you hear something like that? People don't come back from the tunnels. You get that low and you don't come back."

Jenny Haniver doesn't argue, finishes her tequila and watches the dancers. The girl leans close again and her breath smells like cloves and alcohol.

"I scored some x," she says. "You want to do some x with me, Jenny?"

"I have to go," Jenny says and stands, notices a glistening, oily patch on the candy apple naugahyde where she's soaked through the bandages and the nylon body suit.

"Everyone misses you, Jenny. I'll tell Glitch you said hi, okay?"

She doesn't reply, turns quickly and leaves the girl without a word, pushes her way across the dance floor, moving between tattered lace and latex and hands that casually, desperately grope as she passes, undertow of oblivion and need and at least a hundred different hungers.

Jenny Haniver's father never raped her, never laid her open like a live, gray oyster and planted grains of sand for pearls and psychosis; none of that trendy talk-show trauma, nothing so horrible that it would have to be coaxed to the surface with hypnosis and regression therapy.

He was a longshoreman, and her mother had left him when Jenny was still a baby, had left him alone with their child and his senile old mother with her Polish accent as thick as chowder. When he was drunk he hit her, and when he was sober he sometimes said he was sorry.

Once, after a layoff or a fight with his foreman, he backhanded her so hard that he knocked out a front tooth, just a baby tooth and already loose anyhow, but afterwards he cried and they rode the D line together all the way out to Coney Island, to the New York Aquarium. He held her up high and Jenny pressed her face flat against the thick glass, eyes wide and drowning in the mossy light filtering down from above, unbelieving, as weightless groupers and barracuda and sharks like the sleekest nightmares cruised silently past.

*   *   *

After the club and the long, February-cold walk back to her apartment, Jenny stands before the mirror in her tiny bathroom, unframed looking glass taller than her by a head and the walls papered with bright prints torn from library books. Millas' Ophelia and John Waterhouse's Shalott, "The Green Abyss" and a dozen nameless Victorian sirens. She has stripped off the body suit rag, has wound away most of the leaking bandages. They lie in a sticky, loose pile at her feet, stained unforgiving shades of infection and a few bloody smears.

The air is so cold that it moves slow and heavy like arctic water around her naked body, gelid thick, and redolent with the meaty, sweet perfume of rot that seeps from the incisions that don't heal, from the dark, red-rimmed patches down her thighs and legs, her belly. The most recent, only two days old, has already faded, silverblue shimmer traded for a color like sandwich grease through a brown paper bag. She touches it and the cycloid scales flake away like dandruff, drift dead and useless to the floor.

Jenny Haniver closes her eyes until the disappointment and nausea pass and there's nothing left but the drip of the faucets, the bubbling murmur of her fish tanks from the other room. This time she will not break the mirror, won't give herself up to the despair. Instead, she opens her eyes and stares back at the gaunt thing watching her, metallic glint of desperation in that face, Auschwitz thin, the jut and hollow of bones just beneath death pale skin.

You can't win, she thinks, I won't die locked in here.

Jenny Haniver turns her back on the mirror, turns to the shower stall, no bathtub here, and she pushes aside the mildew-blackened plastic curtain. She has to use the wrench lying on the little shelf intended for soap or shampoo to turn on the water and it comes out numbing cold. She stands under the spray until she's stopped shivering, until she can't feel anything but the distant pressure of the water pounding itself futility against her immutable flesh.

When Jenny Haniver was a child, Old Mama talked to the pipes, leaned over sinks and tubs, and the toilet and storm culverts and spoke slow and softly through the drains, microphones that would carry her raspy old woman's voice down into the bowels of the city, the city beneath

the city. Jenny would sit and watch, listening, anxiously strain to hear the responses that her grandmother clearly heard.

"Why can't I ever hear anything?" Jenny finally asked one winter afternoon. After school, and she had been watching for almost an hour from the kitchen table as her grandmother had leaned, head and bony shoulders into the white sink, alternately placing an ear and then her lips against the drain. When she spoke, it almost seemed that she kissed the ruststained rim of the hole.

Old Mama raised her head, impatient scowl and Jenny knew she'd interrupted, was sorry but afraid to say so. The late afternoon sunlight, dim through the dirty kitchen window, had caught in the lines and creases of Old Mama's face, shadowing each wrinkle deeper, making her look even older than she was. Eyes like a pecking bird, dark and narrowed, regarding her impudent granddaughter.

"Not until you begin to bleed for the moon," Old Mama said, grabbed roughly at the crotch of her shapeless blue house dress. She grimaced and showed her gums. Jenny wasn't stupid; she knew about menstruation, knew that someday she would get her period and that then she wouldn't be a child anymore.

"But then you won't have to wait for them to talk to you, Jenny," Old Mama went on, "because *then* they will smell you, will smell you ripe in the water from your bath or when you wash your hands or flush the toilet. Then they will come to take you back."

Jenny was afraid, even though she knew that Old Mama wasn't well, wasn't right in the head, as her father sometimes said, drawing circles in the air around his ear.

"Back where?" she asked cautiously, not really wanting to know what Old Mama meant.

"Back down to the sewers, down there in the shit and dark where Old Papa found you."

Jenny's grandfather had worked under the streets, had told her stories about the alligators, the huge, blind sewer rats that never saw the sun and the cats as big and strong as dogs that lived down there and fed on them. But he was dead, and he'd never said one word about having found her in the sewers.

"You were such a very ugly baby that even the fish peo-

ple that live down there didn't want you. They left you under a big manhole and Old Papa found you, naked and smeared in shit, and he had such a soft heart and brought you home."

Jenny opened her mouth, but was suddenly too scared to say anything.

"Your Mama, *she* knew, Jenny. Yes, your Mama knew that you weren't really her baby and that's why she went away."

Old Mama laughed, then, dry cackle, and waggled one arthritis-crooked finger at Jenny.

"And don't ask your Papa. He is too stupid and doesn't know that his little girl is not a real little girl. If he knew, he would be so angry he would put you back down there now, or he would kill you."

And then she put her head back into the sink and Jenny sat staring at Old Mama's skinny rump, still unable to speak, pinned between the cold, solid knot settling in her stomach and the hot, salt sting of the tears gathering in her eyes. After a while, Old Mama got bored, or the fish people quit talking to her, and she went off to watch television, and left Jenny alone in the kitchen.

After the shower, after she dry swallows two of the green cephalexin capsules, antibiotics she buys cheap on the street, and puts clean bandages on her legs, Jenny falls asleep on her stinking mattress.

And dreams of Ariadne Moreau and the hanging room and taut wires that hold her, suspended high above the slippery floor. A hundred stainless-steel barbs pierce the blooddabbed flesh of her outstretched arms, shoulders and breasts and upturned face, matchless crucifixion. Ariadne holds her steady and draws the scalpel blade along the inside of her thighs, first one and then the other, down the length of each dangling leg.

"The old hag should have gone to jail for telling a kid crazy shit like that," Ariadne says.

Jenny doesn't take her eyes off the point far above where all the wires converge, the mad gyre of foam and salt spray eating up the ceiling, counterclockwise seethe of lath and plaster and rafters that snap like the ribs of dying giants.

"People like that," Ariadne says, "make me sorry I don't believe in Hell anymore."

And then she binds Jenny's ankles together with duct tape and begins to sew, sinks the needle in just above her right ankle, draws fine surgical silk through and across to the left. Closing the wounds, stitching away the scalpel's track and the hateful cleft of her legs.

Jenny Haniver follows 48th Street westward, black wraparound shades against the late morning sun that shows itself for brief moments at a time, slipping in and out of the shale gray clouds like a bashful, burning child. She walks with quick, determined steps, ignoring the sharp jolts of pain in her feet and legs that seem to rise from the sidewalk. Moves between and through the mindless jostle of shoulders and faces, avoids her reflection in the shop front and office lobby panes of glass she passes. The chilling Hudson wind rips at her shabby peacoat, flutters her long, snarled hair.

The way down to the tunnels, the gully between 10th and 11th Avenues that Ariadne showed her months ago, has not moved and has not been sealed. From the edge of a garbage dumpster, Jenny climbs over the chain link fence that the city has put up to keep the mole people out or in; clings to the steel tapestry, the diamond-shaped spaces like gar scales in-between, with bare, windgnawed fingers and the worn toes of her tennis shoes. There is a single strand of barbed wire along the top that gives her a moment's trouble, but the solution costs only a few drops of her blood and a ragged, new tear in one arm of her coat.

Thirty feet down to the tracks, she inches along the sheer granite walls, nothing but scraggly, winter dry clumps of goldenrod and poison sumac for treacherous hand holds. She slips and drops the last eight feet to the gravel roadbed below, lands hard on her ass, heart-pounding and blood in her mouth from a bitten tongue, table salt and pennies, but nothing broken.

In front and behind, the old railroad disappears into the rock, blasted away over a hundred years ago and nothing through here anymore but the occasional freight train. She takes off her sunglasses, stuffs them into a coat pocket, and walks into the darkness on a welcoming carpet of clothing

and shattered green Thunderbird bottles, empty crack vials and discarded needles.

Inside, the stench of urine and human feces is as thick, as complete, as the dark; Jenny gags, acid bitter taste of bile, and hides her mouth and nose in the crook of one arm. She knows that there are people watching her, can feel the wary or stark terrified track of their eyes, and sometimes she can hear faint whispering from the side tunnels. Some-thing whooshes past and a bottle smashes with a loud, wet pop against the tunnel wall, peppers her with glass shards and drops of soured wine or beer.

"Who are you?" a hoarse and sexless voice demands, *"Who the hell are you?!"*

She does not answer, stands perfectly still and stares back at the gloom, feigned defiance, pretending that she's not afraid, that her heart's not thumping crazy in her chest and her mouth isn't dry as the gravel ballast underfoot.

Not another word from the dark, only the far off growl of cars and trucks on the street above, and Jenny starts walking again, thankful for the company of her own footsteps.

There are iron grates set into the roof of the tunnel at irregular intervals, dazzling, checkerboard sunlight from the unsuspecting world overhead that only makes the blackness that much more absolute. She walks around, not through them, but keeps careful count of the blinding, gaudy pools in her head, one, three, five, and at the seventh turns left. The basket handle arch of the side tunnel is faintly visible dim reflection off measured stagger old brickwork, and spray-painted sloppy white above and across the chunky keystone, JESUS SAVES and the tag like a preschooler's goldfish. Jenny looks over her shoulder once before she leaves the light behind and follows the gentle slope of the side tunnel west, down towards the river.

She learned to hear the voices in the pipes three years before her first period, hardly a month after her grandmother had told her about Old Papa finding her in the sewers.

Very late at night, when she was sure that everyone was asleep, her father lost in his fitful dreams and Old Mama snoring like a jackhammer down the hall, Jenny would slip

out of bed and tip-toe to the upstairs bathroom. Would bring a blanket because the tile floor and cast-iron tub were always freezing, and lie for hours, curled fetal, with her ear pressed tight against the drain.

And at first there was nothing but a far-off ocean hum like conch shells, and the sounds of the building's old copper plumbing clearing its hundred throats, the gurgle or glug of water on its way up from the mains or back down to the sewers. The metal-hammered clank of pipes expanding or contracting. Sometimes she would doze and dream in the muted greens and browns of the big Coney Island aquarium, lazy sway of sea plants and anemone tendrils, and the strange shadows that moved like storm clouds overhead.

And then, three nights before Christmas and a fresh blanket of snow like vanilla icing, she heard their voices, so faint at first that it might have been anything else, trapped air or her straining imagination. And Jenny lay very still, suddenly wide awake and every muscle tensed, hearing and not believing that she was hearing, not wanting to believe that she was hearing.

The softest sibilant, mumble, and gooseflesh washed prickling cold across her skin.

Not words, at least not words that she could understand, a muffled weave of hisses and clicks and velvet sighs that rose and fell in overlapping, breathy waves. Jenny fought the fear, slick red thing twisting inside and her pounding heart, the urge to pull away, to run wailing to her father and tell him *everything*, everything that Old Mama had said that day in the kitchen and everything since. The urge to turn the tap on scalding hot and drown whatever was down there.

The fish people who live down there

Jenny Haniver did not run. She squeezed her eyes shut and ignored everything but the wet voices, fists clenched, knees braced against the side of the tub. Tried to wrestle something like meaning or sense from the gibbering. And afterwards, she would come back every night, would spend the house's dead hours listening patient and terrified until she began to understand.

The city beneath the city, accumulated labyrinth of pipe and tunnel extending skyscraper deep beneath the

asphalt and concrete Manhattan crust; sewer and rumbling subway and tens of thousands of miles of gas and steam and water mains. Electric and telephone cables like sizzling neurons buried in the city's flesh, copper dendrites wrapped safe inside neoprene and rubber and lead.

Jenny Haniver walks the anthill maze, walls of crumbling masonry and solid granite. She counts off each blind step, Ariadne's directions remembered like a combination lock's code; forty-five then right, seventy-one then left, deeper and deeper into the honeycombed earth beneath Hell's Kitchen. The air grows warmer by slow degrees, and the only sounds left are the nervous scratch and squeak of the rats, the faint drip and splash of water from the walls and ceilings as the musty air turns damp.

Her eyes do not adjust, register only the ever increasing absence of light, a thousand shades past pitch already; dark that can smother, that seeps up her nostrils and settles in her lungs like black pneumonia. She walks like a stumbling zombie, hands out Frankenstein-stiff in front of her, lifts her feet high to keep from tripping over garbage or stepping on a rat.

Fifty-seven, then right, and that's the last and for all she knows she's lost, almost certain that she'll never be able to reverse the order and follow the numbers backwards to the surface. And when she catches the dimmest shimmer up ahead, she believes it can only be panic, a cruel will-o'-the-wisp tease dreamed up by the rods and cones of her light-starved eyes. But with every step the light seems to swell, faint bluish glow now, and she can almost make out the tunnel walls, her own white hands somewhere in front of her face.

There are new sounds, too, parchment dry susurrance and the moist smack and slap of skin against mud. The air smells like shit and the cold rot of long-neglected refrigerators, and the tunnel widens, then, abruptly opens out into a small cavern or natural chamber, low walls caked thick with niter and a scum of luminescent fungus, and she can see well enough to make out the forms huddled inside. Skin bleached colorless by the constant dark, stretched much too tight over kite frame skeletons, razor shoulders, xylophone ribs. Bodies naked to the chill and damp, or clothes that hang in tatters like a shedding second skin.

Jenny follows the narrow path between them, and they watch her pass with empty, hungry eyes, shark eyes, grab at her calves and ankles in halfhearted frenzy, hands no more than blue-veined claws, arms no more than twigs.

Ariadne Moreau sits by herself on a crooked metal folding chair at the end of the chamber, lion's mane nimbus of tangled, black hair and necklaces of rat bone draped like pearls around her neck. She wears nothing else but her tall leather boots and vinyl jacket, both scabby with dried mud and mildew. Her thighs, the backs of her bony hands, are splotched with weeping track marks, and she smiles, sickly weak approval of relief, as Jenny approaches.

"I knew that you'd come," she says and her voice sighs out of her, husky wheeze, and she extends one hand out to Jenny, trembling fingers and nails chewed down to filthy nubs. "I never stopped believing that you'd come."

Jenny does not take her hand, hangs a few feet back.

"It isn't working," she says, and opens her peacoat, displays her own ruined flesh to prove the point. She's only wearing boxers and all the bandages are oozing, stains that look like sepia ink in the weird blue light of the cave. A few have come completely undone, revealing her clumsy sutures and the necrotic patchwork of grafts.

"I have to know if you've learned anything. If you've seen anything down here," she says, and closes her coat again.

Ariadne's smile fades, jerky, stop-motion dissolve, and she lets her arm drop limp again at her side. She laughs, an aching, broken sound, and shakes her shaggy head.

"Anything," Jenny says again. *"Please,"* and she takes the baggie of white powder from her coat pocket, holds it out to Ariadne. Behind Jenny, the mole people whisper nervously among themselves.

"Fuck you, Jenny," words spit softly out like melon seeds. "Fuck you and fuck the voices in your sick head."

Jenny steps closer, sets the heroin gently on Ariadne's bare knee. "I'm sorry," she says. "I can't stay."

"Then at least let me kiss you, Jen," and Ariadne's arms strike like vinyl eels, lock firmly around Jenny's neck and pull her roughly down. Ariadne's mouth tastes like ashes and bad breath, and her tongue probes quickly past the jagged reef of sharpened incisors. Jenny tries to pull away,

pushes hard and Ariadne bites the tip end of her tongue as their mouths part, bites hard, and Jenny stumbled backwards, almost falls among the restless mole people, pain and the deceitful copper warmth of her own blood on her lips.

Ariadne laughs again, vicious, hopeless chuckle, wipes her mouth with the back of one hand and snatches up the baggie of dope from her knee with the other.

"Get out of here, Jenny. Go back up there and slice yourself to fucking ribbons."

Eyes that are all pupil now, and the dark smudge of Jenny's blood on her chin.

Jenny Haniver runs back the way she came, dodging the forest of grasping hands that rises up around her.

In the dream, the dream that she's had again and again since the first night she heard their voices, Jenny Haniver drifts weightless in silent hues of malachite and ocher green. The sun filters into and through the world from somewhere else above, Bible storybook shafts in the perfect, silting murk. She moves her long tail slowly from side to side and sinks deeper, spreads her silver arms wide, accenting and inviting. And he rises from below, from the cold, still depths where the sun never reaches, the viperfish night, and holds her away in pelvic webs and stiletto spines. She gasps and the salt water rushes into her throat through the crimson-feathered slits beneath her chin.

Jenny sinks her teeth, row after serrate row, into the tender meat of his shoulder, scrapes his smooth chest with the erect spurs of her nipples.

And the voices are all around, bathypelagic echoes, as tangible as the sweet taste of his blood in her mouth.

She had never felt this safe, has never felt half this whole.

Their bodies twine, living braid of glimmering scales and iridescent scaleless flesh, and together they roll over and over and down, until the only light is the yellowish photophore glow of anglerfish lures and jellyfish veils.

She wakes up again, stiff crammed into the dank cubby hole, more blind than in the last moment before she opened her eyes. There's no sense of time anymore, only the vague certainty that she's been wandering the tunnels for what

must be days and days and days now and the burning pain in her mouth and throat, Ariadne's infection gift rotting its way into her skull. She is drowning, mind and body, in the tunnels' incessant night tide and the sour fluids that drain from her wounded tongue.

Jenny Haniver coughs, fishhook barbs gouging her chest and throat, and spits something thick and hot into the dark. She tries to stand, braces herself, unsteady arms and shoulders against the slimeslick tunnel wall, but the knifing spasms in her feet and legs and the fever's vertigo forces her to sit back down, quickly, before she falls.

The rats are still there, carrion patience, waiting for her to die. She can hear their breath and the snick of their tiny claws on the stone floor. She doesn't know why they have not taken her in her sleep; she no longer has a voice to shout at them, kicks hard at the soft, flea-seething bodies when they come too close.

Because she cannot walk, she crawls.

Here, past the merciful failure of punky concrete and steel rod reinforcements, where one forgotten tunnel has collapsed, tumbled into the void of one much older, she lies at the bottom of the wide rubble scree. Face down in the comingled cement debris and shattered work of colonial stonemasons, and the sluggish river of waste and filth-glazed water moves along inches from her face. The rats and the muttering ghosts of Old Mama and Old Papa and her father will not follow her down; they wait like a jury, like ribsy vultures, like the living (which they are not) keeping deathbed vigil.

There is wavering yellow-green light beneath the water, the gaudy drab light of things which will never see the sun and have learned to make their own. So much light that it hurts her eyes, and she has to squint. The ancient sewer vibrates with their voices, their siren songs of clicks and trills and throaty bellows, but she can't answer, her ruined tongue so swollen that she can hardly even close her mouth or draw breath around it. Instead, she splashes weakly with the fingers of one straining, outstretched hand, smacks the surface with her palm.

Old Mama laughs again and then her father and Old Papa try to call her back, promise her things she never had

and never wanted. This only makes Old Mama laugh louder, and Jenny ignores them all, watches the sinuous long shadows move lazily across the vaulted ceiling. Something big brushes her fingertips, silky roughness and fins like lace, unimaginable strength in the lateral flex of those muscles, and she wants to cry but the fever scorch has sealed her tear ducts.

With both hands, she digs deep into the froth and sludge that marks the boundary between worlds, stone and water, and pulls herself the last few feet. Dragging her useless legs behind her, Jenny Haniver slides into the pisswarm river, and lets the familiar currents carry her down to the sea.

"O heat, dry up my brains! tears seven times salt
Burn out the sense and virtue of mine eye!"

—William Shakespeare

One-Eyed Jack

S. Darnbrook Colson

All my life I've blamed what happened to me that night on that blimp-assed Marlon Brando. Him and his famous line in a flick I'd seen when they still had drive-in movies. I was with my hot-to-trot girlfriend, but that's another story. In his incomparable way Marlon had mumbled, "You may be a one-eyed jack, Dan, but I seen the other side of your face." Of course, Brando wasn't fat then; neither was I. But when you fuck-up royal, or even do something just flat-assed stupid, you gotta blame somebody or something.

That night Brando was my *somebody* and his one-eyed jack line my *something*. But booze and depression were the real culprits. Funny how when you're ready to buy the farm, reality kicks in and you finally see stupidity for what it is. It's funny too how unemployed fools with their welfare checks running out can still find it in their budget to buy booze. It's called desperation.

All we wanted to do, for Christ's sake, was keep our weekly high-stakes poker game going. Oh, we could've played penny ante, or just for fun, but not us. Just not exciting enough. Abandon our Wednesday night game? No way. It was about all we had left.

Every time I've thought of that time, I've wanted to shove a deck of cards sideways right up the asses of each and every board member of Kleinhauser Corporation. Now, in retrospect, I laugh to myself about it—more somebodies to blame.

It was Joe Koszinski who suggested that we could play for valuables other than money: those useless silver tea sets that the wives never used, but had to polish once a week, jewelry that was shoved away in the back of drawers and never worn, hunting rifles, cars. . . . It was easy for Joe to suggest stuff like rifles (he wasn't a hunter) and like silver

and jewelry, he was the only one of us not married. His wife had divorced him and split with the valuables years ago. Ran off with a guy whose pecker she could see without a magnifying glass was the poker buddy's joke. Nope, it wasn't Joe Koszinski who would be whacked over the head with a frying pan, kicked out of the house or, worse, cut off from the weekly dose of poontang.

No, it wasn't going to be the household goods. What else? The next most valuable thing was our wives. Sure! Mary'd just love to have Joe or John or Buddy or Big Black Clarrince drop in one Sunday morning to collect his winnings. Then again, maybe she would've, but there was no way in hell I was gonna stand for that. Besides, none of the other guys had anything better to offer than Mary, and she was no beaut. And who would Joe pay up with, his seventy-two year old mother?

The week after our unemployment checks ran out, we met on Wednesday night anyway. The four of us who were married told our wives we were playing just for fun. We all brought booze. Like I said before. It's funny how. . . .

I musta dozed off. Thought for a minute there I'd gone and died. Obviously, I didn't, but somehow I have the feeling that the next time I nod off I won't be waking up— ever. I'm glad I hadn't kicked off yet, 'cause the one-eyed jack was still eating away at me. Maybe that's what hell was: an extension of all the bad things that happen to you during your life. Hah! Me, the big philosopher with a tenth grade education.

Clarrince was the only one of us with a real education, two years of trade school. Can you imagine? A nigger with a better education than us white boys. Guess Clarrince popped into my mind because it was him who came up with the idea for poker stakes that kept the game exciting.

All we had left was ourselves. Seems like everyone knew that, 'cause we all brought booze . . . Did I say that before? Any rate, usually only one of us brought a bottle of hooch or a couple of six packs of beer, but somehow we knew it would take a lot more'n a couple of drinks for the loser to pay up.

We always played in the loft down at Bennuci's Warehouse. Bennuci was Buddy Santori's brother-in-law. Buddy

had sponsored Bennuci when he'd immigrated from Sicily, and Bennuci had ended up marrying Buddy's sister, Teresa. Luigi, that was Bennuci's Christian name, called us the International Poker Cartel—his little funny—'cause Joe was a Pollack, Buddy a fellow Wop, John O'Mally was a Mick, straight from the glass factories of County Cork, and Clarrince was a Jamaican Coon. Me, I was then, and still am— till the ticker stops—a plain old flag-wavin' American. I guess it seemed like a strange mix to Bennuci, but we'd all been living in the same neighborhood, going to weddings and funerals together, and working together for the past dozen years—that is, until these fucks at Kleinhauser did us dirty. The five of us'd played poker together for eight years. We'd tell ethnic jokes and call each other prickhead, white trash, spearchucker, mackerel snapper, potato eater, asshole, you name it, and we never got mad at each other. Oh, we'd get pissed off at the winner, no matter who it was, especially if he took us for a bundle, but I never thought we really got mad. Just let someone outside our group call Clarrince a black son-of-a-bitch, or Joe a dumb Pollack or any of us anything disrespectful, and that big-mouth shit would have five mean mothers busting his face.

I guess that's what makes it more tragic. I thought we all cared and respected each other and would look out for each other no matter what. As it turned out, that wasn't so. I got it worst of all, 'cause I lived to age eighty-two— or will if I make it a few more days.

Buddy made a quick exit. Two weeks after that night, they found him with a .22 rifle slug between the eyes. Clarrince said the damned fool should've tucked his 12 gauge shotgun in his mouth and made it a clean shot. Instead the poor bastard had that low caliber piece of lead bouncing around in his head making scrambled eggs out of his brains. He died in the medivac copter on the way to the hospital, but I'll bet he had a few painful, fractured, parting thoughts on his way to meet the man at the pearlys.

John was next. This was surprising to the rest of them, because he was the most religious of all of us, more Catholic than O'Mally for Christ's sake.

It took Joe five years before it caught up to him. Five fucking years! Then one day they found him hanging in his garage.

Clarrince moved away, for awhile. But he came back . . .

Me, I just blocked it all out—most of the time. When I couldn't keep the memories away, I'd just go out in the woods with my 30.06 and blast away every bird and animal that moved. Didn't give a shit if it was hunting season or not. As whacked out on morph as I am now, I can still smell the cordite and the blood and the . . .

That first and last night of the new-stakes poker game was cold and wet. A front had moved in during the late afternoon, and by early evening, low, black clouds had come in over the mountains, bringing a steady rain. Less than a month later, the same system would bring the first ice and snow of the season. Buddy was already dead and buried by then.

Joe wore his black plastic visor, which he thought made him look like a card shark, but really made him look like a backroom clerk in an old-time bank, one who sits there all day counting money. Maybe that was the idea. Most of us wore plaid flannel shirts, the usual for that time of year: yellows and blues, reds and yellows, greens and blues . . . Everyone except Clarrince, who always wore his black stud shirt with a brown, fake leather vest over it. We all were smokers, including Clarrince, and he said he wasn't about to ruin real leather by dropping lit cigarette ash on it. Everybody knew he was just a cheap son-of-a-bitch.

Bennuci's warehouse was a big old three story brick building that took up half a block on Brockton Street. He had a contract with the railroads to store machine parts for their trains, everything from nuts and bolts to big-assed engines. We held our poker game on the second floor mezzanine in a small conference room across the hall from Bennuci's office. The room had a wet bar with a small refrigerator under it, an oval table big enough to seat six people (although only five of us played—I say this as if the conference room was just for us, Har, Har!), and a big plate glass window that overlooked the open bay area, full with its crates of metal parts. The walls of the "game room," as we called it, were shit-brindle yellow. We could never get Bennuci to repaint the damned thing. Said he liked the color. Said it reminded him of his bedroom when he was a boy. We always made jokes about what the rest of his

house must of looked like: Baby puke green, Menstruation red, and so on.

The wet bar was always stocked with clean tumblers and beer mugs and, on Wednesdays, Bennuci always put five mugs in the refrigerator to frost up. Got them ready for our weekly poker game. Bennuci was an all right guy. He went to his grave never knowing what happened there that night. Never asked why we stopped playing poker either. I guess in Sicily you don't ask nothing about nothing or you get your mouth shut, permanent. Bennuci never lost his old habits from the homeland.

We didn't need the frosted mugs that night. We all brought whiskey. Joe brought Old Crow, Buddy, Wild Turkey, John, some rotgut labeled Ancient Times, Clarrince, Canadian VO, and me, I brought a fifth of Jack Daniels Black Label. Wine—especially wine—was outlawed at the poker games: womens' drink, we called it—was bad enough having to drink it at communion, although I think Joe really liked the grapy crap, and swilled it in secret at home. Buddy broke out the tumblers, set them on the table, popped in some ice cubes, and we each poured up a healthy couple of shots. I can still see the booze in my mind's eye splashing in slo-mo over the cubes of ice, individual drops popping into the air, then falling back, trying to hide themselves in the mainstream of liquid, like I've tried to hide myself in the mainstream of my life. Joe popped a couple of bags of popcorn in the microwave, divvied them up into five plastic bowls and set them around the table.

John had the chips, and we decided to divide them up equally, so's everybody had the same chance at the beginning. Like me, I know everybody'd been thinking about it, dreaming up weird shit to play for. It was funny to think and talk about, but a lot less amusing when it was pay-up time.

I'd brought a new set of Bicycle cards. I broke open the pack, took out the instruction card and the jokers, shuffled them up and we cut for deal. Clarrince, being the wise ass, cut so deep that the rest of us had barely twenty cards left to cut from. John won the deal with a Queen of Clubs draw. My Two of Spades wouldn't of got me a dead bird at a cock fight. A bad omen. I shoulda known.

We all took healthy swigs of our booze. Buddy and Joe

cut theirs with water, the rest of us drank it on the rocks. In my mind, John shoulda been cutting that Ancient Times craps with something thick and syrupy.

Everyone anted a white chip, worth one buck imaginary money. The reds were worth five, the blues, ten. John shuffled the deck and slid it over to Joe, on his right, who cut thin. "Thin to win," he said. John then called for a game of five card stud—my least favorite game—and dealt out the cards. On the first pass, Clarrince, who was on John's left, showed a Four of Spades, I had a Jack of Clubs with and Ace of Clubs in the hole—*my night,* I thought—, Buddy showed a Five of Clubs, Joe a Deuce of Clubs and John a Ten of Clubs. It was *my* bet. I was thinking big and didn't even care that clubs had already gotten mighty thin. I dropped a blue tenner in the pot. Hell, the Ace alone was worth that. Everyone stayed in, no bumps.

On the second pass, nobody seemed to get anything worth bragging about. My Five of Hearts sucked and Buddy's King of Diamonds made him high, showing. My Clubs were busted, so it didn't matter that no more clubs were displayed. Buddy threw in a white chip, worth a buck. Everyone else followed, but when it got to me, I bumped a tenner. "Asshole," I heard Joe mutter as he folded. The rest of them kicked in.

"Got a pair of Jacks, huh?" John said as he dealt out the third pass, not expecting an answer.

All of a sudden there were two pairs on the board. Clarrince had Treys and John Tens. I saw John checking my hand, figuring his Tens were one shy of taking my imagined Jacks. That was good, but it forced me to continue to bet the max. I fondled my blue chips so's John and the others might start thinking too much.

John threw in a tenner and said, "Fuck it, it's only for fun."

Yeah, I thought. *We'll see how much fun it is when it's pay-up time.* Suddenly, my ace in the hole wasn't looking too powerful and I took a healthy pull on my blackjack. Up to the day they shoved a tube up my nose and strapped on a pee bag, I loved the taste of that smokey essence sliding down my throat. Now I gag at the thought of it.

Clarrince, with his pair of Treys, stayed in, and I found myself reaching for two blue chips. I tossed them with a

flourish into the pot and sighed, as if I was sorry for taking the rest of the bastards to the cleaners. Buddy laughed out loud and bumped another ten, twenty more to John and Clarrince, and ten more to me. *Shit!* I thought. *What am I doing in this hand?* John and Clarrince both called and, the smile wiped off my face, I dropped in ten more.

"Last cards," John announced and dealt around.

Clarrince got John's third Ten. My cards went over the minute I saw the Nine of Hearts. I was outgunned showing by both John and Clarrince and, with Buddy's previous raise, I figured he had me too. Buddy didn't bluff much, if at all. John was still high on the board, but he chuckled. We had a rule that it was okay to sandbag—to check and bet. Hell, it's part of the strategy. Makes things interesting. Clarrince fiddled with his cards for a while then also checked. Buddy just smiled that winning smile and dropped in five, afraid that a ten would scare the other two out, figuring a one wasn't worth the effort, and that he might suck another five or ten bucks out of the other two.

They folded and Buddy raked in the pot. Two hundred and thirty-nine bucks, not counting his last five, forty-one of it mine.

At the end of the hour we counted up our chips. The whole time my hands felt like they just came out of a bucket of tepid water. I musta downed three ounces of JD during the count. I had beat out poor old Joe by three bucks. Joe had to pay up. I was so relieved it wasn't me that I laughed like a fool. Later, I remember Joe whispering in my ear, "Who's laughing now, sweetheart."

We cleared the table and Joe was forced to kneel in the middle of the table, unzip his pants, pull out his pecker, piss in his own whiskey glass (we let him go half and half with his Old Crow) and chug down the sweet and sour mixture. He closed his eyes and did it in four gulps.

Everybody else, including myself, half embarrassed, half titillated—half drunk—toasted Joe and chugged down our own untainted brew.

Joe staggered off to the bathroom and we pretended we didn't hear him retching. When he returned, he went straight to the Old Crow bottle, poured a good three ounces in and downed it, straight up.

According to the rules we had agreed on, we drew slips

for the next loser's payment. There was an air of uneasiness, eyes shifting around the table. We recounted out the chips, an equal amount for each of us, and began again.

God, even now at my eleventh hour I ask myself why we did such things, things that were foreign to our very nature. Maybe Joe'd had the urge in him all along, never being married, living with his mother and all, but the rest of us . . . hell, the rest of us were just hard working, hard drinking, church going, family men. We schtupped our wives once a week on Saturday night—or in my case, Sunday morning, right before we got up and went to mass.

I'll tell you one thing. Father Donnigan never heard about our transgressions during Saturday afternoon confessions, not from me anyway.

So, why did we do such things? Abject despair. You gotta understand, we lost the only jobs we'd ever had since high school, and there weren't no new jobs to go to. Kleinhauser wasn't the only company laying off. All that government bullshit about how good the economy was. Yeah, for the rich bitches I guess it was just hunky fucking dory. But for me and the other poker guys it was abject despair. And with that, lack of self esteem came on us real quick; one day we're on top of the world, the next day we're a bunch of loser assholes, lower than whale shit. Couldn't pay our mortgage or rent, couldn't put food on the table, couldn't buy new clothes for the family . . . Just five big dog turds. A hell of a thing, to die feeling like a piece of shit . . .

Whoa! Thought I'd caught the last elevator to the fire pit, but I'm still here. Robert, my son, is still sitting by my side, holding my hand. I wonder if he'd be here if he knew what happened that night.

I really don't remember much now about the specific hands that were dealt, or how the betting went, except for that very first hour . . . and the very last hour. In between, there were four other rounds of card playing, over six hours in all, all the way to half past midnight. We'd promised the wives we'd be home by one-thirty a.m.

At any rate, it was around eleven fifteen and Joe, eyes downcast, was shuffling cards for the last one-hour set. He'd lost two of the five sets, and after he saw what the draw for penalty (a nice way of putting it, we thought) for

the *finalé,* he'd gone bedsheet white. The rest of us weren't too comfortable with it either, 'cept for Clarrince, who just laughed like a friggin' hyena. Joe, though, had just paid the penalty for losing the previous set. Had to whack off onto the table top, then—

I can't even think about it.

Afterwards, he'd killed the remains of his Old Crow, straight out of the bottle, using it like it was Listerine. Then he was bumming swigs from the rest of us. Hell, we were down to the last dregs ourselves, and Joe was using it for mouthwash.

John saved an altercation by going outside and retrieving an extra bottle of Ancient Times from under the front seat of his car—it was rot-gut, but by then we were pretty well juiced up and didn't much give a rat's ass what we were drinking, as long as it made us brain-blind as to what in the devil's name we were doing.

Joe finished shuffling and offered Buddy the cut. "Cut 'em deep and the rest of you fuckers sweep," Buddy slurred out. "What the fuck does that mean?" Clarrince said, and John piped in, "Cut 'em deep and all you guys can weep." "He said, rest of you sweep," Joe mumbled. "Whatever," I said. "Sweep, weep, sheep, don't matter, just deal the fuckin' cards." "You anxious?" Clarrince said, smiling goofylike. "Think you gonna nail my black ass? Think you gonna—"

"Get up, you scum sucking pig," I said in a low drawl, kicking back my chair. There was dead silence, except for the sound of the chair as it bounced and clattered on the green and tan tile floor. Clarrince and the others just sat there pie-eyed. Then, straight-faced, I said, "Rio to Dan Longwood in One-eyed Jacks."

"Huh?" John said.

"Marlon Brando movie. Made it in the sixties."

"He said, 'Get up you scum sucking pig?' " Buddy asked.

"Yup. To Karl Malden."

"Karl who?"

"Don't matter, jut deal the fuckin' cards," John said.

"You anxious or something?"

"Just wanta get this done with."

"Hoping to win or lose . . . or don't matter which to you?" Clarrince said, smirking.

This time, John jumped up, knocking *his* chair back. "What the fuck you saying, nigger?"

"He be saying he *am* a scum sucking pig, just like we thought," Buddy said.

It was all 90 proof booze talking, and everybody burst out in spontaneous laughter like a bunch of fools who didn't have a care in the world.

Joe restacked Buddy's cut, called five card draw, and dealt them out. Clarrince won the hand and the deal went to John. Near the end of the hour I wasn't doing too good and was playing conservatively, just trying to stay ahead of Buddy, who wasn't doing so well either. When it was a couple minutes to the end of the hour, Clarrince had dealt last and passed the deck to me.

A quick count told me that I was ahead of Buddy, but not by much. The rules we made up said that no one could fold on the last hand until the last round of betting. Since it was my deal and I could call the game, I figured my best shot was to go with seven card stud. That way, I could see at least four of Buddy's cards. In reality I was playing against him. It didn't matter if I won the pot or not. The idea was how much Buddy was betting and how good *his* cards looked. The man with the least amount of chip-money at the end of the hour was gonna have to pay the penalty, and it damned well wasn't gonna be me. It was hard enough for me to think of giving the penalty, much less getting it. I remember thinking, *shit, how did I get myself into this stupid game?* Then I remember giggling—the booze—and imagining the look on Buddy's face when he counted his chips at the end and realized what he had to do. I never once thought it would be me—

Then before I knew what I had done, I had called five card draw, one-eyed Jacks wild, Clarrince had declined the cut, and I was dealing out the cards. It was that fucking movie and that goddamned fat Marlon son-of-a-bitch Brando that was sloshing around in my booze-sodden mind that fucked me up. I kept seeing the look on Karl Malden's face, lying there trying to take an afternoon nap, looking through the newels on his porch, seeing Brando riding up to his house; later, Brando conning Katy Jurado out of her pantaloons with that ring he'd stolen in a bank robbery, telling her it was his mother's, knocking her up; Malden

making mincemeat out of Brando's back with a bullwhip, busting up his gun hand with the butt of his rifle; Brando escaping. . . .

Brando never even played cards in that goddamn movie!

It wasn't until I was dealing out the third card that I realized what I had done. Immediately, I rationalized that five card draw *was* my game. It had kept me out of the penalty box for all four previous one-hour sets. I smiled and looked at my cards, smiled again, glanced out of the corner of my eye at Buddy, whose hands were shaking, smiled again, and called for bets.

I was holding a pair of Aces with a King, Queen and Deuce. "Your bet Buddy," I said. He passed, and I sucked air up my nostrils, trying not to be too conspicuous. I probably didn't have to worry. By this time, most of us were too drunk to see past our own hands. But the adrenaline in my body seemed to overcome the booze in my veins; my heart was pumping like a fire hose. Joe passed. John opened with a white chip. Clarrince hadn't even looked at his cards. He just threw in a buck. I nonchalantly tossed in my white chip and Buddy and Joe followed.

I could see tears welling in Buddy's eyes as he discarded and asked for three cards. He didn't even look at them when I dealt him the replacements. He just sat there staring into space, wondering, I suppose, if he could live with himself, afterward, sweating at the thought. *Better him than me,* I thought as I dealt Joe three, John three, and Clarrince, who'd finally looked at his cards, one. It didn't matter to me if I won the hand or not, but it would certainly make me breathe easier if I did. Again, the key was not to lose more chip-money than Buddy; and Buddy couldn't drop out now or he was a goner, unless, of course, Joe dropped a major pile and lost *his* modest holdings. Unlikely. Joe was drunk but not stupid. I discarded the King, Queen and Deuce and drew three cards off the top of the deck, a Nine of Hearts, a Nine of Clubs, and lo-and-fucking-behold, the Jack of Spades, one of the two one-eyed Jacks. *Son of a bitch, an Aces over full house.* Not only was I not gonna lose, but I was gonna take the last pot, big time.

When I think back it was pretty damned stupid of me to worry about winning the last pot. I mean, what was I winning? Nothing! Not a goddamned thing. The chips were

worthless . . . unless you lost more of them in fake dollars than all the other guys. But there I was riding high with the best hand I'd had all night. Hell, it was the best hand I'd had in a month. I had two choices: drop out and hope Buddy had a loser against the other three guys, or bet modest—a one-buck white chip—and see what Buddy would do. Instead, I found myself tossing in a ten-buck blue chip, and if I'da had a cigar, I'da lit the friggin' thing right up and blown smoke in Buddy's face, the fucking little prick. Funny how in a moment, your best friend can become your worst enemy, isn't it?

Buddy finally picked up his cards, slowly fanned them open, and stared at them. Again his hands began to shake and his eyes ferreted around the table as if he wasn't sure what to do. His eyes darted to my cards, which I'd laid on the table, face down. He glared at them as if he were Superman and could see through them with x-ray vision. As I watched him trying to imagine what I held, I had a flashback of the time he suckered me into folding with trip fours, and he lost the pot to John, who had a pair of sixes to Buddy's threes—the little prick. I was gonna win and be the first one to take a piece of his hide.

"See your blue and up it a blue," Buddy said, his voice quavering like lemon jello.

My jaw dropped.

Joe folded.

Chicken shit bastard, I thought, remembering how he always tried to short change the pot when he bet.

John smirked, threw in two blues and said, "I remember those threes, Buddy."

It was easy for him to stay. He had a stack of chips three times the rest of us. John always seemed to win and I was sick of his piss-assed smugness about it.

Clarrince didn't say shit. He just tossed in two blues.

Always was an arrogant nigger, I thought, remembering the time he was over at the house for a picnic and made a suggestive remark to my wife. *Always wearing tight jeans and showing off his bunch. Asshole!*

"You scum sucking pigs wanta play with the one-eyed jack, that's fine with me," I said, tossing in my last three blue chips, representing a mock thirty bucks. I only had three reds and four whites left: nineteen buckeroos.

"Can't do that," Joe said. "Limit's one blue."

"Aw let him throw his fucking money away," Clarrince said. "Thinks he's fucking Marlon Brando."

"And we gonna see the other side of your face, Marlon," John said, the left side of his mouth riding up as if he knew he—or somebody—had me beat.

Buddy swallowed hard and said, "Call," throwing in his last five reds, and five of his last six whites.

I was surprised when John folded.

Clarrince toyed with his cards for a few minutes, then threw in three blues saying, "What the hell, it ain't gonna be me anyway."

It was down to Buddy and me to see who was going to be the biggest loser of this round, maybe the biggest loser of all time. To tell you the truth, I don't know if Buddy or me was sweating or shaking more. I turned my cards over one at a time: the Ace of Diamonds, the Ace of Clubs, the Nine of Hearts, the Nine of Clubs, then slowly, I laid the Jack of Spades face up next to the Aces. "Aces over. Full boat," I said, arrogantly tapping the Jack. "Now I'm the one-eyed Jack around here, cowboys. Now, you gonna show me your threes, Buddy boy?"

Joe was practically crawling under the table; John just laughed; Clarrince glared at me as if I'd just cut his big black dick off.

Hands still shaking, Buddy turned them over: the Ten of Diamonds, the Three of Clubs, the Three of Diamonds—

"I knew it," John said.

—the Three of Spades.

"Don't worry, Marlon," John said flipping over one of his cards, "I had the other three."

The Three of Hearts lay face up in front of John, and I started laughing. Even if Buddy had another Ten, Treys over didn't take out Aces over.

I reached for the pot—and Buddy turned over the Jack of Hearts, the *other* one-eyed Jack.

Four Threes.

Son of a bitch!

I started crying and Joe said, "Let's forget about it," and Buddy said, "Fuck that. He'da been first in line . . . ," and John said, "Bad actor's gotta pay up," and Clarrince just stood up saying nothing and unzipped his pants, and . . .

I was bent over the table and Clarrince pushed John, who shoulda been first, outa the way, and said, "Your wife likes it this way too," and then horrible pain, and then it was John's turn, then Buddy's, and Joe's and, again, Clarrince, and it went on and on, getting easier to take . . . on and on . . .

A few years ago, Clarrince came back. Something about collecting some inheritance or something. It wasn't so. There was no inheritance. Somebody had lied to him. They found that black bastard with his cock and balls cut off and shoved down his throat. They don't know whether he'd bled to death or choked to death. Doesn't matter. He was D-E-A-D.

It amazes me that my son is here with me, holding my hand. Probably wouldn't be if he'd known what I'd done to my old poker friends. You see, it wasn't what they'd done to me that night. It was the fact that I'd *liked* it. *Son-of-a-Bitch!* I *liked* it, and in the following days and weeks and years I wanted more. And those bastards wouldn't give it to me, like they had that night.

I may have been a one-eyed Jack, but Buddy and John and Clarrince and Joe had seen the other side of my face. So, I made 'em pay. Killed 'em all.

And now I'm lying here dying like a scum-sucking—

Elena

Steve Rasnic Tem

DISCUSSION

"You know what your problem is, Elena? Your problem is you're just too damn *receptive*. People see a really receptive person, and it's like an open door they just *have* to go in, you know? And if it's a really *bad* person, well, it's like you're a door to a bathroom, and those types just feel no hesitation doing to you what they'd naturally do in any bathroom."

That was Elena's friend Ann talking, and Elena kept thinking at the time that those were especially odd things for Ann to be saying, since Ann had just fucked her, and it was their first time together. Elena had sort of wanted to, of course—she'd been having those feelings for her good friend Ann for some time, but she never would have done anything about it if Ann hadn't pushed the issue so hard.

"So what you're saying is," Elena mumbled lazily around a swallow of red wine, "is that people—hmm, men especially—feel free to shit on me, fuck my brains out and then shit on me. You're saying I'm easy, and men have no respect for me because of that."

"Well . . ." Ann looked in pain. Elena thought about how naturally beautiful Ann was, even in pain. "I would never use exactly those words. I mean those are *your* words. But yeah, that's the gist of my point, I suppose."

"Well, that's . . . just . . . *terrific!*" Elena threw the wine glass against the fireplace. The anger felt good. The fireplace spat back, glistening diamonds scattered across the thick white rug.

"Elena, I'm sorry, it's just that I'm your best friend and . . ."

"Uh uh. We're *lovers* now, Ann." Funny how quick people were to call her their *best* friend.

"Well I should hope that won't change things."

"Of course it does. It always changes things. I'm a toilet, remember? A 'crapper,' as my daddy would have called it."

"Elena . . ." Elena recognized that Ann's tone would have been cautionary, if Ann had just been a little more forceful about it.

"Sorry. Of all the people I know, I know you care about me, Ann. You love me."

"I *do* love you."

"That's what I said. So kiss me, okay? Right now I need somebody kissing me."

Ann moved herself across the floor so clumsily Elena had to bite her lip to keep from laughing. Ann didn't seem to notice, however, so intent was she on Elena's body.

"Kiss me," Elena murmured, and Ann did, swaying her breasts gently, purposefully, against Elena's own, making the nipples rise. Elena kept glancing down at the contact of nipple against nipple, unable to see very much, feeling the sparks there, knowing that the sparks were real, and might grow too powerful, consume them both in fire.

"You taste like blood, sweetheart," Ann whispered into Elena's mouth, and laughed softly, inserting her tongue as if to lap the blood from the bleeding lip out of Elena's mouth. Elena closed her mouth on Ann's tongue, first imagining it to be a man's penis, maybe even Ann's penis, then imagining it to be Ann's tongue again, then not sure if it was either, or both, or when her imaginings had taken over her life so completely. Tongue or penis, it really didn't matter—Elena was sure that some seed had been planted that would be inside her forever, eventually growing and maturing until it destroyed its host and burst her apart.

"Kiss me. Kiss me," Elena whispered, and Ann did, first her breasts, and then each of her nipples, her navel, then deep into her pussy, and down flickering like a cigarette lighter in the tight opening of her anus, then up into her pussy again.

Elena squirmed on her back across the carpet, moving aimlessly, yet making progress.

"You're holding back," Ann said from somewhere inside

her. "I can feel it—you're still holding back. Why can't you let yourself go?"

Elena had moved herself up onto the shards of broken wine glass and stopped, because that was where she wanted to be. She completely covered the glass, protecting Ann from it, but every time Ann pushed into her pussy with her tongue Elena could feel the glass cutting deeper into her back.

She closed her eyes in relief and gratitude, smiled and moaned, which made Ann move even more vigorously, which embedded the glass deeper into her back, which made her feel even more grateful.

Grateful because of the keen reminder of pain. The reminder that she had been alone, and now she had someone deep inside her, and when the pain stopped she would be alone again. Again and again, the lifecycle of the human being. Loneliness for long periods of time, interspersed with brief, sharp, painful periods of togetherness.

Ann rose over her breasts, over her head, bending to kiss her: Ann's face steaming with blood, her features distorted, the face of a monster.

"The better to eat you with, my dear!" Ann cried, and laughed, and cried, and cried.

SEDUCTION

"You're a monster," Elena said softly to Michael as he began to kiss her.

"What . . . what did you say?" Michael looked genuinely surprised, but Elena knew monsters were adept at feigning surprise. Monsters had only two basic expressions, really: surprise and monstrousness. With occasional sadness when it had been too long since they'd ravished some fair young maiden. "You heard me. I said, 'you're a monster.' "

He just looked at her for a moment. "You're kidding, right? You're tripping on me or something. You liked what I was doing—I could tell."

"Oh, I liked it all right. I liked it very much. But you're still a monster."

Then he smiled his dopey male smile. "I get it! I'm a monster, as in I'm a monster lover, right? As in great."

Elena almost laughed, but stopped herself, held herself

to a light smile. "Of course, lover." She sighed. "You're simply terrific."

"Just like I thought," he murmured, his lips between her breasts.

He was younger than any lover she'd had in some time, a good ten years younger than she, she guessed. There were decided disadvantages to that. But what he lacked in technique he made up for in aggressiveness. And what he lacked in personality he more than made up for in anger.

"Except you're a little slow," she whispered softly into his ear.

Michael pulled his head away. "Slow? I move too slow for you? I didn't think a guy could move slow enough."

"Well . . ." She smiled languidly. "Just a *little* slow. Not much."

"I see," he said, and immediately jerked into her rapidly a few times, so hard it hurt her tail bone. "So how's that? Fast enough for you, sweetie?"

Elena knew what her part was supposed to be at this point. She was supposed to look puzzled, hurt, perhaps even on the verge of tears. She was supposed to ask him, "Why did you do that." Or tell him, "Ow. That hurts." Or look angry and tell him to be careful. Or look sad, and not say anything at all.

Instead, she laughed. "Closer, sweetheart." She laughed again. "That's closer. Now if your cock was just a little bit bigger . . ."

The words were hardly out of her mouth before he rammed into her again. "Couldn't quite catch that, sweetie," he muttered. "Want to run that by me just one more time?" But he didn't give her a chance to speak, kept ramming her as hard as he could, as fast as he could, and she grunted each time, and he seemed to strive to increase the volume and sincerity of her grunts.

It went on that way for several minutes until he was too exhausted to continue. He stopped suddenly, without ejaculation, panting lightly beside her, his forearm up and covering his eyes. His hip still rested against hers, the point of adhesion cooling rapidly. She was quite sore, and raw between her legs. She moved the leg further away from him. What should have happened then was that one of them—most likely she, but possibly he—would get up, get

dressed awkwardly, perhaps leave without speaking. But she wasn't going to let it happen that way.

"You can fuck me again, you know," she said, "that is if you're still able."

If Michael had been a reasonable man he would probably have left in disgust at that point. Probably. But Michael was not a reasonable man. That was why Elena had chosen him to be one of her lovers.

"Whatever you ask for, bitch!" He sprawled over her, holding her down roughly by the wrists, awkwardly trying to thrust his way into her with a semi-erection. The violence of it made her grin. Involuntarily, but she knew he'd never believe that. The longer he failed to enter her the more tightly he squeezed her wrists, until she gasped and tears rolled down her cheeks. Finally, unable to get inside her, he let go of her hands and, using an arm to force her head and arms out of the way, he reached inside her with the other hand, thrusting with two fingers held together like a little boy's pretend six-shooter, jerking them back and forth, the rim of his fist jamming painfully against her pelvic bone.

Elena gritted her teeth and laughed through her tears, the tension in her body releasing.

AROUSAL

"Sex is always an experiment," Elena said as she refilled Dan's wine glass. Dan had elegant wine glasses, and an equally elegant apartment. Dan was the gay guy in the apartment next door. They'd been friends for years, but they'd never discussed sex before. Sometimes she thought he was her one true, best friend, since they'd never slept together. "We always have this vague result in mind, but since we've never actually achieved that result, we don't know exactly how to get there, so we try different things, different ways to get there, with this ridiculous faith that we'll even recognize it when we do." Dan was nodding dreamily. Elena figured he was quite drunk by now. "Most of us practice this meek sort of experimentation, different positions and such, so of course we have no chance of achieving what we want, but we figure that at least we're trying, until someday we figure it's impossible to achieve

anyway and sex gets reduced to this mildly pleasant massaging of our spirits until we get too tired or too cynical to do it at all anymore."

Dan looked slightly puzzled, out of focus. His hand trembled as he put the glass down on a coaster on the coffee table. "Are you a lesbian, by any chance?" he asked.

Elena threw back her head and roared. "You don't get it," she said after she'd regained enough composure to speak. "Sexual orientation doesn't matter, ultimately. We're all trying to get to the same place, even though we have no idea what it's going to look like. We just know we'll feel part of *everything* then, and the joy of that moment will be an orgasm that's unsurpassed."

Dan nodded and fell asleep. His body was soft and rubbery, and it took Elena quite a while to get his clothes off. She wasn't surprised to see the leather underwear or the pierced cock. He awakened now and then through this, giggling, but he was very drunk and obviously had no idea who he was with. He seemed to enjoy the beer bottle but clearly preferred the piece of broomstick she'd cut off just for him. Using makeup she'd found in his bedroom she'd even painted it pink with a purple tip because she thought he'd enjoy the trashy humor of it.

She recounted to him in detail her amorous adventures as she performed various experiments with his body. It would have been much better if he hadn't been so drunk, so that she could have felt completely responsible for his arousal, instead of wondering how much her stories had to do with it, how much the objects she inserted repeatedly into his anus, and how much the wine.

Elena discovered that her own arousal was considerable, and didn't know whether to stop and masturbate, to somehow continue and masturbate at the same time, or to convince Dan that he should have sex with her. Or rather, convince his penis—that was the important thing. At least she had discovered that it made no difference in terms of her own excitement that Dan was gay—that was something to know. As long as she was in control. His penis was long and unusually skinny, waving about like a floating, bobbing straw. And what she did to his body kept it that way. Then he had to spoil it by coming, exhausting himself and ruining everything.

Hours passed while she drank from another wine bottle and watched his sleeping form. Asleep and flaccid, Dan looked like a little boy. He was virtually hairless but she could see no signs that he'd been shaving himself. The ring through his penis looked silly, garish—a little boy playing with his mother's wedding ring. A little boy mutilating himself because he couldn't get what he wanted, because he didn't even know what he wanted.

"Welcome to the club, Danny Boy," Elena mouthed around the neck of the wine bottle. She dropped her hand onto something hard on the couch between them. When she lifted it she saw that it was a cork screw, the spiral of it glinting like fine silver jewelry. "Piggie piggie," she giggled. She glanced down at the garish ring fixed to Dan's penis like a promise or obligation. She bent over and kissed him on the belly button. He didn't stir. She brought the cork screw down beside her head, her ear to Dan's belly listening to the conversations inside. She tucked the point of the corkscrew under a little loose skin by the navel, pressed and started turning it. After some initial resistance and a loud grunt from Dan it entered the skin, and as she turned it more rapidly a row of coils appeared just under the skin of Dan's belly. Elena was amused to see Dan's penis rise a bit, growing firmer, skinny like a trained earthworm. She wondered if she could lower his penis by slowly backing the corkscrew out.

Blood covered Dan's lower belly. When Elena realized this she suddenly grew panicky. The realization also brought her to orgasm. Then she realized it wasn't so much blood after all, simply a flesh wound. And as suddenly she was bored with the whole experiment. She carefully backed the corkscrew out and wiped the blood off—or most of it— with a hot wet rag.

She just left him like that. Elena never heard anything more from Dan. He moved out of his apartment—several big guys in tight pants and T-shirts helping him—a few weeks later.

FOREPLAY

"Spread them!" Elena commanded the woman kneeling on the floor in front of her, her ass up in the air.

"Come on, I paid good money for this!" Of course, she had also paid good money for the woman's token reluctance, and her eventual submission. But both acts of the play were necessary for a satisfying denouement. "Come on! spread both the ass hole *and* the lips of the pussy. You've got long enough fingers, and I know you've had the practice."

Earlier, Elena had been afraid that the woman was going to tell her her name. That was the last thing she wanted, and she'd specifically told the woman that when she'd picked her up on the street. "No names," she'd said, "not even made-up ones," and the woman had just shrugged and sucked on her cigarette a few times, and agreed.

Then right after the hooker had pulled off all her clothes and stood there wearing nothing but a cigarette dangling two inches of ash and Elena had approached her to tell her what she wanted, the hooker had started "Okay, honey, my name is . . ." and Elena had slapped her across the face as hard as she could. And the hooker had just smiled at her and said, "oh yeah, I forgot. What's the next game, sweetheart?" Like getting slapped was a normal, everyday thing.

The next game was this examination, the hooker on her knees spread what was physically possible to be spread, Elena behind her with a bright light and a magnifying glass.

"You want me to start peeing or anything, honey?" the hooker said and barked a short smoker's laugh. Then Elena knew she must be high on something.

Elena had never looked at a woman's crotch so closely before. The inside of the pussy was loose and pink and moist, with folds which seemed to repeat into the deepest part of her. Calling it a "pussy" made perfect sense in this context—Elena had always wondered why men seemed to favor the word—it was like a cat split open, but still alive, the sides heaving. A monster, and Elena knew that deep down most men must see the opening into a woman as some sort of monster. A monster they must pass or kill in order to reach that mysterious sense of explosive completeness which must await them inside.

Not that she hadn't thought of it as a monster herself

sometimes. But more like a monstrous need which she had no idea how to fulfill.

She shone the light as deeply inside the hooker as she could, but still, it seemed, she was far from illuminating the heart of things.

"Do you have a pimp?" she asked the woman while probing her anus with the tip of the light. If it burned her, she didn't show it. An earthy scent filled the air, making Elena think of moist basements and graveyards.

"Sure. Sure, I do. His name's . . . say, can he have a name?"

"That would be fine. In fact, I think I *want* to know his name."

"Jerry. Jerry Phipps. He's handled me since the beginning. Guess you might say he discovered me." She cackled.

"What does he do for you?"

"Protection, mostly. And sometimes he lines up a special customer for me, a guy with 'special needs.' He checks 'em out to make sure they're at least relatively harmless."

"He didn't check me out, did he?"

"He doesn't bother with the women customers. Women are no problem—he knows that."

"He does, does he?" Elena mumbled, switching off the light. "Be right back." She got to her feet and went into the bedroom.

"Okay if I get another smoke?" the hooker called. Elena chose not to answer, but was relieved to see the woman still in the same position when she came back out. "My fingers are crampin', hon," the hooker said wearily. "How much longer you think this is going to be?"

"Not long, just keep them wide open," Elena said, as she started running toward the woman, the long stainless steel phallus strapped to her groin bobbing enough that she had to steady it on target with one hand. It was meant to be an erotic sculpture, but the flanged base had been easy to attach a leather circular pad and straps to.

She'd always wanted to do it as a man, and this seemed like the ultimate male sexual fantasy to her as she slipped into the hooker, and fixed her eyes on the dark wall ahead, imagining an end to this as she went through, imagined what the hooker must be feeling as the steel went in, and through, and came out the other side.

*   *   *
INTERCOURSE

"I'm looking for Jerry Phipps," Elena told the old cab driver down on the street where she had first seen the hooker. Old cab drivers knew everything, and this one didn't disappoint. He directed her to a pool hall down on the corner.

Jerry Phipps was tall and pale and had a scarred face. He was also a bad, and angry, pool player. Elena took one look at him and knew she'd chosen correctly.

She walked up to him and whispered into his ear, "I want you to fuck me."

Jerry looked down at her and scowled. "You got a disease or something. I mean, I could, but I don't usually. I could call somebody . . ." She showed him the five hundred dollars in her purse and he grinned. He threw the cue down on the table. "Let's you and me take a stroll down the street, baby."

The room Jerry Phipps paid five dollars for was cold, the walls gray, the sheets brown. It occurred to Elena that if the power and water were shut off it would be a perfect place to be buried in.

She put her purse on the scarred dresser and removed her clothes quickly. Phipps hadn't moved yet, just watched her. She knew what he was thinking, how she was some crazy bitch, diseased with AIDS or something, and he could just knock her out and take her money. She reached into her purse and brought out the pictures she'd taken of the hooker. The "after" shots. She threw them on the bed. "There." Even in the dim light and from that distance she could see the red. The red of sex. The red of love. If she ever reached that ultimate place she knew it would be nothing like this room—it would be as red as red can be. "You know her. She worked for you."

Phipps scowled and went over to the bed. "I don't like games," he said. "Your kind, you like games. I can always tell." He picked up the photos and looked at them. "Jesus . . . it's Annie. Jesus fucking Christ." He looked at her. "You crazy bitch. How'd you . . ."

"I did that. And I'm sorry." The tears came down, even though she'd sworn to herself that they wouldn't. And still

they came. She was a monster. "I should've known it would kill her. I was paying her for the pain . . . I knew there'd be pain. But I guess I *was* crazy . . . to do a thing like that and not know she'd be dead afterwards."

"Fuck *me* . . ." Phipps said, and Elena at first thought it was a request. It almost made her laugh. Then she saw him pull out the knife. Which was what she had wanted all the time, which was why she had come to him and shown him these pictures. Because she knew he was the kind of man who could do it. Who could stop her. Who could end all the experiments with one, final experiment. Who could give her what she deserved.

She opened her arms as he walked toward her. She readied herself for his kiss.

CLIMAX

The mirror was dingy and brown like the rest of the room. Elena hadn't noticed it when she first came in, hours ago. It must have been hanging on the wall above the scarred dresser where she'd put her purse. She didn't know where her purse was anymore. But of course . . . Phipps had taken it. Phipps had taken a lot of things. She wondered if he had the pictures.

The mirror wasn't on the wall anymore, of course. Wasn't *up* on the wall. It leaned *against* the wall, the part of the mirror that was still there. Elena sat on the floor leaning against the bed, she supposed, but it was hard to tell it was so red, as if she were in that all red place she'd been looking for, a part of everything. A part.

While Phipps had been doing it to her she had tried to tell him of her sexual adventures, her experiments. She had tried to explain how sexual orientation didn't matter, how all the technique in the world didn't matter, how her own experiments didn't matter. How we try so hard to reach this vaguely imagined place, then one day give up and just go through the motions. She had tried, but she'd been crying and screaming and she really didn't know if she'd been able to explain herself very well. She didn't know if he'd been aroused. If he had reached climax as she had reached climax. But how could you ever know?

Elena had never looked at herself this way before. She

tried to lean closer to the reflected red, then realized some of the red was actually on the mirror itself. She'd never looked closely at her own pussy. That word again. It was a word Phipps must use all the time—it was central to the vocabulary of his profession. A pussy all cut open, gutted and turned inside out. A monster you're afraid to touch. But stare at something long enough, obsess on something, and you start to crave it. You don't care anymore about where it might take you, the opening it represents, the wonderful red paradise at the end. You start craving only what you can see, and you can see it in a thousand magazines, and yet nothing measures up to the one you dream about. The pussy they see in their heads.

Elena reached down and started peeling back the layers, staring into the mirror and letting the red reflections guide her. Layer after layer. Sexual orientation didn't matter, nor technique, nor any partner. All you needed was yourself.

Elena pulled and tore and peeled until she could barely feel her hands anymore. Until she could see the first glimpses of bright red, reflected light. Until she could feel herself approaching the enormous beating heart of the ecstatic monster that lived inside.

Family Album

Adam-Troy Castro

The book is bound in soft leather the same shade of brown as your favorite pair of comfortably worn shoes. The word MEMORIES is stamped into the cover in goldfoil tracing out an elegant cursive script appropriate for weddings or births or senior proms.

You're not supposed to have this album. It's supposed to be police property. It's supposed to be in a sealed box on a shelf in a room stuffed to bursting with the detritus of ruined lives. Most of those other boxes also contain photographs: tens of thousands of photographs, depicting the aftermath of enough stabbings and shootings to drown entire generations in torrents of spilled blood. But those other photographs are not your business. These are. And while you're not supposed to have this album, it would be out of place anywhere in the world except in your hands. You haven't stolen it. You've taken it back. Because they can't save him anymore. You can.

Just inside the cover is the title page. MICHAEL in purple magic marker, the handwriting not nearly as decorous as the professionally printed MEMORIES on the cover. The script is downright childish: the sort of thing you'd expect to see drawn on a blackboard by a not-very-precocious first grader. It even misspells "Michael," which was your son's name; he was a very bright seven and could proudly write the word a whole lot better than that. But the word on the title page was not written by a seven-year-old. It was written by a 37-year old man named Emil Hinkins, who had big bright eyes and a goofy smile and isn't even literate enough to know how to spell Michael. Hinkins is now in prison, serving ten consecutive life terms. In his hands, the mis-spelling isn't just an error. It's a violation.

There's only one photograph on the next page. It's Mi-

chael, standing in the corner of a room with white walls. He looks smaller than you remember him. There are glistening tear-tracks on his cheeks, and his eyes are glowing red the way eyes do when flashbulbs light them the wrong way.

You turn the page. Another photograph: Michael still standing in that nondescript corner, taking off his pants at Hinkins' command. His underwear looks sodden. His eyes are only slits, epitomizing the ostrich strategy of pretending that if you can't see something horrible then it really isn't happening. Like hiding your head under the blanket so the big scary monsters in the closet can't find you. It is the only defense open to Michael, and his face is filled with the terrible knowledge that it can't possibly work, because the monsters in the closet are pretend and Emil Hinkins is real.

Next picture. Michael, naked. Still standing in the corner. Miserable. His hands at his sides, stiffly, there only because Hinkins won't let him cup them over his little penis. You recognize the mute apology in the boy's face. He might be directing it at Hinkins—he's just a child, he knows nothing of real monsters, he might still think that Hinkins, who killed six children before Michael and another three childred afterward, is doing this because Michael has been bad in some way. Michael might think that if he acts contrite enough, Hinkins will feel sorry for him and let him go. That might be what all the children thought.

Next page. A naked Michael chained spreadeagled to the four legs of a kitchen table lying upside down on the floor. He looks very small and very cold. A white gas oven, which will figure horribly in some of those photos, looms ominous in the background. You try for the most part not to look at that oven. Michael isn't looking at the oven. He's looking at Hinkins, the mad photographer who will soon devote an entire roll of film to his castration. And he's looking past Hinkins, past the camera, past the film, past five long years of time. At you. Because you're his daddy. And you're the one who really holds your little boy's life in his hands.

Because having seen them once, you don't have to look at the hundred or so other photographs documenting the rest of Michael's dying day. Pictures of Michael being sodomized. Pictures of Michael being blinded. Pictures of Michael having his tongue cut out. Pictures of Michael being

strangled, revived, urinated on. Pictures of Michael screaming. Pictures of Michael being murdered. They're available
to you, later on in the album. But you don't have to look
at them. The important picture, the one you really have to
look at, the one that presents your only chance to save
Michael, is the one on the very next page.

The picture Hinkins took the first time he set the camera
to auto. The picture marking the transition between intimi-
dation and actual torture. The first picture Hinkins appears
in himself.

He's stripped to the waist, bending over the inverted
kitchen table, undoing Michael's handcuffs. Michael's eyes
are thin slits, his mouth a black o deeper than a starless
night. Hinkins' eyes are also thin slits, but he's smiling in
sick anticipation.

You're standing behind him.

You're in the corner where two white walls meet. The
place where the walls meet is a vertical line, visibly cutting
you in half. Both halves of you project years of stored-up
hate—years and years and years of staring at this one picture, needing to be there. Years of watching the vaguely
humanoid shadow in that corner gain color and definition,
becoming first an indistinct blob that might have been anyone and then, gradually, this pale pallid ghost that is only
now beginning to take on the look of a father enraged.

It may take you another five years of single-minded concentration before the version of you in the photograph is
finally solid enough to act.

But he will act. He will.

His hands curled into transparent fists . . .

. . . his eyes burning with transparent need . . .

. . . he faces Hinkins . . .

. . . and it's too early to tell, because the picture isn't
yet clear enough . . .

. . . but he might be smiling.

Having Eyes, See Ye Not?

Sue Storm

Dawn shrugs its way through the lizard trees, painting their trunks a wan gray. Magdalene stands in the door of her tiny aluminum trailer; watching the creeping light with horror. Her eyes are red and swollen from a night spent drinking. The sickly-sweet smell of wine surrounds her like a tangled aura; her face melts into blunted weariness.

(Having eyes, see ye not? And having ears, hear ye not? And do not ye remember? How is it that ye do not understand?)

Sunlight shifts through the dry and empty forest. The ancient lizard trees press down on her with their silence, condemning her. She wants to yell at them, but she is afraid. They are too beautiful. Their beauty catches in her throat, reminding her.

(I am blind to beauty if it has no meaning.)

She grabs her pounding head, tries to focus her dull anger toward God. "If you expected something better, you should have watched a lot closer," she mutters.

Sitting heavily on the cold metal step, she grips the nearly empty wine bottle in one hand. With the other, she traces patterns among the buoyant lava rocks. An ant drags a dead moth into her vision; it is huge, almost an impossible burden for the insect. Like a man carrying his own stupid cross. Perhaps she, the slight, black-haired girl with "adulterer" burned across her breasts, should crush it. After all, they've both been alive since before the lava rocks burst out of the mountain and covered the ground, alive before the towering lizard trees took root. Now, if she wants, she can deliver death.

(Because strait is the gate and narrow is the way, which leadeth unto life, and few there be that find it.)

Perhaps she should—put it out of its misery. She lifts the

wine bottle to her mouth, lets the last of the warm liquid slip down her throat. Her throat was made for wine; it swallows effortlessly.

Surely, the ant would do the same for her.

Rising heavily, she retreats into the still-cool trailer, closing the door on the oozing day. She fumbles in the dimness—there is no electricity, and the kerosene is long gone—and finally locates the last bottle of wine in the back of a dark cupboard. Did she hide it from herself? Hah, she is not so clever after all, this one renegade child!

(I am sick with meaning. Purpose grows in me like a cancer.)

Opening the bottle, she stumbles back to the "bedroom," which is only an alcove filled by a stained mattress and blankets that twist and wrap around her young body at night, like lovers mad with seduction.

(What color is the purpose?)

Her mind refuses to listen (traitor mind), instead parading in Nazi, goose-step fashion, her favorite methods of becoming dead.

(Deadly gray.)

"The river," she says out loud.

(What shape is the purpose?)

She takes out the thought of her body yielding its clumsy gravity to the cool, watery embrace of the river and strokes it gently, like a kitten.

(It is oval, and smooth, like a stone worn by water.)

"Yes, definitely the river." She smiles, back propped against the trailer wall, and tilts the bottle to her lips, savoring the sweet taste of betrayal. Daylight oozes through her windows. From where she sits, she can twitch shut all three of the ancient, musty curtains. She watches dust swim in the velvet light.

(How does the purpose move?)

A mosquito whines just above her knee. Holding her breath, she lifts a quivering hand as it circles and circles. When it finally lands, her hand slaps down hard, smearing its existence across her tawny flesh. Her lips skin back from wine-stained teeth.

"All life is sacred, I have sinned. Damn you!" she yells suddenly. "See that? I have sinned again!"

(It is carried by someone.)

Magdalene removes the shirt she has worn for a forgotten number of days; already, the aluminum heats, forsaken by the dubious shade of the thin lizard threes. She drinks long and deep, desperate for sleep. Panic buzzes across her forehead like another mosquito. Her hand flails in vain. The panic grips her temples and won't let go.

(By whom? Who carries the purpose?)

"Now," she says out loud, her voice lurching drunkenly. "I am a nice lady. I get up at six and shower and dress. At seven, I eat breakfast, let's see fresh-squeezed orange juice and—" The panic moves around her head like a band of iron, it burns through her scalp. "—and toasted English muffins. With raspberry jam. At nine—"

(Who carries it?)

"—the mailman comes and we talk about the weather. At 9:30, I put on my hat and sweater and walk to the store to buy fresh fruit—"

(Who? Who?)

(I do! I do! Me and the others . . .)

She screams and throws the wine bottle at the wall. It shatters, spraying glass across the bed. A large shard slices her arm. She stares stupidly at the blood, at the pink wine dripping down the wall.

"I am bleeding," she announces to the unseen Watcher. "The wall is bleeding. Our blood is mingled, and I've sold my soul for a bed full of blood."

(There are no others)

Falling over on the bed, she raises her hand to the light, gazing at the blue and mortal veins. Blood drips down and wreathes her arm like a shackle.

"Life, pushing on in there, in its own secret rhythm, with all kinds of plans to continue . . ."

Crazy laughter spirals out from her throat, hurting it, as if the laughter is really the broken glass lying all over the bed, and she is swallowing it, again and again.

She wishes for more wine.

"The river," she whispers. "Definitely the river."

Tears leak from her eyes as she drifts into sleep.

(oh god there are no others)

The heat wakes her, the heat like a giant grizzly bear moving into her trailer and taking up all the space. She pushes against it weakly; it does not give. Her arm hurts.

Blinking open gummed eyes, she stares at the blood, the broken glass. She does not remember, but the cut gapes open on her arm, providing entry into a world she doesn't want to see. Carefully, she moves off the bed. The mattress gives, sending the butt end of the wine bottle crashing to the floor. The heretic winces as the sound rebounds inside her head. It is not a hangover causing her discomfort; she's long since stopped having hangovers. No, it is the feeling— like worms curling in her stomach—that she will wake something long dead with her noise.

She cannot afford to wake anything.

Tiptoeing into the rest of the trailer, she slops water from a jug into a pan. The water is warm, splashing over her face *(like blood)* like the slippery remnants of raw eggs hot from the nest. Gently she washes the cut. There is nothing clean in the trailer, not even the water, which she lugs in gallon containers from the sandy well at the store a mile away. She wraps her arm with strips torn from a dish towel that hasn't been washed since she moved in, eons ago.

It doesn't matter

(I am angry)

The fierce slut pulls on a shirt and a pair of shorts. Perhaps she once had underwear, but it is gone now, too, like the hangovers, like so much of her life. Fluff she didn't need; it blew away on the evening breezes.

(I am angry with a God who leaves nothing clear.)

She stares at herself in the mottled mirror screwed on the closet door. Sweat sheens her face, making her look almost as young as she is. She must get out: Her stomach rumbles, and there is no more wine.

"Eat first," she tells herself firmly.

(Eat, this is my body.)

Her face leers back. It knows better.

But sometime during the twenty-minute walk to the store, she, tired and weak, loses the battle with her body and turns her steps to the café. She pushes through the screen door into a clinging, greasy heat flecked with the bodies of flies. Two tiny booths under the south window append the horseshoe-shaped counter.

(For godly sorrow worketh repentance to salvation not to be repented of . . .)

Quickly, she moves with the hunched gait of one wishing

to go unnoticed to a stool opposite the booths. A teenage girl wearing big hair and too much makeup pushes a menu and a glass of water (no ice) in her direction. Magdalene hides her eyes in the plastic-covered cardboard.

(. . . But the sorrow of the world worketh death.)

When the waitress returns, the traitor points to the menu, ordering coffee and scrambled eggs. She does not trust herself to speak aloud in public. Cupping her hands around the coffee, she feels sweat trickle down her sides, between her breasts, but still she is oddly comforted by the thick, white coffee mug, which generates its own heat. Muffled talking and the clink of dishes, the pervasive odor of frying bacon, combine to give her a cozy, almost permanent feeling. The sloe-eyed waitress refills her cup.

(This must have meaning)

She wants to stay forever.

The couple in the booth across from where she sits are fat, and seem determined to prove the loud jollity myth decrees accompanies such girth. He has a gray mustache and a bald head, shining now from the grease condensing in the air. His brand new overalls stiffly refuse to crease; they've not even been washed first. The woman's sun-wrinkled face matches the condition of the blue and purple flowered dress she wears. She shifts uncomfortably; her hands keep smoothing the material nervously over her knees. She only wears dresses on special occasions. They smile and joke with one another thinly, as if they are expected to. Whenever silence falls over their table, the man bellows out neighborly words to the cook whose harried, sweating face shows through a square cut in the back wall. The fallen woman hears them order two "Number Three Ranch Hand Specials with extra large portions."

And then, somewhere in the back, a radio crackles with nostalgic effort: "Put your hand in the hand of the man from Galilee . . ."

Jesus, you bastard, she thinks. You grand and hateful sufferer.

(There are hooks in each and every one of my vital organs and I am being dragged in a river of blood.)

"If You were here right now, I don't know if I'd hug Your knees or beat on Your torn body."

"Huh?" the waitress stands in front of her, the plate of eggs slouched in one arm.

The traitor's fingers fly to her mouth, trapping her betrayal inside. With her other hand, she grabs the plate away from the girl.

Smirking, the waitress turns away.

(. . . dragged in a river of blood . . .)

Suddenly she remembers the river. Her escape hatch: body slowly sinking below the surface, pulled like a long, sweet kiss into the silky depths. Hurriedly, she shovels eggs past a palate that tastes them as effectively as it would cardboard.

Two stools down from her, a man casually fills a spoon with Tabasco sauce and slips it between his lips. He turns to look at her and grins, his teeth filling his mouth like a feral dog's. She shudders and drops her eyes. But that smile draws her. She looks up again, and he is gone. There is no spoon, no tabasco sauce.

(So much pain, oh holy pain! I am yours, you are mine. I asked and you came, came, and came again. Oh God!)

Between her legs, hollowness throbs. It's been too long. But soon she'll be dead (and free), and it won't matter, not anymore. Not any of it. Not you or you or you. Her eyes shoot darts at all the people in the café. Not even you: she turns lasers on the tabasco man, willing him back. Impatient, her feet beat out a silent tattoo under the counter.

(Paper people, all of them, paper people—so fragile, so ready to tear into scraps and blow away down the street like little lost bits of time.)

At last, the lazy waitress brings her check. The betrayer fumbles out a couple of bills, confused as usual by the strange, smeary feel of money. She turns toward the door.

"Ma'am, here's your change."

The teenager's voice is snide, assuming. blushing, Magdalene turns back and grabs the coins. They slip through her fingers, clatter on the floor. Staring down at them, she thinks, I am too young to be called "Ma'am."

(Ancient crosses set against an angry sky. I was there! I was there!, and I ran away.)

She runs through the door, leaving the coins untouched. Heat from an indifferent sidewalk rolls up and hits her in the face. Sweat pastes her shirt to her skin before she's

gone more than a few feet. She heads straight for the store, and its blessed supply of wine. First the wine, then the river.

The sound of a motorcycle backfiring makes her jump. A sunburned young man fiddles with his motor. His red hair and the beginnings of a beard look proudly unkempt. The cycle is piled high with traveling gear. She stares at him, tugged by his youth, by the slippery muscles of his bare back. Gradually, she becomes aware of another, also watching the boy.

It is an old man, meticulously dressed in shabby clothes. The pants are held together by suspenders stretched over a small pot belly. His spotted left hand grips a cane; his right, a tiny, crumpled brown bag. Both hands shake violently, as does his head. The face is heavy, impassive, shadowed by an ancient felt hat. Almost, she feels the gloomy thrust of his eyes as they bore into the boy's back. His body leans forward, describing a mournful arc toward the motorcycle.

Suddenly, the shaking figure droops, seeming about to collapse. Without thinking, she darts forward and grabs his arm.

(But the very hairs of your head are all numbered)

Slowly, he turns his decaying face toward her. The skin is slack and yellow. His eyes fix on hers with a watery vagueness that makes her stop breathing. He shudders with a last, great effort. Tensing, he draws his body up tight; the trembling stops. His look slides away from her as, stolidly, he pulls his arm free. Taking one careful step after another, he moves away, head thrust forward, frozen by great effort into the carved lines of an ancient totem.

The motorcycle roars.

"Hey, bitch! Move it will ya?"

The traitor turns, her eyes burn back at her from the young man's sunglasses.

"You deaf or something? Get the hell out of the way!"

She steps away just in time; the motorcycle swerves by her. It's heat, and the heat of the boy, wash over her.

(I rejoice, I rejoice, I weep with joy at the foot of your wretched cross.)

It is over.

Her body drips, sagging from her bones with peculiar relief. Before she leaves—the store, the wine, the river—

she slips off her shoes. On bare feet, she walks under the lizard trees, all the way back to the trailer.

(Eli, Eli, lama sabachthani!)

With the last of the water, she washes the dust from her tattered, swollen feet. Wadding the blankets into a corner, she lays the sacred objects on the bare mattress and places her naked body next to them. She lies with her legs bent and her feet flat in front of her. Experimentally, she stretches out, arms to each side, knees leaning a bit. It's a tight fit. The surface of the mattress rubs against the new, raw skin on her feet. Sitting up, she stares at them, at the blue veins running along the top like ropy tunnels providing transport for a busy, unheeded life.

The long, steel nails at her side grow hot in the ovenbox of the trailer. When she finally picks one up, it burns her fingers. But she brings it to her mouth anyway, and licks it, scalding her tongue. She tastes iron and rust. The nails; they've traveled with her everywhere, from country to city, from house to hovel. An now they are here, under the lizard trees.

Her right hand closes around the hammer. Its wood is warm and alive against her skin.

Setting the point of one nail against a foot, her gaze focuses completely on the small silver platter of its head. She brings the hammer down hard. Betrayal flows out of her body, soaking the bed. One more foot, and she loses consciousness.

Drifting, warm currents. She's reached the river after all. With an effort, she opens her eyes. A full moon casts pearls across the mattress. She cannot feel the lower half of her body. Something cold rolls against her breast. Groping, she touches one nail, two.

Without help, she cannot crucify her hands.

(Having eyes, see ye not?)

"Yes," she murmurs. "Yes, at last."

Taking up the hammer again, she pounds the final two nails into her eyes.

(How is it that ye do not understand . . . ?)

Sisters in Death

D. F. Lewis

At first there were three sweet sisters in childhood. Then one of them died of diphtheria—and the others, Alice and Esme, missed her deeply. For a time too, in their touching innocence, the pair of them pitied God needing to look after such a mischievous imp as their dear, dead sister.

Still, there was always a silver lining in their thoughts, if no silk edging to their rough blankets. In their really young days, all three had shared a double bed which became—with their femininity filling out—only fitting for two. Their mother scolded the two survivors when they ate too much, for she took reckon of the mattress springs, and money was spent all too easily on such creature comforts. It was not surprising, therefore, to learn that the lights were kept dim which—with grime building up on the nursery window—meant that Alice and Esme had to pore over their improvement books with reddening eyes. Their only affection, each other.

As compensation, their mother allowed a tiny light to flicker during the depths of night. Esme preferred it that way. But Alice thought it made everything more frightening, for the resultant shadows moved piecemeal across the cracked ceiling, the rocking horse traveled from child to child across the generations of its past, and Alice even imagined the ghosts of bodiless wings entangled in the butterfly net which leaned against the wall. In those days, hunger could act as a soporific so, before long, even Alice was snoring, with only dreams of fear.

As time waxed, the girls grew older, in spite—as well as because—of the meagerness of their condition. Esme eventually caught a cold from the years of suffering Alice's nightly nervous tugging the bedcovers off her. It would be hard-hearted to blame Alice, but there was no doubt that

her actions resulted in Esme incubating a sniffle, then influenza with, eventually, fevers building upon fevers—and at the peak of those body wrenching nights, Alice was moved from Esme's heaving side to the mother's room. Alice recalled listening to Esme's rhythmic screeching lungs even a corridor away. Then Esme died, as the dead sibling had once done before her. The family doctor pronounced Esme gone, the faint heart having given up the ghost after finally fluttering for just a few breathtaking seconds amid the trammels of the butterfly net.

Mother shed a few tears, but then took businesslike control of affairs. She allowed Alice a short while with her dead sister, to say goodbye. That was the way things were done since even soft-heartedness must be recognized, if but briefly. The nursery had the usual night lamp beside the bed, making ripples down the rhyming walls. Esme, if one can call a corpse by her name, was resting in carved repose, no longer concerned about the scarcity of covers on her side of the bed. Her hands had been positioned in prayer, as she used to do as a child at the end of a school day, like a closed, fleshy, moth. Her near womanly face was composed, peaceful, forgiving.

Alice was scared. She had been too young to appreciate the significance of death, when the earlier sister had become dead so young. Now, it was the shock of stillness. Abruptly, the corpse that had been Esme sat bolt upright in the bed, hands still poised, its shadow shuddering in the shape-shifting gloom. Even the rocking-horse ceased its light prance of pretense.

Esme's words hissed out: "I can't go away. God won't let me. And I am so very tired. Help me, Alice, please help me. Help me go where I can truly rest."

Alice replied as if to herself: "This must be a dream. I will wake up in a moment, as I always do from dreams . . ."

Esme's voice answered, bristling with irritation: "It may only be a dream to you, dearest Alice, but it's oh so horribly real to me. Think on that!"

Alice smiled, before she calmed the corpse's tongue with her own.

Window of Opportunity

Roman Ranieri

Juan gritted his teeth and shoved harder, the muscles swelling impressively on his thin, fourteen-year-old arms. One step above him eight-year-old Benito grunted loudly as he added his own boyish strength to the task.

A few seconds later, the 12-inch thick, solid concrete block slid up the last step and onto the top landing of the fire escape stairwell.

"Damn! *That* was a bitch!" gasped Benito, leaning tiredly on the block.

"I know, but this was the only thing I could find that was heavy enough. We'll rest here a few minutes, then get ready."

The boys sat down on the cold steel landing, their labored breathing echoing faintly in the dark stairwell. There had once been lights installed above the landing, but the fixtures and the electrical conduits had been ripped out and scrapped for drug money a long time ago. In the low-income projects, the term *necessities* meant different things to different people.

Juan slowly got to his feet. "You hold the door open while I push the block over the ledge."

Benito stared at his brother's face as he pulled open the heavy metal door. The left eye was swollen shut and colored a painful shade of purplish red. A thin trickle of blood ran over the lower lip from the ragged hole where the boy's bottom front tooth used to be. "Does your face still hurt?"

"Yeah, but the asprins are helping a little."

Together the boys lifted the concrete block up onto the outer ledge of the short walkway. The metal door to their left opened into the corridor leading to the various apartments. The door to their right was the stairwell. Supposedly, these narrow open-air walkways between the apartments and the

175

stairs were designed to vent the smoke away from the fire escape if the building started to burn. Up till now, the only serious fire had been on the ground floor, so the engineer's theory had yet to be tested.

Today the walkway on the top floor was being put to a different use. It happened to be directly above the building's front entrance.

The brothers seated themselves on the cramped ledge, the heavy block positioned squarely between them.

"Why did Tyrone beat you up like that?" asked Benito.

"He saw me talking with Angela and he thought I was trying to put a move on her."

"Were you?"

"Fuck, no! I've been going to school with Angela for the last nine years. I was just *talking* to her. That's all."

"Couldn't you just *tell* Tyrone that?"

"Shit! Nobody can talk to that loco fucker anymore. His brain's burned out from all the crack he's been doing."

Juan coughed, then spat on the floor, the saliva was mixed with blood.

"He hurt you pretty bad," said Benito.

"Well, shit! He *is* eighteen, and a hell of a lot bigger than me."

"I know that. I just meant he never should have done what he did to you."

"That's why we're up here. It's pay-back time."

"Are you sure this is the best way?" asked Benito, doubtfully eyeing the concrete block.

"Look, I know you don't remember Papa too well because you were so little when he died, but one of the things he used to say was: *Stay out of a fight if you can, but if you have no other choice, then do anything you can to hurt the other guy. Make sure he knows that even if he wins, the price he had to pay was way too high. If you can do that, then he'll never bother you again.* Do you understand now?"

"But this thing could *kill* him."

"I don't give a fuck! I'm not going to let him get away with what he did to me. It wasn't even a fair fight. He jumped me from behind," yelled Juan, droplets of blood spraying from his mouth. "Besides, what's one more dead

junkie around here anyway? The cops probably won't even ask any questions."

Benito shrunk back from his older brother. When he spoke again, his voice was hardly above a whisper. "Okay. Do it anyway you want to."

With the discussion ended, the boys quietly sat on the ledge and waited. The building faced west. they watched as the setting sun appeared to set the LA smog on fire, turning the sky to a muddy orange color. Down on the street, the evening traffic thinned out to just an occasional car or truck. Most of the working people were home now. In the night hours, the neighborhood belonged to the junkies, the dealers, the whores, and the pimps.

Benito began to fidget. "What time is it? I'm tired of waiting up here."

"He'll probably be on the next bus. Tyrone always gets off work at six on Thursdays."

"How do you know?"

"Because sometimes I hang out at the 7-Eleven where he works."

"What time is it now?"

"Almost seven."

"I want to go inside and watch television."

"We're *both* staying out here, and we're *both* pushing this block over," Juan snarled. "That's the only way I can be sure you'll never dime me out."

"I wouldn't tell no one. You're my brother."

"Then just do this with me, and stop whining. I do favors for you all the time, don't I?"

"Yeah. Okay."

Benito absently caressed the block with his fingertips as he gazed out at the East LA skyline. He didn't really want any part of this, but Juan had taken care of him since their father died. In his heart, he could not refuse his brother's request. Even if it did seem too extreme.

After another half-hour had passed, Juan began to feel foolish. He glanced over at Benito, marveling at the small boy's patience. "If he's not on the next bus, we'll go inside and watch TV. Okay?"

"Okay," replied Benito, smiling.

Ten minutes later the bus arrived.

Only one person got off at the housing project stop; a tall black woman carrying some kind of package in her arms.

"Who is it?" asked Juan. "I can't see too good with only one eye."

"It's Mrs. Washington, Tyrone's mother," answered Benito.

A strange feeling seemed to swell within Juan's heart. It was half dissapointment, and half relief. "Okay. That's enough. Let's go in."

As the boys backed away from the ledge, Juan looked over for a last look. "What the fuck is she carrying? It sure as hell *ain't* no grocery bag."

Benito peered over the side for a few seconds. "It looks like a new basketball. I guess it must be Tyrone's birthday or something."

Juan's lips slowly curled back from his teeth in a savage smile, and his body began to shiver with rage. Benito looked up into his brother's face and gasped. He had never before seen such an expression of cruel, deadly fury.

"No!" screamed the young boy.

The heavy slab of concrete soundlessly began its descent. Although the shove that launched it had been merely a momentary impulse, the speed and trajectory of the block were perfect. There was a wide steel canopy jutting out over the entrance that was sturdy enough to stop the deadly cube, but the plummeting block missed it by less than an inch.

As the boys watched in mesmerized awe, Mrs. Washington warily swiveled her head from side to side, searching the shadows for muggers or other signs of imminent danger.

She never thought to look up.

Envy

Christa Faust

I am waiting for you by the door. Kneeling as always, head bowed, spine held rigid and upright by the strict embrace of the white leather corset you laced me into this afternoon before you left for work. My body aches. My legs tingle bloodlessly. I hear the subtle sound of your key sliding into the lock and a tight fist clenches between my legs. I am wet already.

You are so beautiful standing in the doorway, filling my world with your long legs and the secret smell of gardenias and warm leather. A Goddess. Your chestnut hair is glossed with rain.

Laughing, you shrug off your damp trench coat and drape it across my outstretched arms as if I were a coat rack. Underneath, your long body is hugged by pearly gray silk, conservative enough not to raise eyebrows in the expensive hotels where you conduct your business. Beneath that sober dress, there are many secrets.

I take your coat and your equipment bag and hang them in the closet like a good girl. When I return, I find you sprawled back in your favorite chair. Your elegant, race-horse legs are crossed and your skirt rides high on strong thighs. I can see the darker tops of your seamed stockings. I am entranced, hopelessly in love with you and at the same time steeped in viscous jealousy. Next to you I feel dull and clumsy, hopelessly ordinary beside your exotic brilliance. I want more than anything to dive into your body and look out through your glass green eyes. I will try again tonight.

I kneel before you again, anxious and burning. You nudge me with your high heeled shoe and I catch it in both hands, pressing my lips to its cool surface. So the ritual begins.

I remove your shoes with reverence, lavishing your chilled

feet with hot kisses. The texture of sheer silk is sweet and familiar against my tongue. You make low purring sounds as my mouth follows the curves of your narrow ankles, traveling cautiously over the long muscles of your calves. My body is tense and ready to retreat at the slightest hint of your disapproval, but the lazy movement of your hips encourages me. I can taste perfume in the soft hollow behind you knee.

My mouth has reached that magic place where silk becomes skin. The flavor of your flesh is excruciating. The muscles of your inner thighs are pulled fine and taut as your legs drift apart. I can see the dull gleam of polished leather between them, dark and mysterious beside your pale skin.

I suck in a drowning breath, already resolved to my crime and eager for the consequences. My belly is full of the sick pulse of adrenaline. I kiss your thigh one last time before I sink my teeth in.

"Slut!"

Your hand is fast as a striking snake, catching my face between thumb and forefinger. Your gaze burns me and fills me with shame and sick desire. You slap my face, first one cheek, then the other. When you let go of me, I tumble back, unable to support myself without your strength.

You are standing now, nothing but legs and heels and a disapproving voice from high above like a child's fantasy of punishment. I force myself to look up at you.

There is heat and mischief in your eyes as you toy with the buttons on your dress, opening each one so slowly I feel like screaming. Underneath that thin disguise of respectability, there is leather, revealed in stages. Your breasts are bare but unwelcoming, pointed like weapons tipped with silver rings. they are utterly unnatural, straining out from your boyish chest in defiance of the Y chromosome you were born with. I covet them ceaselessly.

The corset that cinches your waist is black leather, glittering with spikes. I know that you have had ribs removed to make that waist narrower, more feminine. Sometimes I fantasize about your surgeries. In my mind I see you naked and helpless beneath flashing scalpels. I wish I could have been inside your head.

All semblance of normality is gone now, pooled with the gray dress around your feet. I see that you are wearing a

studded codpiece, the stiff leather cupping your most tender secret. The sight of it is painfully erotic, a delicious contradiction.

Your fingers caress my stubbled scalp and I shiver.

"I think this nasty little girl needs to be taught a lesson."

Phrases like this are so ritualistic, I barely hear them anymore. Instead, I focus on the feel of your dark nails digging into my arm as you haul me to my feet and drag me down the hall, to the discipline chamber.

This room is long and narrow with blood red walls and racks to hold the tools of suffering. Sometimes you bring clients here, driving me into fits of aching rage as I listen to the sound of your whip on someone else's flesh. It is easy to hate you for your indifference, but my passion for your impossible body holds me bound in true slavery.

You tie my wrists to a ring in the wall, high enough to pull me up on the balls of my feet. Now that I am immobilized, you stalk back and forth, a thin smile curling in one corner of your mouth. Frustration digs into the vulnerable parts of my body. I crave transcendence and you are in the mood to tease.

You toy with my nipples and it makes me feel sick. I want to bite you again, to invoke the dark passion of your anger and break through your jaded veneer. I want you to open yourself up to me, to let me in.

My skin is slicked with cold sweat and my muscles strain against their bondage. My heart beats between my legs as you search for some implement that strikes your fancy. I am not entirely surprised when you choose a small tray of needles.

So fine and silver they are, flashing like Christmas, like hollow stingers. I am making little desperate noises in my throat, hot with anticipation. I can feel the faintest breeze on the flushed skin on my thighs. I flinch a little at the icy kiss of Betadine.

Gently you part my legs, fingers precise as a surgeon on the slippery folds of my labia. I hiss softly at the first numbing pinch that is prelude to the silver sting.

When the needle slips into my flesh the pain is sweet and fresh as a Fourth of July sparkler, nostalgic almost. I am drowning in its glitter. I have to force myself to breathe.

A second sting and a third and the pain is spreading now,

sending hot silver threads racing over the surface of my skin. Seven needles and then eight and my vagina is a boiling cauldron of razors. I reach out for you, try to touch you with my mind, but you are not ready yet. You feel no passion as you examine the sea urchin you have created between my legs. In your mind there is only detached speculation, smooth and impenetrable. I feel a scream of frustration welling behind my clenched teeth but it transforms into a gasp of shock as you turn me away to face the wall and bring the palm of your hand down hard on my ass. The muscles of my vagina clench, bringing out a bright new blossom of pain.

You let me have a few more warming slaps before I feel the sharp bite of your whalebone crop. The cheeks of my ass feel full and ripe with blood.

Passion finally, slow at first, then building. I can feel it pouring off you in subtle waves like a sound too low for human ears. Your breath warms my throat as you lean close to me, caressing my swollen ass. Your desire weakens the wall, opening a thousand pores like hungry mouths ready to suck me in.

You are using a wide leather strap now, supple but unforgiving. The vicious crack of contact is loud enough to swallow me whole. The pain is bright and echoing, filling me with strength. I think we both are ready now.

At first it is just a flash, like an accidental double exposure, the pale ghost of my own ass superimposed over my view of the gritty wall. I have gone this far before. First, as a child cowering beneath the meaty blows of a folded-over belt. Then, later, with other mistresses. Even before with you a few precious times. But never have I wanted it so fiercely. Never have I tried so hard.

Again a flash, stronger this time. I clutch at this vision as if it were the only way to save my life, sliding in deeper. The curve of my back and hips gains solidity while the pain and darkness slips away like burning cobwebs. The sharp caress of each blow is swallowed by the sure strength of the strap in your hand.

There is more now. The teasing rasp of your silk stockings against your calves. The lingering taste of sweet spices on your tongue. You can smell my sweat and this excites you.

Somewhere far away, there is pain and the aching pull of the ropes but they no longer matter. What matters is the rush of power that courses through your body. My body.

The vast orchestra of sensation is hypnotic to me but I am afraid I will lose my hold on you. My own wretched body pulls me back but I resist, clinging to your mind with hooked insect feet.

Your desire tastes rich and purple like some primal ocean. The blood pounds in your veins (my veins) coaxing unlikely erection from a body soaked in estrogen, boiling away the last resistance.

The curve of my ass burns hot as sullen orange coals beneath you, so lush and tempting. You reach out your hand and slide questing fingers up into the slick crevice between those blood-striped cheeks. When my lifeless body does not react, I feel a cold trickle of fear. Do you know? Can you feel me inside you squatting behind your eyes and drinking in the rich liquor of your experience.

Do you hate it?

You are angry that I do not shiver beneath your touch. You scold me softly but with steel beneath it and when I still do not react you are furious. This anger is red as blood and shot through with veins of lurid purple. You hit me harder, the bright sparks of indignation lighting the inside of your skull like fireworks.

"Answer me when I speak to you!"

The words taste coppery and sharp in your mouth and I savor them as if they were the richest meal. Your anger is huge now, full of black thunder. You reach for a thin bamboo cane, slice through the air beside me, but my body does not flinch.

With fire in your veins, you lay into me with the whistling cane, opening my flesh in long bleeding welts. Drops of blood are strung across my ass like garnet beads, their delicate pattern smeared by each blow. Harder and faster now and blood running down my thighs and I can feel the fury, *your* fury, white hot and out of control. I drink it in like wine and sweet sugar, gorging myself. I am more in love with you now than I have ever been.

The cane breaks, a small sound like a child's bone snapping. The sight of the splintered end cuts through the meat of your anger like a ruby laser and suddenly you are afraid.

You pull my slack body to you and call my name, stinging tears filling your eyes. Your mouth fills with wild apologies. You tell me that you love me and I can feel the truth of it resonate through your belly and your heart, but there is something else now, some strange low throbbing. You touch a fingertip to your temple. The vein there is thick as a nightcrawler, pulsing. Sharp edged light bisects your vision and dizziness swarms up to engulf you. I know that I have overstayed my welcome. If I continue to cling to the fragile tissue of your mind, it will tear beneath my weight. Invaders leave damage, and I love you too much to use force.

Falling back into my body is like diving into a vat of napalm. My disused flesh screams with numb, tingling agony. My lungs are filled with hot ash. The pain of my lacerated ass is like the world burning, but I will endure it for you. I will endure anything for you.

I turn to you and look into your green eyes from the outside. In their stained glass depths, I can see childish relief and even love. Your hands are trembling as you untie my bonds.

I collapse to my knees and cover your feet in kisses. Our session has only just ended and already, my mind is brimming over with thoughts of next time.

Next time, perhaps I can find a way to be more gentle, to stay longer. Next time, perhaps I will be able to hide myself more deeply. Perhaps, some fate could befall my wretched body while I was inside you, next time. Perhaps, then, I could stay with you forever.

I look up into your flushed face and wonder, as I always do. Next time, perhaps.

The Man of Her Dreams

Alan M. Clark

"He'll probably think I'm nuts," she told herself. Rachel had never before said anything about her tormentor to anyone, but lately it had all become too much for her to deal with alone and she needed to talk about it.

Tied up in knots over how Eric would react, Rachel was unable to motivate herself and spent the day gazing out her front window, watching the city of San Francisco go about its Saturday business.

Just as it was becoming dark out, she heard Eric return from work and enter his flat across the hall. Now, she both dreaded and looked forward to his knock on her door.

"Seems like it was about five years ago," Rachel said, feeling like a small child under Eric's scrutiny. "I started getting sick all the time and I was always having these accidents—mostly small ones, but a few took me to the hospital. Then there were other things, like I seemed to be failing at everything I tried, and all my relationships went sour for no reason I could think of. I began to feel like someone was responsible for all these disasters, that someone was out to get me. But I knew he wasn't real, not like you and me." Rachel looked to see how Eric was taking this. Although he seemed a bit confused, he was calm, attentive.

"I think he stalks me in my dreams. I get this deep sense of, like . . . dread, and then I see this figure off in the distance. I never can see his face clearly, though. He doesn't ever do anything to me in my dreams, but I *know* he's the one fucking up my life.

"My mother would tell me," she began and then laughed. Eric smiled gently. "Go on, I'm listening."

"*If* I were willing to talk to her," Rachel corrected her-

self, "she would tell me that it was just God punishing me for my sins. But I refuse to believe that. If God is doing all this, either he's very evil, or *I* am, and I don't want to think about that."

"I don't think you're evil," Eric said. "So If it's not God and it's not the devil, who do you think is picking on you?"

She hesitated as if she knew the answer, but didn't want to admit it.

"I don't know," she said.

"So, what you're saying is that you don't know who, but they're responsible for all your problems. I wish it were so easy to explain away my own. If I could blame someone else for the things that go wrong in my life, I wouldn't have to feel so bad about myself."

"Well, okay," Rachel said defiantly, "let's see, I'll give you some examples—just this week I stubbed my toe six times, the *same* toe! Someone snatched my purse last week and now I've got to replace all my ID and credit cards. In a store yesterday, I broke some stupid vase-thing and it cut the shit out of me and I even had to pay for it. Then I was told that this damn photography course I'm in is no good for completing my major. And hell . . ." she paused to think, "now you're laughing at me.

"Look, I don't blame *all* my problems on this son-of-a-bitch and I don't *know* that this is real, but it sure *feels* that way."

Realizing how all this sounded, Rachel turned away.

One of these days, just like I do with everybody else, I'm going to say or do something that will drive him away.

With chagrin, she remembered her behavior last Tuesday night when they had gotten drunk together in his flat.

"You're my only friend, Eric," she had said, slurring her words, "and I love you. You're the only man I ever felt close to—the only man I have ever wanted to have sex with. But you're gay, you asshole."

One more bourbon and Coke and she had passed out. Eric carried her across the hall to her apartment and put her to bed. She awoke Wednesday to a shame laced hangover, one she felt she deserved. How could she ever face Eric again, she wondered, reaching to feel the deep ache in her soul as well as physical pain in her head. That afternoon, when he came over to "borrow" some toilet paper,

however, he said nothing about the night before and seemed to have forgotten all about it.

"Rachel," Eric said, snapping her out of her reverie, "are you with me?"

"You're laughing at me, and I deserve it. I act so stupid sometimes."

"Come on, Rachel, he said, turning her around, "I'm not laughing at *you*—just the dumb idea of this *tormentor* of yours. I think if you expect the worst out of life, you'll get it, that's all."

Eric parted the dirty black hair hanging over her pretty face. Unable to look directly into his eyes, she turned away, and Eric took her slender hands in his own and squeezed them affectionately. She winced and pulled away quickly when his fingers touched the cigarette burns on her palms. She was trying to think of something to change the subject when Eric did it for her.

"Listen," he said, "If I'm taking you out, you need to be presentable. I know you don't have anything attractive to wear, but the least you could do is take a bath, wash some of that oil paint off."

"Why aren't you going out with your boyfriend tonight?" she asked cruelly.

Eric let it pass with a shrug.

"I told you when you called this morning I didn't want to go out," she said. "Why don't we stay here and talk about you moving in with me. With your boyfriend—excuse me, I meant roommate—moving back to L.A. for the summer, your flat will be too expensive for you and there's plenty of room here. It would be easy just to move your stuff across the hall."

"Look honey," Eric said with as much camp as he could muster, "my motherly instincts tell me it's a good way to keep an eye on you. But I know how you feel about me and I know what you want and it's just *not* going to happen. What you need is the man of your dreams."

Without giving her time to think about what he was saying, Eric gave her a spank on the butt. "Go on now, get ready. Remember, you're my date for the party and I don't want to be embarrassed. And no more about *Faceless tormentors* tonight, okay?"

She wandered off to her room feeling small and silly.

Rachel had known that he would not believe, had somehow hoped he wouldn't, and that this would convince her that it was all in her imagination. She couldn't shake the feeling, however, that someone was watching her, looking for opportunities to make her life a living hell.

Before dressing, she began a series of short scratches on her stomach with a straight pin. As she thought about going out into the San Francisco night, about meeting strangers, she applied just enough pressure with the pin to draw blood.

Her flight from Tennessee had not improved her life. She had thought that this geographical change would serve as a cure-all for her troubles. *Surely he can't climb aboard an airplane and follow,* she had told herself. San Francisco wasn't at all what she had expected or wanted and the evil spirit somehow came up with the airfare and continued to harass her.

When Rachel was not in school at the Art Institute or working at Fazarre's as a window dresser, she spent most of her time alone in her flat thrashing out images on canvas or paper with paint or pencil. Her art was the only thing over which Rachel felt she had complete control. "Here, I am God," she reminded herself daily. Her tormentor seemed to allow her this territory.

Physical pain, self inflicted in minute doses, seemed to help distract her from the larger pain of her emotional existence. The passage of time had become a steep incline with very slippery, blood smeared handrails.

Rachel didn't know anyone at the party but Eric, who seemed to know everyone. She was jealous. And, although she was introduced around, she would not talk with anyone. She tried to sit alone in a corner and get drunk on the punch, but a woman approached and sat down next to her. She looked a lot like Rachel's mother.

"I've always wished that I had such shiny, black hair," she said.

Rachel smiled and looked away thinking that if she ignored the woman perhaps she would find someone else to talk to.

"Excuse me for not introducing myself—I'm Andrea. You're a friend of Eric's aren't you?"

"Yes, I am."

"You're very attractive, although not particularly vain about it," she said taking a pack of cigarettes from her shirt pocket.

Rachel *knew* what this woman was really after. Reaching for an ashtray, Andrea bumped against Rachel's breast. *That* clinched it—she had a perfectly good excuse to leave now. When she saw Eric step into the bathroom, she slipped away from the party and headed for home.

As Rachel walked to the bus stop, a black limousine began pacing her close to the curb. The passenger door on her side opened and she could see the dark silhouette of a man beckoning for her to get in. She turned toward the entrance to an apartment building and the car sped away. She heard the driver's contempt for her in the sharp squeal of his tires.

She glanced nervously from side to side and behind as she moved along the sidewalk. The wind blew her skirt up and she whipped around pressing it back down, vowing never again to wear a dress. Someone whistled at her from a window up the street. She turned around and walked in the other direction an then cut over one block to the bus stop. Running, she hopped on board the bus that was just coming to a stop when she arrived. She collapsed into a seat near the front and, after a ride that lasted fifteen minutes, got off and walked a block to her flat. Closing the door, her fear was shut out in the damp night.

After removing her clothes, she lay in bed reducing her anxiety an inch at a time by making small cuts on her breasts and inner thighs with a box knife. A half hour later, her thoughts calmed, she fell asleep.

Everyone knows that married couples have sex with one another, Rachel thought. Even so, none of the guests at the wedding reception let on that they thought there was anything strange about Rachel marrying her own mother. She held her head high and choked on her shame as the guests, mostly relatives from Tennessee, watched Mama hold her close and kiss her with something more than just a mother's love.

Eventually, they were able to get away from the crowd. Rachel knew what her mother would want from her now that they were alone. It was something she would just have to get used to—she had made her decision and would stick by it.

Mama began kissing her, fondling her breasts, and Rachel felt cold hands parting her thighs. The facial features of the man who suddenly stood in her mother's place did not quite fit together into a whole. A familiar fear welled up inside her. She struck out at the man, the blows connecting without any force. He was no longer just stalking Rachel—his penis was pure terror thrust into her.

She awoke suddenly, heard her own scream and knew that it had been a dream—all but the orgasm which had crested and now broke within her.

Rachel spent Sunday full of anxiety. Although the nightmare/wet dream was terrifying, she had gained some sexual satisfaction. *At least there wasn't the usual "dirty" feeling,* she told herself. She had always assumed that the "dirty" feeling she experienced after masturbating was just another gift from her tormentor, his small way of spoiling even this simple pleasure. The orgasm from the dream was incredible, however, and without the dreaded aftereffect. *Was it just a meaningless dream, or does this mean something?*

Rachel got dressed and decided that what she needed was an Eric fix. On her way out, she noticed a folded piece of paper that had been slipped under her door.

"Doll face," it read, "I've gone to help Tim move to Los Angeles a day earlier than I expected and won't return until Wednesday morning. We'll do something together when I get back. Love, Eric."

Rachel experienced a deep emotional sinking spell. There was only one way she knew to get out of that—she lost herself in her work. Beginning with pencil and paper and no particular idea, she filled two pages with meaningless scribbles.

The third page began the same way, but a couple of shapes suggested themselves and then, although she wasn't conscious of it at first, she was drawing the man from her dream, her tormentor. After she realized what she was doing, she filled page after page, trying to capture the elu-

sive qualities of his face. Her drawings came out looking rather cubist, the facial features disjointed and overlapping at odd angles. She cut the drawings up and tried to piece the features together into a reasonable face. The effort was not wholly successful but the portrait she produced frightened her.

I know this man.

Monday, she was able to lose herself in her work at school and made it through the day without any Eric once again. There was enough to do at work that night to keep her busy as well and she avoided being the center of the universe at least until she hopped on the streetcar to head for home.

Because of the number of people on board, she was forced to stand as it rocked and bounced along. She was considering getting off and catching another car when a man sitting to her right grabbed her by the hips, stuffed his head between her legs and took a big sniff, muttering something about "pussy."

The doors opened as the car stopped and the man ran off into the night with her smell. Sobbing silently, Rachel crouched down and kept her head lowered to avoid eye contact with any of the other passengers. At the next stop, she stumbled off and walked the rest of the way home.

Entering her flat, she headed straight for bed, apprehension causing her to hesitate only a moment before succumbing to her weariness and crawling between the sheets. She made ten, one inch long cuts near her left armpit and dropped off to sleep with the box knife still cradled in her hand.

Tonight, her faceless tormentor came to her as just another passenger on a streetcar full of old friends from high school. She didn't recognize him until it was too late. The others watched with the same interest they might have had for an aspirin commercial as he threw her down in the aisle between the seats, pulled up her dress and stabbed her repeatedly with his box knife-shaped penis.

Rachel felt her scream as it passed from her dream throat through her waking mouth and then came the orgasm—a major quake with multiple after shocks. She lay for a moment clutching the bedsheets as the world swung back into

focus. When she could move again, she found a pool of blood between her legs.

"It's just a dream, Rachel," she said, trying to reason with her battered imagination. She dragged herself into the bathroom and stared at herself in the mirror. "And my period is, what . . . I guess it's a week and a half early."

Tuesday morning, before school, she drew the faceless man once more, trying different poses and various expressions on his face in an unsuccessful effort to steer the image away from looking like the person she had in mind. *The man of my dreams,* she thought with a chill.

At school, what started out as an uneventful day of painting in one of her studio classes, turned into disaster when her professor accidentally dropped his cigarette in her thinner and caught her paints and easel on fire. Horrified, She stood gaping at the flames as they ate up her painting. The professor and several students rushed around looking for a fire extinguisher. Rachel fled, abandoning her equipment. She would not be needing it now that her tormentor had profaned her art—the last thing in the world that was her own. She headed for home.

Preparing for work, Rachel was washing her hair in the shower when the bugs attacked her. Opening her eyes after rinsing, she screamed and jumped backward, trying to get away from the swarm of tiny black insects pouring from the spray nozzle. She crashed through the plastic shower door and lay writhing on the cold tile floor, pain shooting through her back and arms. As she scraped at the black grit clinging to her flesh, she realized there *were* no insects. Reaching up and turning the hot water off, the black sludge stopped and only clear water flowed from the pipes.

Calming down, she cleaned up with cold water, bandaged a nasty gash on her forearm and got dressed. After dialing several phone numbers, she got through to her landlord.

"Sounds like it's coming from the hot water heater," he said. "I'm sorry, but I can't get out there to fix it until next week."

"Mr. Zooker, *please,*" she said, "I can't do without a bath until then."

"What's wrong, Rachel," he said. "Ain't you got any

friends. Go use someone else's shower. Next Monday's the earliest I can make it."

She slammed the phone down in frustration.

Rachel was exhausted after work that night and upon returning home, she went immediately to bed and abused herself to sleep with a pair of needle nose pliers.

As she dreamed, Eric came to her, sat upon her chest and tied her feet and hands to the bed posts. She willingly began to suck on his penis. It was only when the black sludge came spewing out of him into her mouth that she realized this was her nightly rapist, not Eric. She gargled out her screams as he worked her over with a pair of vise grips.

Just as the orgasm awakened her, she began to choke and cough up the gritty hot water heater goo. Screaming, she jumped out of the black-stained bedding. The pliers fell from between her legs, landing with a clatter. She hit the light switch and began to spit black and then to vomit on the floor. When she could breathe easily again and her adrenaline was wearing off, she bent to pick up the bloodied pliers and saw the rope burns on her wrists and ankles.

Two hours later, Eric, just returning from Los Angeles, found her sitting in front of his door crying.

"It's my dead brother," Rachel told Eric.

This had come after Eric brought her into his flat, gave her bourbon to drink and spent an hour coddling her with hugs and tender words. They sat on the floor just outside of the bathroom where she could easily reach for toilet paper to mop up her tears.

"He's the one stalking me in my dreams," she said, "my brother is attacking me in my sleep. I think he wants to kill me. See these rope burns—he tied me up and tortured me with pliers. Don't you see what I'm saying—the dreams are real!"

"Rachel, dreams wouldn't be dreams if they were real."

"That's what I'm saying!" she said, tears of frustration sliding down her cheeks.

"Okay," Eric said, taking a deep breath and letting it out slowly as he waited for her to calm down. "*Tell* me about him. I didn't even know you had a brother."

"He's not really my brother." She said, chewing on the ice from her drink.

He grew impatient as her silence stretched on. "If you won't talk to me, how can I help?" he asked.

The word *help* rang in her head. She *did* want Eric's help. But she didn't have to tell him *everything*.

"After my daddy died, my mama married a man who ran off and left his son for her to raise. His name was Dwight. He was very cruel to me and I hated him."

She paused for a moment and lowered her head. "It's my fault he's dead," she stated flatly.

"Oh, come on, Rachel—how did you do that?"

Her eyes became very cold and hard. "I wished him dead and he died," she said. "And now he's haunting me."

"You can't *really* believe that." Eric was dumb-struck for a moment watching her. Rachel sat rigid, her eyes focused beyond the room in which they sat. "There must be more to this than you're telling me."

"He was a bully," she said a little too quickly. "Mama worked late and I was stuck with him in the house after school until she got home. He would trap me in my room and torture me. I started keeping a butcher knife under my mattress—I wanted to cut his throat." Rachel became red in the face as she remembered.

"Then he was in a car wreck. His head punched a hole in the windshield of the car but his shoulders kept him from going all the way through. When he bounced back into his seat, the ragged edge of the hole cut his throat and he bled to death before the ambulance came. I was sixteen years old and I was the one driving the car.

"You see?" She was becoming hysterical. "I killed him!" Rachel stared at Eric wide-eyed and trembling as if daring him to prove her wrong.

He swallowed hard, his face flushed and then he opened his mouth to speak. "Did Dwight abuse you sexually?"

"Yes!" she shouted. Rachel was horrified—she didn't mean to say that. This was a secret she had vowed never to tell anyone.

She was about to deny it, to tell him that she had misunderstood his question, when a sense of relief spread through her as though a great abscess of emotional pain in her chest had been lanced.

She wiped her eyes and looked into Eric's. His concern for her didn't seem to wave in the face of the "dirt" she just spilled and she realized that the feelings she had held back for so long could now all be expressed.

He reached for her shoulders, pulled her close and hugged her. It was awkward—Eric obviously didn't know what to say or do for her. "Have you ever told anyone else about it?" he asked.

"No," she said. Rachel had intended to put an end to the problem when the car accident had done it for her. She could still feel the sharp edge of the butcher knife, however, could still remember her fantasy of reaching under the mattress while Dwight lay atop her, of bringing the knife out when an orgasm caused him to throw back his head, exposing the pulsing arteries of his neck.

There was an unnerving mix of anger, fear and shame in her eyes and it was Eric's turn to look away.

Rachel was unable to explain that she had never told anyone about the sexual abuse because she had been a willing participant—at least, her body had responded from the very start. Deep down, she felt that, since she had been able to have orgasms while having sex with Dwight, she was morally corrupt, an incorrigibly evil human being.

Eric fixed lunch for the two of them, insisting that she try to eat something. As he prepared ham and cheese sandwiches, he seemed deep in thought. Rachel was confident that he could help her figure out a way to deal with Dwight. She tried to be patient.

When he was through eating his lunch, Eric looked across the table at the sandwich from which Rachel had taken only one bite. "If you're not going to eat that—"

"I'm catching a cold," she said to discourage him She wished he would hurry up and say something.

"Rachel, I had no idea. I'm sorry you've had to deal with this all alone for so long. But you need to move on now, try to put the past behind you. And I'll do what I can to help. Regardless of the shame you might feel, my feelings for you are the same—I love you and I'm here for you whenever you need me."

Eric took a deep breath. "But," he said letting it out slowly, "Dwight's dead and you have to realize how irratio-

nal it sounds—the idea that he's out to get you. Seems like you use him to account for everything that goes wrong in your life—so *you* don't have to take responsibility. Take a good look at yourself, at the way you think and act. As hard as it is for me to say this, I think maybe you ought to consider seeing someone—I think you should get some professional help."

"You *really* know how to kick someone while they're down," Rachel said as she rose to her feet. "Son of a *bitch*—you're saying I'm *sick!*"

Eric was saying, "no . . . no . . . no!" as he stood up.

She picked up her plate and threw it to the floor. It shattered at his feet and he hopped away, looking like he'd been bitten by a snake.

"I don't need this kind of help," Rachel said, spitting the words. She started for the door.

"*Think* about it, Rachel," Eric said as he kept pace with her.

She didn't understand why *he* sounded desperate and hurt; he was the one who had abused *her* trust.

"Wait," he said, grabbing her arm before she could get through the door. "I didn't—"

She stomped on his foot, said, "Go fuck yourself. *I'm* no longer available."

She made it through the door and into her flat. Just before closing and locking it, she saw Eric in the hall, crouched on the floor holding his foot, his expression that of a lost child.

Rachel crawled into bed and pulled the sheets up over her head to shut out the world, but Eric's voice found its way in as he called to her through the door. When one of the other tenants complained about the noise, he became silent. Then, there were only the background sounds of the city and she could think again. *I belong to a cruel husband.* And isn't that what he truly was to her, she thought? They had been bound together many years ago by an act meant to consummate a marriage. *Would he relax his grip on me if I went to him freely?* Could she hang her head any lower?

Work! She had to go to work. Rachel glanced at the clock on the night stand. It said 4:02, time to think about getting ready.

*   *   *

She had made an arrangement of pedestals, hampers, clothes lines draped with fresh linens, an a washer and dryer. Next, she would dress the mannequins and put them in place. The dresses for this display were strapless and so low cut that the only way to keep them up was to use the two clothes pins sewn to the bust line. The breasts of the mannequins, however, had only a suggestion of nipples too hard and slick to pinch with the pins.

Wondering what kind of adhesive would solve her problem, she sat on the edge of a pedestal and leaned back against a plastic body. She adjusted the mannequin's arms so that it embraced her from behind. It then reached up and tweaked her nipples.

She cried out and drove her elbows back into the solid body. The hard plastic arms bruised the flesh over her ribs as she twisted to get away.

Although his face was frozen in an emotionless, plastic smile, Dwight was immediately recognizable. There was the usual fear but there was also something else—she knew that she belonged to him and that he would have his way.

He whipped a clothes line about her neck, wrestled her to the floor and forced her legs apart. His plastic penis then tore through the crotch of her pants and into soft flesh.

The cord prevented Rachel from screaming as the muscles of her vagina spasmed painfully. His thrusts became inhumanly fast while his smiling face bobbed mechanically. She could not get any air and thrashed out, her back arching in time with his movements, driving him deeper with each thrust.

Then the expression on his face changed and he threw his head back exposing his neck. She tried to reach for the butcher knife under the mattress as he erupted, sending scalding hot, molten plastic into her.

An orgasm burned through her like a lit fuse leading to her brain. Pain exploded in her head and she awoke gasping for air, then screaming as her left hand released the bed sheet wrapped tightly around her neck. Her right hand remained in her crotch, prolonging the orgasm with abusive fingers.

Over the sound of blood rushing through her aching head, Rachel could barely hear Eric pounding on her door, asking if she were all right. Feeling emotionally drained as

well as physically spent, she disentangled herself from the bed sheets and rolled over to prop herself up at the edge of the bed. The mattress bulged beneath her. She reached under it and her hand closed on a handle.

Of course, she thought, laughing hoarsely, *it's the butcher knife.* Dwight had put it under the mattress for a reason and she understood his message.

Someone was talking to Eric out in the hall. "Rachel," he yelled, "I'm gonna break down the door if you don't come and open it."

She didn't have much time. She pulled out the knife, turned it until she could see her reflection. *Just one more inch and the pain will be all gone,* she thought and then drew the blade across her neck with one quick motion. The knife had kept its edge.

Rachel dropped to her bed as she heard a crack and a crash from the front door. Eric and a woman named, Nadia, from the flat upstairs rushed into her bedroom. He stopped short, staring silently while the woman moved to the bed and tried to staunch the flow of blood with a bed sheet. "You'll be all right, honey," Nadia said, reaching for the phone on the night stand and punching numbers.

Rachel remained still, kept her eyes on Eric as Nadia spoke into the telephone. Seeing the tears running down his cheeks, she knew that she loved him. She wanted him to know that their fight had nothing to do with this, that she was no longer angry with him, but it was too late to explain.

"Help is on the way," Nadia said, hanging up the phone. She looked to the open window. "Is that how he got in, Honey?"

Eric broke eye contact with Rachel and looked to Nadia. "Who?"

"The one who attacked her!"

He paused.

Apprehensive, her consciousness fading rapidly, Rachel tried to concentrate her attention on him.

"He's been dead for years," Eric said.

He doesn't blame himself, Rachel thought, relieved. *Eric won't allow me to haunt him.*

Her reservoir of pain rushed out through the one-inch-deep gash in her neck. The darkness reached out and took her.

For the Curiosity of Rats

Jeffrey Osier

I could start by telling you about Monica, the glitter of her skin in the tavernlight the first time I ever saw her and the fool I made of myself—trying not even to impress her but just to find enough interesting things to say to justify standing next to her—and the way she took it all in without ever turning her attention away from her friends or the music or all the things that would have been running through her head had I never walked up to her in the first place. Years later, she could still recite my babblings back to me almost verbatim, while I could no longer remember them at all and even at the time she had barely seemed to notice my existence.

Or I could start by telling you about the first time I saw Gretchen, glistening with blood as she burst into the world and began to scream and would not, could not be consoled, in a voice that seemed to know there was no way ever, ever back into that primordial warmth, and who seemed to have discovered with sudden, precise and all-consuming terror the inevitability of death. They laid her on Monica's belly then and Monica cried and Gretchen stopped crying, and I, like an idiot, cried through itching, sleepless eyes, trusting without knowing why that I was a part of all this: I was Father, I was Coach, I was the Sperminator.

Or I could start instead with a crimson 1991 Ford Tempo. The old man driving it wasn't a drunk or asleep or seizuring; he was just a simple, uncoordinated fool who should never have been given a driver's license in the first place.

"It should have been me," was what Monica kept telling me. "It should have been me walking along the curb."

Three years old. At the low end of the growth curve, she was a very small three years old. It's impossible to impress on you how brilliant she seemed to me—how ingenious

everything that came out of her mouth sounded because of that tiny body, the shrill little voice.

I could start any of a thousand different places in the hope that one would be the perfect place from which to carry you through to the end of the tale, but the truth is . . . the end is *me*, here and now, walking through this tunnel. The end is beside the point, *nothing*. What matters most, beyond all else, the one place I have to start, the one thing you have to see if any of this is to make sense to you, is the potty chair.

We didn't buy it new—we didn't buy it at all. Our down the hall neighbors Bob and Cathy Grimaldi gave it to us when they moved out of the building. They'd trained both of their sons on it, and from the looks of the chipped and buckling varnish, the few wrinkling traces of the decal ornamenting the backboard, they'd inherited it from someone else. I stripped it, stained it mahogany and revarnished it; did an absolutely wretched job with it, but still—more than any of the toddler furniture we ever bought Gretchen—it seemed to fit her, the darkness of the wood reflecting the seriousness in her own manner. She seemed to understand it almost as soon as we set it up for her and, while not committing herself to it, she would sit on it and, by her second birthday, was occasionally making a successful deposit. By her third birthday it was so ingrained a part of her household rituals she no longer even announced she had or was about to use it, merely grabbed a book or magazine, sat herself down and pretended to read.

She had this way of furling her brow with what in an adult might have been called brooding intensity, every time she sat on that chair.

And so, for all the pictures we have of her, taken at weekly or even daily intervals throughout those thirty-nine months, when I first stepped into the bathroom after the service and saw that inch of deep yellow urine in the bowl of the potty chair, the face that imprinted itself into my mind was Gretchen looking troubled and introspective far beyond her years. I turned away, could not bring myself to empty the bowl down the toilet. If I had, none of this would have happened.

The week following the service was a churning, viscous fluid through which we were forced to move at a constant

forward pace. We had no idea where we would be once it was over, only that if we stopped, if we surrendered to despair or exhaustion for even a moment, the churning would pull us under, and once underneath we would never be able to pull ourselves up again. I returned to work, Monica was given an extended leave of absence—four weeks—as though those four weeks would make any kind of difference.

I made an arrogant show of pulling myself back together whenever I came home to Monica. At work I could be as inconsolable as I pleased—there always seemed to be someone who'd yet to offer their condolences, who would let slide a few more days all the work I just couldn't bring myself to focus on yet. But once I got home there was Monica: so much farther gone than I was, of course—she'd been there, had felt Gretchen's hand pulled from her own, had *seen* what could happen to a three-year-old so low on the growth curve, pulled under the wheels of a Ford Tempo. But it didn't matter. I'd held her night after night as she cried, screamed out in anger, quaked and thrashed in pointless god-rage. Now . . . I wanted to see her *pull herself together.* It wasn't that I demanded to be taken care of, that I feared she was losing grip permanently. . . . I really don't know what it was, other than to say that I thought—and I realize how stupid this sounds in retrospect—that I could rouse her out of her depths with an inspirational show of pep and enthusiasm.

And so it was that I found myself, twelve days after my daughter was run over by a car, once again standing in the bathroom doorway eyeing the potty chair and its inch of urine, still not emptied, now filling the apartment with an ammonia reek. I winced as I knelt to the seat and slid out the bowl and began to tilt it over the mother toilet bowl.

"What are you doing?" she cried from the doorway, in a voice so alarmed and so out of character with the brittle wheeze with which she'd spoken to me for nearly two weeks, that I nearly let go of the bowl-handle.

Instead I stood to my full height, betraying, I think, not one bit of shock over her intrusion, and gave her a condescending smile—condescending and, yes, a little bit cruel. "I'm emptying this thing out. I'm cleaning it up and putting it away. What else would I be doing?"

"You can't do that." She would not move, just looked back and forth from my face to the bowl, as though I were holding a gun. "Just . . . put it back where it belongs."

"Monica," I said with the cold, velvety patience, "flushed down the toilet is where it belongs. What's the matter with you?"

"What's the matter with *you?!*" eyes blazing. "I'll take care of this. *I'll* empty it."

"Fine," holding it out for her, handle first. She looked at the contents of the bowl with an expression that at the time was so puzzling . . . not quite longing, not quite revulsion, hunger, confusion, sadness or awe, but a rapid-fire succession of all these and many more.

"Not yet. I'll empty it when I'm ready." I had to take another look at the cloudy yellow pool, as though entranced by her own concentration I would see it too, whatever *it* was.

Instead, I slid the bowl back into place. The fluid seemed to have condensed so thickly that it no longer even splashed, merely murmured and gulped

"Do you mind telling me what's going on? Why are we doing this?"

She wouldn't tell me there, in the bathroom, as though it might hear us.

I won't even begin trying to piece together what she told me then. She paced the floor while I sat on the sofa, occasionally looking at the grandfather clock and telling myself, *there's another hour, there's another hour and a half, there's another* . . . There seemed to be no end to it and yet she would never just come right out and admit that . . . well, what we had here was haunted urine. And yet that was the conclusion she hedged around constantly, always referring to *things* that had been Gretchen's—the clothes and toys we'd bought for her, the drawings she'd done for us—as though they were mere artifacts, devoid of any but the coldest, most anthropological meaning without Gretchen here as their common reference point. But by sitting one last time on that little seat and squirting into the bowl, she'd given us a piece of herself (of excess water and toxins her body could no longer use or afford to hold, I wanted to add) and that in a way she had to make me understand, this was really all we had of her, all we would ever have.

Oh, there were so many things I wanted to say, so many cruel and—at the moment, to me at least—extremely clever retorts I could have shot back to her. And you see, half the time I couldn't even hear what she was telling me because I was so busy congratulating myself for not saying anything in return, because I was really coming up with some funny stuff.

Nothing was resolved. I was burning, but I wasn't going to talk about it. I was going to be *understanding*, something else I was so proud of I was able to pay attention to what was really going on around me.

So I said, "Just remember if we ever invite anyone over here and they want to know why we have a bowl of evaporating urine in the bathroom, you do the explaining," and let it go at that.

"But it *isn't* evaporating. It *won't*." I realize now that she wasn't avoiding my point with her reply. She was convinced of her higher agenda, but at that moment I cared about one thing only: attempting to normalize our lives once again, to reduce Gretchen to a somber but palatable memory to which we could refer at artfully poignant intervals. Is this how I saw it at the time? No. It really was Monica I worried about, or at least the Monica that was half of the formula of: Monica Plus Me. I was convinced that I too was grieving in my own way, and there was something noble in my own persona form of grief and that there was truly something Monica could learn from it. I wanted to help her, help her by convincing her to be more like *me*.

Over the coming weeks I exhibited the kind of stoicism one can usually only find in grand opera, a patience exhibited in thunderous silences and in broad, secretive gestures. I recalled a tenderness that had held us together over those first few days after Gretchen's death, but that had disappeared decisively after our scene over the potty chair, and with every day it remained with us, those bonds between us became drier and more petrified. It did no good to bring *it* up, I no longer even wanted to know how she'd respond. If I'd confronted her again, if I'd gone to our friends, to her doctor, her parents, how different might it all have turned out? Instead I withdrew, and looking back on it now, it must have been me who withdrew the furthest, so that on the day I came home and found the apartment

choking with disinfectant and no trace of the potty chair anywhere and Monica in better spirits than she'd been since before Gretchen's death, I no longer knew how to respond.

A subtle but persistent laughter seemed to lace her every word—neither forced nor uncontrollable, but to me who at least thought I knew her better than anyone in the world, the sign of something much more than contentment, resignation. She seemed genuinely happy. She wanted to touch me, to be near to me, with an urgency that was difficult to adjust to so suddenly. Through those first few hours, I was actually afraid of her. It seemed too fragile to question and yet, after awhile at least too genuine to ignore. So, without ever casting a light on it, without even making a casual remark about it, by evening's end I just more or less accepted this sudden transformation, and if there was too clear a correlation between it and the disappearance of the potty chair I chose not to examine it.

We made love that night and for the first time, she was the more aggressive, the more talkative and more easily satisfied. Every touch, every whisper, perhaps even each light gust of breeze through the open window only made her reel all the more, and yes, I was afraid, but I am a man and these are things a man wants to believe he is capable of doing to a woman so yes, I was perfectly willing to believe that I was the one responsible for her pleasure.

Now I became the one who was unable to talk about Gretchen, while Monica seemed to cast the girl and the experience in a light that seemed almost poetic. I realized that the example I'd tried to set for Monica, this model of grave and mature recovery, had been a sham. Monica had been a willing victim to every nuance of her suffering until the moment it played itself out and she was able to re-enter the world. I was actually a bit shocked at how quickly she seemed to have put that suffering behind her.

But she was infectious.

One thing we had lost by bringing Gretchen into the picture was the freedom to go out together . . . spontaneously. Now we went out constantly. Very often, traffic on the north side was so bad that we'd go out to dinner or to a show via the subway, as we had years ago, in the days when we'd never had the money to indulge ourselves the way we were now. Usually, it was Monica's idea. I'd come

home or she'd call me at work or she'd wake me up late on a Sunday morning, and announce she'd just ordered tickets to a concert or a play, or she'd announce she wanted to see a movie and how soon could I be ready?

We went to a movie tonight, in fact. It ended less than ninety minutes ago and I can't recall a single thing about it. But we were there, seated in the center of the row, when, halfway through a series of trailers, Monica had to go to the washroom. She made it to the aisle when she turned and called out for me to bring her her purse. Monica has never been one to talk in movie theaters, not even under her breath, not even during the trailers. So it was the act itself, even more than the traces of panic in her voice, that drew my attention to the tense geography here; her in the aisle, me in the center seat and her purse separated from her not only by my body but the bodies of a half a dozen other people. I looked at her, I looked at the purse, a large crumpled thing next to me, and I looked back at her, choking back this horrid curiosity and I motioned silently to her: don't worry about it . . . I'd look after it. She lingered for a moment and then slowly turned and walked up the aisle.

She was probably angry because she'd realized I was embarrassed over her breach of theater etiquette, when in fact there was probably something in her purse she needed or at least wanted while in the washroom. I grabbed the purse and was about to get up and go after her and then thought better: if she really needed it, she'd have insisted on it. And besides, she was probably in there already, and there I'd be, standing like a fool outside the Ladies Room holding a purse. This appears to be one of the key contingencies of my life—when all other deciding factors are equal, avoiding the potential for embarrassment will determine my actions.

I set the purse in the seat and did not take my hand away. It was a soft, plush leather and I liked the way it felt, liked the delicate, fleshlike quality it gave to the contours of the contents within. I poked my fingers along the outside, trying to guess the identity of the underlying shapes. Book, gum, lipstick, contact case, eyedrops, set of jeweler's screwdrivers . . . and something else, a jarlike cylinder. Now what could this be?

Rather than try to guess the nature of this object, I opened the purse and pulled it out and held it up to the screen-light. It was clear plastic with a blue lid, and looked to me like a hospital specimen jar. Inside, darkening, fogging, warping the face of an actor on the screen, was a thick amber-colored fluid, almost viscous as I tilted it.

Monica showed up just as the film was beginning, apologized to everyone she had to step over and then offered me a cute, clipped "Hi" as she stepped over me and sat, pulling her purse onto her lap. I must have said something back to her, something innocuous because I refused to behave any other way, and yet, the last thing she said to me before the opening music began was "What's the matter?" I shook my head and smiled. "Nothing."

And then I kissed her, an empty, reassuring kiss on the cheek. I thought of Gretchen, who never tired of kissing me on my cheek, and who had been the main reason I'd shaved every day, even on weekends.

Throughout the movie I was distracted by my own thoughts, which were so conflicting and deafening that I wondered how anyone in this or any of the five adjoining theaters could possibly pay attention to anything other than me.

Evidently Monica enjoyed the movie. She laughed and gasped on all the right cues and hardly ever fidgeted in her seat. I couldn't even focus on the screen, follow the dialogue or hear the music as anything more than an annoying cacophony. The one thing I kept turning back to, the single image of that whole moviegoing experience that I will always remember is the sight of Monica, clutching that soft, plush purse to her stomach, one hand gently caressing an unmistakable contour, her eyes on the screen—and yet not precisely: glassy, far away, so very happy to be here and not so alone as she would have been had she only been here with me. Because there were three of us seated in these two seats: Monica, me, and whatever radiance resulted from the conjunction of her mind and that jar of fluid.

When she finally turned to me it wasn't to smile with recognition or to acknowledge the fact that I was looking at her. I'm sure it was because she could hear me grinding my teeth. She flashed me the what's-the-matter smile, and

when I made no response, the smile faded, and she shrugged, returning her attention to the screen, to her purse. To the *third*.

Finally I got up and went to the lobby. I did not go back. I bought a box of Snowcaps, sat on one of the lobby benches and attempted to read the coming attractions pamphlet.

"Jeez, did you really hate it that much?" she asked when she plopped down beside me afterwards. She smiled and nudged me with a kind of a hey-snap-out-of-it-playfulness. I stood and started to walk away. "Come on," I said coldly. Her gaze was perplexed and hurt, and for an instant I decided to give in, to put my arm around her and tell her, yeah, it was just the movie, nothing more. But by the time we were out on the street, I was back in character.

It was late and the fact that we saw a train puling away from the subway stop as we descended the stairs meant there wouldn't be another for quite some time. And the fact that it was a Sunday meant it would be a lonely wait. But it would not be a quiet one. My silence during the entire walk was wearing thin.

We were standing by a pillar, and I was staring up at a semicircular arrangement of limestone stalactites on the concrete above us. They looked like tiny fingers.

"Are you going to tell me what's wrong, Vincent, or am I supposed to guess?"

I didn't look at her. "You know what's wrong. You know exactly what I'm thinking."

"Is that right?" She was trying to sound incredulous. *Nice try, Monica.* I could already hear it in her voice. She knew I knew. How long was she going to try and stonewall me?

I did look at her now. "Yes. You do." Our eyes locked and in that silence, we traded confessions, both knowing that once confessed, any break in that silence would be total, terminal.

A roaring filled the tunnel as a train going in the opposite direction pulled into the station. Doors clattered open, maybe people got off the train . . . I don't know. It was underneath the rumble of that train pulling out of the station that Monica finally said something.

"What?" I demanded, not meaning to make it sound so harsh . . . Or was I?

"I said, congratulations, Vincent. Were you looking for anything in particular, or was it just a sudden inspiration? I was wondering when you'd go rummaging through my things and find it. So now you know. What are you going to do?"

"I'm not sure." I was stalking her now, pacing the platform, moving around behind her, but she did not turn with me. "I should demand that you get rid of it."

"Why?"

"Or at least stop carrying it around in your fucking purse! Don't you realize how—"

"What?! How *disgusting* it is? Let me guess, Vincent. You think I'm deranged and first thing in the morning you're going to call my doctor, my mother. . . . Let's see, who else can we call? My friends? Too bad we're not religious. I'm sure a minister would have a field day with me. Well . . . let me tell you how it's going to be. I'm not giving *her* up."

"Her? *Her!?*"

"Yes, her. I figured you'd think I was crazy. I knew if I sat you down, tried to make you see how it is . . . how it could be, you'd fly off the handle. You'd refuse to even *try* to understand."

"So you figured it was better to just keep it a secret."

"I figured that if all it was going to get me was an edict from you, then it wasn't worth consulting you."

"Not worth consulting me?"

"Vincent . . . your Gretchen is dead. You stopped being her father the moment that car hit her. But I'm still her mother, and she's still my daughter, and everything we ever had between the two of us until right this moment and every moment for the rest of my life . . . is *ours*—mine and hers. And you either accept it or get the hell away from us."

I halted directly in front of her. "How can you talk that way to me? What have I ever done to deserve that? I'm not the one who . . ." I threw my hands up, exasperated, spun about as though I was going to start pacing again and then turned as though I were going to charge her. She backed away, dangerously close to the platform's edge. "No . . . wait. Okay." I took a breath. "Let me start over again—"

"Jesus, Vincent. Are you going to get violent with me?"

"No, listen. Please . . . go ahead. Tell me how it is. Monica . . . don't talk about me getting away from you. I'll listen. I swear I will."

She lowered her eyes, unzipped her purse and looked inside, unsure whether it was really safe to bring out the jar in this cavernous public place.

"You know what I've always really disliked about you, Vincent? I can't stand this self-congratulatory air of yours, all this *hey, aren't I a great guy, aren't I nice to her, and isn't it modest of me to bring it up as seldom as I do?* If I show you this . . . if I tell you everything I can about what this means to me, if I tell you why I will never, ever give this up, and you stand there quietly . . . how do I know you really understand me? How do I know that what you're really doing isn't just nodding sympathetically, and all the while telling yourself on the inside that it's really a fine thing for you to be standing here humoring your crazy wife?"

I thought of the night we'd argued whether to empty and put away the potty chair. "Okay. Maybe I deserve that."

"Vincent . . . if I talk to my daughter, if I spend an hour a day talking to her, if I can feel that she can hear me, if I possess a line that gives me access to her, does it matter if no one else can understand that access? That as long as I know that wherever she is, whatever it must be like for my baby . . . that I can make her happy by talking to her? Does it? I mean, the gist of everything anybody tells me is: *you're supposed to have been miserable, you're supposed to learn to be philosophical about it and get on with your life.* That's fine . . . for them . . . for you. But am I kidding myself if I know that I don't have to be miserable, I don't have to let go, and that it doesn't matter if everybody in the world believes I'm kidding myself or just cracking up?" She pulled the jar out of her purse, holding its base with one hand, the fingers of her other hand glancing the curves *so delicately.*

I couldn't stand it. I tried to step near her as slowly and as unassumingly as I could, but the moment I was within reach, I grabbed the jar. We were both holding it now, but her grip was tight, as desperate as mine. What triggered my reaction? I wasn't even thinking of it at the time, but

looking back at it now, I'm sure it was the gentleness of her touch on that plastic, that appalling transference, the delusion. If I struck out at it, surely I could stop it, burst it like a membrane.

"Let go," she hissed, looking around for help, but there was no one else on that platform.

"I won't. Damn you, Monica. I want you back. If Gretchen's gone, *she's gone.* But I'm still here!"

She tried to pull away from me, her expression aghast and then creased with disgust.

"Is that what you want? An ultimatum? If I want to keep you, I have to give up the one last piece I have of my daughter? If I find solace or maybe even—go ahead and call me crazy for saying it!—a lifeline to her in something you find personally distasteful, I'm suppose to give you up? Is that your masterful solution to all my pain?" She telegraphed her attempt to yank it out of my hands, and in that moment's windup, I yanked it away from her.

"Or it is just your way of taking control of something you have no right to take any control of? Give me that back right now!"

"No." There was a roaring in the distance. Our train.

"You asshole. You spoiled son-of-a-bitch. Hurray! You weren't a totally inept father! Congratulations! You could take care of yourself well enough to survive even though I had a daughter to look after! Jesus, I think you're glad she's gone and the only thing standing in the way of you being really happy is the fact that I've had the gall to grieve for my baby and that having something to remember her by makes me happier than having the privilege of sleeping next to you every night!"

I'd been staring into those strange, milky yellow depths as she spoke. Was there something . . . happening in there? As soon as Monica stopped talking I turned on her again. "Shut up! You just . . . shut the fuck up. Is that how I figure into this fantasy world of yours? Something *this* gives you the stomach to tolerate? Well, thank you so fucking much, Monica! It's been a great seven years, hasn't it?" I was shouting now. Any moment now the light would round that last bend out of the tunnel of darkness.

"Give her back to me, you bastard!" She burst into tears. "I hate you!" She lunged at me and I pushed her back-

wards. She screamed something else to me but I could no longer hear her over the roar of the train. But it didn't take much imagination to read the sentiments behind the rage on her face.

So much uninhibited loathing could not go without retaliation.

I could feel the train at my back, and I could feel the jar in my hand. What I did not feel was the casual backhanded toss—the jar onto the tracks just as I looked at her calmly, as cold as I have ever looked at anyone in my entire life. She leaped at the platform's edge, but I grabbed her in my arms as the train roared into the station, only inches away from my back.

And then she screamed—in my face, at the ceiling, at the train—while her limbs fell into a trembling fit, and her eyes, suddenly so old and so raw, turned to that spot where she'd seen the jar disappear onto the tracks. Now there was only the train, the dulling metallic glare, the smeared glass, a dozen tired, indifferent faces behind that glass, their eyes directed towards the hysterical woman and the man clutching her.

"Monica, Monica," I pleaded, but at the sound of my voice, the trembling lowered into a shiver of revulsion and she pushed away from me. And her face . . . it was no longer anger, no longer hatred, just the horror of a loss that has suddenly bloated to encompass anything in the world that could possibly mean anything to her. She pushed once and then went limp in my arms. If I let go, would she be able to stand on her own? Everything was happening so quickly. "I'm sorry. I didn't mean that."

And then came the moaning, soft and unstoppable, as her eyes peeled even wider and yet seemed to see nothing at all.

The train doors creaked open.

"Monica . . ." I whispered into her ear and then pushed her softly, gently, through the doorway of the train. She didn't look at me until the doors shut between us and I could no longer hear her moaning. She stared at me through the glass the way any woman lost in soul-killing despair would look at a total stranger who just happened to catch her eye.

Except that as the train pulled away, she continued to

stare at me, as I continued to stare at her until she was out of my range of vision. And then the train was gone. And then, I could no longer even hear it.

I looked down at the tracks. There, by the third rail, was the blue lid to the jar. But there was no sign of the jar itself. And as I looked at that blue lid, a rat appeared, hair wet and matted into a chaos of spikes, sniffing at the lid and the ground around it, as though it were just one more piece of interesting garbage there only to occupy a moment of its curiosity.

"Hey!" I hollered. "Get away from that! *Scat!!*"

It ignored me, but it did not ignore the lid, which it continued to sniff, at one point climbing on the top of it, perching as it stared blankly at me.

"Get away!" I screamed. It did not move.

So I jumped off the platform, onto the tracks. Reluctantly, the rat scurried off, in the direction of the next oncoming train. It was late on a Sunday night, and that next train would probably be awhile in coming. So I followed the rat, towards the tunnel darkness at the station's edge.

And that's the end. Thinking on it now, when that plastic hit the tracks, or the train, it was I who should have disappeared, I who should have been crushed out of existence. Does this make any sense to you? I can't make sense of any other outcome.

And yet . . . I'm still here. In the darkness of the tunnel, listening for a train, looking for a sign of a tiny rat, or perhaps something else. Gretchen? Part of me knows beyond any doubt that this tunnel will continue to widen, to darken, that the foul odors and trash will diminish and disappear and that I will fade cell by cell into a quiet, gentle oblivion. And yet another part of me knows that I have only one of two options: either I will arrive at the next station and climb onto the platform, or else a train will come before I get there and I will have to stretch myself against the wall to escape its reach.

But the bigger part of me can think of only Monica and Gretchen. Monica homeward bound on a train without me, perhaps so lost she will never know when to get off or what to do once she does. Or perhaps free at last of my smothering demands for attention, for primacy. Gretchen some-

how far closer to me now than ever before: these tunnels always smell of urine, and yet now, in the wake of my casual act of destruction, all I can smell is her, the sweetness of her skin, her talc and especially baby shampoo. It is almost as though every step is just one step closer to hearing her laugh or seeing the glint of her barrette bobbing through the darkness or calling out to me, that word I will never hear myself called again: "Daddy." So I say the word out loud. And then, just once, in a louder, more desperate voice, I call out her name, just to bask in the luxury of dreaming that there is someone here to respond.

There's that rat again. How at ease the rats are down here, how luxurious the contours of all this rubbish must be, baptized by that last remaining residue of Gretchen's life. I need to confront it and yet I have no idea what I'm supposed to do once I do confront it. I have *never* had any idea what I'm supposed to do.

Fatherhood is such an incredible sham, isn't it? Unless it's men like me who dictate the rules, a man can do absolutely nothing for a child that a woman can't do just as well, not to mention all the things that a woman is to her child for which the father has nothing comparable nor even analogous. A father is no more than a lifetime of fatherly acts, and you don't have to look far to see the bleakness, the ugliness and pointlessness of what passes for fatherly acts in this world. And what constitutes a lifetime anyway? *Three years?* I changed quite a few diapers in those three years, and it was I who heard the click of the spoon against that first tooth, who saw Gretchen step away from the chair and take those first independent steps. But what was that? Nothing a babysitter couldn't have witnessed. And yet, I was so proud of myself for being there for those moments. No that's not quite right—proud that it was me there instead of Monica. Proud that I could claim territorial rights to those moments.

When I was a boy I reveled in destruction, in fire and hammers splintering wood and news footage of dynamited buildings and in fantasies of pounding on the children whom I did not like. I grew to manhood so proud that I had eliminated or at least suppressed these desires, impulses . . . these *interests.* *I* was not a destroyer, I was not a war wager, a murderer, a wife beater, a child molester, all

those myriad things that boys can become. And yet, what's the use of having pride in not being something horrible, as though moral behavior were something that really had to be aspired to? In the end, I destroyed Monica, so proud and so insulted and so demanding that it could not possibly occur to me that there was anything horrible in what I did to her, in what I did to the most tangible attachment she still had to Gretchen, all because I found it so distasteful, so embarrassing, such a distraction from what was truly important—ME.

For in the end, I am no different from those monsters who reduce cites to rubble and the innocent to charred bone, no different from the lesser monsters who've pissed and vomited onto these tracks, dumped their trash and obscured every effort to aspire heavenward that has ever occurred to the human race, reducing it all to nothing more than undifferentiated piles of rubbish whose only lasting purpose is to provide a landscape for the curiosity of rats.

The Stranger Who Sits Beside Me

Yvonne Navarro

SEPTEMBER:

"Excuse me—what are you doing?"

For a moment the young woman on the other side of Lyle Garrett's truck stared at him in confusion. The swimming pool blue of the hood that separated them reflected the strong, sunlight blazing from the west, making it harsher and brighter, sending sharp twinkles of light bouncing off the edges and blinding him in spots. Instead of answering his question, she moved slightly to the right in his field of vision, a small step backwards that put her behind the frame of the door and sent more pinpoints of glaring light spiking into his eyes as he tried to follow her movement. He blinked and rubbed his eyelids quickly, and she was gone when he looked again.

Lyle thought about her briefly on the way home, idle curiosity while he waited for the stoplights to change to green during the eight-minute drive. He could walk the distance—probably should, in fact—but it was so much faster to just hop in the Montero and drive. Cathy had her own car, a black Dodge Caravan that she used to get around in and for chauffeuring the kids. His mind returned to the image of that woman again, nagging at him the same way the thought *Did I leave the iron on?* does, even though you know you shut the damned thing off. The way she'd looked standing next to the hood—make that the *door*—of the Montero, as though she'd been expecting him to unlock it so she could climb in, like it was the most natural thing in the world for him—*them*—to do. Strange. He remembered her taking the seat next to him on the commuter train, had felt with a sort of inbred city instinct the subtle appraisal she'd given him after the initial glance. He wasn't looking for anything, not even conversation, so Lyle had

215

kept his gaze firmly trained on his paper, politely ignoring the fact that her study of him, tactful as she kept it, made him feel vaguely ill at ease. Not that much though; thinking back on it, somewhere around the Bensenville stop he'd become engrossed in an article on the uproar over the exams for Chicago firemen and forgotten about her . . . until, of course, she'd followed him off the train and to his truck.

He saw the curtain in his living room window flutter as he pulled into the driveway of his home and got out; less than thirty seconds later his youngest daughter, Kasey, hurtled down the front steps like a miniature tornado.

"Daddy!" Her four-year-old voice was more a shriek than words, but Kasey was the last of five children and Lyle sincerely believed that his eardrums had finally mutated to adapt to the higher pitches of kidtalk. Now he grinned and dropped his briefcase as Kasey catapulted herself from the too-high bottom step of the front porch and in his direction, never doubting he would be there to catch her. It was a routine that had been fine-tuned over the months of summer and now, as the cottonwood tree next door began to shed its dried-out leaves into Lyle's yard, he plucked Kasey out of mid-air by simple reflex.

"You smell funny," he told her as he gave her a bear hug. "What gives?"

Kasey wrinkled her nose, a cute little twisting that reminded Lyle of Elizabeth Montgomery and the old *Bewitched* reruns. "Mommy made me wash the mirrored doors in your bedroom with vinegar water," she confided. "It was *very* nasty."

"I see." Lyle hung onto her with one arm while he bent and retrieved his briefcase with the other. As he climbed the front stoop, her hair, soft and still that special childhood shade of platinum, tickled his cheek and filled his nostrils with the scent of baby powder, despite the smell of vinegar still hanging on her fingers. "And why would she make you do such a thing?"

"I don't know."

"Do you really not know or are you fibbing to me?" He tried to look severe but it was difficult; at four, Kasey didn't yet understand that a "fib" was the precursor to a lie. Confronted, she usually told the truth.

"I guess I got some fingerprints on them," she admitted reluctantly. "But she's not mad at me 'cause I cleaned them off." Her little brown eyes, the color of paper grocery bags, were wide. "Are you?"

Lyle squeezed her slightly. "Of course not—but only because you cleaned up after yourself. Your mommy's not your maid, you know." Kasey nodded solemnly then giggled as he carried her inside and dropped her lightly onto the over-stuffed couch. In another instant, she streaked away, down the hallway and towards her own room and whatever games would hold her attention for the next twenty minutes. Good luck, Lyle thought wryly.

"Cathy?" he called aloud. There was no answer and he headed for their bedroom, where he shrugged off his jacket gratefully, then took off his tie and shoes. The tang of vinegar filled the air and when he looked, Lyle saw that if the mirror had been full of fingerprints before Kasey's "cleaning," it was now a myriad pattern of whitish streaks. He had to laugh.

"What's so funny?"

Lyle smiled at his wife of nearly eighteen years and pointed to the closet doors. "Housekeeper in training."

Cathy glanced at the doors and chuckled. Her face pink along her cheekbones and on the end of her nose, evidence of several hours in the garden this week. Her hair, a lush dark brown, was pulled up in a wispy bun, a vain attempt to keep cool. Although she refused to wear a hat, the sun never succeeded in lightening her hair, just making her swelter under its nearly black halo. "Well," she said now, "Kasey gave it a shot, anyway. Maybe she'll learn to think twice about where she puts those grubby little hands."

Lyle snickered. "Yeah, in about ten more years."

"A dream is a dream," Cathy said in a deadpan voice. She couldn't hold it though and finally broke into a grin. "How was your day?" She came over and began unbuttoning his shirt for him, her fingers skittering swiftly along the vertical row of buttons.

"Okay, I suppose. Nothing spectacular."

She raised her eyebrows and her eyes, that same paper bag tan as Kasey's, sparkled mischievously. "Oh? Care to spice things up a little?"

"You better be careful," Lyle warned. "I might decide to take you up on your hint."

"Let's go for it."

Cathy's hands moved to his belt and Lyle's mouth dropped open. "What about the kids?" he asked in surprise.

"Kasey's nearly asleep, Brett's at band practice, and the rest of 'em won't be home for another hour. Care to put your money where your mouth is?"

"No." Lyle grinned. "But I'll put my mouth in a few other spots."

"Oooh," she teased, "I *love* it when you talk dirty!"

Lyle rolled his eyes. "Now *there's* an original line." Five more seconds and Lyle forgot the woman on the train ever existed.

OCTOBER

"Good morning."

Lyle glanced up from his paper and nodded absently then looked back down and tried to focus on the newsprint swimming in front of his eyes. It was the same woman, he was sure of it. When had she started sitting next to him every day? This month? Or last? He couldn't be sure; it'd just *happened.* She never explained that incident in the parking lot . . . if it had ever happened at all. He was no longer sure; he'd been too uneasy to ask and she'd never said anything; he'd begun to think he'd imagined the whole scene, some sort of sun-induced mirage on that particularly bright day. This . . . "partnering" on the train had evolved into a routine, the same schedule, the same seat, day in and day out. It had never occurred to Lyle to sit somewhere else, take a different train, or be unaccountably rude by blocking the seat beside him with his briefcase. It just wasn't his way. He let his gaze drift up from the newspaper until it found the window and the fall landscape whipping by at sixty-plus miles an hour; the trees were changing already, dropping their leaves at a frantic pace and signaling an early, harsh winter. The woman beside him said nothing else and Lyle moved his eyes to the right, trying to use his peripheral vision to see what she looked like. No use; every time he tried this—every *day*—everything above her shoulders seemed to fade in a sort of moving, wet haze, like

smoke-dirtied fog. Once he thought he'd glimpsed dark hair, black like Cathy's, but he couldn't be sure. It was an anomaly that worked at his mind all the time because he knew it couldn't be. He knew, too, that he was the only one who saw it and thus couldn't ask for another's opinion. He *did* see this . . . didn't he?

Thinking of Cathy made him frown outright. The two seemed to be oddly intertwined in his mind, as if he were having an affair with the stranger who sat beside him every day. A ridiculous thought . . . no, not ridiculous. *Frightening.* At times.

At others it seemed the most natural thing in the world, as though something had been going on between them for years, too many to think about, second nature. He couldn't have said what that something was, though, only that it *wasn't.* Not an affair, a tawdry, sneaky series of late night motel rooms or lunch hour gropings, never that. Rather, something automatic, intuitive, unquestionable.

Lyle blinked and brought his thoughts back around. Something about Cathy bothered him these days, or rather, something was bothering *her.* She seemed . . . distant somehow, slightly removed from him and the kids, vaguely unreachable. The kids didn't seem to notice, everything was fine and busy, and in the full swing of the school year with thoughts of Christmas and what-am-I-going-to-get-this-year already starting to pop up at odd times. As she did every year, Cathy was working on Halloween costumes for the youngest ones. This year, only two qualified: Kasey wanted to be a pumpkin, so Cathy had devised this puffy orange cotton thing that would be soft-stuffed with wads of tissue paper. At eight Bobby was ready for his fireman's costume, but the one Brett had worn four or five years earlier didn't fit; Bobby would be slender like his mother where Brett had the stockier build of a linebacker. No one but Lyle seemed to notice that Cathy's stitches had lost most of the careful quality of previous years, but what could he say to her? *Gee, sweetheart, that pumpkin doesn't look sewn together as nicely as the Cabbage Patch doll outfit you made for Kasey last year. What gives?* Now there was a surefire way to start the evening with a flash of real Irish temper.

Lyle rubbed his eyes abruptly and saw the Roselle train stop flash by the window, folded his paper and pulled his

ticket out of the holder and tucked it into his wallet. The woman next to him did the same without touching him or trying to make further conversation, and for that Lyle was grateful. When he glanced at her from the corner of his eye, he realized she was working on a needlepoint sampler, the hobby kind that Cathy had made right after they were first married and she was just discovering she had a flair for needlework. The other passenger in the seat wasn't as lucky as his wife had been; after watching Cathy sew for nearly twenty years, it was easy to see this woman was struggling mightily just to keep the thread from twisting below the needle. God knew what she'd do to a real piece of clothing.

"Our stop's coming up," he commented. Whatever muddy shadow had screwed up his eyes was gone, finally, and he could see the stranger beside him clearly now. She looked vaguely like his wife, in a smaller, less robust sort of way.

Lyle didn't know why he felt compelled to remind her, but she smiled at him in response and nodded, began to carefully pack away the hobby kit. "Lost track of the time," she confided. He gave a nod of his own but said nothing else and she turned her attention back to her canvas tote bag and the mini-skeins of embroidery thread. By the time the commuter train rolled into the Schaumburg station, they were both standing in the aisle.

It was raining heavily and while the woman snapped open an umbrella, Lyle was forced to run through the downpour for the Montero. He'd gotten a decent spot that morning so his journey was only ten seconds, fifteen at the most. The Montero had a nifty little electronic lock release and he was inside with barely a hitch, but it made no difference; the rain had been so heavy, he was soaked right through his suit jacket and shirt. Even his keys were wet and he patiently dried the ignition key using a tissue after wiping his glasses. Pulling out of the parking lot was a pain in the neck, bumper to bumper vehicles inching along the slick roadway, their drivers apparently convinced anything over five miles an hour on wet pavement would result in a spin. It took damned near five minutes just to make it to the 53 underpass, with another four blocks and two stop-lights to go before he reached the turn at Irving Park. At

least the water noise decreased under the protection of the bridge. He felt sorry for the people who walked rather than drove and who now waited, looking like sorry, bedraggled puppies, for the rain to let up. One of them, Lyle saw, was his seat partner. His eyes locked with hers briefly and he tapped his fingers against the steering wheel indecisively. Should he give her a ride? He felt like he should, he knew her, sort of, sat next to her every morning and evening. She would do the same for him, surely. Another hesitation, shorter-lived, and he hit the switch to lower the passenger side window and motioned to her.

"Climb in!" The torrent of rain was now punctuated by thunder and he had to shout to be heard. "I can give you a ride home, if you like." How far could she live, he reasoned, if she walked to and from the train?

Her smile was bright despite the rivulets of water running down the sides of her face. Poor thing, her black hair was plastered to her skull, and the short fall jacket she wore looked about as comfortable as a wet wool sponge. She was inside the Montero in an instant, pulling the door closed and snapping the seatbelt in place almost simultaneously. The movements were so efficient it was obvious she was familiar with Mitsubishi's truck style.

"Thanks," she said. "I was afraid you wouldn't offer."

"Of course I would," he said. As soon as the words were out, he knew they made no sense. What was he talking about? It wasn't at all like him to give a ride to a stranger. All you had to do was read the paper to know that killers came in both sexes and any age. "Where to?" he asked to cover his nervousness.

"Irving and Olde Salem is close enough," she responded.

Lyle stopped himself before he could say, "That's close to my house." First, she sits with him every day, then he gives her a ride home. What next? Rain trickled out of his hair and onto the back of his neck, spreading a chill as it slipped beneath the gap of his shirt collar and down the knobs of his spine. Jesus, he thought in disgust, I'm watching too many murder movies. "I'm Lyle," he said just to make small talk. "What's your name?"

"Kathe." Voice soft, she was looking out the window at the downpour and didn't see his shocked look.

"Cathy?" he asked in bewilderment.

"K-a-t-h-e."

"Ah." He could think of nothing else to say. They were headed west on Irving now, finally moving at something other than a worm's crawl. Silence settled between them but it wasn't uncomfortable, just oddly . . . restful. Rather than stall traffic by stopping on Irving, Lyle took the turn onto Old Salem and coasted the quarter block to White-bridge before pulling over. The force of the rain had slowed, but it was still coming down. "Are you sure I can't just take you home?" he asked.

"No, but thanks." Kathe gave him a small smile. "And I really appreciate the ride. My car wouldn't start this morning—darn thing's always giving me trouble."

"My wife has a Dodge Caravan. She's real happy with it." Now why had he said that?

"Really?" She smiled again and looked away slightly. When her eyes came back to his, they were clear. "I'll keep that in mind. Thanks again."

A slam of the passenger side door and she was gone. He stared after her, troubled. There was something about her, a familiarity that he couldn't put his finger on—

He jumped at the bleating of a horn behind the Montero. Glancing automatically in his rearview mirror made him jerk. Cathy's van was behind him. She and Kasey waved from the front seat and Cathy made a motion with her left hand that he instantly understood: *I'll meet you at the house.* He nodded and waved again, put the Montero in DRIVE and took a sharp left onto Whitebridge after check-ing his side mirror. Cathy followed, and when Lyle checked his rear mirror again, he caught a glimpse of the other Kathe, umbrella closed, walking in the rain back the way they'd come.

"Daddy, who was the lady in the truck with you?" Leave it to Kasey to ask the million-dollar question, Lyle thought wryly. Out of the mouth of babes and all that crap. Why did he feel so guilty? He could feel Cathy intentionally *not* looking at him from across the kitchen; did she really think he'd cheat on her? Be serious; he loved this woman more than life.

"Someone in the train station whose car wouldn't start, pumpkin. And you know what?"

"What?"

"She had the same name as your mommy but spelled differently." He grinned at his daughter and winked, let his glance slide over to Cathy. "And she wasn't as pretty." Kasey giggled and tried to wink back, succeeded only in scrunching her face up on one side; Lyle saw Cathy smile to herself and sneak a look in his direction. He smiled back and tickled his daughter's side, laughed out loud at her shout of surprise.

Inside, his head was spinning.

Kathe wasn't as pretty as Cathy, not at all.

Was she?

"Thanks for the ride last night. I really appreciated it."

Lyle studied Kathe thoughtfully for a moment before speaking. "No problem. Funny thing, though," he said slowly, "I could have sworn I saw you going back the other way after I let you out."

Kathe nodded without hesitation. "Yeah, I remembered something I had to pick up at Menard's. That's why I asked you to let me off there. By the time I got out of the store, the rain had let up."

"I see." Such an obvious explanation, he felt like a fool for bringing it up. Should he ask her about her car? Never mind; it was none of his business. "Well, I'm glad I could help out."

She nodded again and he unfolded his paper, starting with the sports section like he always did. Beside him, Kathe pulled out her needlepoint and spread it carefully on her lap, then began working on the small circle of linen. Out of the corner of his eye, Lyle could see her movements, slow and meticulous, precise despite the unpredictable rocking of the train. She must have practiced last night; there was a marked improvement in the stitches that made up the pattern, some kind of stained-glass thing that reminded him of the charms the Pennsylvania Dutch painted on everything to bring prosperity. The way he was peaking at her made him feel a little like a voyeur; God knew he hated it when people read over his shoulder, but he couldn't help himself now. The difference between the work she was doing and how it had been when she'd begun the project was startling.

"My wife sews." It was such a lame thing to say, he couldn't believe the words had actually come from his own mouth.

"Does she." Kathe paused for a second to look over at him, then resumed her work. "What kind of sewing does she do?"

Lyle shrugged, feeling more inane than before. "Clothes, curtains, you know. That kind of stuff."

"Me, too."

Lyle opened his mouth, then shut it. He'd been about to say *but your sewing wasn't that good until today.* Not the most tactful observation. "Do you have children?" he asked instead.

She shook her head and smiled. "Not yet. But I'd like to have a lot. Do you?"

"Five—three boys and two girls."

"Wow," Kathe said admiringly. "That's quite a family. Do you have pictures of them?"

"Sure. It's a required thing." Lyle pulled out his wallet and flipped it open. How many times had he performed that simple motion over the last two decades? Thousands. He slipped the latest family photo from its slot and handed it to her.

"Wow," Kathe said again. "Look at all these kids! What are their names?"

"Kasey, Bobby, Brett, Liam and Catlin," he answered, pointing with his finger as he went.

"Twins!"

He chuckled. "Yeah, they were quite a surprise to Cathy and I, too."

"Kathe?"

"Cathy with a 'C' and a 'Y'."

Kathe peered at the photo once more before handing it back. "Very nice," she commented. "Your wife looks like she's pretty, but the photographer could have done a better job focusing on her."

Lyle smiled in response and said nothing. What did that mean? The photograph was perfect, taken only four months ago on one of those package deals from Sears. Kathe bent back to her sewing and he tucked the photo carefully back into its pocket, then paused and inspected it more closely. It *was* blurry in its upper right quadrant; Cathy's face was

soft around the edges and vaguely fuzzy, as though she were the only subject who'd been shot using a romantic, soft-focus lens. It might have been pretty except it had gone just a shade too far; she was barely recognizable.

They'd picked this photo out of the proofs together, even had a framed fourteen by ten in the front hallway. Why hadn't they ever noticed this before?

Lyle had a dream that night that Cathy was changing somehow, *diffusing*. Fading away at the edges like her picture in their family photograph, until his dreamself swore he could see right through the outer edges of her to the rest of the world beyond. All of the kids were there, popping in and out in that fragmented way that people have of making their presence known in a dream, but no one ever said anything about Cathy or complained or questioned the way she looked. Soon Lyle became convinced that it wasn't a dream at all, but reality, and no matter how he struggled he found he was physically incapable of broaching the subject. It was the fear that stopped him, a black voice inside his head that said it was only *him* believing this, the situation existed only in *his* mind, and did he dare reveal his strange delusions to anyone else? So he didn't, just sat at a table across from his wife and in the middle of a room full of blue sky that looked as if Magritte had been the architect, sat and watched his wife melt away at her edges.

He woke in the morning with a small but audible cry of relief. The shower in the master bath was already running, and when he walked into the steamy bathroom, he found Cathy standing in front of the fogged-up mirror, clawing at it with her fingers as though she were trying to get at something hidden behind the layer of condensation.

When he asked her what she was doing, she looked at him blankly and said, "I'm putting on my make-up, of course."

Of course.

DECEMBER

Christmas in a family with five children was the biggest project of the year. In the eyes of the children, it eclipsed everything else in importance, birthdays, school parties, even summer vacation. He didn't know why, but Lyle had

traditionally been an unconversational train person, not rude, but not particularly interested in carrying on daily dialogue with a fellow rider. But all that had changed since the afternoon he'd given Kathe the ride to Menard's. The train ride on the way to work each day had become a morning report of the events of the night before, with Monday's a.m. account going at the verbal equivalent of 78 r.p.m. so he could describe all the events of the weekend before the train pulled into Union Station downtown. The evening ride had evolved into a quieter, gentler routine, a soothing forty-five minutes of recovery for both he and Kathe after a day of hard work. Lyle considered it wise that he said nothing to Cathy about Kathe, and he assumed that Kathe followed the same routine in her life. He knew little about her and the time or two that he'd asked, she'd given vague answers that led him to believe that whatever the details were, they weren't very happy. Propriety wouldn't allow him to snoop; he let it be known that he was there if she wanted to talk, but she never did.

Dealing with Cathy was becoming more difficult with each passing week but Lyle didn't know why. He felt guilty about Kathe, but, again, he didn't know why; he and Kathe had conversation, not a vulgar affair, and nothing about the two of them seemed inclined to move towards anything else. As the holiday grew nearer, Lyle wondered why the children didn't notice the change in their mother, but not one said anything. Kasey was the most likely candidate to speak up, but Lyle's careful questions were met with uncomprehending looks that made him so uncomfortable he couldn't help but remember that awful dream of two months ago and the fear he'd felt in it, the terror of losing his mind while being convinced the whole time that it was the rest of the world that was crazy.

And wasn't he freaking just a bit? After all, nothing about Cathy had outright *changed*. He talked to her, touched her, ate meals with her. She was the same as always, even in bed, where she generously shared her body with him with the same tenderness and careful attention she always had. She was *there*. Yet . . . she wasn't.

On the last day of the year, Lyle could no longer keep the two of them straight in his mind and he could have sworn that his wife hadn't said anything to him in days.

*   *   *

JANUARY

Lyle couldn't have said exactly when or how it had happened. Lately he'd been having a lot of dreams about fields, always the same, great, yellow expanses of Black-Eyed Susans swaying in a warm, gentle breeze under a piercingly bright sun. Each dream made him wake in the morning with a placid smile on his face and the absolute belief that his mind was gone, it *must* be. Inexplicable insanity happened occasionally, and he was sure that sometimes the person who went mad actually knew it, in an uncontrollable way. Kind of like being a backseat passenger in a car skidding on ice towards the opposite guardrail—nothing in the world could change what *was*. You just sat back, watched the show, and waited for the final act. He thought the day that he brought Kathe home was it, but it turned out to be only the beginning.

Cathy wasn't there anymore.

She hadn't left them, or been kidnapped, or set herself up as the next statistic on the Cook County Sheriff's Missing Persons list. She'd been . . . *replaced*. On the day this occurred, it seemed the most natural thing in the world for Kathe to follow him to the Montero, just as it was perfectly plausible that he should walk over and unlock the door for her, then stand and watch her climb in and buckle up before closing it again. He didn't ask her 'where to?' or try to let her out by the Menard's lot as he had months before. He took her all the way home, *his* home, pulled into the driveway and shut off the engine. By the time he'd climbed out and closed the driver's door, Kathe was waiting for him by the front fender. She followed him up the steps, watched as he unlocked the front door, and stepped into the house behind him without a word. There were a thousand questions rolling around in his mind, but none of them were able to find a way out. He stopped thinking when Kasey ran out of the hallway and saw Kathe, then cried, "Hi, Mommy!" and threw herself into Kathe's arms for a hug.

FEBRUARY

Life was pretty much the same as it had always been. Someone new sat beside him on the train now, a man who looked like he could have been Lyle's older brother and always seemed to be looking for someone. When the man

tried to make conversation one day, Lyle refused to answer, wouldn't even acknowledge his seat partner's existence. Lyle didn't want to speak to him, or get to know him. There were questions that needed to be asked, but Lyle didn't want to ask them; he certainly didn't want to answer them. After that, the new guy still sat beside him every day, but even though the man spent a lot of time staring at him, Lyle learned to ignore it and it no longer made him uncomfortable. Besides, Lyle had learned to become comfortable with a lot of things.

Someone—he thought it might have been a Chinese philosopher but he couldn't have said who, because he'd always had an atrocious memory for facts and dates—once asked if a man who dreamed he was a butterfly might not actually be a butterfly dreaming he was a man. The concept had bothered Lyle the first time he heard it, and now it haunted him nearly every waking moment. Never far from his thoughts, that unanswerable question became as much a part of him as his heartbeat. He doubted he'd know the answer even when he died.

He loved Kathe, but he had loved Cathy, too. Lyle's eyes snapped open in fear every morning and he looked for Cathy on the train each weekday. He cringed every evening when he went through his front door, wondering who he would find putting a Bandaid on Kasey's newest knee-scrape, or expertly working on the line of mint-colored ruffles that went down the sleeves of Caitlin's June grammar school graduation dress. Who would be in his home?

It might be Kathe.

It might be Cathy.

Or it might be that treacherous butterfly.

In Pieces

Deidra Cox

The beans were cold, clinging to the roof of Liza's mouth like tiny rabbit turds. Showboat Pork and Beans. 29 cents a can. Throwing them out would be wasteful and Devon hated waste. So Liza swallowed yet another heaping spoonful. Down the hallway, a shrill cry was quickly silenced. Liza stiffened, teeth clamping down on the sour metal.

don't look

But her disobedient eyes wandered to the closed door at the end of he darkened tunnel. A narrow strip of light peeking underneath, betrayed the frenzied movements within.

Another cry. Sharper, more intense. The tinny voice keen with agony. Blissful agony. It wavered in the air, a butterfly with razored wings slicing through the sky, then falling to the earth.

Liza trembled, dropping the spoon. Her tepid meal scattered. A peppering of tiny stones across the dirty formica surface, but she didn't notice. Her mind was focused on the activity behind the door. The access she was denied.

Hunger gripped her, gnawing at her loins. Long neglected. A dull weight in the pit of her belly. Liza wanted to hurl herself at the cheap wood, pounding till the minor barrier was cast aside, rendered useless.

fuck me please fuck me

The plea was ripe on her lips, nearly ready for the harvest.

Muscles tense, fingers clenched as the lust built.

Before she could act, the door flew open, the knob making a dull thud against the flimsy paneling. A menacing silhouette stood on the threshold, a halo of light surrounding the thick body.

Liza's mouth went dry. Her heart raced. Was it her turn?

"Clean it up," Devon said and staggered into the bathroom.

A hollow numbness sank in her chest and she stared after him.

Please . . .

Shame flooded her cheeks in a hot rush. Unworthy. Lacking. She dropped her eyes to her lap, waiting for the tears. The comforting wetness splashing down her cheeks. The wait was futile.

No tears. No more tears left in her lifeless husk. No juice. She imagined her vagina, shriveled and dry. She shivered.

"Bitch!"

Devon suddenly reappeared, fists drawn. Fire lit his face, burning a fresh glow to the pallid features. Anticipation pressed. She licked her lips and caught her breath. The blistering embrace of flesh and bone. The subtle beauty of welts blooming across her skin.

"Fucking bitch," Devon screamed. "Clean it up!"

The fists swung out, poised for execution. Yes, oh yes. Liza ached for his shattering caress.

Then, the rage slowly subsided, faded from his eyes. The passion quenched, leaving nothing but dead ash. Disgust settled upon his head and he curled his coarse lips in contempt, dropping his arms to his hips.

"I need another one," Devon said. "Better stock, this time."

Liza nodded. Her knees popped as she rose from the table, eager to escape. Her humiliation complete.

don't look at me like that

"Something young. Something sweet," he said, his face breaking into a greasy leer.

The blood drained from her cheeks and she scurried from his sight. Refuge in the shadows. Cool darkness. The blind acceptance of the dead.

The scene which greeted her in the bedroom was vaguely arousing. A broken body of indeterminate sex. Blood dripping from various wounds. Newly constructed orifices.

The skin atop Liza's shoulders itched. Ancient scars screaming for attention. The cold burden of remembrance.

Narrow rod of metal sliding through Liza's flesh. The exquisite torment as she hung suspended above the floor. Muscles ripping. Meat shredded in bloody flaps till she fell

at Devon's feet. Her fever kisses along his swollen ankles. The giver of precious pain.

Liza slowly forced the memory from her mind and concentrated on completing her task. The soiled sheets served as a more than adequate shroud for the corpse. She tied the corners tightly, reached under the bed and pulled out a box of large garbage bags. Drawstrings for disposable convenience. The body slid inside easily.

The trunk was closed. The body secured and Liza wanted the whole unpleasant episode over with as quickly as possible. She needed a chance to redeem herself, something to tip the scales in her favor.

But Devon had other ideas. "I'll be waiting," he promised, leaning against the car door. "Don't disappointment me. There's a surprise for you." His eyes were black marbles boring into hers. Devoid of any emotion.

he's gonna kill me

This realization snatched the air from her lungs and a dark wind roared in her head. She nodded mutely and tried to swallow her fear. Satisfied by her response, Devon allowed her to pass.

he's gonna kill me

yes, oh yes please

no, this time for real

How long had she been with him? Six, seven months. Hands grabbing her from behind dragging her from the dark Wal-Mart parking lot. Filthy rag stuffed in her mouth. Thin wire binding her wrists. The beating. The knife. Violation. She took all he had to give. Welcomed the show of affection.

This surprised him. A willing victim. A novelty which soon lost its appeal. Liza tried. So hard. Urging him on. Treasuring each slice. Each mark decorating he flesh. But it wasn't enough.

Then there were the players. The innocents she helped him recruit. The unspeakable acts she was forced to witness. The hunger they evoked between her legs.

And now, it was over. She read his intentions, the flat expression in his eyes. His refusal to touch her. The absence of any physical contact. Once she delivered the new toy, her life would be expendable.

a final act of love

No, no, no! Liza slammed her head against the steering wheel, listening to the loud thud pounding in her ears. Can't let yourself think that way.

She parked the car by the road. Golden arches beckoned nearby. The happy clown frozen in plaster by the drive through. A steady stream herded by the door. Some clutching paper bags filled with nuked morsels. Some with coin in hand.

A cop strolled to his car, coffee steaming in the cool night air. Liza watched him pull out, black and white making the rounds. Wry smile. Maybe if the pig had been a wee bit more observant, her trials would've been ended.

The body in the trunk. She should . . .

No. Leave it where it was. Eventually, the smell would attract the curious. But would she be in a position to appreciate the attention?

Darkness lightened into early morning and Liza awoke from a troubled sleep, watching. The breakfast crowd. Grabbing a bite on their way to work. Stray napkins fluttering in the breeze.

Across the street, a bakery opened for business. Fresh doughnuts and cakes for the sugar junkies. Another cop appeared, heading for the shop, his badge flashing in the muted light. Liza suppressed a short row of laughter.

She eased the car from its slot, deciding to move on. She drove past the high school. The bank, a sparse cluster of consumers shooting for that early morning deposit. Or withdrawal.

Faces gaped at her as she went by. Empty. Dead. Heavy with the last dregs of sleep. They melted into the dusty glass, their eyes following her as if they knew her soul.

One of the drones stepped in front of the car, confident of her concession. For a second, Liza played with the idea of forgetting to brake. Ramming her foot on the gas. Body bouncing on the hood like a puppet without strings.

But she didn't.

As the heavyset matron crossed, a small boy exited the Rite-Aid. He sprinted past the car, running like the bogeyman himself was hot behind him. Soon, a skinny teen dashed out after him, arms waving, shouts tearing through the morning doze.

run baby run

Liza silently kept pace after them, changing direction, mimicking the chase. The couch potato gave out first, pasty skin glistening with sweat, lips open, gasping for air. Spitting obscenities, the hunter retreated, cowed in defeat.

There, in the alley, hidden from view. The boy was there. Liza could feel him, sensed the adrenaline pumping through his veins like a drug.

Ditching the car, she hurried to the mouth of the alley. Black ribbon, streaked with a potpourri of grease, trash and broken glass. But way back, by the overflowing dumpster, a small head protruded at the side.

Liza smiled and stepped away, pressing her cheek against the wall. Sooner or later, he had to come out and she had nothing but time. The rough brick scratched her skin. Liza closed her eyes, reveling in the bittersweet collage the sensation awoke.

love me daddy please love me

And he did. Whenever the opportunity presented itself.

Glowing red tip hovering near her breasts. Heat searing, swelling. White hot agony spreads, stretches to infinite. Waves of pleasure hurdling over her.

Belt whipping around her legs. Climbing higher, licking at the damp moss nestled between her thighs. Heat building, strap demanding till she begs for release.

please love me

But then Daddy died and she was alone. Till Devon.

A rustle. Footsteps treading lightly along the trash. The child approached. Liza rocked on the balls of her feet, waiting.

The tousled head poked around the edge of the building. Liza's fingers flexed, ready for the kill. Narrow shoulders slinked from the alley and then, Liza pounced.

A wildfire of activity, kicking at her shins. Tiny fists punching her stomach. Teeth bared. Liquid chocolate still gleaming on the babyish lips from the stolen treat.

A quick blow to the head stanched the brief show of resistance and the small body sagged into Liza's open arms. A hasty sweep of the area gave no witnesses and a lull in traffic. Gathering the child up like a sack of flour, she carried him to the car. Lying him in the front seat, Liza strapped the seat belt in place at the thin waist. Delicate eyelids fluttered as hummingbird wings.

"You're mine, now," Liza said. "Get used to it."

A pair of old eyes met hers. She saw the pain and hunger reflected in them as a polished mirror. A kindred soul.

Dirt streaks painted a film of grime over his face and neck. Bony arms, thin, ever so thin, peeked beneath the ragged tee shirt. Angry bruises and ripe cuts trailed to the edge of the cheap fabric and beyond.

five, maybe six

Liza couldn't be sure. Yet she felt that Devon would be pleased with her choice. The boy sat quietly, No hostility. No frantic pleas for escape. Just a vague pliancy. An acceptance of his fate.

The new pet to take her place.

fuck me Devon please

The keys dangled in the ignition, taunting her. Chewing on her bottom lip, Liza considered the possibilities.

"Where are we going?"

The child looked to her and Liza tried to measure the thoughts racing in his gaze. Mentor, master, slave. Which of these? A choice to be made.

Then, Liza smiled. "How about a trip? Or at least until the smell gets too bad."

The boy frowned, unable to grasp the meaning behind her words, but Liza didn't worry. They boy had potential. And he would take everything she had to give. She would instruct him well.

Voices Lost & Clouded

David B. Silva

How could you?

Douglas Hobbs looked up from his newspaper, where he had been reading about a mother who had killed her two little boys and tried to make it look like a car jacking, and he glanced at the television, then at his wife. Someone had said something. He had caught the gist of it, but he wasn't sure if what he had heard had actually been addressed at him directly or if it had been the television or maybe Marian talking to herself.

At the other end of the couch, Marian was working on her checkbook, trying to find the thirty-two cent discrepancy between the bank statement and her checkbook balance. She had been working on it since dinner. Discrepancies, even the smallest of such things, drove her absolutely mad. *There's enough confusion in the world without adding to it,* she liked to say. *Besides, things have a balance of their own, and you don't want to go upsetting them if you can help it.*

"Did you say something?" Douglas asked.

Marian looked up and shook her head. "Probably the television."

"Probably."

He ruffled the newspaper and returned to the article about the mother and her children. They were two boys, age five and four, only a year apart like Douglas and his brother had been before John had died at the age of eleven. *What a terrible shame, Douglas thought, a mother who could do such a thing to her children. A mother's love—*

How could you?

"Huh?" He looked up again, this time directly at Marian.

"What?" she said, buried in her dollars and cents, catching his stare out of the corner of her eye and giving it only cursory consideration.

"You said something."

"Not me."

"Yes, you did. I heard you."

"Don't be silly."

"And you didn't hear anything, then?"

"Hear what?"

"That question," Douglas said. It hadn't really been a question, though. It had been, he thought with a chill that buzzed the back of his head, an *accusation.* A finger pointing. The kind of thing you heard from your mother when you were young and she was shocked by something you'd said. How could you, young man? How could you?

"Are you feeling all right?" Marian asked.

"You didn't hear it?"

"No. No question. And before you ask, yes, I'm sure."

Always sure, Douglas thought disdainfully. Always little miss perfect. Always right. Always sure of herself. A woman whom he had met just out of high school, two young kids with burning hormones and the mistaken notion that sex was the same as love and that love was free. Marian had been thin back then, with a bright smile and a sparkle in her eyes. Her hair had been long, a beautiful auburn brown, the touch of a natural perm, and bangs that made her look younger than she really was. He used to follow her home from the Evergreen Library where she worked afternoons as a volunteer, always forty or fifty steps behind her, thinking she didn't know he was there when she really knew all along. She carried her books in the crook of one arm, pushed up against her breast like a tease. That was what his mother would have called her . . . a tease. And she would have admonished Douglas for even being aware that the poor young girl had breasts. *Get your mind out of the gutter, young man,* his mother would have told him.

"Yes, ma'am," Douglas muttered.

"You're mumbling, Douglas."

"Am I?"

"Like you've got rubber lips."

"Sorry."

He glanced back at the newspaper, gazing past the headlines which, like most things in life, were blurry unless you focused on them directly. Something about the President

making a campaign stop. Something about a drive-by shooting. Something about . . .

How could you?

"Think I'll get something to drink," Douglas said, folding
the front page. He sleeved it over the local section, which
was sleeved over the sports, which sleeved the business section, and tossed the whole mess on the couch between
them. "Want anything?"

"No thanks."

The house was like his marriage, he supposed. Comfortable. Or like his life. Or like the printing shop where he
worked, mostly on the offset press, though sometimes at
the front counter. He came home smelling like ink most
nights, and over the years the house had begun to smell
like the print shop, that strong, not entirely pleasant odor
that didn't settle on the paper alone, but settled under his
fingernails and in his hair, even in the lining of his jacket
that hung on the coat rack all day. It was a smell he hardly
noticed anymore. Not until recently. Recently, it had become more and more noticeable, the smell of something
rotten in Denmark, as the saying went. Where had that one
come from? Something rotten in Denmark?

Douglas held the refrigerator door open.

How could you . . .

"Lie to mom?" he finished, surprised, even shocked that
it had come to mind.

It hadn't been a complete lie—that lie to his mother.
And he wouldn't have lied to her at all if . . . if he hadn't
thought the truth might kill her. It would have, too. It had
been hard enough on her—finding out her youngest son
was dead after an awful accident. John shouldn't have been
playing down there. She had warned him before about it,
but you don't always pay attention to what your mother
says when you're a boy and you're eleven, nearly a man in
your own mind.

The old McBride place had been built years before either
Douglas or his brother had been born. It was a Victorian
that sat back from the road on its own little piece of coun-
tryside, partially hidden by dogwood and sorghum and
horse chestnut, though you could see the white trim framing the roof line and you knew it was back there, old and
abandoned and out of the curious eyes of most passersby.

Ethan McBride had died upstairs in the master bedroom in 1973 after a long battle with lung cancer. He had died alone. Shortly afterward, the courts went about taking away his possessions and the house had stood empty ever since, white paint chipping and peeling, windows broken out, weeds growing over the front steps and up the walls like mold on an old piece of bread.

John hadn't been alone when he had gone down to the McBride house that day. In fact, it hadn't even been his idea. The idea had belonged to Douglas. Douglas had talked him into going there the same way he talked him into all the mischief the two of them got into.

"The McBride house? Mom'll be ticked."

"She's never gonna know," Douglas had said.

"She *always* knows."

"Egg layer."

"Am not."

"Are too."

And that had been all it had taken, a little goading and John had followed along behind, not at all sure whether it was a good idea or not.

The property was fenced. Douglas stood on the middle strand of barbed wire and raised the strand just above it so John could slip through without catching his shirt on a barb, then they started down the gravel road. The McBride place loomed in the distance, a mysterious dinosaur, weathered, two of the upstairs windows boarded over, the front door off its top hinge, hanging askew.

"Race you," Douglas had said.

"Huh-uh."

"Two seconds head start."

"Five seconds."

"Okay," Douglas said, counting the first second on his index finger. "Go!"

John took off running, his thin legs pumping, his shoe heels kicking up road gravel, believing for a moment that he might actually have a chance. Douglas believed it, too, which was why he didn't count to five like he had said he would. He counted to three instead, then took off after his little brother, running harder than he had intended and still arriving at the door half-a-second late.

"Beat you!" John cried, touching the door.

"Did not."

John leaned against the wall, fighting to catch his breath. "You didn't . . . even . . . count to five."

"Did too."

"No, you didn't."

And of course, Douglas hadn't counted to five. That would have assured his loss, and he couldn't have stood the thought of losing to his brother. Not to John, the baby of the family. Not to John who always got his way. Not to Mom's favorite, with those blue eyes of his, with that baby giggle, with that pout everyone thought was so cute, with the way he would crawl into her lap when Douglas was talking to her and make her quit listening. He was . . .

. . . he was everything Douglas wanted to be.

And Douglas hated him for that.

And that's why Douglas had done what he had done that day.

How could you?

It hadn't been something he had intended—*be honest with yourself, Douglas*—just something that had happened, an accident—*no more lies*—Douglas first goading him up the stairs, then into the master bedroom, then into an innocent game of Simon Says, John's eyes closed, his arms stretched outward like a bird in flight, roaming the small area, getting too close to the one window that hadn't been boarded over, losing his balance—*the truth now*—and tumbling out the opening—*the truth*—two stories down, landing full force, his chest against the rim of an old wheelbarrow, his ribs broken, internal bleeding, not an accident at all, but a deliberate—

How could you?

The same way I—

It *had* been an accident, Douglas told himself. He pulled a Michelob out of the refrigerator, closed the door, and leaned back against the kitchen counter. An accident. That was all.

In the living room, he could hear Marian laughing at something on the television as he pulled the tab on the beer and guzzled down half the can. She was always laughing, Marian was. Laughing at the television or something cute one of the kids had said or at life in general. Life was not a laughing matter, he had tried to tell her once when

he had banged his shin on the corner of the coffee table and she had gone into hysterics. But she wouldn't have any of it. Life was too short, she said. He shouldn't take things so seriously. The tension would kill him someday, she said. A lot she knew. It wasn't the tension that was going to kill him. It was the voices.

"What's so funny?" Douglas asked as he returned to the couch. He plopped down, the beer in one hand, and put his feet up on the coffee table. "Sounds like you're laughing yourself silly in here."

"I found sixteen cents," Marian said with amusement. "My error. I wrote one number on the check and a different number on my check stub. At the Target. Can you imagine? Where was my mind?"

"Sixteen cents," Douglas repeated.

"Sixteen more and I'm in balance."

"In balance." Ah, but he knew that couldn't be true. Because nothing in the world was in balance. Douglas had always known that. That was what made him different from everyone else. There was no yin and yang, no good and evil, no right and wrong. The lines were never that clear. There were always exemptions. And exemptions led to uncertainty. And uncertainty led to imbalance.

How could you?

"What?"

Marian looked up from her checkbook. "You're mumbling again, dear."

"Am I?"

"You look restless tonight."

"Maybe that's what it is—restless."

"Something wrong?"

"No."

"You seem kind of . . . out of sorts."

"What's that supposed to mean?"

"You know . . . unhappy, a little on the grouchy side."

"Well, I'm not."

"Just wondering if everything's all right, is all."

"No need," Douglas said, picking up the newspaper again. "Everything's fine."

"Glad to hear it."

"Are you?"

Marian smiled without looking up from her checkbook. "The boys off to bed?"

"An hour ago."

"You check on them?"

"Not yet."

"Um-hum."

That was the word, wasn't it? He was supposed to get up and go check on them now, like he did every night, because Marian not only worked outside the home, but she made more money than he did, and there was a silent agreement between them that money was the measure of power in this household. She had never come right out and said anything of course. But he knew. They both knew.

Douglas looked up from the paper, which was in his lap, unruffled, and glanced at his wife. She was a woman of few words. She had always been like that. In fact, that had been one of the things Douglas had liked about her when they had first been married. But somehow, over the years, the silence had taken on a meaning of its own. He didn't like it much anymore. He didn't like the way it had built a wall between them, him on this side looking in, her on that side, indifferent.

"I'll go check," he said resignedly.

"If you'd like."

He put aside the paper and made his way upstairs, the climb seeming a little steeper this year than it had last. There were four bedrooms on the second floor. The fourth bedroom had been converted from an office, which Douglas still missed on occasion. His mother stayed there, having moved in after his old man had died three years ago at the end of a long battle with lung cancer.

Only it hadn't been the cancer that had killed him, had it?

"It may as well have been the cancer," Douglas muttered to himself.

The old man had been dying for years, having finally succumbed to a wicked combination of booze and cigarettes that had left him bedridden and emaciated, unable to feed himself, unable to clean himself, just a shadow running from the light. Douglas had watched his seventy-two year old mother, the good wife that she was, get the old man up every morning, bathe him and feed him and do her best

to make sure he was comfortable, not so much his wife near the end as his mother. And like the stubborn old cuss that he was, the old man had held on and on and on. Two years of shaving him and changing his soiled bed sheets and spilling broth down his chin because he didn't have the good sense to close his mouth around the spoon. Two years. And then one day when Douglas went over to visit, he found his mother at the kitchen table, looking deluged and pitiful, crying, her face buried in her hands.

"What's the matter, Mom?"

She looked up at him, her eyes red, her cheeks puffy, and all she could do was shake her head.

"What is it? Dad?"

"I just can't handle it anymore," she had said.

Douglas rubbed her back lovingly. "I'll go check on him."

"I'm sorry."

"Don't be. I know it's been hard on you."

Upstairs, he found the old man in diapers on the bed, half his face shaved and the other half still lathered. The razor and a dirty towel lay on the floor nearby, discarded or tossed aside in one of those scuffles the old man had seemed to engage in more and more often of late. Douglas picked up the towel and wiped the shaving cream off his father's face.

"Mom's downstairs crying."

"She's always crying about something."

"She's crying about you."

"I didn't do nothing. I'm just an old man, doing his dying. That's all."

"You didn't nag at her?"

"A little, maybe."

"You didn't hit her?"

"Not so she could feel it any."

Douglas put the towel aside and sat on the edge of the bed. "How much longer you think you have, Dad?"

"The doctor says a month, maybe six weeks."

"Not long."

"Long enough."

"Any regrets?"

"Regrets?" the old man grumbled. "What kind of fucking nonsense is that?"

"No regrets, I take it."

"Listen, I worked down at the mill for forty years, cuttin' and planin' and stackin', turning some of the crappiest pieces of timber you ever saw into something usable. I lost the tips of three fingers, and sometimes there was barely enough money to put food on the table, but we did all right, your mother and me, and you and your brother always had a roof over your head and shoes on your feet. So if you're gonna start laying a bunch of crap on me 'bout how I wasn't always there for you or how I didn't tell you I loved you, well, you can forget it. I ain't buying any of it, and I ain't gonna look back with a pocketful of gee, I wish I would haves. It ain't my nature."

"No, I don't suppose it is," Douglas said calmly. He raised one of the pillows off the bed, and pulled it to his lap, feeling a strange sense of distance, of being far away and looking in, observing, not involved so much as simply curious. "And maybe that's the shame of it, old man."

"Don't you old man me," his father said, his eyes wide and instantly furious. "I can still tan your hide if I damn well feel like it."

"I know," Douglas said in a whisper. He took the pillow out of his lap, placed it over the old man's face, and pressed his weight against it. The struggle was short and weak, a hand flailing out from beneath the covers, a muffled scream that sounded more like surrender than defiance, a kick or two against the bedsheets, and then it was over.

Douglas sat back and shivered.

What had he done?

Now, standing in the hall outside the boys' bedroom, he tried to shake free from the memory. There was an unrealness about it, a farawayness not unlike the way his dreams often felt. Part of him wasn't sure if it had been a dream or not. And part of him didn't care. Douglas opened the bedroom door.

The boys had left the light on. The lamp, which sat on the night stand between the two twin beds, had lost its shade to a pillow fight last summer. He had told the boys that they were going to have to pay for it out of their allowances, but somehow it had slipped his mind, and only now did he realize that he had let them get away with something. They hadn't paid him so much as a single red

cent. You couldn't let kids get away with that kind of thing, not if you were a good parent and you expected them to grow up to be responsible.

Randy was in the far bed, curled into a ball, the covers kicked off, his face turned toward the wall. He looked like an elf in those bright red pajamas. How many times had Douglas tried to talk Marian into getting rid of those damn things? A boy didn't need to wear pajamas to begin with, and he certainly didn't need to wear bright red pajamas.

Justin was in the bed next to the door. He was lying on his back, one arm draped over the edge of the bed, his mouth wide, his eyes open and staring vacantly off into nowhere land, unseeing.

"It's a couple hours past your bedtime," Douglas whispered. "You're supposed to be asleep. You roll on over and close your eyes now, you hear?"

He turned off the light and stood in the doorway, listening to the darkness, hearing not a breath, not a whisper of movement in the room before slowly realizing that something was wrong. It wasn't like Justin not to do as he was told. Not like him at all. Douglas flipped the light on again.

"Did you hear me? You turn over and get back to sleep right now, young man. Before I have to get the paddle."

Justin did not move, not a muscle, not a breath, and Douglas found himself clenching his fists, feeling something terrible gnawing at him from deep inside, the same way that the old man's death still gnawed at him now and then, like rust eating away at an old iron bar. Pay no heed to the fact that the old man had needed to die. Pay no heed that it had made his mother's life sufferable for the first time in years.

How could you?

He glanced across the room at the other bed, where Randy was turned toward the wall, and thought distantly, calmly, that what had happened here had been a father's duty. Spare the rod, spoil the child, the old man had always said. And Douglas remembered now . . . he had caught them in the other room, in their grandmother's room, standing at the foot of the bed, saying things about her. Disrespectful things. Calling her an old sack of bones and telling her, right to her face, that she reeked something awful and why didn't she just die because she was past her

time, well past her time, and it was making everyone in the house a little crazy the way their daddy was fawning over her night and day and . . .

. . . and

. . . and Douglas had heard every word of it. Every ugly little word.

He stared across the room, aware now that Randy wasn't wearing red pajamas. In fact, Randy wasn't wearing pajamas at all, just a pair of shorts. And the red, the red that was everywhere, it was . . .

. . . it was blood.

How could you?

And Justin . . .

Douglas reached out and shook Justin's foot to see if he could bring him back from his vacant stare, out of the silent treatment and back to the here and now again. But Justin wasn't having any of it. He was like his mother in that way, always fighting to be in control, even when he had been wrong and deserved to be punished. Douglas shook him again, harder, and this time Justin's arm fell away from his stomach, dangling lifelessly over the edge of the bed, exposing the handle of the kitchen knife sticking out of his midsection. A red pool of blood had collected around the wound, staining the boy's shirt, and wasn't Marian going to be upset with him about that, and wasn't—

"Douglas? Everything all right up there?"

He glanced through the open door, down the hall at the stairway.

"Douglas?"

"Shhh," he said. "You'll wake them."

He closed the bedroom door, leaving the scene inside locked and sealed, out of sight, out of mind, if that were possible—and started back down the stairs.

"They both asleep?" Marian asked as he entered the living room.

"Isn't that what I said?"

"I didn't hear you."

"You should pay attention once in awhile, Marian. I swear you're getting more like the boys by the day. Never hearing a word unless it suits you."

"Douglas!"

"It's true."

He sat down on the couch again, settling into his little corner the way he had settled into his own little corner of the world. It was comfortable on this end, safe, protected, territory where no one else was allowed to stray. The newspaper, which was no longer folded along the crease, no longer neat and manageable, no longer organized, sat in a heap on the couch next to him. He picked it up, fought to get it back into a recognizable shape, then settled back into his seat again.

Marian had fallen quiet. She was going to sulk now, upset because he had said something that she just as soon would have preferred not to hear. That was the way it went around here, Marian always getting upset about some little thing, then making him suffer through her silence. She knew it ate at him, the way it ate at him when his mother would get upset and quit talking. Women were like splinters, he had come to realize. They knew just how to get under your skin, how to irritate you until you finally couldn't stand it any longer and you had to dig them out.

"All right, I'm sorry," Douglas eventually said.

Marian, the checkbook in her lap, refused to look up.

"I shouldn't have said what I said. Okay? I was out of line. I admit it."

How could you?

"I said I was sorry."

But it hadn't been Marian's voice that he had heard. Douglas glanced up at her, realizing suddenly that she hadn't said a word, then glanced at the television and realized it hadn't come from the television, either. The boys were upstairs in bed. His mother was upstairs, too. It hadn't been any of them.

"Did you hear—?" he started to ask, before catching himself. Marian appeared to have dozed off, her head bowed forward, her eyes closed, though Douglas knew immediately that it wasn't the sandman who had come and taken her. She was wearing the scarf Douglas had bought for her last Christmas, green and gold with little snowflakes, and the scarf was tied snugly around her neck. A little too snugly, he thought.

"Marian?"

He put aside the newspaper and kneeled next to her, raising her chin with one hand, surprised when she wouldn't

open her eyes, surprised at the discolored ligature mark around her neck where the scarf had bitten into her skin and left an indelible impression.

"Marian?"

How could you?

"I didn't," Douglas said, standing up and backing away, feeling suddenly lost, disoriented, not sure what had happened or how he had found himself in the midst of this headlong nightmare. Everyone, it seemed, was leaving him. He backed into the wall and stood there a moment, staring down at Marian, trying to find the rhyme or reason, coming up empty, suddenly not even sure if this woman, dead on the couch, was his wife or someone he had known casually or a stranger or any of those or none of them.

"Mom?"

He backed around the outer edges of the room, afraid to take his eyes from her, afraid to turn his back. Then he made his way down the hall and from there to the stairs, and upstairs he found the second door on the left. It was the door to the room where his mother stayed, and Douglas opened it slowly, at last finding his way home again, home where he could feel cradled and loved and never be alone again.

"Mom?"

She was lying in bed, her face turned toward him, the lines cut deep, the eyes as dark as black agates, her hair thin and gray and wispy, her mouth open, calling: *How could you?*

"I'm sorry, Mother," he said, closing the door behind him. It was the door to the rest of the world, and it was a door Douglas had closed a long time ago. He went to the bed and pulled back the covers, shaking her thin, dry fingers loose from the cloth, then climbing into bed and snuggling up beside her. Her smile was sunshine over the mountains in the early morning of a winter day. Her touch was the soft, warm caress of a wool blanket. Her smell was the sweet young scent of honeysuckle. And Douglas was home. Where he belonged. Where he had always belonged. Safe and loved. A boy in the arms of his mother.

How could you?

How could you have stayed away so long?

If Memory Serves

Jack Ketchum

Patricia sat relaxed in the armchair across the room.

The metronome on the table in front of her had done its work in record time.

"I'd like to speak with Leslie," Hooker said.

The woman looked at him, sighed, and shook her head.

"God! Leslie again. I don't get it. What the hell's wrong with speaking to me once in a while?"

Hooker shrugged. "You lie. You evade. You try to confuse things. If you didn't lie so much, Susan, maybe I'd want to talk to you more often. Nothing personal."

She pouted, leaned back in the chair and folded her arms across her breasts.

"I'm only trying to cover my ass, y'know," she said.

"I know. And I understand. It just doesn't help matters much at this juncture. Let me talk to Leslie, okay?"

The eyelids fluttered. The woman threw back her head and howled. Then gave him a meek bright sidelong glance and began to whimper.

"Leslie. Not Katie."

Katie was a dog.

Only the second such dog ever recorded in the history of Multiple Personality Disorder. Hooker had written about her extensively in the article he'd done for the Journal of Psychiatric Medicine. Speculation mostly and observation of the physical aspects. The crawling, the snuffling, the howls. Katie's connection to the other personalities had seemed vague at the time. Now, knowing what he did, it was clearer.

"Hi, Doctor Hooker."

"Hi, Leslie."

"I guess you want to talk some more."

"That's right."

"I'm not supposed to."

"Why?"

"Patricia doesn't want me to."

"I think she does want you to, Leslie."

"She's scared."

"Scared of what?"

She shifted uncomfortably in the seat, a typical teenage girl wrestling with a problem. Like all the personalities who had emerged so far other than the dog Katie and Lynette, who was only five years old and of course Patricia herself, Leslie had come into the world at sixteen and sixteen she remained.

"They said they'd hurt her, remember? If she talked. They said they'd kill her."

"I remember."

"So?"

"So that was quite a long time ago, wasn't it."

Twenty-two years to be exact. The woman sitting in front of him was thirty-eight and the mother of two, both girls, ages eight and ten. Until her divorce a year and a half ago she had been a successful editor for a large paperback book company and then a chronic alcoholic who finally had sought therapy after having beaten her oldest child with a soup ladle across the face and head and then not remembering doing so. Four months into treatment the first personality—little Lynette—had emerged.

"I don't know about this, doctor."

"You've done fine so far, Leslie. Why stop now?"

"I don't want to stop."

"Then don't. Believe me, it's going to help Patricia enormously in the long run. Enormously."

"I'm scared."

"Don't be."

She thought for a moment and then sighed.

"I guess I owe it to her."

"Yes."

He allowed himself to relax. It was a crucial point. Had she balked here it might have been weeks before she allowed herself to address all this again. It had happened before.

And today, finally, he had Patricia's permission to record their sessions.

"You were talking last time about how they—the Gannets—'passed her around' I think you said."

"Uh-huh."

"And you were talking sexually passed around, correct?"

"Yes."

"Can you tell me who her mom and dad were giving
her to?"

"Lots of people. That whole group they had there. Mr.
and Mrs. Dennison, Judge Blackburn, Mr. and Mrs. Siddons, Mr. Hayes, Doctor Scott and Mrs. Scott, Mr. Sey-
mour, Miss Naylor."

"The schoolteacher."

"Right. And Mr. Harley. There were others. But those
were the main ones."

"Her mom and dad, did these people pay them for this?"

"No. They just . . . allowed it. It was just okay by them."

"And this was when Patricia was how old?"

"Three. Maybe four."

He suspected it was five. Lynette's age.

The age she'd started hiding.

"So then what would these people do to her again?"

This was all familiar territory but he needed it for the
tape.

"Well, she would be naked pretty much always and they
would put their fingers in her, in her bum, in her vagina,
and some of the men would put their penises in her and
sometimes make her put their penises in her mouth, you
know, and they would spank her real hard and Doctor
Scott, he liked to put these long needles in her . . ."

"Acupuncture needles?"

"I don't know. Big long needles."

"Go on."

"He'd put them in her, stick them everywhere. And Mrs.
Scott always wanted her to lick her vagina."

It was a hallmark of Leslie's personality that none of this
seemed to embarrass her in the slightest. She treated this
catalogue of childhood horrors with a detachment that was
almost clinical. Admirable in a way, he thought, were it not
so sad and frightening.

"Mrs. Siddons liked to twist her nipples until she cried.
And Miss Naylor always wanted to have her breasts sucked,
like Patricia was a little baby and she was her mommy. Mr.

Hayes would put her in the tub and pee on her and one time he shit on her too. On her belly. Sort of stood over her and bent his legs a little and dropped it on her."

"And there were other kids involved, right?"

She nodded. "Danny Scott, Ritchie Siddons, the Dennison twins."

"Did Patricia ever try to resist at all? Ever try to run away?"

"A couple times she tried. But she was too little to go anywhere. The Gannets beat her bad for it. So after a while she didn't try anymore."

She stopped. Tears were rolling down her cheeks in a sudden stream.

"Leslie?"

Her chin trembled and the large brown eyes were doe's eyes, liquid, innocent.

"Lynette? Is that you?"

"They hurt me! Mommy and Daddy . . ."

"I know. It's all right, Lynette. Mommy and Daddy won't hurt you any more. I promise. I swear."

That was true enough. Mommy and Daddy were dead in a car accident nearly ten years before. The father was drunk, the telephone pole unforgiving. As far as Hooker was concerned, good riddance.

"They hurt me!"

"I know they did, Lynette. But that's all over now. Mommy and Daddy can never hurt you again. You understand?"

She sniffled. The tears abated.

"Are you okay now?"

She hesitated, then nodded.

"Good. If it's all right then, can you let me talk to Leslie again?"

"Oh for chrissakes, fuck Leslie!"

The voice was deep and husky.

Sadie.

Only the third time she'd appeared.

The first two times were trouble. He could see this was not going to be an exception. She was out of her chair and striding over.

"You want to talk sex, honey? You feel like a turn-on? Is that it? Then you better talk to me."

He was halfway up out of his own chair when she reached down and pushed him back again.

Then lifted her skirt and straddled him.

"Sadie . . ."

"I know. We been through this before. 'It's inappropriate for a patient and therapist' blah blah blah. Loosen up, will ya?" She shrugged off her jacket.

"Get off me, Sadie."

"Loosen up. You know you want little Sadie."

"What I want is to talk to . . ."

"Yeah, Leslie. I know. But will Leslie do this for you, Doc?"

She pulled the sweater off over her head. Underneath it her breasts were naked. They were lovely breasts, full and firm despite her age and the fact that she'd born two children—and judging by the size and shape of the nipples, breast-fed at least one of them.

They were lovely but for the scars.

Small puckered burn-scars. Over a dozen on the breasts alone. Many more on her stomach, neck and shoulders.

He could still make out the swastika carved just above her navel.

He had never seen the evidence of what they'd done to her first-hand before.

"You want to talk about those, Sadie?"

She laughed. "Talk about what? My tits?"

"The burns. The swastika."

She pushed off him angrily and scooped up the sweater and walked to the window. Slipped the sweater on. Walked back to her chair and dug in her purse for a pack of Winston Lights.

Sadie smoked. The others didn't.

"I don't allow cigarettes. You know that, Sadie."

She gave him a look, disgusted, and tossed the pack back into her purse. Sadie would rebel, but only so far. Then like all the others she'd been trained to obey.

"Oh, fuck you, Doc. Talk to your precious Leslie. Have a great time. You asshole."

She dropped into the chair and looked at him. The eyes softened. Her face went slowly neutral.

Leslie again.

Now if he could just keep her here for the duration.

The session was running long. He could see that already. The clock on the wall above and behind her read two-fifty. But this was all much too productive to quit in ten minutes. He had a first-time patient who was probably already outside there in the waiting room, his three o'clock appointment. It wasn't the best way to start a doctor-patient relationship but the man would have to hold on awhile.

It wasn't just Patricia who had something on the line here.

This case was going to make his reputation, there was no doubt about it. The first article, published six months ago, had gone a long way toward doing that already. AP had picked it up. My god, the *New York Times* had picked it up. For Warhol's classic fifteen minutes he and his unnamed patient were famous.

Soon they'd be more so. His first paper was only the beginning.

"Leslie."

"Hi."

"We were talking about all the sexual things they did to Patricia. But there were other things too, weren't there."

She nodded.

"Would you mind going over them for me again?"

"All the witchy things," she said.

"Like what?"

"They taught her all these chants and stuff, and they would all dress in black and sometimes they'd visit graveyards at night and sometimes they'd dig up bodies and do stuff with the bones and the dead person's clothes, make up devil potions for the Feast of the Beast or Candlemas or for calling up spirits and . . ."

"What do you mean, 'devil potions'?"

"Pee. And wine. And blood."

"Whose blood?"

"Theirs. Anybody's."

"Go on."

"Well, most of the time though, they were in the basement of the Gannets' house. They had a really big basement there. And everybody would be naked. And everybody would have to kiss Mr. Gannet's penis before things started, like all in a line, you know? And then

there'd be chanting and people would eat and drink a lot and then they'd bring in the sacrifice."

"What was the sacrifice?"

"Chickens. Cats. Mostly dogs."

Dogs like Katie.

It was amazing and highly unusual. Patricia had created this personality in total identification with the dead or soon-to-be dead.

The dead taken inside her, made one with her.

A remarkable exercise in compassion.

"And then there was that one time," she said. "You know. Her initiation."

The voice was small and not nearly so matter-of-fact as before. Unsure. A little frightened.

He knew that tone.

Because it was at this point that Leslie's information had almost always stopped in the past, here or only slightly further on. Something about the initiation had been highly traumatic. Hooker knew from sessions past that Patricia had been sixteen years old at the time, the age at which most of the personalities erupted out of her all at once, guardians at the gate of her sanity. He knew that the initiation had occurred in her parents' basement. And that was about all he knew.

He looked at the clock. Three exactly.

To hell with the time, the next patient. He needed to try.

"Leslie, in the past you haven't wanted to tell me about this, I know. And I understand that it's difficult for you. But this time's going to be different. I'll tell you how and why it's different. You see the tape recorder on the desk there beside you?"

She looked and nodded.

"What's different is that this time I'm taping this. And next session I'll play the tape back for Patricia. When I do, Patricia will know and understand what they did to her. She'll understand why she's this way, why all of you are this way. And can you guess what happens then?"

She shook her head.

"The pain stops. A little more time, a little more therapy, and it will stop."

He looked at her, gave it a moment. Thinking, trust me.

"Tell me about it, Leslie," he said.

For a moment he thought it wouldn't happen. Then she leaned back in the chair and closed her eyes and when she opened them again she was remembering.

"There was a boy," she said. "I don't know where he came from. Not one of the usual boys, I mean. Not one of theirs, one of the circle. Cuban or Mexican, about Patricia's age. Patricia'd had all these drugs and so had the boy and they both were naked and they put her down on the table, on the alter, with the boy standing over her, everybody chanting while he put his penis in and started doing it. He was doing it a long while and it was hurting. And then Mr. Gannet reached over with this knife, this sacrificial knife which was very, very sharp, and he cut the boy . . . you know the place, right between the . . . you know, the balls and the . . . the hole? that skin there?"

Hooker nodded.

"And there was blood running out of him, all this blood running down his legs and dripping off the altar but I guess because of the drugs or because he was doing it, into it, I don't know, he didn't know he was cut at first, he just kept doing it to her. But Patricia knew, she could feel it pooling up under her real warm and sticky wet and finally the boy got it too, he started screaming and went to pull out of her but by then Mr. Gannet was around the side of him and cut him across the throat with the knife and Patricia was screaming and the boy was coughing up blood, it was all over the place, all over her, she could taste it, and all the others were around them catching the blood in bowls, drinking the blood from his neck and from between his legs and she could smell his shit by then and they were catching that in bowls too and smearing it across their faces, across their mouths, and instead of coming inside her he just released, you know? I mean, he pissed inside her.

"Well, then the boy fell on top of her, he was dead, and Mr. Gannet handed Patricia the knife and told her to stab him in the name of Our Lord Satan and she was so scared and so mad at the boy—it was weird—so really completely mad at him, that she did. She stabbed him over and over and over."

She stopped, puzzled.

"I wonder why she was so mad at him? And not at them."

He let her consider that a moment. There wasn't time to get into it now though he knew perfectly well where the anger of one victim toward another usually came from. Save it for another session.

"What happened then?" he said.

She shrugged. "They ate his heart. They smeared her with his blood. Then they did it to her one at a time. Then they let her go upstairs to shower and then they let her sleep."

Ten minutes after three. They'd got through it. My god. It was over.

He felt shaken. Elated too. He couldn't believe what he had here.

"I'm going to count to five, Leslie," he said. "When I get to five I'll be speaking to Patricia again and she'll be awake, rested, relaxed and comfortable. And she'll remember none of this. You did very well. Thank you."

"Doctor?"

"Yes?"

"Patricia's scared again."

"She needn't be."

"She knows I told. That I told you everything. They said they'd kill her if I ever told."

"That was years ago, Leslie. They're gone now. All of them, gone. Patricia's going to be fine, believe me. I'm going to count to five now, all right? Close your eyes."

He counted.

Patricia opened her eyes and smiled.

"How'd we do?" she said.

"You did beautifully." He returned her smile. "I want to go over this with you as soon as possible. But I've got another patient outside now."

He consulted his book.

"How is three o'clock Wednesday? Day after tomorrow?"

"Fine."

"We've made a breakthrough here, Patricia. You really ought to know that."

"Really? Then can't you . . . ?"

"No. I'm afraid not. Not right now. This is going to take some time. I'm scheduling you for two hours Wednesday, all right?"

"All right."

He handed her the jacket on the floor in front of him. She didn't even ask how it had gotten there. She was practically an old pro at this by now. She gathered up her coat and purse and stood to leave. Hesitated and then turned back to him.

"Should I be worried?" she said.

"About what?"

"I don't know. Just . . . worried."

"Not at all. We're already through the worst of it. There are some very difficult issues to face, I won't deny that for a moment, but now at least we know what we're dealing with. We know for sure. It's going to take some time. But you're going to have a life, Patricia. A full, integrated life. Without hiding. And without fear."

She smiled hesitantly. "See you Wednesday, then. And I guess . . . well, I guess we'll just . . . see."

She stepped through the door to the waiting room and closed it gently behind her. He walked to the table beside her empty chair and turned off the recorder. Pushed the rewind button and heard the sibilant hiss of tape which was her voice and his so that he knew it hadn't failed him and then heard it click back into the start position. He unplugged the recorder, walked to his desk, opened the top drawer and slipped it away.

In the waiting room outside he heard a chair thump against the wall. His three o'clock was probably impatient as all hell right now, would probably need some soothing of ruffled feathers. That was all right. At the moment he felt up to anything. He walked across the room and opened the door.

The man crouched over her, a big man all in black, jacket, shoes, trousers, crouched over her so that Hooker could see her lifeless eyes and wide open mouth and the back of the man's head moving side to side just below her chin. There was blood all over the walls and the landscapes hung there to set his patients' minds at ease, blood still pulsing up from out of her neck over and around both sides of the man's head, drenching his long black greasy hair and the man looked up at Hooker and grinned, his face a thin bright mask of red, teeth dripping paler blood thinned with saliva. Hooker saw the knife in his left hand and the blood-stained silver pentagram swaying, dangling from his neck.

"Session's over," hissed the man. "Your patient's cured."

Hooker fell back through the doorway to his office as though he'd been pushed. Tried to slam the door. The bloody left hand shot out against it with a crack and thrust him farther into the room.

The man stood on the threshold.

For a moment as he approached Hooker thought of all the people, all the structure, all the wealth of invention and will to survive that had just died out there in the waiting room and his only pitiful solace was that the tape would outlive them, the man would not know about the tape, his work would go on in a way, and in a way so would she go on, despite and not because of his ambitions for them both though none of this was enough, not nearly enough for either of them or for her children. He thought publish or perish, or both because of course that was finally what had done it to them, the *New York Times* for god's sake and then heard the whimper of a dog which was his own whimper as the knife came down and down.

The Tears of Isis

James S. Dorr

It entered softly, creeping in the gray, mist-like place between languid wakefulness and dream. It entered silently, almost. But then the sound of its weeping grew louder, although remaining just on the edge of actual hearing.

Copper's eyes opened.

She *had* been dreaming. She rubbed her eyes as she stretched on the bed, then felt for the huddled, thin body beside her. So many drugs, she thought. So much liquor consumed in her past life—consumed the past night, as far as that went, at the unveiling party—she never was quite sure what was just dreaming. Except this, the figure that stood by her window, the sad-eyed woman draped in white gossamer, jet black hair gleaming in the still bright, reflected lights of San Francisco's North Beach section, this, she was sure, was not just some drug vision.

She turned to her lover and shook him awake. Her lover and model of the moment, an eighteen-year-old boy, but smooth of face and slender of torso. Able to pass for perhaps only fifteen—not that she hadn't had lovers that young before—which was the age that her son would have been. The son she'd been dreaming of.

"Ramon?" she whispered.

Eyes as black as the figure's hair opened. "Huh—what?" her lover said.

"Look," she whispered. She pointed to the lingering figure that, even as she spoke, was fading. And yet whose tears still seemed to spot her carpet.

"What?" Ramon said again, rolling toward her. He muttered as he rolled, *"La Llorona."*

"Ramon, what?" she said as she shook him again. The figure was gone now.

"A Mexican superstition, that's all," he said, still half in

his sleep. "La Llorona—it means 'the weeper.' A kind of ghost woman." He had been drinking as well, Copper knew. Perhaps more than she had—Copper had watched him telling a young woman, nearer his age than she, how he had posed for her sculpture at last night's Union Square showing. And now, as he mouthed the words in his sleep, she felt suddenly afraid.

Not for the ghost, though. She didn't believe in ghosts— God knew there was enough that was tangible to be afraid of, if one wished to fear it. In fact, the symbols of these fears were what she sculpted, like last night's statue, called "The Grave Lover." Or the one before that, "The Vampire," called by the art critics her greatest work.

The model for that one *had* been only fifteen, an unprofessional that she'd picked out from the North Beach crowd. Trying to look older, with his hair dyed black, ears pierced and jangly, black rouge around his eyes, fingernails grown long. A hopeful musician . . .

She tried to remember—after his sculpture was done and she'd thrown him out. After his eyes had started to wander, just like Ramon's last night, but, unlike Ramon's, back to his old girlfriend.

She stared at Ramon, now on his back, the covers half off him, his light-muscled chest rising and falling in the dim shadows of her bedroom. She moved her hands over him, stopping suddenly when they struck something that fully distracted her.

Ramon's erection.

She thought again, oddly, as she mounted him, taking advantage of the moment, of what her son might have been like had she not miscarried that night fifteen years ago. Not that she hadn't had fifteen-year-olds since, and more than just once. But she could see *this* boy in her mind's eye, a face just like Anthony's—Tony her brother, their parents both dead, who she'd not even written a card to for how long a time now?—stark-featured and perfect. His boy-body slimming out into young manhood. His little cock stiffening . . .

She moaned as she thought of what might have been as she leaned to her work, kissing her love awake, kissing his eyelids until they were slippery and glistened as much as the carpet's tear stains. The stains that were gone now.

And Ramon responded—thrusting her fears away. If she had *had* fears.

They slept late that morning, Copper and Ramon, but she often slept late with whatever lover. Ramon. Frederico. Johnnie before them. Before them all, the ones at college—when she'd been just eighteen. She didn't remember, not everything anyway. So many lovers, just like the parties, the drugs, the liquor. They took their toll from her.

But when she awoke with Ramon in her arms, she saw in her mind what would be her next sculpture.

It wasn't a woman—or part of it was, but that wasn't the focus. Nor was even that part draped in white, like last night's vision, but rather a strange, twisted kind of woman with shadowy arms that were somehow wing-like. Hovering, maybe. Sexy, yet horrible. Shielding within them a figure. A young boy.

She didn't know yet the whole composition, nor any but the most broad of its features, but that was the way creation worked for her. She got out of bed and, still naked, she padded downstairs to her studio. She set up cameras and, behind them, mirrors, remembering vaguely the night before and how she and Ramon had fought at the party until, exhausted, they'd made up and gone home. How even then they hadn't made love until after her dream—her vision—the thickening of fog through her open window—whatever it was that had caused her to wake him.

She shrugged. When Ramon came down, she had him take pictures of her standing unclothed in the place of the shadow-armed woman of this, her new vision. She picked up a drop cloth and whirled it around her, having it flutter as if it were feathers. She didn't know yet what it *was* she was posing as, nor what she posed him as after she had him recline on a couch and began her preliminary sketches. That, too, was the way creation worked for her.

But Ramon was sullen, even after they'd paused for breakfast. The work didn't go well. Even after she'd resumed her sketching her hands felt stiff to her.

She called a halt finally and let Ramon dress and go about doing his things for the day. She stared at her hands,

then, still not yet dressed herself, stalked to the largest of the mirrors.

She looked at her body long and hard, from every angle. She thought of Frederico, her lover before Ramon. He of "The Vampire." He with the past girlfriend, even if he had been only fifteen.

And of what had happened after their love had cooled.

So many lovers . . .

She wasn't that old—in actual years she was nearing thirty-four, but she could still pass easily for being in her mid-twenties. Yet, Ramon was just eighteen.

And, she thought suddenly, even with Ramon's still-childlike looks, she would need someone younger than that for this new project. Younger than fifteen, like poor, lost Frederico. Perhaps even thirteen. Even if she didn't yet know what it was.

So many lovers. Frederico, the hot-blooded Los Angelino who, after she'd thrown him out, went back to Columbus Avenue and slashed his old girlfriend. Wilhelm, the German boy, subject of "Parsifal, Slain by Dragons." And others, not models. Some not even boys, like Michelle, her roommate back when she'd been in college in Boston, across the country. Before she'd decided she liked boys better.

And dark-haired Consuela. Hot, dark-eyed Consuela, so much Copper's twin, who'd moved out to Phoenix and bought "The Vampire" for the Heard Museum's new expansion. She owed her a visit—they did keep in touch, unlike her and her brother—and Phoenix was less than two days drive away. Much less, if she pushed it.

And driving, especially on the second night, through the desert, helped Copper collect her ideas together. Thus it had always been, she thought, the bleakness around her blending into a whirlwind of reds and tans, yellows and grays, as she pushed her Mercedes up to its limit, crossing the last of the mountains at twilight—even on trips, especially on trips, she liked to sleep during most of the day-time—and taking the worst of the desert in darkness.

And then morning, Phoenix, and Consuela's arms for old times' sake. But only a little. "I'm working on something," she explained that night while they were out drinking.

"I understand," Consuela said. "Tomorrow, though. We will go to the museum. Would you like to see your exhibit?"

Copper nodded. Yes. Often she didn't like to see her sculptures after they'd been sold. She preferred, rather, to put them behind her. Just like her lovers.

But some, like Consuela . . .

Who'd persuaded her boss at the museum to buy "The Vampire," in spite of their love rather than because of it. The sculpture stood alone in its own room, darkened by velvet drapes. Track lights shone on its focal figure, that of a teen-ager, tender and white-skinned, a hint of the plumpness of pre-pubescence still on its smooth features. And yet, above, shadow. The shadow of . . . *something.*

The lighting was clever—it never was quite seen. The eye didn't linger. A bat-like construction of wires and metal, but drawing the eye down and back to the focus, this time to soft lips that just started a half grin.

One sharp tooth just showing . . .

She'd drunk blood herself before it had been finished. She'd mixed with the crowd on Columbus Avenue and Broadway, the would-be Satanists, and, after that, so they'd both see what it *really* would be like, she and Frederico had opened each other's veins.

Only a little, though. Not like after, when the police had broken Frederico's girlfriend's door down and found her throat slashed open, bloodied lip prints over her chest and arms. One breast half bitten off.

Copper shuddered, reaching reflexively to touch her own breasts. She'd seen photographs of the body, using a part of what she had seen, in fact, in "The Grave Lover". It wasn't *her* fault, though. Frederico had fled, perhaps back to Mexico—she hadn't seen him either before or after the murder, not since she'd quit with him. Just as she'd fled from Boston after . . .

After Tony had raped her.

But after that, also. The son she might have had . . .

"You ever hear from Anthony these days?"

"What?" she asked, startled. They had left the exhibition and were walking out through an older part of the museum, featuring native art from Africa.

"Your brother, Tony. Is he still in Boston?"

She looked at Conseula. Why had *she* thought to bring up Tony? Then her eye lit on a figure behind her, a small wooden statue of a reclining boy.

"What's that?" she asked.

Conseula turned. "Oh, that," she answered. "It's a figure of the god, Horus. It's sub-Saharan, though. Not Egyptian."

Copper looked again. Yes. *Her* statue. Her new-planned sculpture—this was the key to it.

"Horus?" she asked.

"Yes," Consuela said. "You know. The son of Osiris and Isis. After Osiris died. After—who was it?—Set tore him to pieces and Isis had to put them back together. Except one was missing."

"Uh huh," Copper said. Her mind was racing. Her brother, Tony, was an Egyptologist she remembered. After he'd left school three years after her. She'd already gone to New York by then, to study art there, and then for a time to the Nelson Gallery in Kansas City before she'd finally moved to San Francisco, but friends had told her. Most of them gone too by now, of course, except some who still kept in touch, like Conseula.

And off and on, like Michelle. Ex-roommate Michelle, who had also loved Tony.

Michelle had gone west too, Copper thought as she raced through the night on Interstate 10. She'd been a psychology student at first—the only one of their group not in the arts—until she'd switched majors at Tony's insistence. This was after Copper had left, and Tony, always bright for his age, had entered the university early. Not that he hadn't been hanging around the campus anyway, ever since Copper had started classes.

Copper laughed. *That* had been a romance that was even shorter than some of her own. She thought about Michelle and how she would have done better to stick to her Jung and Freud. And then about Wilhelm, her dull, stolid German. And how he might have been more Michelle's equal. Careful. Methodical. Until that night, afterward, when he'd stolen a Porsche from somewhere and crashed it in flames in San Bernardino . . .

Copper swerved—fast! A truck barreling past her, her train of thought lost. She looked down at her speedome-

ter—the bastard must have been doing a hundred!—and,
instinctively, slowed her own speed. And then, to her right,
by the side of the road, she saw . . . La Llorona.

The woman was weeping—yes. Swathed in gossamer, as
if she'd just popped out of her house still wearing her night
dress. And in her arms—what? A skull? A body? A tiny
child's body? One half of Copper's mind raced with the
image, knowing now it too—or parts of it, anyway—would
after all be part of her sculpture while, with the other half,
she swerved out again, missing the figure by less than
inches.

She stepped on the gas. In the rear view mirror she saw
it waving, no longer holding—whatever it was!—but beckoning hopefully for her to stop as if it were trying to flag
down a ride.

She stepped on the gas harder, noticing now that her
hands were shaking. Tall, thin, long-haired—hair cut straight
across its back, square at the edges—the figure *was* that
which had been in her bedroom. But now in the desert.
And weeping—she'd known that—tears glistening in moonlight—and yet she'd not seen a face, neither here nor in
San Francisco, but rather a hole where a face might have
been. A nothingness. Staring . . .

She slowed her car down again, but only after she'd
topped a rise and knew that the figure was far behind her.
Then when thirty or more miles farther she saw the lighted
sign of a motel, she pulled in and stopped.

The next morning was sunny, a day for enjoying life. Nevertheless, Copper still felt frightened. Frightened enough, in
any event, to stop in the motel lobby and call, not San
Francisco, but Consuela's number back in Phoenix.

"You're Mexican, aren't you?" she asked as soon as the
phone was answered.

"Wh-what?" a sleepy voice replied. "Oh—is that you,
Copper?"

"Yes. And aren't you Mexican? I mean, your family?
Last night I saw something and Ramon—you know, the
boy I'm with now?—said it might have to do with some
kind of Mexican superstition."

"The boy you intend to get *rid* of, you mean, from what
you told me," the telephone answered. "But no, I'm not

Mexican. How would a Mexican get to go to college in *Boston*? I just ended up here afterward, that's all, and now my mother won't let me forget it. 'Surrounded by Mexes and Indians,' she says, whenever I call her. 'Is this how you get ahead in life, Consuela?' But, if you just mean am I Hispanic, yes. I'm Puerto Rican."

"I'm sorry," Copper said. "And I knew that, too. From back in college. But anyway, in Puerto Rico, do you have a belief in some kind of ghost called 'La Llorona'?"

The phone was silent, so Copper went on, describing the figure she'd seen in her bedroom as well as the previous night on the highway. Finally, Consuela interrupted her.

"Yes," she said. "The 'Weeping Woman.' That's what we call her in Puerto Rico. The woman who searches for her poor lost children—or at least that's how *one* legend about her goes. But what you saw on the highway last night, that's another version. It's one that comes up in the North as well, called the 'Phantom Hitchhiker.' "

"You mean what I saw were two *different* ghosts? But they looked so much the same . . ."

"They are the same," Consuela answered. "But two different aspects, don't you see? How can I explain it? Like maybe a statue that looks one way in one kind of light, but if you turn it or change the lighting then it looks different. Or maybe the same, but two people describe it in different manners . . ."

"I think I see, yes," Copper answered. "But why am I seeing the thing at all? I mean, I don't believe in ghosts."

"Some say it comes when a person feels guilty." Conseula laughed. "Knowing you, though, I doubt *that's* the reason. But anyway, the way the myth goes, that's because the woman is guilty of losing her children in the first place. Or, in other versions, for killing them. Or, in yet others, for killing herself, or sometimes she's just been in some kind of accident and maybe doesn't know yet that she's been killed. You see how it goes? Others will say it's a sign of the future, that someone you know is going to be killed, or maybe will kill himself. But, in your case, Copper, what I would say is that you were tired from too much driving—and frightened as well from that truck that almost pushed you off the highway—and just *thought* you saw it. That would be this time. As for the first time, you're always

telling me how San Francisco has so much mist and fog, and how it billows and sometimes looks solid, like something had just stepped in through one's window . . ."

Copper laughed as well. "You mean that I—me, the artist—the one who creates them—just saw an illusion. Or *two* illusions. And maybe—of course I was still half asleep the first time it happened—when Ramon babbled about phantom women, my mind just put the different things it was told together."

"Something like that, yes," Consuela answered. She let her voice trail, as if she were thinking. "Or, well, you say you often do your thinking when you drive alone. It could, perhaps, have to do with your sculpture . . ."

"My sculpture?" Copper asked. "But I hadn't been thinking about that when I saw the vision. And anyway—weeping women and Horus?"

Copper could almost see Consuela nod as she answered—Consuela, the pedant, even in college. "Not Horus, of course, but rather his mother. When Osiris died and his parts were scattered—Set had them scattered around the whole world. And Isis, who still loved him, had to search for them her whole later life. Because of her sadness conducting that search, Isis, just like your ghostly hitchhiker, has often been depicted as weeping."

Guilt, Copper thought as she sped the last miles back to San Francisco, still hoping to get in ahead of traffic—guilt was what Consuela had said caused the phantom's weeping. At least in some versions. But she'd been thinking of Michelle when she saw the vision and, if there were any guilt attached to Michelle, surely it would be Tony's guilt, not hers. Not that her own loves weren't tragic either.

She ticked them off as she drove. Frederico's girlfriend. Poor, stolid Wilhelm. Consuela, who should perhaps have ended up teaching at some major university, writing about if not doing art herself, burning out early. Ending instead in her Phoenix backwater.

Tony in his way, no longer painting but switching to studying Egyptian history. Perhaps for his guilt, too, for what he had done to her. Even if after . . .

They *had* loved after—she tried to remember. Brother and sister, after that first time . . .

He a few years younger, much like Ramon. Sweet, child-like Ramon who, if he hadn't realized it yet, she'd have to tell their affair was over.

The others. How many? She *couldn't* remember. And were they all tragic or, at least, marked by some long-lasting sadness? At least for her lovers when she had to let them go?

Copper shook her head. Perhaps. But perhaps it was *she* who was marked by misfortune. And hardly guilty for how her loves ended, unless it might be for choosing partners too weak to accept the inevitability that love *would* end.

Or, like Michelle, who chose wrong . . .

Copper parked her car a block away from her town-house, then took her time getting her gear out the trunk. Michelle? she wondered. Again her thoughts had come back to Michelle—Michelle who had gone to Kansas City, searching, like Isis, to find some part of Copper still waiting, except she herself had moved farther west by then. And so Michelle stayed there, much like Consuela, in her own backwater . . .

Copper shrugged. Jesus, she thought, I'm getting morbid. Or weepy in old age. She thought again of La Llorona—the first time she'd seen it—and how Consuela had also said it might not mean guilt, but rather portend some future misfortune. Like . . .

She opened the front door of her townhouse and dragged her things in, then crossed the hall to her downstairs studio. She called out, "Ramon?" She hoped he was in—he could help her carry her suitcase upstairs. And then, perhaps over an intimate supper, she could tell him . . .

She saw something glinting. Some hint of movement in one—no, in all ten—of the studio mirrors. Some shadowy thing—her eyes were tired and not yet adjusted to the room's dimness.

She turned first to the half-open window, thinking for a moment it might be the woman again. But then it resolved itself. Ten separate images, no single one giving a complete picture, but adding together to what she saw now.

Ramon's body, hanging.

She would see no more ghosts. At least not hitchhiking on the highway. That she resolved after the police finally

left her, having asked questions, but, afterward, doing their best to comfort her. Certainly not *blaming* her—not for this. Her lover, jealous. Afraid.

He might lose her. It happened all the time.

One policeman in particular was most attentive, one of the younger ones, blond and baby-faced. Someone, perhaps, she would get to know later.

But not for now, she thought. When she'd been filling out forms for the police she'd also been thinking. Thinking of Michelle and Kansas City. Thinking they were a key, one more key to the project she planned. A key like the statue of Horus in Phoenix.

It *had* been Michelle she had been thinking of back on the highway. Normally at this point in a project Copper would go, perhaps to the library, to do book research. To add details in to what was becoming, if still not completely formed, the work's broad image. But visions—especially non-drug induced ones—did not appear without some reason. Not to a creator's mind, like Copper's.

And so her next stop was Kansas City, but not by road this time but by plane. And not even thinking—she'd made a point to take barbiturates before she took off so any visions she might see *would* be dreams. But Michelle was solid enough when she saw her, apparently having put on weight when she'd settled down and bought a small shop near the Art Institute and School of Design. At first she'd sold art supplies—Copper had known that from the occasional letters she'd gotten since. Art and then, later, dope—or at least drug culture paraphernalia—as it evolved into sort of a head shop from which Michelle pursued, if not art, art students. Both men and women.

"You look good, Michelle," she said, smiling.

"Oh?" Michelle answered.

Copper nodded—a sudden picture came to her now of a skinny Michelle, her eyes filled with tears, the way she might have looked when Tony dumped her. "I mean it," she said. "Your figure's filled out. On someone like me it would look fat, but you can carry it."

"Oh?" Michelle said again, but then she smiled back. "Well, if you say it, since you're the artist I'll accept it as being flattery. How have you been, though? And what brings you back here—after *how* many years?"

"Well," Copper said, "I've got a new project." She told her ex-roommate about her vision—her various visions, both of a sculpture having to do with Egyptian mythology and La Llorona and phantom hitchhikers—as the two of them closed up the shop. They went to a place Michelle recommended for dinner and drinks, then back to the shop and the rooms Michelle kept on the second floor.

"Try some of this," Michelle said as they talked, lighting a small pipe and placing it into Copper's hand. "It's kind of Egyptian, or Near Eastern anyway, so maybe it'll help bring more visions. You know, like you're looking for?"

"Mm-hmmm," Copper said, after she'd drawn the smoke into her lungs and passed the pipe back. "It *is* good, Michelle. But what I don't understand—I mean I already know about Isis weeping, but why don't I see *her*? You know, directly? Instead of these other phantom women? And even with that, if what I'm really working on is focused on Horus, why don't I see *him*?"

"Well, you did, you know," Michelle said. "The statue in Phoenix. But also—remember that back in college I studied psychology, including courses on myths and symbols—you *are* seeing Horus, in all of these visions."

"I-I don't understand." Copper puffed on the pipe again when it came back to her, then put it down. "I mean, I know the Mexican stuff and the hitchhiker turn out to be the same thing, or so Consuela said, and that they both have to do with children. And Horus is the child of Isis, who sometimes cries too. But still, all we're talking about is coincidence . . ."

Michelle shook her head. "Do you know who Osiris was, Copper? I mean besides being Isis' husband. He was her *brother*. Like you and Anthony. But that's not all, because in some versions Horus isn't a separate person, but a reincarnation of Osiris, just as, to stretch a point, your weeping hitchhiker is the reincarnation of Isis. You see, the way myths work, they all eventually point to the same thing. The earliest versions—Osiris and Horus are both the same, both child and lover, and brother as well. The earliest version, that's what you must look for . . ."

"Like me and Anthony." Copper nodded, picking the pipe up and having another toke, then passing it back to

Michelle. Like her and her brother, who she would have to see for the next clue. Her brother, Tony, the Egyptologist.

She started to giggle. "You ever hear from Anthony, Michelle?"

"Jesus no," Michelle said. "He never writes to me. God, how I envied you, with your talent—the reason Tony and I broke up was because when I switched to being an art student like he wanted, I couldn't even draw a straight line. A fucking straight line, you know?"

She giggled harder. "A *straight* line, Michelle?" she asked. "What with you and me, no matter what we did when we went out, always ending in bed together."

Michelle stared at Copper, then started to laugh too. A harsh, robust chuckle. "God, yes," she sputtered. "You and me and Tony—and your Spanish bitch-friend, Consuela. Until you got pregnant."

Copper suddenly sat up straight, as if she'd been slapped. Osiris and Horus.

She'd *hated* her pregnancy. But she'd concealed it, at least till the sixth month. She remembered telling people how she'd just been gaining weight. Until the seventh month.

"And then I miscarried," she said, not realizing she'd spoken out loud. This time Michelle sat up.

"No," Michelle said. "And then you aborted it. Don't you remember? You came home that night drunk. Carrying more bottles of what you'd been drinking. You'd called up Tony and told him to bring his friends. Including one you'd slept with at least once or twice, from Harvard, a pre-med student . . ."

She did remember now. Part of it, anyway. Some kind of drug she'd gotten hold of. Drinking more with it, because she feared the pain. Suddenly, possibly for the first time in her life, Copper felt shocked.

"You mean I *caused* it?" she asked. With part of her mind she felt Michelle's arms, tentatively at first, circle her shoulders.

"Uh huh," Michelle answered, kissing her more boldly now on the cheek. "I'd been drinking as well, of course. We all got drunk that night—the stuff you brought with you. Terrible tasting stuff. And I don't think Tony ever forgave you . . ."

"Forgave me?" she mumbled. Another memory—fighting to come back.

Michelle's voice softened.

"It would have been his son."

She bought a pistol before she left Michelle. A Beretta, small enough to fit in her purse, where she transferred it from her luggage after she landed at Logan Airport. She *had* to see Anthony. But, as Michelle warned, even after so many years he might not have forgiven her.

Nevertheless, he was the next key. Of that she was certain. The final key to the "Birth of Horus", the sculpture that she was equally certain would be the greatest of her creations.

She kept an eye out for weeping women, ready to welcome the visions now since they were a key too. She made a point of not taking drugs, of being cold sober, even refusing cocktail service on the long flight from the Midwest to Boston, but was disappointed. At least for the moment. The process, she thought, the artistic process was always marked by a certain perverseness, and then she giggled. She felt high on clean air.

A certain perverseness, she thought, just as she was—a certain sadness, perhaps, left behind her. A Ramon. A Wilhelm. But, always, she went forth to new creation.

A Johnnie. A Lisette—a French girl she'd met one night in Cambridge, at a party she'd gone to at Radcliffe. A Donna and Marty, twin brother and sister. The memories came back as she rode the taxi, first to the Fenway where she stopped at the Museum of Fine Arts. She got an address there—her brother was listed on the staff as a free-lance consultant—and then to the backside of Beacon Hill and a narrow alley that twisted off Charles Street.

She paid the cabbie and carried her bags herself up the steps of a crumbling brick building. A Michelle. A Tony. She thought of Michelle and the week she'd just spent in her still eager arms as she climbed the stairs inside, three flights up to the tenement's top floor. She thought: "The Grave Lover". Ramon and Frederico. "The Vampire". "The Lust of War", one of her earlier pieces in which she'd used parts of Consuela.

"The Birth of Horus". She saw the Woman now, shad-

owy, indistinct, on the top landing. Drifting to—through—a door. Leaving a trail of tears.

Knowing, she followed—that Anthony was the key. Probably the last key. Putting her suitcase down on the hall floor, she clutched her purse to her, checking to make sure the pistol was still inside, then knocked on the peeling, white-painted door.

She heard no answer. She rattled the knob and found it was unlocked.

She thought about models, young boy-like models, as she eased it open. And found, confronting her, a painting.

She gripped her purse harder, and gazed at the painting, huge and primitive, depicting a vulture-winged woman, a savage woman, her face smeared in blood. Her breasts, bare, blood-smeared too.

She exhaled loudly—the wings of her sculpture! Then heard a soft cough from an arched doorway to her right.

"Tony?" she whispered.

A thin-faced man entered, tall and imposing yet frail as well, as if he'd been ill a very long time. A man younger than Copper, and yet with his hair white. "I—Copper?" he asked. He coughed again, louder. "I-I recognize you from your eyes. Their dark intensity—who could forget them? The lines of your cheekbones. Time has been good to you, better to you than me."

Copper began to laugh, thinking of the fear she'd had that this man might kill her. "Anthony," she said. "I recognize you, too. But what's happened to you?"

"Aging before my time," he said. "The Boston winters . . ." He hesitated, then coughed again. "No, that's not entirely true. You, my sister—you've used me, Copper. I might have painted, studied the models, gone to Egypt. And yet I stayed here . . ."

"You speak of using!" Copper was angry—suddenly angry. She clutched her purse against her breasts, gripping the hardness she felt inside. "You *raped* me, Anthony! When I was just eighteen."

Now it was Tony who laughed out loud. "Sister," he finally said, gasping to catch his breath, "don't you remember? I was just *fifteen*." He gestured toward his crotch. "I wouldn't even have known what to do with it, if you hadn't shown me how." Then his voice softened as his eyes

tracked her, appraising her body. It took on a cultured tone.

"Still," he continued, "time *has* been good to you. And not so bad to me. And now you're famous." He winked and smiled. "Do you think you'd like to seduce me again, Copper?"

Copper shook her head, looking for a desk, a table, something to lean on. "I'm confused, Anthony. But . . ."

But the memory came. Yes. She had raped *him*. And then, the abortion . . .

"Then you're not still angry?" she said. "I mean, not just that—but it was your son. Afterwards I told myself I'd miscarried."

Her brother spoke gently. "We thought it was my child, yes. But the abortion was my idea, Copper. What drove us apart was what you did after."

"After?" she asked.

Her brother nodded. "Well, we were all high most of the time then. And you thought it might knit the group more together. And so, when the fetus came out, bleeding as you were you still stumbled around for a big pot. You . . ."

"No!" she screamed. The memory of *that* began to come back too. She reached in her purse and pulled out the Beretta.

Anthony stepped back, putting his hands up in front of his face. "No, I'm not lying. You ate it, Copper. You cut it in parts and fed it to us, too. Michelle. The other girl you went with—the Puerto Rican. Georges. My friend, Henry. You'd had us drink tequila first—you'd just discovered it and bought, God, I don't know how many bottles.

"Except I couldn't stand the taste, so I was still sober . . ."

"You mean"—the gun wavered—"I, you, the others . . ." She started to turn the gun to her own head. "My baby— I made us *eat* . . . ?"

"Yes. Just like Isis. I'm probably the only one who really remembers."

Her hand froze in mid-motion.

"Isis?" she whispered.

Her brother nodded. "Yes. Isis as vulture. The cannibal mother. The eater of dead." He turned and pointed toward the painting she'd seen when she entered his apartment.

"That's what the wings are. In the earliest myths of Isis she tore the dead Osiris apart with her own hands, burying parts of him in the ground to assure its fertility.

"Except for his manhood . . ."

Again the gun wavered. "You mean his penis?"

"Yes. Like your fetus. Our son. The part *you* ate. She devoured his manhood and brought it forth again from her womb as Horus. The new Osiris."

"Then . . ."

"Yes. In later versions, when she tried to find the parts Set had supposedly scattered, that's why the phallus was always missing. Because it was part of her."

"That's why she wept, then?"

"Because she'd never find it again, yes. But *you*, Copper . . ."

Copper pushed the unfired Beretta back in her purse and closed it firmly. "I'll never weep, Tony."

"I know you won't, Copper. At least not until you're very old."

Until she was very old. But she was still not yet thirty-four—and could pass for her twenties. Her son would have been fifteen, going on sixteen. And she had her sculpture.

La Llorona—Isis—the Hitchhiker—Osiris—Horus were all the same. She and Anthony—they were the same, too. The vulture wings over all, but beneath them the new Osiris, nurtured by Isis, and yet entwined with her as lover also. And at her feet, earlier incarnations, Ramon and Wilhelm, Frederico and his murdered girlfriend, Michelle and Consuela doomed in their own ways in soul if not body, but, above all, Isis. Isis and Copper, her own face that of the Weeping Woman. But smiling, as she smiled now, as she took Tony's hand.

"Brother," she said, "I will *never* be very old. You ought to know that." She placed her purse on the table behind her, then took his other hand in hers.

"And now," she said, "about that seduction . . ."

Stick Around, It Gets Worse

Brian Hodge

You weren't there when it happened, but you've spent so much time imagining what she went through during those final moments that she was aware of the world around her, you feel as though you were. You know the details pieced together by forensics experts analyzing the crime, and these feed you plenty of insight, but you knew her as the experts never could.

Remember the swoop of hair that would mask her left eye, and the way she'd always be pushing it back with two fingers, never three, and how that eye, when revealed, seemed to notice something worthwhile in you that no one else could recognize? Remember the way she would listen to music, sitting with folded legs upon the floor, doing nothing, just *listening?* Remember her penchant for giving money to downtrodden panhandlers and her tolerant smile when you complained, a smile that made you feel so small, so petty, so much less formed a creature than she was? Of course you remember, you remember everything, and still so clearly. Somebody has lied—time hasn't healed a thing, not for you.

The experts only knew her post-mortem, knew her unconscious, bleeding in the wreckage of her car, knew her clinging to life while her head was undergoing emergency reconstruction; knew her in the morgue's cold stainless steel drawer. Knew her just enough to tell you that she never once regained consciousness during those last nine hours. Knew her just enough to assure you that even had she lived, she'd never be right again, not the person you married, because the brain damage was just too extensive.

And you?

They didn't even know you at all. If they did they wouldn't have tried to make you see her death as merciful.

You've lost track of how many times you've found yourself right there beside her. She's driving her customary fifteen miles per hour above the speed limit on the Landry Expressway, and bust with the radio, while notched between her thighs is a tall paper cup of Thai iced coffee, her summer drink of choice. Thinking of work, or getting home, or later in the night the way you will feel together, another joyously fevered coupling to make a complete world between your flesh, just the two of you and nothing and no one else. You're flattering yourself, naturally, imagining her last thoughts to be of you, but that's all right; it's allowed; something in you, never touched by daylight, needs to ache so much it makes you groan in still, small hours.

She approaches the overpass and you see it coming from miles away, it feels like, but no matter how loud you scream warnings it never does any good. How little it would take to change things, a flex of her wrist and she'd be in another lane, and that *might* be enough. Somebody else would be bearing this burden, and right now you'd gladly wish it on him. But it's yours, always and forever. It became yours the instant the brick thrown from the overpass smashed through the windshield and pulverized the left side of her head. You wonder, crazily enough, if she just didn't see it coming because her hair was in the way.

Vandals, a young police officer told you. They're pulling these stunts all the time, and he doesn't think they have any real appreciation of the kind of damage they can cause.

The hell they don't, you thought, didn't bother saying. They know exactly what can happen, it's what they're hungry for, and the only thing that might've bothered them was that she didn't kill anyone else when her car went out of control. Ruining the lives of others, they've made this the mission of their own.

At the funeral, family and friends and clergy were brimming with the same big question that, in a moment of weakness, scrawled itself on the front of your brain as soon as you got the phone call: *Why?* Everyone wanted to know why. A few, desperate to dredge up some comfort at bargain basement cost, spoke in platitudes—God's will, all shall become clear one day—and you would force yourself to swallow the bile, if only for *her* sake, knowing she wouldn't have wanted you punching anyone at her funeral.

"God's will?" you contented yourself with repeating, after hearing the phrase one too many times. "I can't decide what's more monstrous: a god who sends little thugs up onto a freeway overpass with bricks to do his dirty work . . . or the way people believe that a god like that actually exists."

Their blind trust has never made sense to you, nor the meager delusions to which they cling as proof of being rewarded for their faith. It's not quite in you to feel smug because you know better, but lately it's not quite in you to pity them their superstition, either. Mostly it's disgust that you feel. They call you lost, but that's just projection, you deduce, because *you're* the one who's comfortable right where you are, realizing there's no reason for anything that happens, ever. How they hate that, because it grants you a freedom they will never know. A freedom that would paralyze them if they did.

You remember something you read years ago, written by Stephen Crane, and how deep within you resonated the chord it struck: *A man said to the universe, "Sir, I exist!" The universe replied, "That fact has not created a sense of obligation in me."*

You take your comfort in the oddest places, don't you?

By autumn grief has become something permanently affixed to you, like a boil grown too thick to be lanced, drained. It must grow until it bursts, or turns to silently consume you from within. Your friends understand—she truly was everything to you—while you in turn understand their reluctance to be around you these days. You just aren't that much fun anymore.

She was the last straw, that broke the camel's heart.

It's got you thinking—you've never really know anyone who's died of natural causes, have you? Parents and grandparents, plus friends and neighbors and casual lovers, they've all left you too early, and in such ghastly ways. Cancers and violence, accidents and congenital defects, aneurysms of the brain and psyche. You've heard of people who've slipped peacefully away in their sleep, or in their favorite easy chairs, after ripe octogenarian lives, but suspect they must be mythical, in the company of unicorns and mermaids.

If you didn't know better, you'd think there was a delib-

erate methodology behind it all, a gradual pattern of calamity spiraling inward until, at last, you're the only one left to be dealt with. You could be expected to think that, but don't, because you still keep your wits about you, thank god—

So to speak.

While fall's vainglorious colors deaden to rusts and browns, and drab wet shadows lengthen across the city, you feel yourself trapped in freefall. The most appealing thing you can think of is the end of it all, by chance or by your own determined hand . . . yet a spark of hope lingers on, that maybe there's something out there worth surviving for, if only you could find it.

It turns you into as restless a wanderer as any junkie hoping to score, as an insomniac, as one of Arthur's knights looking for the Holy Grail. Shoes married to the pavement, you submerge within the wretched refuse; the teeming shores begin at the stoop of the building where you used to live with *her*. Where you sleep, still, although you seem to have quit living months ago.

You don't even know what you're seeking, do you? Only that it's entirely up to you to find it, to make of it your new life and purpose; nothing and no one else can do this for you. You take heart, for it *can* be done: life, like death, can be as random and abrupt as a brick hurtling from overhead.

"Now you take me, for instance," says the old gentleman whom you've come to know as Stavros. "My whole family killed in the war and me just eleven years old. Would I be coming to this country if this hadn't happened? No, no, I don't think so. All this life I've had here? It would be unknown to me."

Mornings, before work, you've taken to stopping by a sidewalk cafe where Stavros holds his solitary court, drinking cup after cup of coffee. Against the autumn chill he wears a bulky knit sweater and on his head a flat billed cap, and if back in Greece he would look like any ordinary fisherman. Here, though, he seems exotic, a rogue and an adventurer.

"Do you ever think you'd been better off if things had just stayed the same?" you ask.

He laughs, showing his great mouthful of strong, stained

teeth. "Never. God rest their poor souls, every one of them, but these were people, let me tell you, who'd clutch a child to their bosoms 'til it suffocated. It wouldn't have been a bit different with me." Stavros peers into his coffee, the twinkle in his eye sharpening into something more cunning. "I was . . . *liberated*. Freed to become all the things that my first life kept away."

He tells you stories, as he does each morning since you first paid him attention; tells you what it was like to cross an ocean and see the world unfolding with eleven-year-old eyes. You listen, and you breathe in the scents of coffee and buses, watching both his seafarer's face and the brisk sidewalk passage of everyone who, unlike you, is going to arrive at work on time this morning.

He's the only friend, new or old, who doesn't seem to mind being around you. And you wonder: Which of you is more desperate for a companion?

You're not sure when you first became aware of it, only that it seemed to imperceptibly creep up on you; something you might've noticed the moment you sat down but only acknowledged after nearly an hour: someone is waving at you. Across the busy street and down one building; a second floor window, ornately archaic, in contrast with the more modern storefront below. Few ever pay any mind to the extinct architecture above their heads. Amazing, the way gargoyles can hide in plain sight.

It's no one you know—you're quite sure of it, just as you're sure it's you this woman is waving at. Even from across the street you can see how white and pasty her skin is, her thick and naked shoulders sloping beneath greasy straggles of dark hair. Modesty isn't her virtue, obviously, and you watch, half-fascinated, half-repulsed, as her breasts squash against the window.

A vivid red grin, the only true color about her, splits her face when she realizes that you notice her.

"Do you . . . see that?" you ask Stavros, and point.

But even as you ignore her frantic overtures for you to come up, come up and join her, you have the feeling that just as this invitation is for you alone, so is the sight itself.

"See what?" he says.

"I . . ." You shake your head. "I should be getting on to work," and when you're halfway down the block curios-

ity gets the better of you, and you turn around to see her waving goodbye—or at least until next time.

The skin condition begins like a common rash, spreading and intensifying from there, from scalp to face, down to your neck and shoulders and chest, you back and arms. A great portion of your waking hours are simply spent scratching an itch that never feels sated, and within days you can scarcely bear to pass before a mirror. Scaly red patches, some crusty from too much scratching . . . you don't wear them well, but then who does?

The dermatologist diagnoses psoriasis. What's causing it, you want to know, *why?* Together you rule out food allergies, various environmental irritants to which you may have exposed yourself; you've not changed these sorts of routines in quite some time.

"Of course," says the doctor, "we can't overlook an emotional component of this outbreak."

Swell. You're not even supposed to grieve properly?

Treatments begin, oral dosages of etretinate and sessions of out-patient ultrasound hyperthermia, but you don't seem to make any improvement; to the contrary, you seem to be getting worse. It gets to the point where your boss thinks it would be a fine idea if you'd take sick leave. You're not the only one relieved, this is welcomed by an entire office full of people to whom you must be becoming terribly aberrant. And at whom you've been increasingly tempted to scream, "None of you knows just how lucky you are, not a single complacent one of you!"

Starvos is the only one who doesn't mind your appearance, but you're wearing a hat pulled low these days, with your coat collar turned up, and bandages whenever your busy fingernails have left your face oozing. Camouflage has become a vital skill.

"No improvements," he says, not quite a question, seeming to mourn for you.

You shake your head, wondering with shame who's staring and who's averting their eyes. When you're not occupied with this you usually glance at the window where the strangely repellent woman waved to you; although as far as repellent goes, you definitely feel a new sympathy toward her. You didn't know what repellent was then.

You think maybe you've seen her since, grinning from

the other windows, other doorways; catching your eye, then disappearing, as if teasing you. But there's a certain innocence in teasing, and hers was lost long ago, if ever she possessed any at all.

Luring you, then? That's more like it.

"If your doctors do you no good," says Stavros, gritting that mouthful of brownish ivory, "then maybe you should go to another kind of doctor."

"A second opinion . . ." you murmur. You're reminded of an old joke. *You want a second opinion? Okay: You're ugly, too.* "I don't know any other kinds of doctors."

And from the way Stavros smiles, you know he's about to make one of his stranger pronouncements.

You're not the type who would ordinarily frequent those who don't hang M.D. shingles from their walls, but, relieved of your office duties, you have all this extra time. And Stavros speaks so glowingly of her, and she does live in his building, so you don't have much of an excuse.

Ellen Medicine Crow is her name. Her father, Stavros told you, as a boy was given tutelage by the legendary Black Elk, although you're not sure if you believe this. Quacks never stop seeking ways to boost their own stock.

"A shaman," you say upon first encountering her. The irony isn't lost on you. If your rationalist friends could see you now.

"I prefer healer," she tells you. "It doesn't sound quite as presumptuous. Or as intimidating."

Intimidating. She's that already, this Lakota woman. She must be near fifty, if not past it, but carries herself tall and strong and supple in a way that's agelessly young. The only giveaway are the crinkles around her eyes. Her hair reaches her waist, black but threaded with strands of gray. Ellen Medicine Crow inspires your first sexual thoughts since *she* died, which frighten you with their suddenness, their *power.*

It's no easier when you learn she wants to come stay with you for a few days. There's so much she has to learn about you before she can help—*if* she can, she adds, which is the main reason you give in. You rather like the honesty of this kind of medicine, of someone who, unlike your usual physician, may be perfectly willing to declare your case a lost cause.

It feels strange having a woman around again, although her presence is hardly like that of a roommate; rather, a bird or some other creature which watches you with bright, all-seeing eyes. And at night she sleeps by your side, although there's no touching but for accidental brushes. You turn away whenever an erection raises, yet you feel sure she must know what you're thinking; too, she surely notices your shame over such traitorous skin, but has the grace to pretend she doesn't.

You distract yourself some of the time with the photo albums that accumulated before the hurled brick changed everything. Page after page of memories, some fresh, some seasoned by years, all of them capable of bringing tears if you look at them just right.

Ellen Medicine Crow lingers behind you as you bow your head at the table, weeping, and you feel her bend lower; feel the light touch of her hands on your shoulders, the press of her forehead at the back of your neck. She's just sharing in your grief, but you drink in her touch with a terrible fear you'll never know anything so tender again.

Perhaps she knows this too, and this is why she mourns.

"Why did you decide to become a healer?" you ask her later, with a drier face.

Hair shimmers as she shakes her head. "I didn't decide. I had nothing to do with it. It decided for me. The most I ever did was choose not to fight it."

"Suppose you wanted something else, that this wasn't what you wanted to do. Wouldn't you have fought it then?"

She's patient with your honest skepticism, has undoubtedly encountered it before. "But how could I? The universe creates what it needs. All I had to do was grow. There's no reason to make it all so difficult."

You laugh, not cruelly, mostly you wonder why you had to turn out so enlightened. "I just can't buy into that," you say, but no more. This hardly seems the time to get yourself into a reasoned argument against determinism.

Although you *can* see the appeal: the illusion of hands moving behind the scenes; accountability, someone or something to blame for the wretched turns life takes in this fucked-over world . . .

And you're angrier than you have any right to be, aren't you?

On the third day Ellen sends you out on an errand, something you must do by yourself. Go find a rock and bring it back, these are her instructions. At least the size of your fist, a rock you feel compelled to pick up more than any other rock.

You've never given rocks much thought before, wanting only to duck them when they're thrown, but she's the healer. You find one a few blocks away—it's a tougher order to fill in the city than you might think—half-buried in a nest of weeds beside a stagnant ditch. It passes Ellen's approval and she has the two of you sit on the floor, facing each other. Her face is serious, clouded even, her focus upon you total; you are the world. And you are in trouble.

"It's more than just your skin," she says. "It's everything, everyone you lose and everything that breaks for you. You wonder why. Why it happens to you. Don't you?"

You shake your head. "I already told you, I don't believe—"

"Lie to yourself if you want, but don't lie to me."

Your head lowers a bit. And you suppose, possibly, you may at least entertain the sometimes notion of believing in reasons, that coincidence stretches only so far. You nod miserably, wondering if Galileo felt this way, forced to recant.

"Then ask the rock."

You stare at her. "Ask . . . the *rock?*"

"Ask the rock, then stare at it. Stare *into* it, so that you see more than just its surface. Wait until you see the patterns and the shapes it shows you. When you see something . . . tell me what it is." She takes pity on your failure to grasp any purpose here whatsoever. "The rock will tell you what you already know, but cannot or will not admit to yourself yet."

So you feel like a fool, holding this flattened slab in your hand. Talking to it. Staring at it as if it's going to talk back. Except . . . it does, of a fashion. Stare long enough and shapes *will* arise, minutiae of texture and shading, and suddenly you realize what's actually going on here. Basic psychology, fundamentally no different than staring at ink blots. Okay, you're back on track, you can accept this after all.

"I see the top of a skull, without the lower jaw—these

dark spots are the eye sockets, and there are the teeth—
do you want me to show them to you?"

She shakes her head, directs you back to the rock.

"There's a snake crawling from a broken eggshell . . .
and that's an axe head . . . there I see a little guy, it looks
like he's caught in the jaws of this primitive-looking fish."

That makes four from the top of the rock; she stops you
and has you turn it over. Your orient yourself to the new to-
pography and keep going: A curved dagger. A branch with
decaying leaves. A butterfly leaving its cocoon. Screaming
faces in profile.

"That's enough," she says, tougher to read than any doctor you've ever been to. What must she think of you? Does
she reserve judgment at all? You watch her lose herself in
thought so deep it could be a trance.

"So . . . what's, what's next? You can't contain yourself.

"Next?" she says, and shrugs as if wondering how you
could be asking this in the first place. "Go put the rock
back"

You're feeling different even before you reach your door
once again, as if you've been less than vigilant, let slip a
crucial guard. You've as much as admitted there may be
more to the world than you give credit for, a wizard behind
the curtain of Oz. One slip is all it takes; which facade will
be the next to crumble?

What better proof than this: You didn't cheat. You returned the rock to the precise spot where you found it, as
if somehow Ellen would know if you conveniently tossed
it in the nearest lot.

Her bag is packed and by the door when you return, and
she's obviously been waiting for you, dreading the need to
look you in the eye. She does it anyway, for you are the
world. And you are in worse trouble than you ever
dreamed. Her gaze is brutally honest.

"I'm sorry," she says. "But I can't help you."

No. Of course not. She's got you talking to rocks—
where can you go from there? And why are you crying?

"Think of what you saw. The symbols, their meanings."

Again, they drift forth. Images of transition, of death to
old lives, emergence into new. Pain and torment and tools
of their infliction. These weren't in the rock and you both
know it, just as surely as you know their true origin.

"You're undergoing a change," she tells you. "You're becoming someone or something else. I'm sorry. It's not for me to interfere with this."

"Because," you murmur, "the universe creates what it needs. And you wouldn't dare tell it it's wrong, would you? That it's got no right to do this to me. *Would you?*"

Your voice grows more ragged as she backs away from you, and how you wish her eyes looked younger, less knowing, less certain.

"What does it want from me?" you scream as Ellen takes flight down the stairs. You're sliding to the floor, arms wrapped around yourself in defense of the cold you suddenly feel. *"What does it* want *from me?"* Her footsteps fade, leaving you with empty stairs and hollow corridors, where even your kindest neighbors must now hide behind their doors if they don't want to see what you've become already.

You spend days dwelling on all the people and institutions and ethics into which you placed your faith, only to have them now failing you. Not that you cast blame—it isn't in your nature to blame. You come to realize that the city is the only thing which hasn't let you down. Solid and grey, it's always there; not that it takes notice of you, but at least it doesn't spit you back. These days that's a lot.

So it's inevitable that it becomes your true home after you return from a movie one night to find that your apartment building has burned. And you cry not for yourself, but for *her,* the way her existence has been systematically erased. Even her clothes are now ash, plus all the photos that kept her alive. She might now have been no more real than a daydream.

You sleep in your car, park where you can, walk when you're no longer able to tolerate its confines. Your crusted skin becomes a barrier between you and them, all of them, with their safe and placid lives. You used to be one of them, but no more—perhaps this is why they no longer see you.

You could get away with a lot, with this new invisibility.

You wonder what it all means, and why you were chosen to play the fool's role in this grand illusion. This whole city a stage, with so few of its players even aware of their own parts.

That most peculiar woman continues to wave at you from afar, her hideous red grin more lascivious now; sometimes she seems to laugh. She knows, oh, she knows all right. Your secrets are hers and always have been. Does she find you during your random travels or do you naturally gravitate to wherever she happens to be?

Does it even matter, when in all likelihood you're destined for each other.

The next time you see her she's waving from the third floor window in a monolithic old apartment building of gray stone. Its gables and cornices look heavy, vast, crumbled by the decades; its walls stand mottled by years of water, seeping and trickling. It looms over you, set against a blue-gray evening sky threaded with hints of dying rose. The block you're in is a gauntlet of bare trees; their leaves underfoot weave a ragged, wet carpet, slick and spicy with decay.

A few steps closer, a shift of light and perspective—you now notice the gargoyles perched on the building's corners and nestled above its eaves. Winged, horned, they hunch and squat above you in silent dominance, caught there like corrupted souls, or grotesque children birthed from granite.

They alone watch your entry to the building.

You find the stairs, and the stairs beckon you up. One floor, two—what a chill this building holds, a mausoleum in the middle of a world that only *looks* sane and ordered. Cabs and cable TV would never know how to find this place.

The third floor.

Hallways are many, but you follow the most likely one, that will lead you to her. Your footsteps are small clicks in a greater hush made not of silence absolute, but small echoing murmurs heard through the walls. Someone is crying somewhere, and someone else laughing; elsewhere children are singing, but it's no song you've ever heard, and not a song for children's throats.

The door you decide upon is stout, peeling, as scabrous as your face. Unlocked, naturally, but you knew it would be. Another hand might not find it so, but for yours the knob twists easily.

It stinks in here, of mildew and unwashed bodies, but nothing you couldn't get used to. Sometimes you crave a

friendly touch so much that you think you'd accept it from
a leper.

And you thought this place would be more empty than
you're finding it. At least two dozen people are here, along
the walls, but there's no furniture to speak of, and no one
sits together, no one talks. Mostly they stare at the base-
boards and the floor, some the ceiling, like gray strangers
in a doctor's office. Waiting for their name, their turn, the
expected surrender of their bodies.

In another room you find no one alive, just a jumble of
blue limbs, bodies with hands bound behind them, thumbs
tied together with wire. You can't see their faces clearly
because all the heads have been covered by plastic bags,
then cinched around the necks with rubber bands. Most of
them died with their mouths open wide, straining against
the plastic, sealed forever.

One of them looks like Stavros, but you can't be sure.

You find her in a room glaringly lit by a naked bulb
dangling from the ceiling. A moist, yeasty smell surrounds
her, but maybe that's just imagination, because her skin
reminds you so much of dough. A roll of fat bunching
about her thick waist, she kneels on the floor before a middle-aged man who lies naked and trembling on a tabletop.
Her arm, her right arm . . . you can't find it, and for a
moment think she must only have one. Then you realize:

She's working it up inside the man. He shudders, groan-
ing, as one bony foot pedals ceaselessly in the air, like a
tickled dog.

You watch, a voyeur, until at last she grins at you. Red,
so red. A tangle of greasy hair obscures her eyes, and she
licks her lips as if she'd like to kiss you.

Not yet; not yet. You're not that desperate yet.

"Get started anywhere," she tells you. Her voice is low
and, for a woman, almost gravely; not unerotic. "That's the
one thing about this place, the work's never done."

"I . . . I don't understand." At least you're being honest.
You think.

And she laughs, fisting her arm another inch into the
man. "I remember when I was like you."

"How . . . like how?"

She grins again. "Asleep." Then she tilts her head back,
and you know her eyes must be closed in something like

ecstasy. Her mouth curls into a sneer, lips skinning back, and she's gritting her teeth, little gray pegs that rim her jaws.

"So few innocents," she says, "and so much time."

The man cries out, suddenly and sharply, and with the thick sound of membranes giving way she yanks her arm out. It glistens, and in her hand is clutched what may be his heart. It's so hard to tell, though—you think it should be red, but mostly it's clotted black, as if riddled with disease.

"Thank you," he breathes, head lolling back, and at last his leg drops prone, exhausted, spent. "No more, please, no more . . ."

She rests the organ on the sparse gray mat of hair sprouting across his sunken chest. "You know better than that. With men like you, there's always more."

She has her arm back in up to the elbow before you can turn to run, run from the building into the welcoming night, where you have no name, no longer even a face.

In the months since *she* died you've frequently found yourself driving the Landry Expressway, even when you have no good reason for being here. You drive it one direction, turn around at an exit chosen at random, drive it the other. Giving in to a need to linger where your one true love met her end, you suppose. Or perhaps your need is baser still—tempting fate, catch me if you can.

Red-eyed, red-faced, you burn gas this night as if there's no tomorrow. And maybe there isn't. The world has surprised you, has shown you things that a year ago might not have even been allowed through the filters that all brains keep in place to strain out that which cannot be tolerated. Now, though, you've been prepared, and it will take so much more to surprise you.

Traffic has been thinned by the lateness of the hour, but here you are in white line fever. When you see something hurtling at you from above you don't even swerve. The windshield explodes, a brief storm of safety glass pebbles showering your bed, your home, the final sanctuary left to you. The brick ricochets off the passenger seat, slamming into the ceiling, then the dashboard. Surprisingly, you feel little fear, knowing that you can't be killed. Not here, not like this. You've come too far; something has invested much cruel effort on your behalf.

You're standing on the brakes; the car spins out across two lanes of screaming traffic, and then you've broadsided a chainlink fence that shears apart to let you through. You've barely come to a rest on the other side before your equilibrium is restored and you scramble from the car. Others have slowed to look, to marvel, as you emerge as unscathed as anyone can expect. Dusting yourself clean of glass, seizing the brick that was meant for your head . . .

And you run.

Backtracking, running parallel to the expressway, you pound toward the ramp that lets drivers on from the overpass. The city, the night itself, has turned red in your eyes, and you wonder what they're saying about you in those cars that swerve to miss you on the ramp. They notice you now, don't they, these people who once were you.

You crest the rise, stand for a moment beneath a sky full of gathering clouds. Down below you can see the fresh loops of rubber left by your tires, and on the other side of the overpass you see them, two figures running from the scene of the crime, and now you obey the purest and most instinctive impulse you've ever felt.

Whatever has filled you, they're no match for it. Run as they might from the expressway, deeper into mazes of brick and asphalt and corrosion, you gain on them in a matter of minutes, until they are close enough to bring down like deer before a wolf. You hurl the brick while yet on the run, and it arcs past the shoulder of the nearest fugitive, toward the leader, thudding solidly into the back of his head. Was there ever any doubt? Something guided it there, as surely as it was first guided through your windshield.

They go down in the street, one tripping on the other. The one you've struck doesn't get up; the other scrambles for his feet but you're there, upon him. He rolls over to face you, eyes feral in their terror; he can't be more than fourteen years old.

He thrashes beneath you with skinny stick limbs and unkempt hair, and you retrieve the brick. In your grip it feels light as a dream, heavy as an anchor. With the first downswing you crunch the boy's eye socket; the second unhinges his jaw, the third staves in his forehead and stops him from moving after one final, frenzied convulsion. He makes a

much easier target, until there's no more point left to hitting him.

The other one is trying to crawl away by the time you finish, legs dragging weakly behind him, knees too weak to support his weight. The back of his jacket is already slick with the cascade of blood from where the brick first connected. You wonder who his parents are, how they let him end up like this, with no more regard for the other people than bugs on which they might drop stones out of boredom. You wonder if they'll miss him. Or instead shed a few token tears, then go on their way, creating other monsters, other demons who haunt these lands, these canyons, these buttes.

Demons. Yes, that's it. That's what he must be. You know what they look like now. You know what makes them. And most of all you know why they're needed.

He doesn't give you any trouble at all.

And soon after you stumble away from them, the rain begins, disgorged by swollen black clouds, falling to rinse you clean, and to wash away the worst of the slick you've left in the street for rats and other eaters of the dead.

There's no longer any need to scan the windows for a glimpse of she who has been luring you for longer than you even realize. You know just where you'll find her, where she's waiting, and if you don't quite yet understand *why,* you've learned that everything comes to you in time.

What a life you've led. What a life you've been liberated from. What a life into which you've been sent, not like a lamb to the slaughter, but the one who holds the knife.

The universe, after all, creates what it needs.

The immense building stands as solid as a fortress, its stone walls gleaming black in the rain. Her window is vacant, but that's all right; you have faith. Your only welcome comes from the gargoyles, watching as you near this one place in the world where you belong.

Does the rain fall harder just before you enter? Maybe. Maybe it does.

At the last moment you cross a weed-choked lawn to the corner of the building, where three floors up a squatting gargoyle serves as a downspout. From its mouth vomits a continual deluge of water, and for a timeless respite you stand beneath the flow, to let it wash clean the last of what-

ever clings to you from what you used to be. There you stay, until the final tears are rinsed from your eyes, and you can no longer grieve for a lost love whose only purpose was to teach you those things that truly begin tonight.

And then you turn for the door, to join the fellowship of gargoyles, to confront your reason for being, to assume your place in the scheme of all things in heaven and on earth.

Voices in the Black Night

Larry Tritten

Kern decided to go the main branch of the public library to see if he could find a book he had looked for in used book stores casually but persistently for years. It was a novel titled *Bravo, My Monster.* He had found it originally in the tiny library at an army post where he was stationed. It was a surreal horror story, something of a philosophical parable about freedom and bondage. And he remembered the name of the author, I. Tarcov, and that the book was a translation from Polish. Recently memories of the book had made him determined to find a copy of it, as one might undertake to seek out an old friend one hasn't seen for years.

Kern hadn't been to the main library for a couple of years, although he occasionally went to the small branch library in his neighborhood. The main library, a huge three story edifice of gray stone downtown, had always struck as a cross between a fortress and some sort of vast sepulchral institution worthy of a story by Kafka or Ligotti. It had also at some point, he remembered, inexplicably become something of a headquarters for a variety of vagrants, panhandlers, and winos who lounged and loitered along the short bleak strips of worn lawn surrounding it, on the broad steps at the entrance, and even on the benches in the cavernous hallways and at the tables in its solemn reading rooms. Kern remembered thinking that these derelicts were not unlike most of the old volumes on the library shelves, timeworn, deteriorated, musty. Such antiquity made him feel gloomy. Kern much preferred the brightly lit new book stores with the warm colors and striking designs of fresh paperback covers. This was where smartly dressed and lovely young women were encountered in aisles more often

than the academicians and shambling derelicts of the main library.

Kern took the street car from his neighborhood to the Civic Center, and when he got off noticed that the sky had shifted from a soft blue to the color of old cement and an annoyingly harsh wind now flailed at pedestrians along the block. He walked the two blocks to the library, noting with revulsion as he approached the shabby men all along the side of the building, some with bedrolls, one trio passing a wine bottle back and forth. Kern went through one of the heavy glass doors and into the vault-like lobby. The main stairway, between the two antique elevators, was palatial in scale, and as he went up the broad steps he noticed a few homeless types even here, at the sides of the steps, looking aimless and dispossessed. He thought of the French Revolution, the lower class taking over the palace. Christ, he thought.

In a central room on the first floor the card catalog was contained in three huge banks of long wooden drawers. Kern had never learned to use the catalog with exact precision, its very size being somewhat intimidating, and he was just independent-minded enough to prefer not asking for assistance, so he decided to search and browse the shelves where the fiction was, assuming that he could gradually zero in on the book if it were here. He enjoyed browsing and was in no hurry.

Kern headed for the wing at the other end of the floor, where fiction was kept. The huge room was filled with books shelved in the walls and bookcases on both ends, these flanked by a few reading tables, a librarians desk in the middle of the room. A heavily sedate atmosphere seemed to emanate from the combination of the resolutely silent people reading at tables and the cumulative blend of muted colors from the hundreds of old rebound books. Kern wandered between two rows of bookcases, glancing at the authors' names, seeing that they began with the letter "P." He kept scanning until he found himself among the "R's", then followed those around into the adjacent aisle until he came upon the "T's". There was nothing by I. Tarcov on the shelf. Of course, Kern thought, if they had the book it might be checked out, and it could also be in a more specific foreign collection in another section. He

realized with fleeting irritation that he would have to appeal for help from a librarian. As he glanced about his attention was suddenly lured by a man sitting alone at one of the reading tables. He wore rumpled black slacks, an old pale green shirt that gave the impression of having laundered over years into a state of near colorlessness, and a baseball a cap with "BUDWEISER" printed on it. He had the care-worn look of incipient old age, though he was probably no more than fifty, and his abstracted expression as he sat there, with no book or magazine before him but merely looking into space, identified him as one of those fugitives who came to the library not read but to linger.

Kern decided to check the bookcases on the other side of the room, where perhaps he might find foreign authors. As he walked past the table where the man he'd noticed sat he felt something brush lightly against his belt and glanced down in reaction, realizing that the man had reached out to get his attention by giving him a momentary, distracting touch. "Sorry," he said apologetically to Kern in a carefully modulated low voice. "I . . . wonder if you . . . have a match."

Kern said "No," and gave the man such a penetrating glance that he responded immediately with a virtually abject smile, then said, "Uh, oh, I wouldn't light up *here*. I was going outside. For intermission."

As Kern reflected on the odd choice of words, the man spoke again, "I need an intermission now and then, like it was a play, or a long movie. Need a smoke. All those voices can be pretty . . . exhausting."

Kern nodded politely and started to walk away, but the man said, "You don't smoke, then?"

"No." Again Kern started to leave, but the man said, "Maybe you should."

"Smoke?" Kern said, transfixed by the outrageous suggestion.

"Yes, I know what they say," the man said, "But it relaxes me. Maybe one day it'll be discovered smoking is one of the healthiest things we can do."

Kern looked at the man's sincere expression with mingled amusement and perplexity. He looked around to see if their exchange was distracting anyone, but the man's

voice was so carefully quiet and they were so far from the nearest reader that no one was paying any attention.

"You think that's silly," the man said, and Kern saw that his expression had changed from being self-effacing to vaguely wily. "But I've got thousands of ideas." He indicated the bookcases behind Kern with a gesture. "I've listened to all of these books." He smiled, then made an expansive gesture that presumably indicated the whole library. "To most of the books in here. You know what a polymath is?"

It was one of those words whose meaning Kern had known at one time but forgotten. "No," he said, irritated at his faulty memory.

"*See??* And *I* never went to college!" The man's smile was complacent but cordial. He motioned with his hand. "Please," he said. "Sit down."

Christ, Kern thought but to his surprise he found himself sliding onto the chair across from the man. He was the sort of person salespeople could trap with their spiels because he was not forceful enough to cut them short with an emphatically negative remark.

"What're you reading?" the man asked.

"Reading?" Kern repeated, blankly.

"What book?"

"Nothing," Kern said. Cursing himself for having sat down, he resolved instantly to excuse himself and leave.

"It's good to hear the living talk," the man said, smiling. He looked at Kern so appreciatively that Kern hesitated again, and the man went on, "I live alone, and pretty much just come here days. I don't have a TV, or even a radio so I listen to *them.*" He motioned to the bookcase behind Kern. "The ones who have died, I mean, and become voices. Of course, they aren't really dead, are they? That's the point, they're immortal. So long as a book contains their voice." He smiled at Kern, and went on, "I know, I know, every linguist will tell you writing and language are two different things. You can't use the phrase 'written language'. But the books by those who have gone do have voices, the writing does talk. It can even *sing!*"

Kern shifted uneasily in his chair, confronting the man's piercing gaze with one of his own that revealed no attitude, although he was thinking, *Jesus Christ!*

"In the beginning," the man went on, "all the voices of the dead but immortal writers blended together, hundreds of them, and it was sort of like the sound of a dark river flowing, loud, *loud*, or like applause, an *avalanche* of applause. But, then, sometimes it sounded like song, too, like all of them singing at once, beautiful voices but *dissonant*. But then after a while I got so I could separate the voices. Like if you were looking at a whole storeful of TV screens all on but finally you just focus on one, on one at a time." He gave his head a thoughtful little shake. "In a way all of the voices are in competition. Writers are almost as vain as actors. But, then, that's because they've got *something to say*, you know. And they end up in libraries talking to those of us who have been chosen to hear them. One of the things that fascinates me is finding out how a famous writer's voice sounded. I'd never heard Hemingway's voice until his stories spoke to me, and I was amazed by how feminine his voice is. Ironic, huh? You'd be amazed by some of them. Lincoln. Shakespeare." He smiled. "Demosthenes."

Kern found himself divided between the impulse to flee and being captivated by the bizarre quality of the man's lunacy.

The man stared down at the table and an edge of uneasiness entered his tone as he continued, speaking even more softly, "Sometimes, though on gray days, it seems like they're *screaming*, or crying, disembodied screams, as if he voices are unhappy not to have bodies, as if being immortal as just a voice, with its thoughts, isn't enough. Writers like Hemingway, for example, or London who were very physical, very sensual sometimes seem to just moan and moan. When I hear that I'll go to the philosophy section, because lots of those voices tend to be very *thoughtful*, you know, resigned." The man gave Kern a half-smile. "It's really a sort of graveyard here. The books are like tombstones, but with long epitaphs that just go on and on. Even when The End stops a voice, there's just a pause before it starts again. It's like a *living* graveyard, full of not quite dead demi-corpses . . . You know what?"

"What" Kern asked in a quiet, dry voice.

"I wonder what it's like at night when nobody's here, you know? When there are no readers to hear them, the voices just going out to darkness. Like actors performing

in an empty theater. Voices in the black night. That must be lonely. But then the library opens in the morning. That's when they sing. They know life is nigh. Even Papa Hemingway sings like a songbird, a love lark, in the morning hours. Happy as if he'd just been embodied and killed a gazelle."

Kern saw that the man expected some sort of response from him, so he strained out a weak smile, nodding almost imperceptibly.

"Some of them, the most likely immortals, are in hundreds, thousands of libraries, which means their consciousness is layered and suffusive in the metaverse. Of course, if somebody had just one book in one library and it was destroyed there would be a final death and oblivion for that one."

Listening to the man, Kern decided that this would be his last visit to the main library for quite a while. Time, he thought, to cut this nut short. He said, "Well, it's time for me to get going, I'll let you have that smoke . . . Nice meeting you."

"What smoke? I got no matches," the man said as Kern started to get up. He frowned, adding, "And we didn't meet. What's your name?"

"Charles," Kern said reluctantly, losing his patience now. He stood up.

"Aren't you going to listen for a while, Charles? See if somebody talks to you?"

"Got to be going," Kern said.

The man gave him a look that was both annoyed and importunate. Get stuffed, Kern thought, and walked abruptly away from the table. Outside the room he exhaled a deep breath and chuckled audibly. Christ! Enough of this library, he thought. A quick pit stop in the men's room downstairs and he was out of here.

On the ground floor Kern went into the men's room. He was pleased to find it empty and went to stand at the last of a row of urinals against one wall. He unzipped his pants, aligning his aim, and gave a pleasant little shudder of relief as the stream began, then grinned and shook his head with vexed amusement as he thought about his encounter upstairs. Moments passed while Kern stood there, and suddenly he had a premonitory sense of something different

in the room and became quickly aware of another presence. Without looking he was sure someone was standing just behind him.

Irresistibly, he looked. A man stood within arm's reach, someone who reminded him of the stereotypical prospector in western movies. He wore shabby, nondescript clothes, had red-rimmed eyes, a partly white unkempt beard, and was holding in one hand a nearly empty olive drab duffel bag. "Spare a buck?" he asked.

Kern closed his eyes for a moment, repressing a sigh. He zipped up his pants and turned around.

"C'mon," the man said.

Kern was deliberating on whether to yield to the undertone of menace by handing over some change or being true to his irritation when something incredible happened. There was a swift diverting movement of the man's hand, a momentary glimpse of something shiny, and he looked down with extreme disbelief at the switchblade knife that had disappeared up to its grip into his stomach, then watched as it was withdrawn, slowly it seemed, as if time had assumed the quality of a slow-motion film. Then a bright, ravishing pain blossomed inside him. An amazingly bright floral pattern appeared on the front of his white shirt and he regarded it with a confused fascination, suddenly feeling powerful indignation as he realized it was his blood. He was being stabbed! The knife delved again into his body, receded again.

"Horse's ass!" the man grated.

Kern took a step, swaying like a marionette with half of its strings cut, then faded down, slowly, slumping over on the cold tile floor. He grimaced as he had a fragmented vision of the man kneeling to remove his wallet from his pants pocket, then standing up. He seemed to be receding to a very remote distance, like a figure seen through the large end of a telescope.

The door to the room closed with a long sigh and Kern lay beneath his soggy shirt, staring at the ceiling. Some time passed, then he saw a face above him. The face of the man upstairs.

"Gee, Charles, you're hurt *bad*," he said. "I best get help."

Yet he remained motionless, staring at Kern. "Oh, you're

done," he said at last, with finality. He shook his head sympathetically.

"Too bad you aren't a writer. You'd just go *on* and *on* . . ."

Kern's body was lacerated with fierce pain that made his mind career, thought dimming. His fingers plucked at his jacket pocket, got inside it, hauling out the book which he dropped onto the floor.

The man picked it up and Kern heard him very remotely, exclaim, "Hey, a diary!"

Kern had intended to go to a coffee house later, have a cappuccino and write about yesterday.

When the police had gone, and the ambulance had gone, and the crowd dispersed, the man Kern had talked to went into the room in the library where the biographies were shelved. He wandered around for a while, casually pretending to read the titles of books, and when no one was looking at him he moved furtively over to a corner. He pulled one of the small stools beside a bookcase over to the wall and stood on it, stretching up to reach with Kern's diary and tuck it onto the very top of a high wall shelf back out of sight where it might easily remain for years before anyone noticed it. Then he went to a table and sat down, folding his hands, and waited to hear Kern's story.

Being and Nothingness. Sartre's title described the "sensation" perfectly. Kern *was,* yet he felt like *nothing.* Because he couldn't *feel.* He could somehow hear himself projecting his words, it was like hearing himself read his diary. He remembered with what complete joy he made that last diary entry, describing as lovingly and poetically as he could making love to Moira all through the night, his nerves translating his mind's love into a consuming continuity of ecstatic sensation. *Love.* He was relating that love to someone now, he was aware, but the thoughts were oddly flat and distorted to him because he had no way to *feel.* So memories of the love were as imperfect as a great work of art seen through waxed paper, vague, frustrating, purely frustrating. He could not *feel* his words.

Cogito ergo sum? Wrong, Descartes, wrong . . .

Kern had the impression of hearing himself crying

through the flow of his words, mental tears seeming to overwhelm his words, his lonely and unfelt words that would, he suspected, be the whole of his dreamlike reality for a very long time, if not forever.

Stealing the Sisyphus Stone

Roberta Lannes

Projected before him was the image of two young girls examining their genitals in a mirror, sending his lust factor into the stratosphere. Electric current buzzed up Steve's leg to his scrotum. Grown used to the amount of juice the doctor had been sending him, rather than inhibit his erections, it provoked and enhanced them. Only problem was, as soon as he had a hard-on, the ring regulator registered it, zapping him with a jolt hot enough to fry frozen sausage.

"Aaaah! Jesus fucking Christ! Off! Turn it off!"

The room went dark. Steve swore he saw the blue glow of current illuminating his cock like a light saber from *Star Wars*.

"Cut it!"

Dr. Bragg's throaty growl came over the intercom. "Steven, you blew it. What happened to following my directions?"

"I'll follow directions, jus . . . jus . . . just turn the fucking thing off!" She was such a sadist.

"I need your commitment, Steven."

He shouted as loud as he could from between gritted teeth. "I fucking promise!"

It quit. He felt the after-buzz as his cock deflated onto the naugahyde chair. Shivering, he pulled the paper smock close.

"You can remove the unit, Steven. The demulcent cream is in the anteroom."

"Thanks." He whispered derisively.

"I want you in my office. Four minutes to get your clothes on and get here, Steven. That's all you have."

He looked back over his shoulder to the one-way mirror. He knew she was behind it, grinning at him, mocking him. God, he hated her.

And he needed her. If she didn't okay him for release

into prison after the treatment, he was going back into the state hospital. He wasn't crazy, he was sick. Every asshole in the hospital was unbearably bugfucking nuts. He never wanted to go back there again. Never.

He gingerly removed the bands and wires, balled them up in his fist and threw them at the wall. Yeah, he was angry. More pissed at himself than at the therapy. He should be better by now. Five months into it, and he was still chronically whacking off, even when he wasn't thinking about eight-year-old pussy.

In the anteroom, before he put on his baggy pants and t-shirt, he wiped the anesthetic cream onto his penis. His cock went hard instantly. The cream went to work quickly, but Steve was faster. He wiped his jism on the paper smock and shoved it into the trash. Dr. Bragg would have the smock checked for semen, but he didn't care. Not at the moment.

Her voice came on the intercom. "One minute, Steven." He hurried into his clothing. "Thirty seconds."

He grumbled as he closed the anteroom door and dashed to her office down the hall, the security guard assigned to him in pursuit.

Cynthia Bragg sat behind her metal desk, her figure hidden in a *Whitehall Institute and Treatment Center* lab coat. Her arms folded over her chest, her forehead set in a semi-permanent frown of disapproval, she licked her lips.

She sniffed the air. "Sit down, Steven."

Damn. She smelled it on him. He looked at his feet.

"You masturbated, didn't you?"

He shrugged. "I guess."

"Steven, you are the most resistant patient I've ever dealt with. Do you realize I have less than a month to show enough progress on your chart to justify continuing treatment? If not, you know what's going to happen."

"I know, Dr. Bragg. I don't want to go back there." He looked at her plaintively. "Nothing's working with me. It's like my shit adjusts to whatever you throw at me."

She put a finger to her temple, her face softening. "Yes, that's obvious. I'm glad to know you can make a conscious connection. That's encouraging."

"It is?"

"Yes." She opened his folder, looked at the computer

screen across her desk, then tapped at the keyboard. "I've run out of options, Steven. You've got a Sysyphaen obsession. The only thing left is . . . well, it's a last resort."

"What the hell is a Sissy-fishing obsession?"

"Don't play dumb with me, Steven. You were the one who came in here months ago whining about Eros, Thanatos, Electra and Oedipus, barking about why psychologists had to mix the Greeks up in something as stupid as mental pathologies."

"I did? Must have been a phase." Steven shrugged. "So what does that mean?"

"You're saying you've never heard of Sisyphus?"

"Sure, I've heard of him. I just don't get the connection."

She frowned, thinking. "All right. Sisyphus was condemned by Hades to roll a stone up . . ."

"I know this. What's it got to do with my sickness?"

Dr. Bragg reigned in her frustration. "You weren't born as you are now. Something affected you, your sexuality. You may not know what it was, consciously, yet, but you've been acting out the trauma compulsively since puberty. Your sickness is your stone. You're condemned to this state for rebelling against the past, just as Sisyphus was for returning to the land of the living to get his revenge on his wife, and refusing to return to Hades."

Steve looked at his feet and mumbled, "I never left Hades." Then he recovered. "Hey, what's this last resort?"

She watched him a moment, then sighed. "Simply put, we call it *The Treatment*." She emphasized the words as if they carried a lot of weight. "The therapies we've used have more specific names because they are used as common practice."

"What if *The Treatment* doesn't work?"

"Steven, it's always worked. Eventually. It's just that it's not preferred. It's still somewhat experimental and rather . . . rigorous."

"And that shit isn't?" He pointed toward the shock room.

"They're not comparable."

"What is it?"

"It's a combination of psychotropics with virtual reality and aversion therapy. No electro-shock. It's complex. And it's tailored to the participant."

"So it's designed for a freak like me?"

She closed his file. "Freak? You mean a sexual deviant."

"Yeah." Steve shrugged. He hated formal labels.

"The most stubborn of all compulsive behaviors to treat are sexual, Steven, we've discussed this. The Treatment was designed to work with the limbic portion of the brain, which is difficult to access through conventional methods. For men with these behaviors, it's nearly a no-fail remedy."

"So why not use it up front when a guy like me comes in?"

"Because the therapies we've done with you usually work to a beneficial, measurable degree." Head down, she looked at him from under her eyebrows.

Steve read her expression. "That's not the only reason, is it?"

She became genuine, concerned. "Steven, The Treatment is serious medicine. It sometimes cures more than just the ailment. The origin of this sickness is deeply rooted, and in order to change the pathways the sickness travels, we have to mess with some integral neural network."

It was the first time he saw anything close to compassion or vulnerability in her. A childlike quality. His dick went hard. He had to keep his act together.

Then her tone changed, went dark. "But it's unpredictable."

He went flaccid. "What do you mean . . . unpredictable?"

"With each treatment, there's some additional affect loss. Something other than just the locus of disease. A patient may, for instance, lose the desire to masturbate completely. Or lose the desire for . . . female partners." She looked away. "It's different every time. Rarely is the loss of affect the same."

Steve stood. When he got nervous, he began running his fingers through his long wavy hair, and trembling. He was shaking like crazy.

"So, if some guy lost his thing for women already doing this shit, it's not going to happen to me?"

"I can't say." She was impatient with him. "You can refuse The Treatment, but you know what that means."

"Shit."

"Steven. I wish there was another way."

He whispered, "Yeah. What else is there, castration? No

way." Wiping his face with his hands, he resigned. "Okay. Let's do it."

Benjamin Nakamura and Claire Butterworth sat at their computer stations, their chairs turned to face one another. Claire threw a wad of print-out at Ben. It bounced off his palm as he batted it aside, grinning.

"You shit. You designed that virus so Purdue's revised program will vomit *all* of its previously accumulated data whenever the user accesses that file. That's cruel."

Ben grinned at her. "You're just jealous. If you'd have thought of it first, you wouldn't be so mad."

"I'd have found another way to sabotage it. Something more subtle, but just as ingenious. They don't deserve complete free reign of our program."

Ben leaned back in his chair. "Yeah, what's three years of intensive research to them if they don't have to do it? Lazy bastards. Some rich alumni donate a million plus to Whitehall and expect us to fork over any new programs we develop. It's more like extortion."

"It sucks."

A feathery ding came over the intercom. Claire pressed the speaker button on the phone.

"Butterworth."

Cynthia Bragg sounded anxious. "Claire, it looks like I'm going to need you guys. Can you and Ben meet with me in . . . say fifteen minutes?"

Ben nodded to Claire. "No problem. Your office?"

"No. There. I'll come over there."

The two exchanged glances. Claire chuckled nervously. "Whoa, must be serious."

"Nothing less. It's Treatment time."

"See you in fifteen." Claire released the button then spun in her chair, yipping with glee. "Oh boy, we've got a live one!"

Ben grinned. "I'm ready."

She stopped suddenly, gripping the table's edge. "What if this is the psychotic she promised us."

"Claire, we've been working on the program for more than four years and the bugs are worked out, believe me. If this is her psychotic, we can do it."

"Yeah, all the bugs were worked out up through patient

X-8. Not quite. Maybe there are more irregularities we need to address."

"Look at the diminishing affect-deconstruction we noted. X-8 left us with complete freedom from bedwetting, and only moderate revulsion of excretory function. That's the best yet. How much more do you think we can improve the program?"

"I want zero affect loss. The margin's still too wide."

"And I thought I was a perfectionist . . ."

"Anal-retentive, maybe . . ."

Ben wadded up paper and flung it at Claire. She caught it, then scooted her chair next to his. Putting her hand to his cheek she touched her lips to his. He grabbed her out of her chair and onto his lap. They kissed long and deeply. When his hand began to grope under her lab coat for a breast, she pulled away.

"You want us to get caught, don't you?"

He tickled her and she shrieked. "You started this."

"Okay. Okay, stop. You're right. Sorry." She straightened her coat and oozed back into her chair.

"Shit, look what you did to me." He squeezed the lump in his khakis.

The tapping at their door broke them both up into giggles.

"Down, boy."

Claire went to the door and let Cynthia in. The three of them moved to the conference room. Cynthia set down the disks and hard copy files on Steven Saterfield, then pushed them toward Ben.

Ben rubbed his hands together. "This the psychotic for us?"

"Sorry, no. He was transferred back up to Atascadero."

"What've you got?"

"Resistant pedophile with mixed sexual deviations. Young girls, mostly. He's mildly anti-social, moderately narcissistic, and manic-depressive with the manic being the primarily expressed mode."

"Yeah? How'd you get him?"

"He kidnapped a seven year-old retarded girl and kept her for three and a half months. Never penetrated her, can't maintain erections for intercourse, but compulsively masturbates. Had the girl manipulate and fellate him to

orgasm. Reached the ability to feel remorseful in standard therapy, but was clearly unable to control the compulsion to offend. He asked for help, so Dr. Alcaron sent him here, knowing our success rate with resistant cases."

Claire shifted in her seat. "Why was he in Bellevue and not in prison?"

"He got a publicity-hungry attorney who got him tried with an insanity defense. You might recall. It was all in the papers. Turned into a big deal because it worked. Got him committed. But he doesn't want to go back to the hospital, my Steven Saterfield, so we're left with The Treatment. If it works, he's willing to finish his time in jail."

Claire steepled her fingers, frowning. "Sounds perfect for what we do."

Ben nodded. "I can tailor the program, just let us have his charts and your notes."

"Everything's on the disk, but I'm leaving copies of my notes, just in case."

"When do you want us to meet with him?" Ben reached for the disk.

"I don't. He's a state commitment and there's a problem if we run this like a private consult. If you want, I'll send over some of the videos of his therapy sessions and deduce what you can for your program. Sorry."

Claire flipped open the file. "Hey, we don't want our work thwarted because some state boy cries unfair practices, do we?"

"Claire, Ben, this guy really wants to get help. I've seen the core personality and he's worth it."

Ben caught Claire's eye, then looked to Cynthia. "We get the picture. Leave it to us."

Cynthia stood. "I trust you. Thanks."

They stared at the door after Cynthia closed it behind her. Neither spoke for a while. Ben reached over to Claire, put his hand atop hers. She flinched ever so slightly.

"I can do this one without you, Claire. You don't have to subject yourself to this monster."

Claire turned to him, her eyes hard. "What about you?"

"I'm going to be fine. I can focus on the outcome. You know, think of this in terms of cleaning up the program, making it ready for sale. I'm concerned about you. How it'll affect you."

"Do I appear to be crumbling like a cookie to you?"

He snapped at her. "Dammit, Claire, no one knows better than I do about what happened. I know *you.* You put on a tough face."

She took his chin in her hand and squinted at him. "Ben, I wouldn't miss this opportunity for anything."

Ben felt the chill travel up his spine and shivered. "I don't know . . ."

"I do. Case closed."

The dream came to Steve almost every night. It was Paola, the retarded girl, sitting in the ratty chair he'd given her, wearing the communion dress he'd kidnapped her in. As he'd trained her, she sat with her legs spread, hooked over the arms of the chair at her ankles, the white froth of polyester lace pulled up over her head exposing her perfect little body from belly to bottom. Her peals of laughter were like the ringing of glass chimes.

Steve was on his knees before her, hands clasped in prayer at this shrine of his making. In the dream he couldn't smell her, nor could he taste her, which frustrated him to the point that he couldn't get an erection. Nada. He put his nose to her hairless mons, let his tongue anoint her virginal pussy, yet he was denied the clean essence of her. Her innocence. He always woke then, angry.

Dr. Bragg had turned her pie-shaped middle-aged face to him upon hearing of the dream and asked him if he saw the dream as a kind of penance for his lust. He'd laughed heartily. Perhaps he'd never had any formal education beyond high school, but he was well-read and intelligent. Certainly smart enough to know the dream was his unconscious expressing the continuing anguish over his own lost innocence and the defeat in his attempts to take someone else's to replace it. Shit, he'd read psychology books.

This morning, the dream had ended differently and he was still reverberating from its effect as he sat in group therapy. Dr. O'Dell was the facilitator, a tall, gaunt man who wore bow ties and custom oxfords, one with a thicker sole to accommodate a defect. The group consisted of two drug addicts, an insomniac, an impotent guy and an alcoholic.

Steve watched as the lunatics took over the asylum.

Nothing of depth or purpose went on in group. The others bickered and complained and he hated their whining. He just went into his head, thinking about how he never wanted to go back into the loony bin, re-experience the horrors of it. It was only during these hours when he felt that fear he wasn't plagued with his fantasies about the girls, or fighting the urge to jerk off.

Today, while the other patients fought, he thought of the dream's end. At the point just before he awoke, it had turned strange. He'd felt Paola's tiny hands on his head and looked up. She was glaring at him over her crinolines, her dark eyes flashing. Suddenly, she was his mother, growling at him, then pulling his face toward her foul-smelling crotch. He was being smothered, and he awoke gasping for air. It made him sick, and reliving it brought back the revulsion.

"What's with the face, Steven?" Dr. O'Dell's voice broke through.

"What?"

"You had a grimace on your face."

"Oh, sorry. It wasn't about what you were saying."

The insomniac made fists in his lap. "*I* was talking. Don't you listen? That's what we're all here for."

"I said I was sorry."

Dr. O'Dell clasped his clipboard. "Can you try to stay with us now, Steven?"

"Yeah." He averted the stares. He had to tell Dr. Bragg about the new ending. It meant something. Just nothing good.

"Steven, this dream of yours has finally produced some useful insight. What do you think it means?" Dr. Bragg played with an over-permed ringlet of mousy-brown hair.

"That my mother did this shit to me?"

"I can't tell you that. Only you know if she did."

"It was so real. I mean, I can't smell the girl, or taste her. That's the frustrating part. My mother, man, whew! I could smell her, taste her, and she was nasty!"

"How old were you when she left you with your grandmother?"

Steven let his mind drift back to those hideous years

with Gram. "I was in fifth grade. I had to be . . . around ten, eleven."

"Do you recall sleeping in your mother's bed as a child?"

He remembered. It was what he'd felt most deprived of when he went to Gram's. The warm bare bottom, the arms around him in the night. "Yeah." The breasts he suckled well past the time he'd fed at them. The soft lips and tongue on his little dick. The tricks she taught him to help her fall to sleep. The smell.

"Oh, God!" Steve began to shake. Not the usual tremblings. Violent tremors, wracking him, causing his gorge to rise. He retched into the waste basket at his side, heaving so hard he thought his intestines were coming up. Dr. Bragg placed a stack of napkins on the desk when his heaves had gone dry.

"I'll just set this in the hall for an orderly to pick up." She took the basket to the door. The guard immediately responded. Dr. Bragg whispered to him.

Steve was thirsty. "Hey, can I have a cup of water?"

She leaned into the room. "Just a second. Relax." She disappeared behind the door.

What was happening to him? How could he have spent so much time in the hospital and in the treatment center, with all the talk and therapies, and only now recall what his mother had done to him? His first thought went to The Treatment. He didn't want it. Remembering was his way of making sure he wouldn't have to. That had to be why.

He noticed the message light flashing on Dr. Bragg's phone. When she returned, cup of water in hand, she noticed it, too.

"Drink up."

"Aren't you going to get that?" He nodded to her phone.

"What we're doing right now is the only thing that interests me."

Steve shrugged.

"Do you know what just happened, Steven?"

He nodded. "Some kind of breakthrough. One of the guys in a group talked about his . . . remembering how his dad tortured him with burning cigarettes. He didn't puke, though."

"I bet he went into a rage, huh?"

Steven grinned. "Yeah, how'd you know?"

"Some things go together, psychologically and physiologically. Your reaction is typical. This is what we've been working toward, Steven. Are you glad about it?"

He shivered. "Ah, I don't know." He drank down the water. It made him feel a little sick. "How can I be glad I remembered something so fucking gross?"

"Because it may be one of the root experiences your sickness grows from. It was most certainly a life changing and heartless way for a mother to show affection to her son. Don't you think?"

Steven felt the rage, but instead of acting out on it, he felt it burn a hole through his heart. He didn't want to hurt Dr. Bragg, or his chances of getting out. And he knew he would if he let himself go.

"The worst." He turned away. He could feel the hostility leaking out his eyes. He didn't want her to see.

"Do you feel the urge to masturbate now, Steven?"

He thought about it. Felt around for the yearning. It wasn't there. "Uh, no . . . I don't." The reality was strange, disconcerting.

"Our time's up, Steven. This was a turning point session. We may be looking at avoiding The Treatment, after all."

"Huh? Oh, yeah. That'd be great." He turned back to her, the rage already flowing through his bloodstream, ripping the fabric of his defenses. The grin he gave Dr. Bragg was the best he could fake. He vanished behind it as she led him out.

Ben picked up the phone as Claire sat with the VR helmet on.

"Nakamura."

"I got your message, Ben. It's Cynthia."

"Yeah. Claire's just putting the finishing touches on the visuals for your patient. We can start The Treatment on Monday."

"Wow, I knew you two were good, but I didn't know you were so fast. What's it been, three weeks? Only . . . listen, we may not be needing it."

"Cynthia, you know you're abusing the system if you set a patient up with us and then renege. We put a hundred twenty hours into this program. How're you going to recon-

cile that financially at the end of the month if you don't put it to use?"

"Ben, the guy's suddenly coming out of denial. What am I supposed to do, submit him to kamikaze VR when he's finally at the brink of some real productive processing?"

"I can appreciate your position, but consider that his recent sudden recall may be reaction-formation in lieu of going through The Treatment. It's not the first time patients have absolute memory access on the eve of the last resort."

Ben spun his chair around to see Claire, her mouth set in a hard line, concentrating. Her fingers worked like dancing spiders over her keyboard.

"Ben . . . you may be right. Okay. Monday. Shit. I want him to understand why I'm still having him do it, and I'm not sure myself."

"Trust me, Cynthia. This is more usual than not. We'll run him through part one and so on, break it up. Fair?"

"Fair. I'll see you Monday. Nine-thirty?"

"Nine-thirty."

Claire had removed the headset and was listening to the last few words. "Cynthia?"

"Yeah. She was going to pull her guy out. He's having sudden success."

Claire winced. "You talked her out of that."

"Oh, yeah. I read this guy's files, watched his tapes. Even if I didn't know what I know about what happened to you and . . . you know, I'd endorse The Treatment for this one. He's a real piece of work. Evil, Claire. Nothing more. Pure evil."

Claire pulled Ben out of his chair and stood to meet him in the aisle. She let him hold her, her gratitude mixing with her anger.

"Ben, if we can fix one. Just one."

"You'd better have one hell of a program for him."

She kissed his neck then looked into his eyes. "You bet I do." She gauged him, then went on. "Don't be upset, now, but I watched the tapes, too, Ben."

"What!? We agreed you'd let *me* give you the filters on the behaviors, Claire. I didn't want you re-stimulating over this creep."

"Ben, stop." She put a finger to his lips. He frowned. "I had to be able to build the filters from his stuff, not mine,

and not yours, either. It's what I'm best at. I know you wanted to protect me. I did, too, at first. But I wasn't getting *him*. Now, I believe I have this Mr. Steven Saterfield."

Ben picked up the helmet. "Mind if I do a run through in the helmet?" He was still suspicious.

Claire sighed. She knew he would object to some of it. She hadn't remained completely detached. "Yes, I do. You'll know soon enough whether it'll work. We have a mutual goal here."

He shrugged. Setting down her headset, he went to the door of The Treatment room. "What's real time on the entire program? I want to set the timers."

"Each segment runs forty-five minutes, give or take a few seconds. It's within parameters."

"You clocked it twice?"

She pouted. "You don't trust me."

"Actually, Claire, I do. Too much."

Steve hadn't masturbated in twenty-eight hours. Fear of The Treatment had leeched every sexually compulsive desire from his mind. He'd been isolated, as instructed, for twenty-four hours. He could have given himself ten climaxes during that time with no one to stop him, but all he did was tremble. He couldn't eat or sleep, and in a few hours, he'd be hooked up from toe nails to dick to eyebrows in a VR suit, unable to do anything, even take a piss.

All this time in isolation, he thought about his mother and Gram. Totally permissive Mom, to completely repressive Gram. He had memories now of Gram catching him when he was twelve, his hand around his cock, standing at his cousin's window while she bathed. He could almost feel the sting of her switch on his backside and his genitals remembering it. She'd threatened to cut off his penis if she so much as caught him with a boner. As a result, Steve couldn't keep it down—whether Gram was walking down the hall towards his room, glancing over her shoulder while she cooked him dinner, or following him to the bus stop. Just knowing she might see his prick, made him rock hard.

She'd never allowed him near girls his own age, either. When he was fourteen, Regina Bunce began hanging around. She was a year older, actually, and since the time she turned eleven, just about every male virgin in the neigh-

borhood had gotten his first nut off with her. Gossip had it Melvin Temple, the thirty-year-old delivery boy for Crenshaw's who still lived with his mother, had finally lost his to Regina. Steve was anxious to do the dirty deed with her and Gram was sure to stymie any attempts.

Regina had the brilliant idea that she would sneak over on Gram's quilting night and slip into Steve's bed. But Gram had nailed shut every window in the house and laid yarn at every portal, in the event Steve had any ideas of his own. Regina didn't care, nor did Steve, really. What was Gram gonna do, worst case scenario? Spank him raw? Well, they decided to do it in the backseat of the broken down Dodge in the garage. He never could figured out how she'd known, but Gram arrived home at the precise moment Steve slid into Regina. Gram seemed to materialize right there at the rear window in that exquisite instant, the flashlight going on in their eyes so they couldn't see her bulk, her fury, and her oak switch anymore.

Regina backstroked out from under Steve, screaming. Gram let her run out, naked. When Gram turned her fury on Steve, she left no flesh unscathed. When he was sufficiently healed, she forced Steve to wear Regina's clothes for a one-man parade down Smithy Boulevard, a humiliation he never forgave her for. When she died, she left him a penny and the rest of her estate, a whopping two hundred thousand dollars, to the ASPCA. He'd never told anyone what he did after the will was read—not Dr. Alcaron, not Dr. Bragg, not even Paola who'd have listened even if she'd never have understood.

Steven Saterfield dug Gram's coffin up out of Pennington Cemetery at three in the morning, opened it, and shoved that penny up her tight ass. Then, he jerked off on her face. He closed the coffin, re-buried her, and told her to rest in peace. That, he told himself, was retribution.

Now he was remembering his mother's abuses. No wonder he was so sick. As scared as he was of The Treatment, he knew he'd never get better fast enough to save him from going back to the nut house without it. No, he'd take it. And they'd let him go. They had to.

Ben watched Steven pulling on the VR suit with its wire rigging and tubes snaking. The psychotropics would be

kicking in shortly, and he knew Steven had to be fully suited and belted into the chair before that.

"This thing isn't gonna shock me, is it?"

"No, Mr. Saterfield, it has three purposes, none of which will be conducting electrical shock. First, you move in it and it tells the virtual reality computer program you'll be watching in the helmet how to react. And vice versa. Then it's there to register bodily responses, and send us readouts such as your body temp and pulse rate."

Steven slid the last sleeve over his arm and velcroed the neck as Ben had instructed him. "You said there were three purposes."

"Oh, yes. Three. The third conditions you. No electric shock, just rewards." Ben took the headset off the counter and handed it to Steven.

"Rewards?"

"Yes, it gives you pleasurable feelings when you make healthy choices."

Steven grinned wanly. "You got these suits for home use?"

Ben frowned. "This is no joke Mr. Saterfield."

"I know. I was trying for some lame humor. Anything to lighten this gig up."

"Fortunately, I take this work very seriously." Ben helped Steven place the helmet on and secure it, then led him to the chair. Once belted in, Ben went on.

"We read every movement at our computer terminals. We can also hear you, so that if you have extreme pain or discomfort, say so. We can adjust the output.

"The psychotropic Dr. Bragg administered to you a half hour ago, will take effect any moment. Your first sensation will be of relaxation, then elation. I understand it's quite pleasant. Within ten minutes, the boundaries of your mind will fall and we can begin working with the sickness. The visuals and what you hear, have been tailored to your specific areas of deviancy. The drug will aid you in producing the necessary enzymes to process the information."

Steven chuckled. "So in dumbass terms, I'm in for the ride of my life."

"Mr. Saterfield, this is going to be disturbing, as well as helpful."

"Whoa." Steven writhed as the drug hit. "Nice."

"Once The Treatment begins, it will not stop. We can only adjust it. Good luck."

Steven mugged. "I'll score one for the gipper."

Ben closed the door, checked the room temperature, then sat down beside Claire. "You ready?"

She shuddered, then nodded. They both looked at Cynthia. She shrugged.

"Here we go."

The fear vanished, replaced by euphoria. Steve wanted only to close his eyes and enjoy it, but the sounds began.

Crying. Deep weeping. Male, but young, maybe eight, nine years old. Over that, a woman's seductive voice calling his name.

The suit was gone, cool air wafted over his body, almost like hair, tickling. He thought he could smell birch and pine, dry earth and mildewed rugs on rotting wood floors.

He opened his eyes and saw the boy on his bed, face in his pillow, naked, body covered in welts. The cries came from the boy. The blood on the sheets was his. He was nearly an adolescent. Steve went to the bed and sat down. The boy felt the weight of Steve's body tipping the mattress and rolled onto his side, regarding him. There was recognition on the boy's face. Sudden passivity and resignation.

"What do you want me to do, Mom?" He looked up at Steve, eyes saying "yes," body shrinking from its duty.

Steve was stunned a moment. Then it was easy to be a woman. He lie down on the bed beside the boy and took the boy's hand. Touch me here, he said in his mind. The boy began lightly teasing his nipple. Now, touch me here. He guided the boy's hand to his crotch. Her crotch. Yes, that's it.

There was no pleasure, just a sort of detachment. Steve let the boy replace the hand with his tongue. Suddenly, he felt a surge of lust, not localized in his groin, but in his entire body. And a new sound.

A deep resonant voice, like the pulling of a gut string on a bass, said over and over, "This is wrong."

Filled with shame, Steve pushed the boy away and stood. He stared up at Steve, eyes moist, wondering what he'd done bad. Steve told him he didn't want him to touch him that way. It wasn't right. The boy grinned and hurried out

of the room. As the door shut, Steve felt a steady stream of liquid warmth flow from his penis into his legs and belly. The pleasure increased, the feeling of a hundred soft tongues caressing to bring him to orgasm. His grunts and moans were muffled by the headset.

Then The Treatment changed. His Gram walked into his sixth grade classroom, a yardstick in her hand and anger in her eyes. The teacher called Steve up and stood him before the class. He was ordered to take down his pants. Steve could feel the cold air on his bare buttocks and stiffening penis. Gram saw the erection and shouted to the students, "Steven Saterfield is a pervert!"

The class responded with cat calls and jeers. One girl, he remembered her as Holly Mercer, walked to the front of the room, faced him, and lifted her dress. His cock ached as he stared at her virgin pussy, just beginning to show hair. Gram began hitting him in the backside. It burned! The more Holly wiggled, the closer Steve felt to coming, and the harder Gram hit him. The teacher stepped behind Holly, pulled down the girl's skirt, and pointed at Steve's erection. "Steven Saterfield is a pedophile! Take this!"

The teacher lifted her straight wool skirt and spread her legs. Gram stopped hitting, came around, and got to her knees to begin fellating him. The closeness of an orgasm remained un-relieved. The teacher reached down to her labia and exposed her moist home to him. She began masturbating, the hair on her mons mutating into thin writhing snakes.

He looked down and saw Gram, her lips around his cock, her eyes showing pleasure, and she became his mother. When he looked up, the teacher's crotch was an inch from his face as the snakes began striking, their bites painful. His orgasm was as elusive as an escape from this hell.

"Stop!" He yelled.

His mother let his cock fall, the teacher backed away, the snakes going with her. Steve was panting, the erection still throbbing.

"Stay away." He managed when he saw them stepping forward toward him.

Again, the liquid ecstasy dripped over and around his cock, bringing him joyfully to orgasm.

A soft voice. "Mr. Saterfield, we are slowly bringing you

out of VR. The drug will be wearing off rather quickly, now. Music will replace other sounds, and visually, you'll be treated to neutral scenic images. Relax."

When the helmet was removed, he was astonished that only forty minutes had passed. It had seemed like four hours. Ben monitored the removal of the suit, commenting that Steven might be surprised to find there was no jism in the suit, that actual orgasm had not occurred. When Steve examined the suit, he found a wet stain and sniffed at it. He'd pissed.

As he walked into the terminal room. Dr. Bragg was waiting for him, grinning.

"You did extremely well for a first treatment, Steven. I'm pleased."

Steve grinned sheepishly. "Yeah?"

"Tomorrow you'll be upgraded to the next level."

Steve didn't think he was going to mind this thing after all.

Claire cuddled next to Ben on her bed. Her success with the pedophile in the first two stages had made her hot and she'd screwed Ben's brains out. He lay purring in sleep.

She'd been fair, she thought. Four stages of treatment. Four opportunities for the perv to make the right choices. The consequences getting worse at each level. He'd made all the right choices now for two sessions, but his reaction time lagged at the end of the second. If he failed at all at the third level, the punishment was severe enough that he might not make the same errors in the last level. At least she hoped not. The fourth level guaranteed that the destructive affect problem they had with The Treatment would be used to its full disadvantage.

She stared at Ben's sweet, peaceful face. Trusting, loving Ben. When it was all over, if the perv made it through and was changed by The Treatment, Ben would know she was as good as he at caring for them. If the guy didn't make it, well, then Ben would understand. He was like that. He listened, he cared, and most of all, he hated the pedophile as much as she did. Maybe even more.

Ben rolled toward her, his arm going around her. Neither of them was ever going to let anyone hurt the other. Never again.

*   *   *

The isolation session almost over, Steve sat in his room waiting for his appointment with Dr. Bragg and the Japanese computer jockey. He'd taken his psychotropic and felt great. He actually enjoyed the work. He had no desire to masturbate, even when he woke up hard. When he let himself think of little girls, he still got excited, but he was so close to a healing. He knew it. He did the visualizations Dr. Bragg had given him to replace the girls, and even that was helping. One more treatment. One more and he'd be cured.

The door opened and Dr. Bragg stood beside the security man. "You ready?"

Steve nodded. "I'm almost there."

"I'm proud of you, Steven. So proud."

The security man velcroed Steve's hands behind him, then ushered him out, behind Dr. Bragg. Steve was elated.

Ben was waiting for him.

"Hey, Mr. Nakamura, this it is. I graduate today."

"Maybe. The fourth level is the most difficult."

"I can do it."

Ben handed Steve a new suit. "This is a fourth level suit. It operates just like the others, only there's a separate sheath for your penis and testicles that attaches to the suit."

Steve examined the sheath. There were no electrodes, no pins or exposed metal. "Seems harmless."

"Only if you make it through with the right choices. Now please hurry. Last time the drug took effect before we hooked you in."

Steve stripped, put the sheath around his genitals, and let Ben snap it to the suit. It was elastic and slightly binding, but once the suit was on, he didn't notice. Ben handed him a different headset. This one enclosed his head entirely.

Once in the chair, Ben shuffled out. That woman's voice came on over the intercom system, the woman who never let him see her, though she was part of the team.

"At the fourth level, we go for fifty minutes. We increase the pleasure function and introduce a rather unpleasant consequence for poor choices. There is a pressure pad on the end of the right arm of your chair. If you fear you're

He felt her climbing up, settling there, each wriggle sending waves of pleasure coursing up his prick. "Here, touch my poony." He felt her hand go around his forefinger and guide it to her tiny vagina. The slick, warmth of it around his finger began the first spasm of an orgasm.

Light flared, the child's vagina was now a huge tarantula, his fingertip was in its maws, the bite quick, fierce. A molten heat coursed from his fingertip to his chest and he couldn't breath. It was as if he was standing in a blast furnace and every molecule of oxygen was burning, being sucked from his lungs. There was a sudden grabbing in his groin and he thought he saw the glint of a knife blade. He looked down and saw his cock and testes spurting blood, and the pain was unbearable.

The pad. Press the pad.

Instantly, the heat was gone. He was aware only of his wound. He tried to stop the bleeding, push his balls back into place. Sobbing, he begged for help.

The scene changed. He was standing with a little boy, both of them naked, staring at a bed full of sleeping little girls. The pain in his groin was ebbing and the gore was gone. The little boy began wanking himself. Steve was breathing as if he'd just run a mile, his heart racing. He wasn't into this anymore.

The boy crawled into the bed and began turning each girl onto her back, spreading her legs and fucking her. The girls woke up, and began responding in an adult fashion, the sounds of orgasms banshee screams in his head.

The door to the room flew open and Gram stepped in, nude, her breasts sagging like soup drippings on the side of a pan. She ripped the boy out of the bed and began spanking him. The boy bullied his way out of her grasp and knelt before her.

"Let me, Gram. I'll fix your pain."

Gram put one foot on the bed, opening herself to the boy. The girls on the bed curled up afraid. "Eat me, boy."

The boy began lapping at her, making sounds of enjoyment. Gram threw her head back and moaned. With that, Steve felt a tingling in his cock. It wasn't electrical. It was chemical, like a drug flowing into it. His penis swelled as he came around and sat on the bed to watch the boy at

Gram. As he sat, the girls were all around him, yet he could only look at Gram. And his prick grew.

Gram licked her fingers and massaged her nipples until they were as big as brown marshmallows. The boy's tongue worked as his body became gradually more mature. Steve felt as though he could come any second, but the pleasure was so great, he kept watching.

The girls whined and cried until they annoyed him. "Get out of here." He told them. As he felt them scurry around him like rats, the pleasure increased.

The boy became a man. Steve stared at the man's prick, then his. They were the same. The man turned his head slightly. He was Steve. At the moment of recognition, Gram came and so did Steve.

It was a climax that wrecked him, stole his power, then left him at his Gram's feet. He could smell her crotch in his face, the vile elixirs dripping onto him.

"Let Gram watch you jerk it, my baby boy." She lifted him as though he weighed an ounce onto the bed. She lie across from him, rubbing her still swollen flesh.

Something was wrong here. The pleasure came from Gram, from smelling her, seeing her, pleasing her. He'd chased the girls off. Right choice, but he was being punished with this.

"No, Gram. I can't."

"You'll be sorry." She grinned toothlessly at him.

"No, I won't." He tried to get up. He was paralyzed. The harder he struggled, the quieter and darker the room became. Finally, he stopped trying.

He heard the voice. "Steve, look." He turned in the direction from where it came.

Standing on a brownstone stoop, was a girl with straight black hair and dark almond eyes. She was young, six or seven, but small for her age. She wore a coat over a snow suit, and heavy black rain boots. When Steve approached, she grinned.

"Hiya, Steve. I was scared you weren't going to come. My dad's working late again."

Steve took her hand and walked her up the steps and into the foyer of the brownstone.

"Will you make me hot chocolate?"

She smiled. "Really?"

"Yeah, now you can lick it all off."

She giggled and began licking. He felt nothing. No pleasure, no pain. She licked more and more enthusiastically, laughing, enjoying herself, until his cock was clean, and still she licked him.

The key in the lock startled him and he tried to pry the girl away. She was immovable. Her tongue working him. Suddenly he realized his hand was in the bottom of her snow suit, probing her tiny pussy, and he couldn't get it out.

Her father walked in, his eyes going right to Steve and his daughter.

"It's not what you think, man . . ."

The dad went to the sink and pulled a dirty knife out. He went right to his daughter and yanked her away. Without a word, the man hacked off Steve's penis. *That* he felt. His scream was real. Loud and real.

"Help me!"

The woman's voice. "Steve, look."

His hands went over the bleeding stump of his cock. Standing beside him was a young woman, Asian, beautiful, slender, serene.

"You did this to a little girl like me. You. For that you will never use your penis again." She pointed at the bloody mass in his hands. "My father pretended he never saw what the man did. He never wanted any trouble. Just like he did with my brother and our Aunt Rose. She scarred him forever, too." She turned so he saw only her profile. "I married, took my brother to live with us. But my husband was sick, like you. We left, both of us beyond repair. Now, Mr. Saterfield, you are beyond repair."

"Why are you doing this to me?"

She grinned, something evil then in her eyes. "Why? Because you deserve it. And . . . because I *can*."

She disappeared and Steve found himself on an operating table. Little girls were putting stitches into him without anesthetic. His mother was coaching them. Where his genitals should be, were thick dark stitches. The girls frightened him. No, terrified him. When he tried to tell them to stop, he realized his lips were sewn shut. A scream caught in his throat.

He reached for the pad on the arm of the chair, but his fingers were sewn into a fist. Then everything went black.

Claire watched as Dr. Bragg led Steven Saterfield out. His eyes flicked onto her, a glimmer of recognition there, but it passed quickly. They wouldn't know if the fourth level was successful until Cynthia interviewed him, but Claire was fairly certain it had been. His hands were balled into tight fists, his lips screwed firmly over his teeth. Yes, the deconstruction was complete.

Later, when they were alone, Ben leaned his head into his hands. Claire curled around Ben and whispered in his ear. "Don't be angry."

He embraced her, kissing her neck. "I'm not mad. I guess I expected this. Anyway, I understand. You know I do."

"I did it for you, too, Ben."

He nodded, turning to her. "I know."

"Doesn't it feel good? Knowing we got one back? That he'll probably never be able to think of a child, or even a woman, and feel aroused again?"

Ben shrugged, his eyes holding hers. "It will. I just have to get used to the idea of having this much power."

She smiled. "You will, Ben. No more being a victim. Not for either of us."

She kissed him on the mouth, his tongue touching hers, the yearning growing. "I can't believe we've always affected each other this way. That we still do. Always will. Only you."

"Only you, sister." He whispered to her. "Only you."

For H E

The Nightmare Network

Thomas Ligotti

Classified Ad I

A multinational corporation is dreaming. We are an organization of more than 100 thousand souls (full-time) and are presently seeking individuals willing to trade their personal lot for a share of our dream. Entry-level positions are now available for self-possessed persons who can see beyond the bottom line to a bottomless realm of possibilities. Our enterprise is now thriving in a tough, global marketplace and has taken on a life all its own. If you are a committed, focused individual with a hunger to be part of something far greater than yourself . . . our door is now open. Your life need not be a nightmare of failure and resentment. Join us. Outstanding benefits.

An Opening Scene

Dawn in the rain forest. Sunlight begins flickering through the green luxuriance and appears here and there as radiant pools upon the soft, dark earth. A tribe of hunter-gatherers lies sleeping near a shallow stream. The camera pans from one inanely tranquil face to another. Thus far no noises of any kind occur on the soundtrack—no rustling in the underbrush, no burbling of the shallow stream, no screeching from the rain forest's animal life. While surveying the sleeping tribe, the camera moves in for a close-up of one hunter whose face is anything but inanely tranquil. It is not even the face of one who lives in the rain forest. Although the man is practically naked, and a sharpened stick is lying within reach of his sleeping form, his skin is pale and his hair neatly styled. Now his features are becoming contorted, as if he is experiencing a nightmare. He seems to be talking in his sleep, but thus far there are no noises of any kind on the soundtrack. Finally the silence is broken by the spasmic drone of an alarm clock. The eyes

of the hunter suddenly open and stare in panic; his pale skin is running with sweat. The alarm clock continues to sound.

Orientation Video

A pretty, dark-haired actress in a business suit is standing amid a maze of desks, talking to the camera and expertly gesturing. The occupants of the desks are seemingly oblivious to her presence. At the end of the video the actress smartly crosses her arms over her chest, fixes a stern expression on her face, and utters the corporate motto which introduced the video as a title ("Think Again"). As she continues to stare into the camera the scene around her begins to change: shadows drift about the maze of desks and the faces of all the employees become rotten and corroded, as if they are being afflicted with leprosy in fast motion. One by one they rise from behind their desks and succumb to the strange fidgety conniptions of a danse macabre. Under the stress of these fitful, brittle movements their limbs break off and fall to the floor, where the shadows move in to devour them. Noses and ears quickly wither, lips peel back to reveal broken teeth, eyeballs shrivel in their sockets. The pretty, dark-haired actress continues to stare into the camera with a stern expression.

Memo from the CEO

As the forces operating in today's marketplace become more shadowy and incomprehensible we must recommit ourselves every second of every day to a ceaseless striving for that elusive dream which we all share and which none of us can remember, if it ever existed in the first place. And if anyone thinks that, as all the world races toward the same elusive dream, our competition isn't fully prepared to gnaw off its own genitals to get to the promised land before us and keep it for themselves . . . think again.

From a Supervisor's Notebook

. . . And if I were determined to live solely on the flesh of my own staff, with no access to the staffs of other surviving supervisors or any other personnel, the greatest challenge to present itself would be maintaining each of them in an edible state, while also regulating my consumption of these bodies. Perhaps I should try to keep them all alive; in that case I could simply restrict myself to ingesting only those elements capable of regeneration, such as blood. Even so,

I do dream about their armpits and elbows . . . those of
the men as well as the women. I think that within the first
few days of cannibalistic survival I would devour all those
tender wrinkly parts.

The Hunter

The green doors of an elevator slide open, revealing a
man in a dark business suit. He is standing dead center in
the framing shot, and his hair is noticeably neat and well-
styled. In his right hand is an automatic pistol with a nickel-
plated handle. He holds the weapon close to his side as he
steps out of the elevator and begins walking swiftly down
one brightly lit hallway after another. A series of offices
with open doors passes on either side of him. At the end
of one of the hallways he stops before a door that is closed.
He removes a security card from the inside pocket of his
suit and pushes it into the thin slot beside the door. There
is a soft, droning sound as the man opens the door and
walks inside, leaving his security card behind. Beyond the
door he moves within a maze of desks, at each of which a
man or a woman is seated. The man stops at the center of
the maze, which now seems to spin around him like a car-
ousel. Cacophonous music in waltz time begins rising on the
soundtrack, becoming louder and faster as it approaches a
painful crescendo. The music is then cut off by the sudden
report of a single gunshot. The room stops spinning. The
man lies dead within the maze of desks, his shattered skull
pouring blood upon the floor. Later the coworkers of this
man disclose that for some time he had complained about
hearing barely audible messages on his telephone every
time he made or received a call in the office. Officers of
the company merely shake their heads in condescending
sympathy. The following day they authorize financing for
the installation of a new telephone system.

Classified Ad II

Major Supercorp in the process of expanding its proper-
ties and market-base has limited openings for Approved
Labor in domestic and off-shore sites (real and virtual). We
are among the biggest legitimate multi-monopolies around
and our Corporate Persona is one that any AL can adopt in
good conscience. Experience in sensory-deprived conditions
preferred. Knowledge of outlawed dialects on the Nightmare Network a plus. Standard survival package of benefits.

Prehistoric AL's okay with biologic documentation from transport agency.

The Farmers

An unplanted field beneath a gray prehistoric sky. The camera slowly pans from left to right, revealing several figures at various positions in the foreground and background. Each of them is wearily gouging the earth with crude implements typical of the incipient age of agriculture. They are clothed in tunics made from animal hides which are tattered and filthy. Their long hair and weasly beards are matted and lice-ridden. The camera pauses for a long-shot of farmers and field to reinforce the profound tedium of this panorama of Stone Age planting season. Almost simultaneously the figures all freeze and then look up from the earth upon which their eyes have been previously fixed. What they have seen is the greenish, glowing dome that now hovers over the field and has closed off its perimeter. Some of the farmers begin running about in panic-stricken hysterics, while the rest fall to the ground unconscious or dead from the shock of the inexplicable phenomenon which, given their quasi-feral instincts, they perceive as an overpowering menace. Shafts of greenish light begin to shoot out from various points of the dome, seizing upon each of the farmers and levitating them high above the field. Even the dead bodies are captured and carried beyond the inner surface of the dome. The field now stands empty, the primitive farming tools lay abandoned on the ground. Superimposed on this scene the following legend appears: THE NIGHTMARE OF THE PAST BECOMES THE DREAM OF THE FUTURE. ONEIRICON: ONE WORLD, ONE DREAM.

On the Nightmare Network

Our names are unknown and our faces are shadows drifting across an infinite blackness. Our voices have been stifled to a soft murmur in a madman's ear. We are the proud failures with only a single joy left to us—to inflict rampant damage on those who have fed themselves on our dreams and to choke ourselves on our own nightmares. In sum, we are expediters of the apocalypse. There is nothing left to save, if there ever was anything . . . if there ever could be. All we desire (in all our bitterness) is to go to our ruin *in our own way*—with a little style and a lot of noise.

The Harvest
The main grid at Security Central indicates that there is a crisis situation in sub-cube six-o-six, which is located several hundred kilometers below ground level. A minor security officer explains to his supervisor that, for an undetermined period of time, the Nightmare Network has been engaged in undetected communication with all one hundred and fifty of the AL's in six-o-six, feeding them images and data on their computer screens. A hasty check of all monitors reveals that personnel in that particular sub-cube have been in a malignant dream state for at least seventy-two hours. Signals to the monitors had been altered so that visual and auditory data from sub-cube seven-o-seven were substituted for those that were supposed to emanate from six-o-six. The system was not programmed to indicate an alert after detecting the duplication of data, an oversight that would be corrected in the future. In the present, a heavily armed security force descends to six-o-six for the purpose of assessment and possible remedial action. What they discover there causes some of the new recruits to vomit into their helmets. The entire cube is in an uproar, and there are mutilated bodies everywhere. The AL's who are still alive are running amok within a maze of computer terminals. Most of them are naked and covered in blood; some have adorned themselves with entrails that dangle around their necks or have wrapped flayed skin about their heads. Many of them are eating the flesh of the dead and the dying. An influx of blood and other bodily fluids has caused short-circuits in many of the computers, which are spraying sparks and occasionally electrocute one of the servicing AL's. The computers that are still in working order have the same message upon their screens. In flashing, luminous letters all of them read: GREETINGS FROM THE NIGHTMARE NETWORK.

Classified Ad III
OneiriCon requires Employment Units with autonomous or semi-automonous programming to oversee workforce of Nonconscious AL's. Some contact with Noncons or their semblances may be involved (visual desensitization or nihilization for all EU's paid for by OneiriCon). Remember: there are no bad dreams if there is only one dream; there can be no outlaws where there is only one law. Artificial

entities from the Nightmare Network that attempt to impersonate Employment Units will be discovered and reprogrammed to exist in an eternal state of hallucinated agony. Imperfectly functioning EU's will be discovered and mercifully deleted. Possible elevation to part- or full-time status as cyberpersonage (with commensurate benefits and restrictions).

Masters and Slaves

Twilight in an ancient desert land. The slaves have all been gathered before an enormous, semi-circular platform. Behind the platform the spires and towers of the great palace are outlined against a fading sky. Before the platform is a sea of loin-clothed slaves kneeling in the desert sand, which has grown cool with the setting of the sun. The camera focuses on the central part of the platform, where a number of slaves have been tied to a row of freestanding pillars. From the crown of each pillar emanates a clean, steady flame that provides generous illumination for the entire platform and places special emphasis on the restrained bodies of the slaves. On either side of the platform are the seated figures of the royal family, priests and high-priests, high-ranking military officers, and other notable persons of the kingdom. After the sun has disappeared behind some distant sand dunes, leaving tens of thousands of slaves in total darkness, the proceedings finally commence. The head executioner and several of his assistants now ascend the enormous platform from a stairway to the right The camera follows behind them as they approach the flaming pillars where the bound slaves await an elaborate regimen of torture that will continue throughout the night and end with their simultaneous deaths at sunrise. But when the head executioner reaches the center of the platform and turns to receive a sinister-looking instrument held out to him by one of his assistants, he suddenly freezes in position—a statue with outstretched arms and open hands. At this point, one of the slaves kneeling toward the front of the massive audience rises to his feet and jumps onto the platform. No one makes a move to stop him. The slave walks up to the flaming pillars and scans the horrified faces of his fellows who are anticipating a night of agony and ultimate death. After a while he simply shrugs and turns away from them. Stepping over to the head executioner,

the slave looks the frozen figure up and down. With the fingers of his right hand he probes beneath the wide gold neck-band which the head executioner is wearing and which is symbolic of his office. Some moments pass with no change in the gruesome functionary's state; the slave now appears to be slightly exasperated. He removes his fingers from the gold neck-band, and with the heal of his right hand gives the statue-like figure a sharp rap on the side of the head. The head executioner then goes into motion once again, seizing the proffered implement of pain and picking up where he left off. Before leaping from the platform the slave glances around, as if to see if any of the other persons there might require maintenance, excepting those tied to the flaming pillars. He then returns to his place among the other slaves, who do not in any way acknowledge that he was ever absent from their ranks. Briefly deferred, the long night of torture and death can finally begin . . . followed by a feast upon the bodies of the dead.

Within the System

Having absorbed or destroyed very one of its competitors, OneiriCon begins to deteriorate. It is then that its Governing Executives conspire to create a number of puppet entities which would provide a degree of competition for the organization, thus reinfusing its lower-level executives and other conflict-driven personnel with a sense of purpose once more and staving off total degeneration. (The majority of OneiriCon's employees—the billions of AL's and greater percentage of EU's—have existed in a benign dream state for so long that they seemed to require no external stimuli of any kind, although this remained a matter of debate among the organization's scientists, who are highly adept at providing themselves with trumped-up mysteries and challenges.) For a time Project Puppetcorps succeeds admirably, and some of the artificial corporate entities do quite well in the marketplace, or what is left of it. In the end, however, they too are absorbed or destroyed by OneiriCon. Unable to reconcile themselves to the prospect of terminal stagnancy for an organization that has always subsisted on the principle of ceaseless growth, many of the Governing Executives voluntarily submit to devolutionary brain surgery and afterward join the ranks of Noncon AL's. Others have themselves transported to the

distant past, where they become slaves of society governed by automatons, thus affording their competitive spirits with new objects of resistance and a low point of orientation from which they can once again work their way to the top. The remaining GE's occupy their time by playing extravagant and intensely cruel practical jokes on one another. In this manner most of them are killed off or are so severely damage that they can no longer function at any level of the organization. Then all of a sudden a solution seems to present itself to one of the highest-ranking GE's, who is an old-timer recovering from a major substitution procedure in his own private medical cell. At some stage of his convalescence the ancient exec is made to regain consciousness of himself and his surroundings, a situation that is not supposed to occur during the normal course of these procedures. When he becomes fully awake he is surprised, and somewhat horrified, to find that grafted to his torso is the head of a corporeal Noncon. This state of affairs seems to him to exceed even the wildest of the pranks lately being perpetrated at OneiriCon. The head of the Noncon does not appear to be alive, so the old man is startled when its mouth pops open and begins to emit a long thin strip of paper much like those produced by ticker-tape machines of the twentieth century. With a sense of atavistic nostalgia, the GE picks up the tape and reads the words printed upon it. The words are these: "How about letting the Nightmare Network have some fun?" Possessing the innovative vision and cunning genius of administrative life-forms through the ages, the old Governing Executive exclaims: "We are saved!" Then he dies, his body succumbing to the trauma incurred by its assimilation of the Noncon's foreign tissue. Fortunately a video record of the entire incident is preserved.

The Dreams of a Double Agent

There is considerable resistance at OneiriCon to the proposal that the organization join forces with the Nightmare Network. None of the surviving GE's denies that the concept of a *hostile merger* with one's own anti-entity, corporately speaking, is a risky venture. On the other hand, admitting such a parasite into the system for the strict purpose of revitalizing aggressive impulses—an inoculation, as it were—seems the only alternative to the progressive atro-

phy and ultimate shut-down with which the organization will otherwise be faced. It is therefore agreed (at the highest level) that all personnel at OneiriCon (of every level and status of reality and consciousness) will also be in the employ of the Nightmare Network. This initiative will in effect make everyone in both camps of these long-conflicting entities into a double agent. In a telepathic memo, one of the most powerful GE's warns his peers: "Obviously there can be no official sanction at OneiriCon of our so-called merger with the Nightmare Network, since the sole purpose of this arrangement is that of a motivational strategy for our employees, both real and illusionary. This organization certainly has no intention of becoming mother hog for an overpopulated system of deadbeat operatives (as well as their semblances) who are drawing an easy paycheck coming and going and everywhere in between, whether they try to pass counterfeit data through the OneiriCon circuits or inform on their own semblances for attempting same." Thus, infiltration of OneiriCon by the Nightmare Network, and vice versa, has to be pursued simultaneously, taking place in a most surreptitious manner, one recruit at a time, until there is a perfect similitude between the two entities. This process is swiftly completed throughout the Nightmare Network, where individual and collective values tend toward subversion without regard for rational pretexts. All of them being natural-born losers and saboteurs, they run crotch-first into the bargain, some even adopting multiple identities so that they can experience more than once the monstrous thrill of selling out their own futile aspirations. The camera pans a crowd of faces whose eyes are bleary with sedition and a lust for self-destruction. To no one's surprise, the response of the personnel at OneiriCon is identical to that of their counterparts at the Nightmare Network. Subsequently there ensues an epoch of complex, proliferating intrigues and conspiracies among the ranks of double agents, whose agendas become so densely intertwined that they are virtually indistinguishable. Even the Governing Executives of OneiriCon, many of whom were defectors from the Nightmare Network, have thrown themselves into the depths of the new order and lose all sense of identity in the ever-expanding nebula of blind agitation, which possesses a power and impetus that belongs

entirely to itself. After a time no one can be sure whom they are serving whenever they commit any given act of either sabotage or support. There are no longer two distinct entities in well-defined opposition; there is only a great chaos or confused purposes churning in darkness. Each entity is disappearing into the maw of the other, thereby realizing their most cherished dreams and worst nightmares of oblivion. At last, it seems, they will have managed to close the whole thing down.

Classified Distress Signal

Vast organization of delirious images and impulses seeking Sustenance Input for its decaying systems. All data considered, including polluted discharges from the old Nightmare Network and after-images of degenerated EU's and AL's (Con, Noncon, or OneiriCon). Total atrophy and occlusion of all circuits imminent—next stop, the Nowhere Network. Your surplus information—shadows and semblances lying dormant in long unaccessed files—could be used to replenish our hungry database. No image too hideous; no impulse too attenuated or corrupt. Our organization has a life of its own, but without a steady input of cheap data we cannot compete in today's apocalyptic marketplace. From a rotting mutation, great illusions may grow. Don't let us go belly up while the black empty spaces reverberate with hellish laughter. A multi-dimensional, semi-organic nightmare is dreaming. . . .

The signal repeats, steadily deteriorating, and then fades into nothingness. Long shot of the universe. There is no one behind the camera.

Fiends by Torchlight

Wayne Allen Sallee

I'd like to say that I wish the children hadn't been killed along with the rest, but that truly is not the case. We are taught to live with our actions, however it plays out. And it's not as if I strapped their little bodies into kiddie seats and pushed them into some lake, whining to the country how a black man took my babies, the way she did.

As I said, I live with my actions. When I was clocked by the Oklahoma trooper doing twenty over in a sixty, I pulled over to the side and let myself be taken in. And you know where it went from there, from that one day in April like no other, at least that is what you're all being led to believe. How I was discovered to be the perpetrator, the mastermind behind this heinous bombing in the heartland.

I walked out there past the crowds and the cameras and the jeers, not once pissing and moaning about my plight, my innocence, my insanity, or any of the other "my's" in this country of people making excuses for their each and every action.

Nor did I speak in judgmental tones about those of a different race or religion. I did make certain derogatory comments about the way I, and others like me, are dissatisfied with the government, but that was all part of the show. And it was unfortunate that one enterprising reporter from Kansas City quoted me as blaming the military, the thing about an implant in my buttocks. I realize now that he must have retrieved that information from his files after the discovery of my being stationed at nearby Ft. Riley. Somehow, during the recent desert skirmishes, he must have found a source who mentioned the implants.

I digress here: you think what I say is far-fetched *this soon in my narrative,* well, let me quote from a recent pet brochure from a New Jersey company. (Okay, it is run by

my employers; at least a division of them.) You know, if using their program, cannot lose your dog or cat because there is a microchip the size of a grain of rice in their ears. Each chip has an identification number that can be scanned. Or, the chip can be implanted beneath shoulderblades. The scanners are the same you see in the grocery stores.

The scanners and chips are already used unwittingly by veterinarians and deliberately by "animal control specialists," the latter being those who run the pit bull fights through those who experiment with huntaviruses.

I am involved in "people control," if you will.

The implants in military personnel are real, but not for mind control, that Manchurian Candidate stuff that lone gunmen theorists are wont to believe as gospel. The government controls it all, and each of us simply dances the dance of the day. The tiny steel and manganese receptors are placed in our buttocks so that a specific satellite could monitor us if we were taken prisoner of war during the bombing of Baghdad.

Yes, I was there. I was in quite a few places, although you only know my face from the Oklahoma situation. Oh, the implants are even placed into specific test subjects, taken from a pool of the civilian population fringes. These nodules are placed into the left nostril, and take on the appearance of a polyp. Thus, alien abductions are given more credence, and sightings of boomerang-shaped unidentified flying saucers are reported from upstate New York to the Wisconsin-Minnesota border.

Joe and June Taxpayer made to believe they were the celestial chosen when all they were looking at was the Stealth Bomber or the Black Manta. Fly it in plain sight, what the hell, no one knows about the military hangars outside Ladysmith, Wisconsin. Even the Amish population there believes Nathan Twining Air Force Base to be a defunct copper mine, and you sure as hell are going to see the latter mentioned that way with Rand McNally and friends. And it still amazes me that fringe novelists are so quick to believe that the government must only be running black projects in the deserts of Nevada and New Mexico. Whatever happened to those who believed in the Hollow

Earth Theory? Only, think of it as the Abandoned Mine Theory.

Then you'll have it.

Now go get that Road Atlas. I'll wait.

Back to the "realistic" reasons for the implants. I was a chosen one, all right. Not by the star-people, but by those who need to set things right, to make this century end on a stable manner. George Orwell's 1984 is as obsolete as the initial origin of Superman.

April 19th, 1995 is a different tale. The so-called militia I supposedly adhere my beliefs to might rant about government involvement in the private sector—as if there were one—but it is much deeper than that.

The people I work for manipulate events the same way our sister offices in Lantana, Florida do with every tabloid they publish. Disinformation from the highest levels in one of the most accessible forms; check any supermarket aisle.

Okay. Except for the Elvis sightings.

And, by the way, I never exchanged love letters with the crazy broad that drowned her kids in South Carolina. Over a *man*.

Those kids at the day-care center in the federal building died for their *country*. I'm explaining this now, after all these months, because it is all out of control. The way things are now, well. It makes *The Missiles of October* look like *Pee-Wee's Playhouse*.

Those that employ me have caused the suicides of several high-raking individuals "recovering" at the Bethedsa Naval Hospital, as well as blatantly pulling the trigger on booth presidents and presidential candidates.

The people I work for call themselves skull carpenters. They have divisions called "The Pain Detail," "Walt Disney Dreamland," and "Visiting Hours." The latter two deal with all that new age crap that our office in Lantana fuels. The main headquarters are in that mysterious "F-Ring" within the Pentagon's substructure. The newspapers told how I stole guns and fertilizer in Arkansas. What I stole was provided to me within that five sided structure.

Where am I headed, people? Terrorism faked to catch the Unabomber, make him flustered and angry into giving away clues to his identity within his manifesto? *We made him.* Terrorism to get a better handle on the militia? Close.

But why the Murrah Building? Why the day care center? I'll be getting to that.

The recent past in ellipses . . .

I wasn't executed until July of 1996. There were no appeals, although one judge was removed from the trial early on. This was a token nod to getting the public to believe the outcome. And I am only writing from my viewpoint, those who were listed as co-conspirators are probably running a casino in Las Vegas right now.

My death was carried out by DC5C, a procedure involving the vibration of pixels and the subtleties of morphing that was invented by the Melpar Division of the Naval Intelligence Support Center in Suitland, Maryland. Three hundred thousand picture elements to play with and make me writhe in the first televised execution.

Of course it was pay-per-view. What were you thinking?

While I was incarcerated at El Reno, my employers busied themselves with causing a newspaper strike in Sterling Heights; and starting the infamous careers of the Interstate 88 Killer and the Sabine Slasher; and even playing a small part in what happened to Bob Packwood after he resigned from the Senate.

Meanwhile, I was allowed to read books that figured into my future assignments. Like the one I'll be attending soon. If I listen closely, I can almost hear the coming crowd outside my window, carried by the Chicago winter winds, much like the angry villagers ready to storm Castle Frankenstein.

Fiends by torchlight.

The judge was taken off my case, my superiors argued for a fair trial, and off I went to another prison in Lawton, three counties west. Having a few stumblebums from Tulsa acting out their Jack Ruby fantasies didn't hurt my situation any.

The prison was named for a fellow named Packard who wrote books on subliminal manipulation in advertising in the early fifties. Baby boomers on up read articles in the newspapers touting Kane Packard as some war hero or something. So Packard Correction it is. Like serial killer Ted Bundy—not one of ours, surprisingly—told a biogra-

pher before his execution in 1989: "In one hundred years, no one will remember either of us."

The closest Kane Packard got to combat was rubbing elbows at a Legionnaire's convention. God, it was all so simple once I left El Reno. The warden on down to the final witnesses. Just for fun, one of the Joint Chiefs-of-Staff "pulled the switch" on Old Sparky, jerking me to Jesus.

My death was viewed by more people than those who watched the final episode of *The Fugitive* or O.J.'s wild ride in the white Bronco. My last meal was the same thing I still eat every night while I watch syndicated reruns about a vampire cop in Toronto.

All right, then. The angry villagers are closer now. They play their parts well.

Why was the Murrah Building bombed in the first place? The children, of course. Another experiment gone awry. Like the skull carpenters, when they let the Green River Killer get out of control. I was sent to Sea-Tac to sanitize the situation. As I was sent to cleanse the heartland of America twelve years later.

The Oklahoma City children were test subjects; another variation on the memory implants. The only real way to cover our tracks was to, well, vaporize the test subjects. It didn't hurt that we got to screw around with the militia yahoos after that. Remember Waco! How pathetic was *that* rallying cry?

The Pain Detail. The Skull Carpenters. Hell, I haven't even mentioned Axeman's Carnival. All the best stories start out in somebody's head. So believe what you will of my tale.

They are pounding on the doors downstairs now and it is time for to go and be amongst them.

Chicago:
12 September 1995

. . . & Thou Hast Given Them Blood to Drink

& They are Drunken with the Blood of Saints & with the Blood of Martyrs . . .

t-Winter Damon & Randy Chandler

(A Passion Play for Resurgent Atavists)

"The whole world's going to Hell . . ."

Yeah, how many times a day a week a month, whatever, do you hear *that* phrase? Usually it's just the preamble for one more rote recitation of the motormouth litany of the world's ills. But how many straight-john citizens really BE-LIEVE it? The true-believer fundamentalists no doubt do. It's their *raison d'etre,* justifying whatever persecutions their current witch hunt, real or metaphorical, they're pushing this week. The televangelists sure give it enough lip service—of course, they're lining their pockets off the gullibility of P.T. Barnum's one-born-every-minute rubes. Crusading politicians. But they've got the same bullshit credibility scam . . .

So, sure it's an overused saying.

But.

Believe us.

There *are* other True Believers.

Count on it . . .

Let's talk-out a couple more hackneyed truisms.

The quasi-Zen thing about tossing a pebble into still waters & watching the ripples circling outward . . . ?

& that bit about the ostrich hiding his head in the sand . . . ?

Hang tight. We've got a point we're tryin' to hammer home. Before we get down to the meat of it. Before we open our Trickster's Little Black Bag o' Magick Tricks, ask you to kick back & pop a cold one, derm a fresh hit of Divine Messenger, brain-boot into the Tarahumara Patterns of the Waking Dream, throw back a handful of screamin' black beauties & yellowjackets, & let that ol' neurosystem sing the hightension-wired chainsaw song electric, let Old Pete dream your *reeeeealll* good, pop the holy spike, hang out with Mary J. & those Rainy Day Women, whiff those poppers, listen to the Omen-voice fire-whispering inside your skull, or maybe fire up a pipe of ice, or maybe you're into the *painfix* thing?—slap on a pair of nipple clamps, give those labial or scrotum rings a brighhot whitehot tug & twist—*heh, just do it*, whatever your jones is . . . down'n'-dirty or designer . . . Before we maybe show you a few new steps in the old bone dance *American Bandstand & American Graffiti & American Gigolo* never showed you . . .

Okay. Are we straight, yet, or what?

Let's take the one about the pebble & the ripples. Not too obtuse. It's about cause & effect. It's the heart-essence of sympathetic or homeopathic magick—the infinite spider-web-matrix of charm & taboo. An action performed on the microcosmic scale ripples outward to affect & effect within the context of the macrocosm . . . Deep shit, yeah, but bear with us.

Now about the ostrich. They make some nice Tex-Mex-type boots out of 'em, right? Lizard. Snake. Give it a shake & skin that bird . . . But that's *not* what we're rappin' about. We're talking now about consensus reality. The party line & how Mr. and Mrs. John Q. Buy it. & what goes on behind our backs, 'cause if you don't BELIEVE in things maybe they just don't exist. Clap your hands & save Tinkerbell's tight little tush from Oblivion City, right? You remember the scam. The Freudian faerietale gig about Priapic Peter & the Great God Pan? Not the way *you* recall it? Don't sweat you're headed for Alzheimer land instead of Never Never . . . Or timetripping'n'consciousnessslipping, flashing on Canned Heat doin' "Goin' Up Country" . . . It's called "encoding" & "metaphor" & "sublimation." It

cuts both ways, though. People figure if they don't BE-
LIEVE in them nasty thangs, they just don't happen . . .

We'll hit you with a few examples. Cops didn't used to
believe in serial killers, so there wasn't no such beast; now
the FBI admits there's about 200 running loose, & the glass
teat's chock full of 'em—total overkill. Court system & the
whole Insanity Factory didn't used to believe in physical
child abuse as a massive, underlying concept in god's country, no way, called it "family discipline," kid couldn't take
a little discipline & did the runaway, heh, you tacked that
"incorrigible" tag on 'em, threw their asses in juvie, gave
'em a poke of the broomhandle, whatever, right?; now everybody *knows* the nature of that twisted beast, everybody's an instant expert. Society didn't used to believe in
child sexual abuse & incest & shorteyed Scoutmasters &
pervert priests & the kiddie porn network; now it's a daily
talkshow topic, lawsuits estimated to hit the Holy Roman
Catholic alone for maybe four bil in damages, you know
the score. Stranger child abductions didn't happen, not her
in the good ol' appliepie'n'mom U.S. of A., no way; since
the sixties kids've just been running away by the thousands,
sure, seven- & eight-year-olds & the whole enchilada, &
nobody believed in the snuff underground, either. Straight-
8 J. Edgar didn't believe in the Mafia & he hated queers &
commies; now we know they had him by the short'n'curlies,
while he was worrying about whether his boyfriend or him
was gonna be on top this time . . . & the fucker was maybe
THE BIGGEST blackmailer in North-Am polit history . . .

Let us tell you this little fable about this gimpy-eyed
Montgomery County, Virginia boy, a convicted serial slayer
named Henry Lee. Copped to something like 1,000 kills,
though nobody ever believed more than maybe 360 or so
of 'em. He was the Texas Rangers' main man. Same song
with the FBI, & agents from hundreds of nationwide juris-
dictions were whispering sweet nothings in Henry's ear, trying to coax him into laying down the straight skinny on
their own unsolveds. They bought his tails of sex slayings &
necrophilia. But a funny thing happened. When he & his
partner, Ottis, started spilling their story about cannibalistic
orgies & a secred society called "The Hand of Death," &
hundreds, even *thousands* of child abductions this outfit
masterminded, & how the two of them had been doing a

brisk biz in subterranean cash-per-kiddie snatches & custom orders & border runs . . . well, suddenly the door slammed shut—BANG! Shot their credibility all to Hell. Cops didn't use to believe in cannibals any more than they did the Tooth Fairy. Still don't believe in The Hand of Death. Still don't believe in the major weight in angels moving south for the sex-slave & heavy S&M & snuff markets down May-hee-co way . . .

Now, ol' Henry Lee's recanted all, gone born-again, & admits only his involuntary murder of mom. He wasn't scared when they gave him the death sentence convictions. But there *is* something that scares the holy shit out of this stone killer. THE HAND OF DEATH . . .

Reality check:

Guy named Dahmer, up in Detroit, kinda shoved their collective noses in the cannibal shit . . . Arthur Shawcross, too, up in Gennessee River country—did two kids in a sex 'n'snuff/cannibal/necrophilia bit, the moke does *15-fucking years* & he's back on the fucking street, offing hooks by he dozen, doin' the nastybit with the I FUCK THE DEAD NUMBER & doin' the sexual mutilation thing, excising boxes & painting 'em like ol' Ed Gein, usin' 'em like those rubber jobs in the clipout ads in the sex books, dowhackadoo, doin' the cannibal bit—heh, man, it's *SOCIETY THAT'S CERTIFIABLE*—now *he's* locked up they've got *another one,* & it's like oh well they're only hooks, right, it's not like they're *our* kids, think the kill count's up to twenty-odd & climbing . . .

Oh, & they don't have the *half of it*—no way, José!

One last thing we want to mention, before we get down to it—

You remember David Cronenberg's brilliant cult classic, *Videodrome,* don't you? Sleazoid pirate cable TV station owner Max Renn (James Woods) is looking to hook his customers with a little rougher programming, something to give their libidos a jump start. He "accidentally" discovers the S&M straight-snuff VIDEODROME signal, falling down a *very dark* rabbithole, explores a mindfucking wonderland of edged-out pervs & perps, is seduced into boffing & torturing Debbie Harry (rough, man, rough!) playing mondo-bizarro pop psychologist Nicki Brand, witnesses her murder, begins to hallucinate, flagellate, mu-

tate & transcent the limits of past existence, shedding the old flesh, becoming the new flesh, & suiciding so he can complete his transformation . . . "THE BATTLE FOR THE MIND OF NORTH AMERICA WILL BE FOUGHT IN THE VIDEO ARENA," Professor Brian O'Blivion the Media Prophet confesses: "THE TELEVISION SCREEN IS THE RETINA OF THE MIND'S EYE . . ." "THEREFORE THE TELEVISION SCREEN IS PART OF THE PHYSICAL STRUCTURE OF THE BRAIN. THEREFORE WHATEVER APPEARS ON THE TELEVISION SCREEN EMERGES AS RAW EXPERIENCE FOR THOSE WHO WATCH IT. THEREFORE TELEVISION IS REALITY & REALITY IS LESS THAN TELEVISION." IT'S A KIND OF BIO-ELECTRICAL HEROIN. YOUR BRAIN HAS ALREADY BECOME AN ELECTRON GUN. YOUR RETINAE HAVE BECOME VIDEO SCREENS. YOUR REALITY IS ALREADY HALF VIDEO HALLUCINATION." Do the image accumulator—Accumicon—& the VIDEODROME transmissions create a brain tumor or a new sensory organ as the Professor suspects? A convoluted conspiracy-theory flick, weaving a demented web of descent into perversion & paranoia . . .

But the group mind, the collective conscious, the consensus reality does not readily embrace conspiracy theories. It took thirty years to shake our ostrich heads out of the sand & look around & see that the one-gunman J.F.K. assassination theory just didn't wash, that Marilyn was murdered to shut her up, & most *still* haven't gotten wise the Bobby Kennedy snuff was a two-shooter deal *despite* the admissions of ex-FBI agents, bullet-hole-riddled walls that outcount a single magazine-load & angles-of-trajectory that belie the possibility Sirhan Sirhan acted alone, vanishing evidence, a massive cover-up by the same LAPD hierarchy that time's proven ultracorrupt & racist . . .

Back to *Videodrome.*

"REMEMBER: IT'S ONLY A MOVIE!, right?

Yeah. It is an extended metaphor.

But Life *does* imitate Art.

Don't believe us? How about if we admit we've got the inside line. Henry Lee's Hand of Death exists. We *know.* We *belong* to it . . .

Now we can get down to it. The wet stuff you've been
waiting for . . .

*   *   *

POV: PAN in TIGHT: REZ up: (x1):

Interior of cloistered conference room (?). Wide & flat.
Shaped like a cigar box's interior. Windowless. Damp-
stained with unhealthy yellow splotches, the low ceiling's
erratic patchwork of slightly canted & slowly parting acous-
tical tiles keys the image of an inverted stack of cards or
papers, marked by the ancient spillage of strong tea . . .

Centered, dark wooden lectern standing atop low podium. Illumined by a recessed spotlight directly above. The
glare deepening the shadowed background into a morass
of interwoven Rorschach inkblots, suggesting much but di-
vulging *nothing* of the truly tangible, leaving the perceived
to the interpretation of the viewer's own unconscious
urgings . . .

Flanking a central aisle, rows of stereotypical folding
chairs—metallic mauve paint scraped & wear-worn battered & dented almost imperceptibly through years of
jolted, clattering contact with their neighbors—are aligned,
rank-&-file . . .

(LINE BREAK)

A well-dressed throng trickles into the room. Men dressed
in three-piece suits & freshly buffed & polished shoes.
Women in similarly conservative attire: business suits &
suit-dresses & dark, flowing evening gowns.

Attendees at an alumni-meeting (?). Real estate sales'
presentation (?). Investment counseling session (?). Religious function (?). Poetry reading (?) . . .

They sit. Assuming seemingly familiar places. They chat
quietly among themselves. The air seems unnaturally still.
Charged with expectation. The crowd swells to room
capacity.

Precise in the number of their attendance. No more. No
less. As if answering the needs of some intricately complex equation.

The moderator steps from the background shadows.
Takes his place behind the lectern. He is a tall man, dressed
all in black. An *imposing* man. At his appearance, the room
hushes itself to total silence. His presence is a looming
shadow among shadows.

The tall man gestures a silent greeting to the crowd.
His motions are fluid. Graceful.

*   *   *

POV: CLOSEUP OF MODERATOR'S FACE: (x 5):

His skin is rich, dark, olive-bronzed in the harsh glare of
the spotlight's focus. His hair is jet black, glistening like
freshly-oiled tarmac or the lacquered finish of an antique
coffin, silvered at the temples, backswept from his high
forehead, accenting his pronounced widow's peak. His
neatly trimmed mustache & beard are studiedly sinister in
their effect. Save for the eerie mask of cobalt-blue mir-
rorshades that he wears, he could be a far darker vision of
Vincent Price. But he is decidedly some blend of Latin &
Asiatic:
Filipino, to be precise.
& the poetry he will invoke is a Hell-black tapestry of
swirling evil . . .

POV: STEADY at CENTERSTAGE: (x 1):

The lights begin to slowly dim. Only the bulb above him
now spills forth its harsh radiance.
**& the yellow-white glare phases gradually cold & deathly
blue . . .**
The crowd is a gathered silence. Ominous.
One hundred feet above this room, traffic surges through
the night streets of Manila, a neon cesspool, steaming with
every conceivable form of vice that this lust-petty, insectile
swarm of slithering underbelly humanity can dream.
The soldiers of Golgotha await whatever miracles this
night's Passion Play shall reveal.
All is darkness save for that single bulb above the stage.

POV: CLOSEUP OF MODERATOR'S FACE: (x 5):

With his left hand, he strips off the black-framed convexi-
ties of his mirrored lenses, in slow, graceful pantomime . . .

POV: CLOSEUP OF MODERATOR'S FACE: (x 25):

. . . exposing the hollowed pits of eye sockets gouged
blank & apparently *unseeing* . . .
**(but even the most obvious of appearances can prove dan-
gerously misleading)**
The Hellpits of his punctuated stare strip bare the Inner

Dream divining the secret World of Correspondences, beyond.

(Those blank hollows of finger-gouged eye sockets are the self-altered gateway into far *deeper* visions, a ritual act of self-mutilation that transcends the limitations of pale existence anchored in the meat . . .)

POV: CLOSEUP OF MODERATOR'S FACE: (x 25):

The hollow pits of his eye sockets fix the waiting, expectant crowd with their blank stare that seems to bore into the blackness of their sold souls with the deathly certainty of a .44 Magnum "Dirty Harry Special":

POV: DILATE FIELD: TRACK TO
ROOM CENTER (x 5):

The dark pit of Rorschach inkblot shadows dissolves into a slowly growing flickering of blue . . .

In the extreme background, upright against the rear wall of the subterranean chamber, stand the pitted wooden beams of a cross. The stations of the cross are dark with aged, deep-soaked stains.

"Bring forth the Lamb!" the moderator orders.

Two hulking figures step forward from the shadows as if willing themselves into existence from the substance of stealth & nightmares. They wear black leather vests, unfastened to expose their thickly corded chests & midriffs, shaved & oiled to slick glistening sheen of rippled flesh. Tattoos of dragons or coiled serpents swirl across their forearms & biceps. Skintight leather pants of the same butter-supple black satin lustre as their vests encase thick, muscular thighs.

Their faces are both masked with bug-eye lenses of iridescent cobalt blue.

Black motorcycle boots with scuffed brass rings thonged to the ankles' outer curve clump & clatter on the surface of the wooden podium as they drag the struggling body of a young boy centerstage.

Their hands clench the boy's wrists like iron manacles, half-tugging, half-carrying him, obviously against his will . . .

The room echoes with his shrill screams of terror.

He is, no doubt, some vagrant urchin of the streets. Snatched as he ferreted among the city's stinking refuse for

something to fill his belly. Or, perhaps, he had sidled up to a stranger, offering to turn a homo trick, to sell his street-wise mouth or ass to buy a place to sleep & maybe the promise of a hot meal . . .

He is *young*. But there are far younger children of the streets willing to play bumboy for even less remuneration. Boys & girls willing to sell their only assets. Flesh. Home-less waifs. The losers in civil strife, where the lucky, like their parents, are mercifully *dead*.

He is thirteen (?). fourteen (?). & his shrieks of terror climb in a crescendo of torment as the two men hammer rusted spikes of iron into his wrists & ankles . . .

POV: PAN in CLOSE: TIGHTEN FIELD:
MAGNIFICATION (x25):

Young boy's face, contorted into an exaggerated mask of agony. Each strand in the cords of straining musculature is engraved in relief beneath the thin, taut-stretched surface layer of still childish yet hunger-wasted flesh & exposure-weathered, olive-bronzed skin. Like one of those portraits-in-copper, whose features are hammered into the blank sheet of metal from *within*.

The lids of his eyes are crinkled tightly shut with the extremes of his suffering, as if by blocking out the light, some inner darkness might help to soothe away what can-not, in reason, possibly be borne . . .

The saltbrine of his anguished tears brings no hint of pity from the intent crowd of onlookers. Only a thrall of silent fascination.

The tiny pores of his face are dilated pits, flooding with the ice-chill sweat of excruciating pain, flooding with the pheromones of bowel-twisting, feral FEAR.

The caked layer of dust that had grimed his street-urchin/ tainted-angel face is etched into a jagged terrain of terror by the acid rivulets of trickling sweat . . .

His mouth shrieks open in a gargoyle-scream that threat-ens to rip the whitened flesh of his tender young lips, at the narrow juncture where *upper* meets *lower*.

But his raw larynx now betrays the gut-clenching primal scream that seeks escape from some incredibly deep pit fear far beneath the bottom of his human soul. The only

sound that he is capable of making is a mewling gurgle that can voice neither words nor gestalt of his anguish.

A drying rind of snot half-clogs the opening of his left nostril.

POV: DILATE FIELD: MAGNIFICATION (x 10):

His slender body convulses. again. & again. Wracking shudders of grand mal intensity, *induced* through the dark magicks of his *transformation*—

His *becoming*—a living sculpture of hideous beauty, transcending the limits of mere flesh & bone & . . .

The blood of his stigmata flows black in the deathly wash of ultramarine blue light spilling from the ceiling lamps above him.

"Witness the sacrificial Lamb—" the moderator says.

& the crowd claps in perfect unison. & they cry out in perfect unison a dark invocation: *"So be it to all Men!"*

"Now," he whispers, **"this *Passion Play begins* in *earnest*—"**

From the hidden doorway in shadows a tall, voluptuous woman with long, black, flowing hair sways out onto the stage—

the spikes of her impossibly high heels click like sharpened prongs of bone or thick thorns of bloody red, stained purple-black as livid bruises in the Death-blue light of deep-sea caverns washing the stage

the garment that she wears is skintight leather, a slashed webwork of taunting deceits & exposes of bared flesh & hidden promises of seductive evil—the shaved, bulging furrow of her vulva, the dark dimple of her navel, the lust-swollen nipples of her jutting breasts, the perfect, jiggling globes of her buttock cheeks, provoking lurid fantasies of necrophilic longing

the leather, bloodred transmuted to bruise-purple in the Death-blue light of subterranean Hells

She carries a purple velvet robe & wreath of glittering barbed wire

"I *am* the *WHORE* Eternal!—" she cries out to the gathered crowd.

"So *be it* to *all* Men!—" they respond.

She bends, slowly, provocatively, & lays the robe of pur-

ple at the base of the cross, beneath the twitching, palsied feet of the crucified boy.

The leatherclad Whore straddles the crumpled robe, squatting obscenely, & looses a gushing, splattering stream of urine onto the velvet fabric, drenching it with dark, soaking strains.

"So *be it* to *all* Men!—" they again respond.

"Say OHM, O ye outlaws & outlanders OHM to that onomatopoetic ontology of orgasmic onus, OMNIVOROUS PUSSY, say OHM to that Olympus of electric orgies, amen. O Man. Omen. Ye Sons & Daughters of this Neon Babylon. O ye fornicating filth. Ye muthafuckers & babyrapers—" the voice of the moderator is a babbling wail of near-incoherent invections, invocations & obscenities.

The whore crushes her own full, tempting lips to that silently screaming cavern of the crucified boy, kissing him long & passionately, flickering the soft tip of her tongue into his open mouth . . .

"So *be it* to *all* Men!—" the crowd respond.

The Whore withdraws her lips from the boy's mouth. She dips the cupped fingers of her left hand into the naked swell of her groin, wetting her fingers with her own urine, then lifts them slowly, dragging them across the young boy's dry-parched, pain-contorted lips.

"I anoint *his* lips with *vinegar*—" she taunts.

The whore impales the wicked, shining crown of barbed wire into the flesh of the boy's forehead, until the spikes strike solidly on bone . . .

"& the fifth angel sounded, & I saw a star fall from heaven unto earth: & to him was given the key of the bottomless pit." The moderator recites.

"So *be it* to *all* Men!—"

"& he opened the bottomless pit; & there arose a smoke out of the pit, as the smoke of a great furnace; & the sun & the air were darkened by reason of the smoke of the pit."

"So *be it* to *all* Men!—"

"& there came out of the smoke locusts upon the earth: & unto them was given power, as the scorpions of the earth have power."

"So *be it* to *all* Men!—"

"& in those days shall men seek death, & shall not find it; & shall desire to die, & death shall flee from them."

"So *be it* to *all* Men!—"

"& they had tails like unto scorpions, & there were stings in their tails: & their power *was* to hurt men five months."

"So *be it* . . ."

"& they had a king over them, *which is* the angel of the bottomless pit, whose name in the Hebrew tongue is Abaddon, but in the Greek tongue hath *his* name Apollyon.

"So *be it* . . ."

"For their power is in their mouth, & in their tails; for their tails *were* like unto serpents, & had heads, & with them they do hurt."

"So *be it* . . ."

"& the rest of the men which were not killed by these plagues yet repented not of the words of their hands, that they SHOULD WORSHIP DEVILS, & idols of gold, & silver, & brass, & stone, & of wood: which neither can see, nor hear, nor walk:

Neither repented they of their murders, nor their sorceries, nor of their fornication—"

"So *be it* to *all* Men!—" the crowd screams.

**POV: DILATE FIELD: TRACK to
ROOM CENTER (x 5):**

The crowd of precisely twenty-four gives the moderator a standing ovation.

But his litany is far from finished:

"& I looked, & behold a pale horse: & his name that sat on him was Death, & Hell followed with him. & power was given unto them over the fourth part of the earth, to kill with sword, & with hunger, & with death, & with the beasts of the earth."

"So *be it* to *all* Men!—"

"& there appeared another wonder in heaven; & behold a great red dragon, having seven heads & ten horns, & seven crowns upon his heads."

"So *be it* to *all* Men!—"

"& there was war in heaven: Michael & his angels fought against the dragon; & the dragon fought & his angels."

"So *be it* to *all* Men!—"

"& the great dragon was cast out, that old serpent, called the Devil, & Satan, & Lucifer the Bringer of the Light, and

Baal Zebub the Lord of the Flies, Our Lord & Master, who bringeth Truth unto the world: he was cast out into the earth, & his angels were cast out with him."

"Cur*sed* are *those* Days!" screams the crowd.

The moderator unzips his trousers, & draws forth a huge, bobbing penis like a grotesque, blind, one-eyed serpent, & the image is fixed by the tattoo in varied shades of blue, coiling & writhing down his abdomen, & the serpent has a head—

& the Whore bows to him & kneels in supplication.

"& the serpent cast out of his mouth water as a flood after the woman, that he might cause her to be carried away of the flood."

The moderator grasps his penis in his hand & guides a hissing, splattering stream of hot, brine-salty urine into the Whore's eagerly opened mouth.

"& the earth helped the woman, & the earth opened her mouth, & swallowed up the flood which the dragon cast out of his mouth."

"So *be it . . .*" roars the crowd.

"& I stood upon the sand of the sea, & saw a beast rise up out of the sea, having seven heads & ten horns, & upon his horns ten crowns, & upon his head the name of blaspehmy."

One of the two hulking, leatherclad men who had crucified the boy struts into the blue flood of the spotlight.

"So *be it . . .*"

"& they worshipped the dragon which gave power unto the beast: & they worshipped the beast, saying, Who *is* like unto the beast? Who is able to make war with him?"

The second of the two leatherclad tormentors struts forward, also.

"So *be it . . .*"

"& I beheld another beast coming up out of the earth; & he had two horns like a lamb, & he spake as a dragon."

A third joins them on centerstage, along with the moderator & the kneeling Whore.

"So *be it . . .*"

"& he had power to give life unto the image of the beast, that the image of the beast should both speak, & cause that as many as would not worship the image of the beast should be killed."

The first man lies back upon the podium, his thick, tattooed serpent of a penis rearing. & the Whore straddles his hips & squats with her legs widespread, splayed to offer her bare pubis for the public joining of their flesh. & she lowers herself, impaling her shaved vulva on his upthrust member.

"So *be it . . .*"

"& he causeth all, both small & great, rich & poor, free & bond, to receive a mark in their right hand, or in their foreheads:

& that no man might buy or sell, save he had that mark, or the name of the beast, or the number of his name."

The second man takes out a razor-sharp stiletto, & slits the taut-stretched leather where it spans the sensuous, wriggling globes of her buttocks. He rips the thin, supple leather of her outfit with his powerful, pawl-like hands. & he mounts her from the rear, in the fashion of those of Sodom.

"So *be it* to *all* Men!—" the crowd echoes.

"Here is the wisdom. Let him that hath understanding count the number of the beast: for it is the number of a man; & his number *is* Six hundred threescore *and* six."

& the third man climbs upon the back of the Sodomite, & mounts him as a pederastic priest might rape some pretty young altarboy.

"So *be it . . .*"

"& I beheld, & lo, in the midst of the throne & of the four beasts, & in the midst of the elders stood a Lamb as it had been slain—"

"Notwithstanding I have a few things against thee, because thou sufferest that woman Jezebel, which calleth herself a prophetess, to teach & to seduce my servants to commit fornication, & to eat things sacrificed unto idols"

"So *be it* to *all* Men!—"

the moderator takes the stiletto from the outstretched hand of the first Sodomite. He holds its gleaming blade up to catch the blue light in cold, deathly sparks on razor-honed metal.

Then he plunges it into the young boy's side, as he spasms, nailed upon the pitted wooden cross.

He twists the blade, thrusting it *upwards,* to puncture the throbbing, spurting heart . . .

The savaged Lamb gives up his ghost, the death-rattle gurgling in bloody foam from between his slackening lips.

The blue light seems to strobe & flicker . . .

The moderator slits the boy from groin to breastbone. He tears out the still-beating heart with his bare hands, then slices off a bit & swallows it . . .

"& when they shall have finished their testimony, the beast that ascendeth out of the bottomless pit shall make war against them *that stand against the Lord of the Flies*, & shall overcome them, & kill them."

The moderator slices another piece of heartflesh, & hands it to the first of the crowd to file up to him to receive the benediction of the beast—the wine & wafer of the slaughtered Lamb.

"So *be it* to *all* Men!" whispers the crowd.

"& their dead bodies *shall lie* in the street of the great city, which spiritually is called Sodom & Egypt, where also our Lord was crucified . . . & in Manila & Hong Kong & Port-au-Prince & London & Amsterdam & Chicago & San Francisco . . ."

"So *be it* to *all* Men!" the crowd roars.

"All shall kneel before *The Soldiers of Golgotha*!"

POV: ZOOM in on CENTERSTAGE: AMP-up OLFAC-TORY & TACTILE LINK TRANSMISSIONS (x50): MAGNIFICATION BOOST in RPID JUMPCUT
(x 5—x100—x5):
(x5):

Shadows boil & part for an eternal instant.

Three brute-clones drag three teenage girls on-stage. Nude. Oriental. Struggling. & screaming. Brothel inmates (?) street whores (?) or kidnap victims (?) . . . their past is now but dream their present nightmare their future nonexistent—

(x10):

The Whore in Scarlet & Purple enters. Taunting deceits & exposes of slashed leather webwork bare jutting breasts & stiffened nipples, jiggling globes of too-perfect bottom checks, dimpled navel, & the razor-bald furrow of tapering mons veneris . . .

(x15):

The supple rose branch descends. Thorn-barbs rake naked flesh. More screams. High & shrill. Pinpricks &

bloody zigzags speak the unspeakable upon the vellum of their pain . . .

(x25):

Each curved leaf of living flesh quivering in rise-&-fall of breath in captive wriggling beneath the scourge . . . each a tome a canvass of suffering transcendent in its passages of beauty . . .

(x50):

Droplets of blood & tears & perspiration mingle black beneath the blue-lit bulb . . .

(x75):

Pores dilate. Huge flies of emerald & sapphire crawl lazily across each girl's quaking curve of bared belly, swarming down inside the sweet-damp sweat-damp crater-rims of navels, black wire legs & mandibles forever twitching as they explore the sparse foliage of pubic forests, the ridgeline of Great Divide between each pair of mammoth thighs, then throng within the parted gates of Venus' Temples, disappearing deep into each Womb of Darkness, feeding on the mingled musk & nectar, feeding on the douche of milk-&-honey flooded there before the Passion Play began . . .

(x100):

Faceted eyes reflect the scene a thousand-times-a-thousand-fold . . . reflect the tortured innocents & the Moderator & the Whore in Scarlet & the five brutes & the audience beyond . . .

(x5):

Three wooden stakes loom like colossal upthrust phalluses upon the blue-lit podium.

Three brutes lift three struggling captives. Raise them above their dragon-coiling skulls. & ram them groundward. Monstrous shafts impaling ravage anuses . . .

The pole-sodomized girls shriek until it seems their lungs must burst, as their soft, round heels beat out the Devil's Tattoo of their death throes on the unrelenting oaken shafts or in midair.

& each of their three brute-captors unzips his fly, draws out his own threatening length, grips one victim by her slender hips or rounded globes of pole-split bottom, then thrusts his penis deep into the dying fires in tidal rhythm,

joining the flies that crawl within her Holy of Unholies her defiled vestibule & sacristy . . .

The mingled incense-scents of rose & musk & sweat & blood & voided human wastes break across the senses with tsunami-wave intensity.

POV: STEADY at CENTERSTAGE: DILATE OPTICAL FIELD: (x5):

The twin brutes who earlier had flanked the Moderator return from the boiling background shadows dragging two black ewes by silver choke-chains.

"For they have shed the blood of saints & prophets, & *Thou* hast given *Them* blood to drink; for *They* are worthy—" The Moderator says.

"So be it to *all* Men!—" the Soldiers of Golgotha cry out in response.

The brutes mount the beasts as would two rams.

& I saw three spirits—

"(They that burned with the Fever of Azoth the Leprosy of Perfect Transformation)

"—like frogs *come* out of the mouth of the Dragon, & out of the mouth of the Beast, & out of the mouth of the *Eyeless* Prophet *Who Speaks the Truths*—"

"So be it to *all* Men!—"

& the brutes join their flesh with the ewes' & draw tight the chains about their necks, causing them to beat their hooves upon the wooden planking of the stage & to struggle & to trash their bodies in mindless terror—& the sound of their drumming hooves *is THE DEVIL'S TATTOO* . . .

& the Moderator opens wide his mouth & spits out a huge leopard frog & the Moderator is silent but the frog swells its throat & bellows in a deep, rumbling voice:

"For *They* are the spirits of devils, working miracles, *which* go forth unto the kings of the earth & of the whole world, to gather *Them* to the battle of that great day of *Final Judgment*—"

"So be it to *all* Men!—"

& the frog puffs out its throat again & speaks: "& I shall make testament to You of *The* Woeman *Dressed in Purple & Scarlet Which Sat Upon the Beast*—"

"So be it to *all* Men!—"

& The Whore strides forth from the boiling shadows to

the clicking of spike-thorned heels, & in her right hand she holds the silver chalice & in the other a leash of human skin dyed brilliant cobalt blue, & she leads a great black billy goat.

"& there came out of the seven angels which had the seven vials, & talked with *Me,* saying unto *Me, Come hither; I will shew unto Thee the Judgment of the Great Whore that sitteth upon many waters*—"

The Whore squats down upon the stage & voids Her bladder in a gushing torrent.

"So be it to all **Men!**—"

& the Moderator reaches down, then holds aloft in His cupped palms the Exalted Frog who testifies: "With whom the kings of the earth have committed fornication, & the inhabitants of the earth have been made drunk with the wine of her fornication—"

"So be it to all **Men!**—"

"So *He, Lord of the Flies,* carried *Me* away in the spirit into the wilderness: *& I saw a Woeman sit upon a Great Black Beast with beard & curving horns, & I knew Him to be the Manifestation of Our Most Holy Lord Baphomet*—"

"So be it to all **Men!**—"

The Whore kneels upon the stage & Her white flesh glows blue in the ambient light, & Her breasts & Her buttocks are as if carved jewels of sapphire exposed beneath the slashes of Her purple & scarlet leather, & She whispers to the *Great Black Billy Goat,* the male manifestation of that Beast Lovecraft visioned in his dreams & termed "SHUB NIGGURATH, *The Black Goat with a Thousand Young . . .*"

& the Woeman was arrayed in purple & scarlet color, & decked with silver & precious stones & pearls, having a silver cup in Her hand full of abominations & filthiness of her fornication:—"

"So be it to all **Men!**—"

The Whore sets the silver chalice before Her, near the stage's edge. One of Golgotha's Soldiers steps forward from the seated crowd. Grasps the chalice. Kneels with his right knee cocked. Touches the glistening curves of metal to his forehead—the Sigil of Baphomet burns blue on the flesh it has caressed.

& the frog bellows: "BLESSED BE!"

"So be it to *all* Men!—"

The Soldier tips the vessel to his lips. Then passes it to the next supplicant, who repeats the ritual & furthers it along . . .

"& upon Her forehead *was* a name written, MYSTERY, BaB-y-LON THE GREAT, THE MOTHER OF HARLOTS & ABOMINATIONS OF THE EARTH—"

"So be it!—"

& The Whore spreads Herself to the Beast & thrusts Her hips back lewdly in mock coital thrusts, & again She whispers to Him in some sacred, secret tongue . . .

& the Exalted Frog continues: "& I saw the Woeman drunken with the blood of the saints, & with the blood of the martyrs of *The Epileptic One;* & when I saw Her, I wondered with great admiration.

"So be it to *all* Men!—"

& the Great Black Beast mounts The Whore & joins His flesh with Hers.

"The Beast that Thou saweth was, & is not; & shall ascent out of The Bottomless Pit, & go into Perdition: & They that dwell on the earth shall wonder, whose names were not written in the book of life from the foundation of the world, when They behold the Beast that was, & is not, & yet is—"

"So be it to *all* Men!—"

& the room burns blue and flickers, & the two black ewes are nuns, their habits drawn up about their hips to expose their blue-white rumps obscenely to ministrations of the bald-shaved- &-tattooed brutes, & the Black Goat sprouts seven heads & He is no longer *black* but *scarlet* . . .

"& I saw a Woeman sit upon a scarlet colored Beast, full of names of blasphemy, having seven heads & ten horns—"

"So be it—"

"& here *is* the mind which hath wisdom. The seven heads are seven mountains, on which the Woeman sitteth—"

"So be it—"

"& there were seven kings: five are fallen, & one is, & the other *has cum*; & when he *cummeth,* He must continue a short space—"

"So be it—"

"& the Beast that was, & is, & is not, even He is the eighth, & is of the seven, & goeth into Perdition—"

"So be it—"

"& the ten horns which Thou sawest are ten kings, which have no kingdom as yet; but receive power as kings one hour with the Beast—"

"So be it—"

"These have one mind, & shall give their power & strength unto the Beast—"

"So be it—"

"& so, You shall learn that all this world's philosophies that do not honor *Him* are but falsehoods, He *was*, & is *not*, & is . . . for He *is* Splendor & He *is* Wonder & He *is* Illusion—"

& the frog cupped in the Moderator's palm is once more but a frog, & the ewes that the brutes use are no longer nuns but only sheep, & the *Beast that Sitteth upon The Whore* is once more nothing save a great black billy goat in rut . . .

DISSOLVE to:

A field of blue writhing through a spectrum of unnatural variety: every conceivable hue that the human mind has identified & catalogued & labeled with a name, of shades & tones & resonations that have no name in any spoken language . . .

A FLICKERING BLUE EXTREME. . .
FADE to BLACK

Yeah. The world *is* going to Hell . . .

We're here to see that it does.

We're True Believers.

Part of the Conspiracy of the Great Night.

Each does what they have to in the furthering of the Cause. Some are just streetlevel mercs & assassins, like us—the Hand of Death. Some are the elite strikeforce, the Media People, the prophets & politicos—the Soldiers of Golgotha.

"Golgotha": cool word. We like the way it rolls off the tongue.

You know about Golgotha, right? Calvary, the place where the Epileptic One was crucified. Its meaning has broadened over the centuries to include any burial place, any place of agony of sacrifice.

But what it *means* is derived from the Hebrew word *gulgoleth*—"A SKULL. THE PLACE OF A SKULL."

Remember what we were saying about that old ostrich with his head shoved in the sand. You get the picture, right?

Remember what were saying about the pebble thrown into the pool spreading its circling ripples? Oh, yes, *we've* been making a big splash, a silent splash, 'cause nobody's been listening . . .

Ripples of sympathetic magick.

In a way, it answers that tired philosophical paradox about "what if a tree falls in the forest, but there's no-one there to hear it fall . . . ?"

You see their effects, but you're lost as to their cause.

Others have tried before us.

Hitler & his SS & his Werewolves tried.

But his assault was clumsy. Too involved in the material plane for his magicks to succeed.

Ours *will* succeed. Because it relies not upon brute force, but merely harnesses it, wields it, bends it to the Thelemaic Doctrine: DO WHAT THOU WILL . . .

The New Age *has* come. 1966 marked its advent. The Age of Satan—

The Kennedy assassinations? The death of Monroe? Of Mansfield? Of Martin Luther King? Of John Lennon?

Ripples.

Serial killers: Manson? John Wayne Gacy? The Green River Killer? Henry Lee Lucas & Ottis Toole? Berkie, the .44 Killer, the Son of Sam? Richie Ramirez, the Night Stalker? (You didn't know *he* was an experiment in *programmed* slaughter, did you . . . ?) Jeffrey Dahmer? Artie Shawcross? All the sleight-of-hand ones you *haven't* caught yet?

Oh, yes.

Those Guerrillas of the Great Night—

Like the Zodiac.

Like the Unabomber.

Like how the deathdealing Four Pi ("for to make disorder"; 4×4×4 . . ."; "the Power of the Elementals cubed . . .") of the sixties & seventies has transformed into the FC ("for Chaos") of the eighties & the nineties . . .

Showing but three tombstone hands of the Hand of Death . . .

Ripples.

Each is a *nexus of power,* focusing & amplifying the ripples into waves . . .

The Khmer Rouge? Lat-Am Death Squads? The Middle-Eastern Conflict? The Jonestown Massacre? The dissolution of the balancing power of the U.S.S.R? The slaughter in Serbia & Bosnia? The reuniting of Germany? The Gulf War? The rising swell of the Fourth Reich?

Storm waves.

The World Trade Tower Bombing? David Korresh & the Branch Davidian bloodbath? The Supreme Truth's sarin nerve gas assault on the Tokyo subway system? The Oklahoma City devastation? Yeah, & all the shit that lies ahead . . .

Tsunamis.

The pebble has been cast.

& the world is going to Hell.

Remember how we were talking about Cronenberg's concept of VIDEODROME, & the image accumulator, & the brain tumor?

Trust us, Life *does* imitate Art.

The Great Night found the way to transform the old flesh into the new flesh . . . & the new flesh *is* the *Black Snake* shedding its skin & awakening . . . & the new flesh *is* the *Way of the Werewolf* . . .

Take it from two True Believers.

The Soldiers of Golgotha hold the power.

Take it from two Believers.

Thou hast given Them blood to drink.

& THE WORLD *IS* RUSHING HEADLONG INTO ITS DARK TRANSFORMATION.

FANTASY COLLECTIONS
FROM [RoC]

SHORT STORY COLLECTIONS
FROM [ROC]

☐ **SISTERS IN FANTASY Edited by Susan Shwartz and Martin H. Greenberg.** This collection gathers together fifteen all-original and thought-provoking stories by some of the most highly regarded women writing fiction today. From curses confronted and paths not followed to women gifted with magic as ancient as the earth itself, these powerful tales provide insight into sacrifices made and obstacles overcome. (452925—$4.99)

☐ **SISTERS IN FANTASY 2 Edited by Susan Shwartz and Martin H. Greenberg.** From ancient spells unleashed upon our modern world to the equally powerfully thirsts for romance and revenge, here are all-original stories written especially for this volume by twenty-two of today's bestselling and award-winning women fantasists. (455037—$5.99)

☐ **DARK LOVE by Stephen King, Stuart Kaminsky, Ramsey Campbell and 19 others. Edited by Nancy A. Collins, Edward E. Kramer, and Martin H. Greenberg.** There is no safe hiding place on this fictional turf where burning desire and dark terror meet, where ecstasy merges with agony, and eros and evil spawn unholy horror. These macabre tales give new meaning to being madly in love. (455509—$5.99)

☐ **THE GALLERY OF HORROR 20 chilling tales by the modern masters of dread. Stephen King, Eric Van Lustbader, Ramsey Campbell and 17 others. Edited by Charles L. Grant.** Some galleries specialize in the arts of painting, or sculpture, or crafts. But the gallery you are about to visit specializes in the most irresistibly riveting art of all—the art of horror. For connoisseurs of classic chills for whom no leap into unknown evil is too bold or too scary. (455150—$6.99)

Prices slightly higher in Canada.

Buy them at your local bookstore or use this convenient coupon for ordering.

PENGUIN USA
P.O. Box 999 — Dept. #17109
Bergenfield, New Jersey 07621

Please send me the books I have checked above.
I am enclosing $_____ (please add $2.00 to cover postage and handling). Send check or money order (no cash or C.O.D.'s) or charge by Mastercard or VISA (with a $15.00 minimum). Prices and numbers are subject to change without notice.

Card #_____ Exp. Date _____

Signature_____

Name_____

Address_____

City _____ State _____ Zip Code _____

For faster service when ordering by credit card call **1-800-253-6476**

Allow a minimum of 4-6 weeks for delivery. This offer is subject to change without notice.